The Conscious Virus

First Novel in the Aedgar Wisdom Series

By MIKI MITAYN

To M-L who understands the importance of light and shade.

And makes the flowers shine brighter.

Aboriginal and other language and other local, medical or less-usual words are listed in the GLOSSARY at the back of the book.

NEXT PAGE: **Map of Australia** shows East Coast (from North): Brisbane, Byron Bay (and Lennox Head), Sydney, Wollongong and Narooma.

In Central Australia, Uluru and Kata Tjuta, Yulara and Alice Springs.

And Broome, Geraldton and Perth on the West Coast.

Newman and Port Headland in the Pilbara Region. Broome, Fitzroy Crossing and Kununurra are in the Kimberley Region.

Distance of each one-way, east-west car trip is equivalent to New York to Los Angeles; or Berlin to Athens and back.

Distances of Christmas Island and Cocos-Keeling Islands (Australian territories) west from Darwin are 2,800 and 3,700 kilometres, respectively.

2800 km from Darwin
2300 km from Perth
Christmas Island
Cocos Keeling Islands
Indian Ocean
Kimberley
Broome
Derby
Great Sandy Desert
Port Hedland
Newman
Western Australia
Geraldton
Kalgoorlie
Perth
Nullarbor Plain
Katherine
Northern Territory
Gibson Desert
Alice Springs
Yulara
Kata Tjuta
Uluru
Great Victoria Desert
South Australia
Ceduna
Adelaide
Victoria
Melbourne
Tasmania
Pacific
Queensland
Winton
Longreach
New South Wales
Canberra
ACT
Sydney
Wollongong
Pacific

CHAPTER 1

Newman Hospital, Palyku Country. The Pilbara, Western Australia

Thursday January 9, 2014

'So, you drink a slab of beer a day?' Dr Nerida Green asked with a barmaid's smile. Her client, a ruddy-faced man who looked older than the age on his record, had headaches and insomnia.

'Oh no, doc. I don't drink much. A slab will usually last me two or three days. I would drink thirty-six cans in a day on the weekends, though,' he admitted. 'Less on Sunday because I get to church when I can.'

'Is it a wonderful church? Kind people?'

'Aw, not really. I just go because people expect it. Mum did. Now, she's passed, I feel like I should. Her church was better though. She fit in. I don't fit in anywhere except I've got a can of beer in me hand.'

'Your body's suffering. Can you be kinder to yourself?'

'Like how?'

'Find people who like you for who you are. You're a decent person and good to other people. Have you ever tried giving up the grog?'

'No, doc. Been drinking since I was 14, when I started work in a boiler factory.'

Nerida smiled sincerely now. 'My first job was in a battery factory. Lead and zinc dust on everything. I was fifteen. I had a hole in my spirit I was trying to fill up. Loneliness. Confusion. I didn't drink. Just ate too much and got fat. Nobody talked about feelings in those days. We hardly knew what they were.'

'Yeah. Mum died when I was twelve. Everyone said she was with God. Thirty years later, never did find him at church.'

They sat together as equals. There was a hum, roar and thump of big machinery outside the thin-walled building. In the near distance, a child played the recorder tunelessly.

Nerida enjoyed her morning, even if she was tired. She spent fifty minutes with the man and asked him to make a long appointment next week. Alcoholics Anonymous didn't have a branch in Newman. *I'll talk to community health about employing a drug and alcohol worker,* she thought. Hurrying for a toilet break, the argument with her coffee-filled bladder got louder.

No sound, but instinct made her look into the treatment room. The patient was floppy. Her mouth moved like a fish drowning in air.

'Anaphylaxis!' Nerida's voice boomed down the hall. 'This patient has an allergy.' Ran to the bed. Leaned on the red alarm button.

'You'll be all right. We've got you,' she whispered. Pulled the IV out of the patient's arm. Blood spilled on the bed, the floor. Brown iron splashed on Nerida's dress.

'We had her on ten-minute obs,' the nurse said, rushing in.

Voice still low, Nerida said, 'The trolley behind you. Top drawer.'

The patient had her mouth open. Air going in made a scraping noise.

'Check this?' The nurse showed Nerida an ampoule.

'I need my glasses.' Scrabbled for them. Noted the drug, the expiry, the dose.

'Give it.'

The sister pushed the needle in the patient's thigh.

'This will make you better,' Nerida murmured.

Nerida found oxygen tubing in a basket too high to see into. Felt for it. 'Adrenaline again in four minutes. Find it. Draw it up, please.'

She put a mask over the patient's gasping mouth. Connected oxygen. Turned it on full blast. Soft voiced, 'You gonna be all right. That medicine made you sick. Breathe now.' Touched her forehead.

'Thanks, Doc,' she gasped. Her brown eyes very wide.

Nerida looked in the nurse's face. Noted her purple-streaked hair. Repeated, 'Have you got another dose of adrenaline? In case she needs it. We can give it every four minutes. I'll put a sats probe on.'

'I'll put a cannula in,' the nurse said. 'Now that the doctor pulled your other one out.' She smiled wryly, calming them all. 'The right thing to do, of course,' she added. Gave Nerida a direct look of gratitude as the needle went in.

'What fluid do you want?'

'Normal saline. One litre. Open it up.' Nerida reached into the cupboard and pulled a bag out. 'Are we alone here?'

'Lunch,' she passed Nerida a second vial of adrenaline, read her the expiry date.

Nerida wasn't sure she would have coped with this emergency on her own. 'I'm sorry, I don't know your name.'

'I'm Sarah.'

'Nerida. I'm the doctor.' She touched the patient's hand. It was warm. 'How's your breathing now? You look a better colour. That was scary, eh?'

The patient breathed quietly. Deeply.

The room smelled of blood, iron and sweat.

'Sats are ninety-eight percent.'

'Good.' Nerida consciously put her shoulders down, took a deep breath, too.

'What happened?' asked the young woman. Her skin was a rich brown, fingers wrapped around Nerida's café au lait hand.

'You had a bad reaction to the iron. An allergy. If a doctor ever asks whether it's anaphylaxis, say yes. Because you had trouble breathing. That's the word they use for it. I'll write that you're allergic in big, red, letters on your record so that everyone knows never to give it to you into the vein again.'

'Yes, please. Thought I would die,' she whispered.

'You'll be right. You needed another medicine. Rest now.' Nerida held onto her hand. 'We'll keep you here to make sure you're all right. We'll talk about what happened when you've had a rest. I want to move you into a different bed, so you're closer.'

To Sarah, 'Let's put her in the resus area, just for peace of mind. I'd like her on a monitor for the next hour or two.' She skipped from one foot to the other. 'Excuse me, now. I must go to the loo.'

CHAPTER 2

A Western Desert Aboriginal Community

Thursday August 2, 2014

Mari sat on the edge of the bed and unclipped her prosthetic leg. She placed it carefully, foot on the floor, and briskly rubbed her stump just above where an ankle would have been.

Stretching on her back, she said, 'I took my leg off at school today. The kids loved it.'

'Oh yeah?' Nerida said, tipping water in the humidifier. She noticed the muscles in her wife's brown arms, her cheeky smile. 'What brought that on?'

'I like them. Even if Thomas and Stella are always naughty and Misty is always late. They sit down on the bus for me. Getting on the bus every morning is a pleasure for them. And then they get so excited to go home.'

'What's that got to do with your foot?'

'Stella and Thomas went off chasing a lizard. I took my leg off to show Misty and Paul. Then the others came running back.'

Nerida smiled broadly as she pulled her nightie over her head and let down her hair, running her fingers through it. She leaned over and kissed her wife on the mouth. Lay beside her, fell against her, on the saggy bed.

'Did you tell them a doctor chopped your leg off because he was an idiot?'

'I wouldn't tell them that. You're their only doctor. They love you.'

'They're scared enough of me already.'

'I told them it was a crocodile attack. They might be more careful when they go swimming now.'

At work the next day the clinic receptionist had a smile just peeping out when she said, 'Ms Snow from school wants to see you.'

Nerida finished the sentence she was typing. 'Who is she again?'

'The deputy. Says Mari did something horrible. Says kids are traumatised. Says Mari should have asked parents' permission.'

'What a load of bull. Why doesn't she talk to Mari about it?'

'She's scared of her.' She showed a dimple.

Nerida was earnest. 'Just about every family in this community has someone with an amputation. Or gone blind from diabetes. Poor old Fred—two stumps and his wheelchair that won't work in the sand...'

'He wants to see you again today, too.'

'Yeah, alright. Why don't you go and get Fred? Maybe I can get him sorted before the school ma'am comes.'

Later, Nerida listened to Ms. Snow talk about her eczema for a long ten minutes.

Dr Nerida looked at a scaly red mess on her ankle. 'That would itch like blazes at night.

'This cream will help but you must only apply it thinly. You've got dermatitis on your scalp, too. I can give you something for that. You must be stressed.'

Nerida shifted in her chair. 'I hear you're upset with my wife?'

Ms. Snow flinched. Her pale blue eyes had a permanently startled look. 'Your 'wife' has to understand. These children have been through a lot. She might give them nightmares. She's only the casual bus driver. She doesn't get to say what my teaching plan should be. It was all they talked about this morning. Some of them were hopping around in the playground, pretending they had only one leg.'

And you say that as if it's a bad thing.

She leaned forward so that Nerida smelled mouth rinse and hairspray. 'Was it really a croc?'

'It was a story more terrible than you want to hear. We might need half a bottle of wine to share it.' Nerida joshed. Wine was taboo in the Dry community. 'Sounds like you're doing a great job. What was your lesson this morning?'

The matron considered whether to share. 'We were talking about how much sugar there is in cool drinks. Using that to reinforce arithmetic for the little ones and talk about advertising for the older kids.'

'What a good way to teach them. Kids are interested in stories.'

Nerida ducked her head and spoke softly. 'Most of the drama and disability they see comes from ordinary things. Alcoholism, depression, not enough to eat, too much stress and misery. People not going out hunting or tending their gardens because they're too sad or overwhelmed. Diabetes comes from taking the land away, too, you know.'

Ms Snow snorted.

'No, it's true. Aboriginal people needed to keep their blood glucose high for a long time. Especially this mob, desert people. They might walk for days to hunt an animal. Might have a few berries or yams or bush bananas to keep them going. People travel long distances between the fat-and-plenty places.'

Ms Snow tilted her head. She granted that. One of the old fellas arrived home after walking about eighty kilometres in four days, despite the desert heat, last Summer. He was fine. 'Car broke down,' he said. No one went looking because no one was expecting him. 'I'm all right,' he said proudly, when Nerida saw him at the shop. She bought him a hand of bananas to celebrate his survival.

'You couldn't be collapsing with hunger,' she added. 'It was an evolutionary adaption. It makes those of us with European ancestry look maladapted, if you look at it that way.'

White people liked it when she referred to her English and Irish ancestry. It helped them with the puzzle of how she identified with her Aboriginality, with her fair skin and grey eyes.

'Nowadays we like to eat every day—' she continued.

The teacher looked down at her round belly, reassured that Nerida had one, too.

'—and the foods people eat, well, some of them aren't really food at all. No wonder Aboriginal people get diabetes now. Some of this mob don't understand that you can be sold something as food that's not nourishment.'

The teacher agreed. 'Like cool drinks.' That was the local lingo for soft drinks, soda. *She has to learn something from the kids.*

'Exactly. Colonisation has only happened here in the last four generations. Some of the people my age—' this woman was ten years younger than Nerida, even if she was bossy and fussy, '—born in the 60s, spent their childhood on the cattle stations.

She could see Ms. Snow's eyes glazing over. Nerida was going to educate her anyway. 'Their parents got flour and sugar and tea for wages. Maybe a bit of offal. Tobacco and alcohol. Chronic diseases of colonisation, all packed up and fed to people.'

She finished writing Ms. Snow's details on the labels of the creams and potions for her dermatitis.

'You're doing well teaching the kids not all that's sold as food makes them stronger.'

'It's not just white people's fault,' Ms. Snow said.

Nerida agreed. 'The diseases? No. People from Asia brought leprosy.' Her eyes widened with emphasis. 'We've still got to check for that.' She distracted Ms Snow from her defensiveness by scaring her.

Those startled blue eyes. 'What? Here?'

'No, up north in the Kimberley. People who were leprosy contacts in the 90s still need check ups.

'But you're right. Nothing is just white people's fault. I'm not even sure if there's any such thing as white people, really. Everybody comes from somewhere.

'In my family Irish and English people married into our Aboriginal clan for love, for more than one generation. My mother is third generation Australian from England. She loves my Dad. My white grandfather loved my Goori nana, too. They were good together.'

'One of my ancestors was a convict,' Ms Snow said with quiet pride. 'He went to live with the Blacks.'

Nerida put her pen in her pocket. 'There's always been good people. Always been English that wanted to learn. Open-minded people like you. You've probably got Aboriginal ancestry yourself. It's not likely that a family lives here for two centuries without marrying into the Original people.'

'Do you think so?'

Nerida rose, guiding Ms. Snow to the door. 'If you can use me at school, I'll come and talk to the older kids about diabetic amputations, people going blind and all that. Not to scare them, to help them understand. If the parents are happy. Would we need consent forms?'

That evening at home, Mari served up crumbed chicken. 'What did you say to the snow queen? She was sweet as sugar this afternoon.' She grinned, putting down their plates. 'I got a commission today. Ryan at the Art Centre asked me to take photos of the artists doing their work.'

Nerida felt a thrill of happiness.

'You should see the artists' shed, though. It's horrible. If it's forty degrees outside, it'll be fifty in there.'

'No wonder people move slowly, eh.' Nerida speared a potato. Broke and buttered it.

Mari sat on their second chair, within arm's length. 'Some of the paintings are huge. Like, as big as this house. The men make a painting together. The women make a different one. They each have their country and stories they paint about. And they connect them together. Ryan calls it a collaborative.'

'Magnificent paintings.' Nerida glimpsed the works as she walked by sometimes. She got up and poured them each a glass of wheat beer. It was non-alcoholic, but the taste made them feel good.

'I can only stay in that shed for an hour though. It's too hot for me. How do they do it?'

'People here have stamina. And they were born into this climate. They pace themselves. Have you ever seen people walk so slowly? It's magnificent. You're right, though, it has got hotter here,' Nerida said.

'Ryan has to be patient. Everyone brings their dogs. A couple of the very old people have like a retinue of dogs.'

Nerida laughed. 'We have fights in the clinic all day to keep the dogs out. Great opportunity to shout and wave my arms. I yell at them in language. They're unmoved by English.'

'In the Art Centre, nothing moves them. Dogs walk on the paintings, sit on them, roll around. Ryan cleans the damage off and makes the artists start again.'

Nerida said, 'I s'pose if people are paying tens of thousands of dollars, the painting needs to be very good. And hairless.'

Mari chuckled. 'I'm hoping the photos could be great. I've got the settings right to show people's dark brown faces. It's tricky because the light is so strong around them. A lot of photographers don't know how to capture dark faces, you know?' She pulled the last bite of meat around the sauce on her plate. 'The beef here is so good.'

'It is.'

'Sorry it was sold out and I had to buy the chicken.

'Ryan told me he asked the old people to make smaller paintings. He thought they might sell more if they paint some, instead of, you know, these three by five metre masterpieces. "Come on. Try it," he said, "People don't have big houses for such big paintings!" But the old men say no. One said, "I've got big country. Paintings gotta be big for my big story!" They're onto a good thing.'

'True, people here aren't silly.' Nerida gathered the plates, turned around to wash them.

Later they lay together under the air-conditioner, profoundly relaxed in the darkness of the desert night.

Nerida felt the old mattress supporting her. The earth beneath the house holding her. *It must be after midnight. I'll be tired at work tomorrow. But this feeling's worth it.*

Mari, turned towards the cool wall, had fallen asleep without pain, for once.

She wrapped her arm around Mari's waist, slipping her hand in the warm, sweet valley under her breasts, to feel her ribs rise and fall with each breath. Nerida moved strands of her wife's damp hair to nuzzle the nape of her neck. She felt her life replete with riches: the joy of being alive, having purpose and love.

A breeze travelled all the way from Antarctica, thousands of miles to the south, over waves and whales, rattling the donga walls. Nerida got up, careful not to disturb her wife. Opening the shutter and the small window in the bathroom, she inhaled the breeze, fresh on her face and chest.

The stars seemed near. Powerful enough to influence life on Earth. She saw colours in them, brighter than diamonds in the clear desert sky.

CHAPTER 3
TIME SLIP 1: Future

Gundungurra Country. Formerly known as, 'New South Wales'

Sunday March 16, 2036

On another night, the bed in their accommodation was hard, hot and lumpy. Nerida couldn't tell if she was asleep or awake. She heard Mari's gentle snoring, the distant dogs barking at the moon. But her brain and spirit generated voices and images in her head, racing away. Took her to a far place.

She saw a wide sky in her dream, felt herself travelling at speed.

Over the mountains, Nerida drives into plains of dry, silver-grey trees and straw grasses, heading west. She is in a car, but it's a different kind of vehicle. In this dream or vision, she knows her vehicle can connect with others, making a kind of train in urban areas, but that's east of the mountains. Here she drives it manually for the enjoyment of it. And, she realises in a flash, to be disconnected from the satellites, rudimentary as they are now. *So we can't be tracked*, she thinks.

'Straight into the sun. That wasn't good planning,' her wife comments as she flicks a switch to tint the windscreen. 'That's better. Can you see?'

Nerida realises that she is driving because Mari's vision is unreliable. *Sometimes she sees, sometimes she doesn't.*

Houses are few, far from their path and low to the ground. Kangaroos lift their silky heads at the rushing sound of the hydrogen car's tyres.

'What do people do for water here?' Mari asks. The sun lights her white curls, shows fine lines on her olive skin. She's wearing square sunglasses with dark green glass and a gold frame. Mari speaks seven languages, five of them fluently, and could calm a shark while diving. But life on dry land was opaque to her curiosity.

'They collect rainwater. And they pull drinking water from air.'

'But it's so dry.'

'The trees still breathe out moisture,' Nerida replies. 'Maybe you should come and stay here a while. Call the rain.'

Mari, head up, surveys the surrounding hills and the horizon. The earth opens to her senses like a bride.

'People living inland need a patch of trees,' says Nerida. 'To generate water when humidity is low. Condensation from the morning sun, you can catch that, too. It gets good and cold here at night. Makes a fog.'

'The underground water's poisoned, of course,' Mari coughs.

There's a scent of baked earth and dust from the drought-stricken country.

'I can smell apples,' Mari says. 'Somebody's brewing cider somewhere.'

Nerida can't smell it. 'We need to be in Naarm tomorrow, so let's drive until the light's gone,' she says. Mari's going to channel at a meeting of scientists, technologists, craftsmen. *And unclassifiable weirdos like us*, she thinks. People seeking connections between different disciplines.

Nerida wants to keep Mari happy and well for the upcoming meeting. *I'll brew herbs to help her sleep with that cough.*

And I need goldenseal on this breast. She lays a hand gently on her four-day-old injury. It throbs.

She mentally locates the bandages she'll need. Calculates where they'll next stay long enough to do a proper laundry before the conference.

Mari notices her pain. 'If I cross paths with the bastard that hurt you, I'll kill him. *Des kotzd me à!*' she swears in one of her mother languages.

'You can hate his stupidity, but it won't change him. He thinks he's Spock with a phaser,' Nerida says dryly. The pain of the wound is tiring.

'*Den knüpf i an de Eier nuff.*' Mari scowls. She wants to hang him up by his testicles.

She gently rubs Nerida's shoulder near the hole. Her touch erases the pain momentarily. Mari looks into her face, concerned. Nerida returns a quick, thin smile.

A roo leaps across the road in front of them. The car bleeps, slows itself. 'Just don't hit one,' Mari says. 'I know they're supposed to bounce off these cars, but I don't trust it. We're quiet and they get curious. This path should be fenced by now, really.'

The car is so noiseless they can hear each other breathing.

'*Dhunuwi yalaan*,' Nerida says softly in her Aboriginal language. 'The sun is going down.'

About the upcoming meeting, Mari says, 'What annoys me at these conferences is people who chase me outside of the sessions, telling me 'Ask Aedgar this,' or 'What does M'Hoq Toq think about that?'

I have to tell them over and over that I don't have a personal ear to the spirits. I don't hear what they say.'

Nerida turns on music: Bessie Smith jumps over a century, leaving grief and worry behind, her throaty voice deciding between lovers of different genders, taking none of them too seriously.

The clunking piano resonates in the vehicle.

'Should be right this time,' Nerida says. 'I've written it in the abstract. That they need to come to see you channel if they want to hear what our friends say. Or ask obscure questions.' She peers at the path ahead, around the white sun. 'It's scientists. There will be numbers people.'

Someone with a formula, for sure, that needs to be reduced to constituent concepts in our friend's response. Someone from the quantum club asking about the second gesture on the 57th dance of the muon.

'And there'll be someone asking the colour of their true love's eyes,' Mari says, reading her thoughts. 'You've told me before that Aedgar handles them all gracefully. It's true, isn't it? Much better than I would handle the stuffed shirts.'

We're going to meet people who listen, Nerida assures herself. 'People going to this summit do important work,' she says, flipping a sunshade down to her side as they turn, cruising south.

'They're desperate,' Mari comments coolly. 'I won't forget that *Grasdackel* that kept asking me about graviton spin at dinner the

last time I channelled for physicists. Why ask me? Why ask anyone
if you think you know it all?'

Nerida smiles. A *Grasdackel* is a moron, but literally a grass
sausage dog. 'You never forget anything. I know.'

Her wife's curls are lit by the sun beside her now, making a
frizzy halo. Nerida only glimpses Mari's strong, sharp-featured
European face, but she feels her warmth beside her as the
surrounding air cools. She puts a hand on Mari's arm, caresses it
through her bamboo sleeve.

'They're interested in what Aedgar and M'hoq Toq and
Bartgrinn have to say,' Nerida says with a buzz of pride.

'Yeah, it's good. Conferences aren't about free pens and tax
deductions anymore,' Mari adds.

They cross a narrow wooden bridge where a deep creek runs
after rains.

'Is your passport still valid?' Nerida asks, suddenly nervous.

'Of course, it is. It's digital. Self-renews unless someone decides
to stop you. Are you still back in the 2020s?' Mari smiled, gazing
across the plain. 'Look out.'

Nerida slows for an echidna ambling along the path in the
grasses. The hedgehog triggers an alarm on the dashboard, which
she switches off. 'I am a bit nervous. Sometimes I have to remind
myself we need our passports to travel here. Which names are we
using?'

'We can use our usual names. We're legal here.' Mari keeps up
with details of their legal status in different districts.

She coughs. 'Remember back in 2020, when the rental
company offered us an upgrade? And we were pleased, but then
the car had Victorian plates? Even though we were driving in other
states.' Mari settles into her seat.

'New South Wales people gave us the death stare whenever we
stopped at traffic lights.

'As if we were from the Melbourne outbreak. I thought that
one prick might smash the car windows venting his anger on us.
Did you forget how he pounded his fist on the hood?'

'I had forgotten that. Sometimes we felt like outlaws, then,
already,' Nerida reflects. The sun is getting low now, turning

orange. 'That was before the big Sydney wave. The states and cities still had their Colonial names.'

Mari narrows her eyes. She points out camels lining up to go back to their shed for the evening. The smell of them wafts through her cracked open window. She closes it, opens an air vent. Nerida notices that she sees well today.

It never occurred to either of them, back in the 20s, that someone might want them followed and wish them harm. That word of the 'voices and visions' could have wafted like incense from the cribs at Newman to the penthouse boardrooms in Meanjin. Nobody could be too careful since that moon fiasco.

The 'gougers,' an epithet for the remnant resources corporations, were still on the lookout for those that undermined them.

'I went to the Post Office that April to pick up my Australian passport.' Mari warms to her story. She has that Romany way of getting nostalgic about drama and conflict. 'I needed it to apply to get into Western Australia. And the woman there said, "Aren't you sweet? You know, darling, Western Australia is part of the same country."'

'They wanted my Australian passport number in the permit application forms, though, so I could go there with you. I was right. I needed it. And she was the one who had no idea.'

'True.'

'No travel without citizenship!' Her eyes spark. 'We're all in this together,' she sings. 'Huh! One country where being a migrant or resident was never enough. So much meanness and ignorance at the end of the world. Look at the way Aboriginal people were treated then.' Mari scowls into the sun.

'Some things are fairer now, eh,' Nerida concedes.

'We got the exemption because you're a doctor. That was a good trip.' Mari turns to look behind them to the north, where an eagle swoops, scooping a lizard or a small snake in its talons.

'I remember lots of pressure,' Nerida corrects her. 'It was gruelling. We needed permits to cross Queensland and the Northern Territory, each lasted only hours. Getting up at 4am four days in a row to drive a thousand kilometres each day. I was exhausted by the time we got to Western Australia for quarantine.'

'Well, I drove, and I liked it. No one else on the road. Driving across the country, even passing through the cities and towns, took no time at all.' Below the dashboard, Mari points to specks of reddening cloud on the horizon. Makes a gesture towards gathering them together for rain. But she is only playing. 'And two weeks locked up with you wasn't so bad.'

'We were both crying by the end of that one,' Nerida reminds her.

'Oh, yeah. The bed bugs.' Mari scratches at the thought.

'After the summit finishes on Wednesday, we've got two appointments on Thursday. One for imaging, then in the afternoon we'll see the scientist. About stem cells for you.'

Nerida mentally rehearses conversations with the researcher she's never met. *The fella who'll give us the tools to regrow Mari's foot.* She feels the impact of the thought of it in her belly, hope surging from her heart to her head.

Solar lights by the path switch on. 'Might be forty minutes of light left,' Mari interrogates rest stops they pass.

A safe spot with food, fresh water and a view, Nerida visualises. She hasn't seen anyone else on the road and feels relieved as the sky darkens. Keeping the cars lights off, she uses its sensors to navigate.

'Aren't you glad that they're producing whole cars in that neighbouring country over there now?' Mari ponders after a while.

'You talking about *Palyku* country, in the Pilbara over west?'

'Yeah. Not shipping out truckloads of dirt. They just make the whole car. Great use of sugarcane and chaff. People have the skills. Growing up and living where they're born helps. People learn more in depth.

'Plenty of room to store hydrogen in some of the old mines. Remember how it was all about the economy? All about the vaccinations? And now there are so many fewer people living on this planet.'

Mari swats at a mosquito as it comes through the vent. For a minute or two she's grabbing the air like a puppy, then smacking herself on the neck. She kills it. 'Bastard! Look, it's got blood in it already,' she says. 'Fly times finished. Mosquitos have woken up.

'Some didn't believe in it. But they were forced to have those vaccines. They didn't work,' Mari says. She holds up a hand,

hushing Nerida. 'I know you'll say they were a promising attempt.
But they shouldn't have approved them all before the guinea pig
stage, you know? All the humans were the guinea pigs.'

'We were in a difficult situation. Pressure to get vaccinated was
enormous. All the evidence said it was the sensible thing to do. But
our friends were telling us otherwise,' Nerida says.

Mari shakes her head.

'You know that virus is clever. It's got consciousness. It just
changes. I wish it could have fallen in love with the mosquitoes.
They could have eradicated each other.'

*Sometimes Mari claims ideas she channelled years ago as her own. It
seems like her mind opens to the Beings' ideas when she'd tuned in to the
rainclouds. Or the country.*

'Don't bring any rain yet. Just hold off,' Nerida says. 'I smell
lemon eucalyptus. We'll make a smoky fire to keep the mozzies
away.' She pulls the car into a protected clearing, the wheels
crunching on stones. 'Let's sleep here.'

'No flames, hidden embers,' Mari insists.

CHAPTER 4

Resume Linear Time: Recent Past

Western Desert Community

Saturday October 18, 2014

It was Saturday. They slept in past the closing time of the community's only shop. Jolted awake by the roaring air conditioner labouring against the searing heat.

Nerida felt disoriented. Was that a dream or a vision? *Is my subconscious looking for reassurance that Mari and I have a future, feeling safe together? Or giving reassurance to me? From a real future?*

*But we were fleeing surveillance. Mari had a problem with her eyes. I'd been hurt. Something about vaccinations…*Fragmented images flew around her head as she got up, disturbed.

She went to pee.

Her eyes looked intense in the dull, metal mirror as she washed.

She filled the calcified kettle, feeling like she wanted to remember the vision's vivid conversations but leave behind the knowing unease of it. It felt so real. Cups clattered. The spoon chimed. She didn't care as much as usual if she woke Mari.

Soon after, a neighbour started their washing machine. The vibration of it shook their house because the shipping-container units they lived in were joined by a rickety metal fence. Mari got up, strapped on her leg, put on her shoe. She took the sweet coffee Nerida offered gratefully, her black curls wild as Einstein's.

Nerida put her head against her wife's chest and drew her into a hug, smelling the scent of her skin and the soft cotton of her worn t-shirt.

After coffee, Mari offered to go into trance. She slipped her spirit out her body easily.

That big blue waterhole she goes to must be cool today, Nerida thought.

The Medicine Man M'Hoq Toq flowed in.

Mari had been channeling his words for about fifteen minutes, with Nerida listening, mesmerized, when the spirit murmured, 'Something stopped—couldn't tell you what it was.'

Nerida's tablet had died. She was surprised he noticed. She didn't. 'It's a machine to help me record our conversation, as well as writing notes down.'

'It sounds like the flow of water when it runs on rocks—' he said.

That's interesting. To me, it makes no sound at all. She wondered whether spirits heard through Mari's ears.

She met M'Hoq Toq in 2012.

That was the easiest of his many names and she still didn't get it right. For a while, in the early days, she spelled it M'Hoq N'toq. Then M'Hoq Tauk.

Eventually she had to ask Monica about it, who accepted Nerida's spelling on the old man's behalf. Even if most spirits said names didn't matter (Monica was one of them), that old soul took his names seriously. He was the only spirit Nerida met who proudly recalled many of his names from manifold lifetimes. Names had significance in his cultures.

A noble being, he was a Native American Healer, and a man, in most of his lives. Monica had given her a list of about a dozen tribes and countries he'd inhabited in North America. He came as a woman only twice, he told Nerida when she asked, for the sake of a rounded education, but had found living in a female body hard.

Nerida felt a special freedom and sharp respect with that non-physical being. He expressed values and concepts that resonated with her Aboriginality. She used to be scared of him. Still was, sometimes. All three spirits Mari regularly channelled were direct, truth tellers. Each was confronting in their own individual way. M'Hoq Toq was able to scold her, to get her onto her path gently but powerfully, in just the way her Aboriginal grandmother, her father's mother, did.

She straightened her spine, marshalling questions.

Her mind was with people suffering on another continent. 'There's a terrifying sickness in Africa. Thousands of people have died already,' she said.

He took his time. 'There will be quite a few more.'

M'Hoq Toq kept Mari's eyes closed when he spoke. Nerida felt his energy shift, as if inside and far away, the way she sometimes felt a patient 'go inside' when they were seriously ill. Or, mundanely, the way they used to when she worked in the factory, long before she studied to be a doctor. She and her comrades would talk all morning as their hands moved over the metal plates, then say, 'I'm going inside now,' and become meditative on the production line. *It's as if he goes to consult a book or a scrying glass*, she imagined.

'It will spread—mainly south,' he foretold. 'You'll have a few sufferers in the other directions as well, but it will go mainly to the south. South all the way to the water, east all the way to the water.' He indicated each direction with a slight movement of Mari's chin.

The strange coastal desert of Angola and Namibia, all the way across forests and plains to tourist beaches of Mozambique. And then to South Africa. Ebola in South Africa's cities and townships? All this cannot happen.

She rocked to keep the blood circulating to her legs on the narrow, hard chair. Mari's form was opposite her, with the unearthly relaxation of her muscles that only came when she channelled, or sometimes, rarely, when she slept.

Pain made Mari frown and toss when she slept. It bedevilled her neck, shoulders, hips and legs.

Days she channelled, zoned in to her photography or paintings, or when they went swimming, had sex or got stoned, those were easier days. But then she did too much and it came back, meaner.

The heat outside made cracking noises in the metal and plastic roof. The small desert community of mainly Aboriginal people was deeply peaceful. Most were sleeping. The air conditioner and fridge, machinery of survival, seemed loud.

'Should be seen as a warning,' M'Hoq Toq said, focused on the Ebola virus.

'The trouble is, it's not the same as it was before. It has changed to spread more easily. You can catch it if someone talks to you closely. You don't even need to touch the person.

'It comes with a breath,' he made a starburst with Mari's long fingers, 'out of the lungs.'

Ebola. The name made Nerida's neck prickle. Her shoulders ached.

'The trouble is it can survive in liquid and air. And it survives longer than it previously did. It likes heat and moisture, that's why it mainly spreads to the south. It can't survive heat when it's dry. Strong heat kills it.

That's a relief. This place is hot and dry. The Australian western deserts had scorching summers, with winters cold enough to put the reptiles to sleep. 'What about cold?'

'It becomes inactive and will reappear if the temperature rises. Can survive in the ground as well as in fresh water. Doesn't like salt water or sea water.'

'I see.'

'Animals can spread it.'

'Really?'

'Farm animals, herds of animals, domesticated animals. Some wild animals, too. If you get too close to those, you'll rather get killed by the animal than the disease. Quicker.'

'Where does the disease come from?' She asked, thinking bats, monkeys.

'Created.'

'By people?' She sometimes found it hard to process the damage humans caused.

'People started it, but it transformed. They lost control.'

Her morning coffee and bread sat in her belly like a stone. 'So it's true that they started it as a means of warfare?'

M'Hoq Toq sighed. 'Many things are said to be done in the name of science. There were ideas about warfare, but it was not the primary reason.

'They tried to fight a different disease. They planned to strengthen the body's immune system, make antibodies. Except the creation was stronger than they thought.'

'Is it true that they got the virus from monkeys?' She tried to recall. *Simian origins of Ebola—in science journals. Something about using the viral coat of monkey viruses with medicine inside them to treat HIV.*

Nerida was cautious about genetically engineered viral shells and fragments since what happened to Andy. They were medical students together in the 90s. He was by her side in some classes: his big, soft, easy presence.

That morning, they came out into the sunlight, onto fresh cut lawn, from their Biochemistry and Physiology lectures. 'Are you coming to the experiment?' Andy asked, his face open.

'What are they doing?' Nerida looked up.

Andy frowned behind his glasses. 'Some kind of injection to see how your immune system reacts. Shellfish protein in a viral coat. Sounds delicious, eh?

'They take baseline bloods, then they inject you. Then you come back in six weeks to get your blood checked again. I'm gonna ask if they can check my liver function and get my valproate level done while they're doing it.'

'You can go to any doctor for that.'

'Yes, but this mob will pay me for it.'

'I don't think it's worth it,' she said. 'You know what a viral coat is, right?'

'They take all the virus out of it. It's only the shell—to get the good stuff into the body. All the viral DNA is taken out. It's brilliant, what they do! It'll be all right.' He grasped her small hand with his giant paw, radiating youthful, male confidence. 'They're paying seventy dollars, sis. I need that money for food. We've got nothing at home. And the phone's been cut off.

'If I've grown a prawn head when I see you tomorrow, you'll know why.'

Despite his rich stories of spiritual experiences—he was an Aboriginal man with epilepsy and not averse to a toke—Andy was a man of science. He joined the experiment willingly.

We could never prove a connection between that injection and his illness, she thought.

CHAPTER 5
TIME SLIP 2: Past

A University near Sydney, Eora Country

Monday August 16, 1993

She heard about Andy before she met him. She wasn't sure how she would like him.

Nerida was finishing her science degree, completing compulsory subjects. She knew more about Chemistry and Physics now than she did the first time she studied them, and understood concepts her younger peers did not, but memorising facts for exams still came hard. She felt as if her teachers hefted her a bulky phone book, saying, "Learn this. We'll be testing you on seven of the numbers." Having a record of multiple failures didn't help her confidence.

Andy was already a graduate psychologist with honours, she heard. A Wiradjuri man, he'd studied on his own country at a small, rural campus before moving to Sydney to study medicine. She met him on his way out from their interviews at the medicine faculty.

He was like a glass of sparkling wine, bubbling with success. The Dean of Medicine was thrilled. A bright, young Aboriginal man with a first-class honours degree and a charming personality, Andy put anyone he met at ease. Who wouldn't love him?

Andy was tall, brown and cuddly. As they walked, he put his warm hand on her shoulder. 'We'll be right sis. We'll be in Medicine together. We'll help each other.'

Nerida had no such open door into Med, even if her grade average was high.

She gained high distinctions in Aboriginal Studies. She had distinctions too, in ethics, biology and the history and philosophy of medicine and science.

The Dean grudgingly agreed to admit her to medicine if she achieved credits in all the subjects she previously failed.

Maybe the Dean saw her shouting speeches and slogans out of a megaphone outside the campus library, demonstrating against Black Deaths in Custody, increased student fees or the Australian invasion of East Timor.

Andy claimed attention in the Aboriginal students tearoom that first day. He had a booming voice. He stood hands on hips, with attitude, full of joyous banter. The Student Centre's small lounge was overfull with Aboriginal and Torres Strait Islander students. Many were studying law, eager to participate since the Mabo decision acknowledged Indigenous ownership of Australia, just the previous year. Some were aspiring engineers and accountants.

She followed Andy outside for air. From the wooden verandah they could see part of the hospital. 'Isn't it grand? See that back door there, sis? That's where we'll slip out to see the sky when we work there,' Andy pointed to a dock where orderlies were loading laundry into a van.

At 23, he was six years younger than Nerida. Learning hard sciences and memorisation came easier to him. And he had no children. She was not prone to envy. But he spiked some in her.

Later, Andy told her about his honours project for his psychology degree. 'I examined the relationship between suppressed homosexual desires and religiosity. People came and did this survey, then watched porn.

'You know how psychologists can measure people's sexual arousal? We put sensors on their genitals and their heads.' He indicated where the electrode dots would go with a grin.

Nerida couldn't help a smile. *This guy is bold.* 'So, what did you find?'

'The people who were most religious were most turned on by the porn. And the Christian fundamentalists were most especially turned on by the gay porn.'

'They got paid for that?'

'Of course. You can't ask people to make such sacrifices in the name of science without paying them.'

'Well, people being turned on by what they think is forbidden is not a new dynamic, is it?' asked Nerida.

'Yeah, it was fun though. And it's only an undergraduate honours degree. It wasn't supposed to change the world.' Andy chuckled.

Nerida enjoyed her studies that last semester in science. Chemistry was easier with two Nigerian women, far from home and their young children, tutoring her in the lab.

'We have over five hundred languages in our country,' said Adaku.

'That's brilliant,' said Nerida. 'Aboriginal people used to, before the British came. We have about two hundred left. My language has died. English was my first language. We still know our countries, though.'

Adaku and Nnenne had been well-taught by nuns. They modelled fluency in using burettes, pipettes and volumetric flasks. And they gave Nerida perspective on the sacrifices people made for education. Living in Public Housing an hour or two from campus and working part time to support herself and the kids was easy by comparison.

Nerida enjoyed being a student. *Such a privilege to be somewhere that ideas matter.*

When she met Andy weeks later for lunch, he'd already started some subjects in medicine. Nerida ate salad. He had two hot dogs and chips.

'I should be eating healthy like you,' he said. 'But this is so much cheaper. How much was that?'

'I'm just starting to like salads,' she smiled. 'You have to get a bit older and drier to appreciate them, I reckon. Salads and monogamy are for older people.'

Conversation with Andy was easy. He was interested in everything. In one of her elective subjects, she studied the history of the industrial revolution in Europe.

'I knew the English ruling class did to the Scots and the Irish first what they did to us,' she said, sprinkling pepper from a paper sachet.

'And did the same in India. And Canada. Fiji, you know. Divide and rule. Set people up against each other by favouring one group over another. Degrade people by stereotyping their appearance and culture.

'But I didn't understand before how the English themselves were removed from their land and had their growing and cooking cultures destroyed. All their connections to their own histories were smashed up. It was the first place the factories started, right?

'It helps me understand why Australia is so broken. And why the British food is so bad.'

Andy met her grey eyes with his hazel ones, listening carefully.

'Working class people lived twenty to a house, with big sewer pits in the courtyard. Drinking gin and beer with laudanum in it. There was alum in the flour.'

'What's alum?' he asked.

'It's a metal salt they used to whiten flour. Stops you getting vitamins out of the food.'

Nerida reflected. 'This is the 1850's, when Irishmen lived here together with my Aboriginal clan. They shared the land for about three or four generations without too much trouble. People with a common enemy in the redcoats, sharing drinks, songs and stories.'

'That's about when my English ancestors would have come to Australia,' Andy mused. He didn't talk about his white father much. 'Might be a clue, you reckon, as to why that side of the family was so violent?'

Nerida folded a piece of ham with her fork.

'In England, the children were the only ones who could work in the factories for decades because they fit into the machines. They built the machines small.

'They'd work for twelve hours, then sleep for four hours. Parents had to wake kids to go back to work. Can you imagine? Kids fell into the machines, asleep. It was barbaric.'

'Whitefellas don't know they've got intergenerational trauma, do they?' he said.

'They've got no idea. At least we know our history. Or we push to find it.'

Her voice hardened. 'We know there were massacres. My great-grandmother witnessed a big mob of our people murdered by being forced over a cliff.' Angry tears sprang in her eyes. 'My aunty told me how the women used to go to man traps near the river. Big pits with sharpened wooden spikes. The men fell in to slowly die. Women took them food and water in the night.'

'Why were they built?' Andy asked.

'The invaders used our river to transport timber easily to the coast. Cut down all the magnificent trees. Sent them to furnish Sydney.'

Across the cafeteria a noisy group of students played with food, getting sauce on each other's hair and clothes.

'They treated our men like vermin to be cleared out. Destroyed the hunting grounds and shut off access to water and fishing.'

They sat with the sadness for a minute or two. Their surrounds were noisy enough for privacy.

Andy put a blob of florescent orange sauce by his chips. 'It's supposed to be chili sauce. Just tastes like vinegar. And something bitter,' he said, smacking his lips.

'It's the colour of cane toad ovaries.' Nerida laughed.

'Have you been dissecting cane toads?'

'And tapeworms and liver flukes. And looking at spider's eyes and sperm packages. Invertebrate zoology is amazing!'

Andy raised his eyebrows and gave himself more sauce from the single-serve plastic shell.

'Cane toads are pretty inside. Orange gametes, bright yellow guts. And you don't feel bad about cutting them up, since they're so poisonous they kill everything that eats them.'

'How do they kill the toads? Gas?' Andy asked.

She shook her head. 'Freezing. They go to sleep. There's hundreds of them in freezers next to the morgue, downstairs in the science building. I'm glad we can learn from them.'

Andy understood. 'Do they squirt poison at you if you try to kill them?'

'I don't know. I've never had to kill one. When we get them one of the lab techs has cut out their poison glands. They're still toxic to touch. They're the biggest toads in the world, you know. Easier to find your way around than the inside of a flatworm.'

She was warming to her subject. 'Cane toads live for ten or fifteen years in the wild. Strong animals.

'The fella next to me dissected out his dead toad's heart. It was frozen, right?'

Andy nodded, licking salt off his fingers.

'When it thawed the heart started beating again! I showed it to the tutor, "What's that about?" "Oh, it's just a chemical reaction," he said. Those bastards are hard to kill.'

'There has to be some use to them. They're part of Nature,' Andy said.

'The skin was tough to cut. You could make something from the leather of the big ones, maybe. But they are toxic all through. Should never have been introduced here.'

'People say you can get high by licking the poison on their skin,' Andy said.

Nerida put her fork down. 'That's disgusting. I mean, we used to smoke the threads out of banana skins. Some of my stoner friends wanted to smoke broom flowers once, which is really dangerous.'

'Broom flowers? Causes neuronal death in rats, I remember,' Andy said. 'Kills the cattle.'

Nerida's lips curled in revulsion. 'It causes cardiac arrhythmias.'

Andy packed up his cardboard plate and serviettes, getting up. 'Yeah. And cane toads kill dogs, eh?' He laughed. 'The things people do to try and get high. They're always gonna do it.

'I'll be a harm reduction doctor, Nerida. They should legalise yarndi. A bottle of wine and spliff and I'm feeling no pain.'

CHAPTER 6

Resume Linear Time: Recent Past

Western Desert

Saturday October 18, 2014

A hot, dust-laden wind was making the kids and the dogs excited outide. Nerida saw that one of the dogs had caught a lizard. The children were shouting, excited. *Probably planning to cook it.* She smiled.

M'Hoq Toq was still looking at Ebola. 'They tried it on monkeys.

'They created it from three different, what you call, viruses, taking the strongest part of each of them and creating a new one.

'They planned to test it on monkeys first. Back then, they thought the monkeys were closely related to humans. They were small monkeys, though, not tiny but small. Not very similar to humans at all.

'They figured it didn't work, so they stopped. Except their creation didn't stop.

'They realised. They noticed they lost control.

'From our point of view, they never had control. They were playing with things they knew nothing about.'

'That's why you say it's a warning, huh?'

'Yeah. Stay away from creating viruses.' He paused, and she felt him looking deeply. 'There have been some other trials in other places with other animals as well, much earlier than that.'

Out the window, Nerida saw a kite dive. The windows had heavy, horizontal shutters—for protection against sandstorms, lightning or kids throwing rocks—propped up in the daytime like an awning. She couldn't see much of the sky.

'Arabia, 1200, probably,' he said.

'Hmm.' *Does he mean 1200 BC or CE? Does it matter? Long time ago.* 'How did that go?'

'Bad.' He whispered. 'There are remnants still there.'

If it was Common Era, she realised, *that's less than a thousand years ago.*

'If it gets activated again, that would 'solve' a lot of other problems in the region. People would have to reunite, no matter what religion, to fight it, to survive.'

What a strange concept.

'Just as well the climate is much drier there now,' he said. 'If it gets humid again, as it was back then, there will be another 'creation' emerging again out of that dust and sand.

'Nothing to look forward to.'

'No.' She had trouble comprehending the idea that a thousand-year-old human-created virus could wake up out of the desert sands of Arabia. She wasn't sure she wanted to know. It wasn't something she could call anybody about. *It was humid there a thousand years ago? People created a virus there then?? When did humanity start experimenting with diseases? Could any of this be true?*

'It will take a while. But the climate will change more. It will get rougher.'

In the Arab countries? How could that get any rougher? Or does he mean on the planet? There were floods in Brazil recently. An avalanche at Mount Everest killed sixteen Nepalese guides in April when the snow melted due to global warming. Thousands of people were buried in mudslides in Afghanistan and India. Wildfires in California were the most destructive on record, destroying hundreds of homes. 'It's getting rougher already,' she said.

It goes on and on, she thought. *Last week there was that cyclone. An avalanche and a blizzard caused by the cyclone killed 40 people in Nepal on Wednesday.*

'You think? You have no idea. This is just the beginning. Tiny beginnings.'

I hate him saying that. 'Is that because the earth needs to sustain or protect itself?' She tried to see the bigger picture.

'The planet needs to regenerate some different energy, to get back into some kind of balance,' was all he replied.

Perhaps he senses my difficulty in comprehending all this, she thought.

'So,' she said, 'we were thinking about travelling next month to the other side of the world.' They planned to travel with the money, or credit really, that they earned from working in the remote community. When she was working, Nerida topped up her credit card balances then used them to travel again. They might go to Germany to visit family. From the western side of Australia, where they were, they could go via South Africa.

'Don't travel to that special part of the world, especially not south in this part,' M'Hoq Toq warned.

'The south of Africa?'

'It's affecting a big part of this continent,' he said.

'Is there anything we can do medically to help these people?' She asked.

She heard children playing. Out the shuttered window, they built a tree house with a cardboard box in a long-dead mulga tree. The tree stood tolerantly in the yard between the desert dwellings.

M'Hoq Toq took a sharp intake of breath. 'We have to think about this some more. This will be a challenge.'

She realized she was impatiently clicking her pen.

'We are thinking of a combination of fungi. Two.

'With minerals. Three… Silver.'

Kids shouted and laughed as their treehouse fell out of the tree with one of them in it.

'And one acid,' he concluded. 'Two fungi, three minerals, silver, one acid.'

She was curious. Was he really suggesting a formula for treating Ebola? 'Silver is one mineral?' She knew silver as an effective antibacterial.

'No.'

'The fungi, are they the ones that we are using already to kill germs, to kill bacteria? Those sorts of fungi? Antibiotics?'

'Yes,' he said. 'The disease weakens the body. The body eventually can't fight the bacteria—that's what the fungi are for.'

'How do the minerals work?'

'Blocking the connections of a disease on the tiny base of the molecules. Like a blocked pipe.'

He says molecules slowly. Perhaps it is a new word for him. I wonder what Native American concepts of quantum physics are?

The sound of a lizard moving on the roof brought her back to the moment. 'Uhuh. Stops the disease connecting, so to say?'

'Ya.'

'Is the acid one which is normally eaten, like a vitamin? Or is it something to activate the other ingredients?'

'Activate,' he agreed. Then added, 'Charcoal as well.'

Am I the only one that knows about this? That can't be. 'Are there people working on this already?'

He took his time to answer, as if he surveyed the globe. *Looking for what? An energy connected to the endeavour? Researchers' thoughts?*

'Two groups, working in one direction each,' he said. 'They should combine what they have.' Then, 'I can see a yellow colour acid.'

She saw sulphur yellow in her mind's eye and blurted, 'Sulphur? Sulphuric acid?' *Sulphur is yellow, but the acid isn't.*

'No smell. From a plant.'

'Like lemon juice?' *Vitamin C, ascorbic acid?*

'No fruit. Root. Grows in the Americas—in the big southern part.

'Does it grow in the forest or on the plains?'

'Forest. It can be found in the bark of that plant as well. Root is stronger.'

'But it's not cinchona, for malaria? Different one, eh?' she asked.

'Different but similar.'

The neighbour's washing machine hummed and shook their house like a wire. Nerida felt it in the metal chair. It was too hot outside. The kids had gone into one of the big family houses, looking for iceblocks.

He continued, 'Acts like a poison if you use too much. It will be a challenge now—because that thing has changed—to find the balance.

'So those victims don't get killed by this acid. But you need enough to kill the creation—the virus.

'The other thing that kills it is fire. So, if you have the disease on other things, you need to burn it.'

Nerida visualised health workers in the Democratic Republic of Congo online, wearing hazmat suits, burning everything that belonged to an Ebola victim. She asked, 'Can it live outside the body on objects? You said it can live in the dust.'

'Yes, it can live in the water as well. High temperature and moisture, that activates it. It can sleep for a very long time. Until you get the exact factors that wake it up.

'So, in areas where there's lots of it, they should find this medicine for the victims, mix it up for them. And burn the area. It can't survive dry heat.'

'We tried sometimes to kill things with a breath of boiling water,' he said.

Steam. I love expressions from his lifetimes on Earth. Experiences on Earth matter, we take them with us. We never lose who we are and what we learned.

'It doesn't work for this because it's not dry,' he mused.

'Mmm. What about the chemicals that we splash around to kill germs and viruses? Do they help?' she asked.

He shook the head.

'Nothing?' All her colleagues, cleaners, nurses and doctors, using their enormous bottles of acrid chemicals to clean and disinfect, believing lives depended on it.

Lives do depend on it. Basic hygiene is the most important force we have for good public health. She rebelled against being associated with a stance that disregarded the benefits of disinfectant and proper cleaning.

She also knew Mari, a fastidious cleaner, would hate that.

'They help people with their thought.' M'Hoq Toq explained. 'They think they do something that helps. It makes them feel better. If they feel better, they might not feel weak, so they might not get it.'

Okay, so there's a placebo effect.

'The disease itself is not impressed by it. Just goes to sleep again for a while,' he said.

Nerida leaned back in her chair, trying to understand the bigger picture.

She could be scholarly. At least she tried hard with books, like all doctors.

She studied channelling as best she could.

She read some of the *Seth* books, trying to understand the phenomenon when Mari learned to control her channelling in 2012.

They travelled to the US then, so that Mari could find out if she was a channel, and whether she could negotiate with the spirits. So that they would talk in English, at least.

Monica helped them then. Magnificent Monica was a non-physical being, channelled by Dawn, a sweet-natured and sharp-witted, former sports teacher. Nerida found her on the net, found that Monica, in phone consultations, knew things about her that no one else did.

She remembered the inner happiness she felt when she woke the next day, thinking, *So, we really do have past lives. We are souls. Spirits in the material world, she sang to herself.*

She had told some friends about her discovery. Most never spoke to her again. That still hurt. She felt sad that they couldn't tolerate the change in her when her worldview expanded. It made her cautious about sharing her experiences now with other doctors and scientists. Or old friends she didn't want to lose because of a difference in ideas.

In her reading that year, Nerida was impressed by how many fundamental New Age concepts came from Seth. He was a non-physical being. Perhaps he was another kind of Earth spirit, as Nerida sometimes thought of the beings Mari channelled.

Monica referred to Seth's writings. Her endorsement of another spirit's body of channelled material spurred Nerida to grapple with the books.

The idea that thoughts create reality, that consciousness precedes manifestation, that we are all immortal souls having an adventure to learn in a material world: all this was there in Seth's sometimes austere writings.

She was encouraged and inspired too, by Seth's medium, a fiery, talented poet named Jane Roberts. Her dedicated husband Robert Butts, an artist, transcribed the Seth material.

Robert used a typewriter and carbon paper, sometimes writing from notes made in shorthand, he documented and created a huge body of work.

The couple had the earnest openness of the 60s and 70s. They were not pure. They were not religious. Jane chain-smoked while she channelled Seth.

Some people came to sessions stoned or tripping. Some people came to channelling sessions to talk to and listen to Seth every week for years.

The group made experiments to try to fathom the reality and reliability of the channelled material. They brought questions from their lives and from the broader society.

Jane and Robert had a passion for each other. They had sex before she channelled, every time. *That sounds good. But exhausting,* Nerida thought.

Nerida was relieved that Mari was able to 'let go' without that. Without any ritual really, beyond fasting, quieting and grounding herself. And the spirits Mari channelled were restrained and dignified compared to Seth's loud flamboyance.

Above all, Nerida appreciated Jane and Robert for showing a way, their own personal way, to respond to and integrate this strange phenomenon of deep trance channelling into their lives.

For Mari, as for Jane, the ability to channel was an unsought gift.

Like Mari and Nerida, Robert and Jane were atheists before they began their spiritual work.

And for Nerida, Robert served as an example of a partner whose life was devoted to sharing and promulgating the channelled material. Seth's words had an effect in the world.

She learned a lot in her reading, even if she didn't agree with everything asserted there.

Nerida struggled with the concept that each soul's death was a choice. Or that people enduring injustice had chosen to do so, whether to learn or teach others. *Such human misery and so many deaths are wrong. All that needless suffering. If it's true that each soul has made their own choices, what's the point of fighting injustice?*

Monica told Nerida years ago, before she even met Mari, that she had lived over 256 lifetimes on Earth.

Nowadays, she wondered if Monica was toying with her then, telling her any random number to teach her the concept of many lives lived. *And make me feel wise. It doesn't matter.*

The point was that she'd been born in the company of other souls she knew, had lived as a child and then as a parent, as a gay and a straight person, male and female and in between.

She'd been diverse races: Aboriginal, Asian, Central American, Native American, Polynesian. Different kinds of European and African. Even Lemurian and Atlantean, names she'd barely heard and thought to be fantasy before she talked to Monica. Continents that were still unknown to her.

She lived rich lives and poor, bright and simple, successful and hopeless. She or he had been handsome and plain, able-bodied and not. He'd suicided, she'd been the murdered and the killer, they'd been the inquisitor and the victim. So many ways of being human.

The spirit that was now Nerida had been and learned from them all. *Haven't other people?*

CHAPTER 7

The Donga in the Desert

Same Day

Now, out in the desert where she worked to keep people well, Nerida asked the ancient spirit: 'Tell me about the lives of the people who are suffering, those contracting Ebola and dying from it—what things are they learning from this experience, those souls?

'Surely most of us have been through plague already in other lifetimes?'

'Some have,' M'Hoq Toq reflected sadly. He took a breath. 'Our people died from what you call chicken pox and the measles.'

'That's right. Terrible.' He triggered memories of the mass deaths in Eora country, now called Sydney, when the British arrived. They brought smallpox and influenza. Syphilis, too. Tears suddenly pricked her eyes as if the ancient being shifted her intellect into true emotion.

Still the intellectual, she asked, 'What does a soul learn from this kind of experience?'

There was a deep quiet.

I wish I hadn't asked him, she thought. When he eventually replied, the words were slow and grave. She had visions of the desperation, of people enduring plague and genocide, as he spoke.

'Nothing is for granted.

'Never feel safe.

'Observe what's happening around you.

'Try to learn from what you see.

'Try to choose a different path that takes you somewhere else.'

'That's horrible,' she said. *You can tell he's been there. Does he mean choose a different path in a new lifetime?*

'You can't see everything as "souls have chosen to die there,"' he explained. 'They will learn that they suffer or leave this planet because of other humans' actions.

'It doesn't take a war to kill someone. Many are only in the wrong place.

'And most likely, it wasn't them that created the rise in temperature and humidity that made them vulnerable.'

Nerida saw her neighbours, seventy metres away across the red earth, preparing a fire on their concrete verandah. The grandmother sat down in a camp chair with a cup of tea. Nerida recognised her height and shape. The children teased the dogs, who barked and jumped, throwing up dust in the late afternoon light.

Summer's approaching. It's getting too hot to live here in Summer now.

Nerida thought also about people on islands. She'd been to places in the Indian and Pacific oceans where people watched sea levels rising, their homes disappearing forever as the Earth warmed. As the planet tried to adapt to poisoning, to changes made by industries, and cars and cows, far away.

'It's about learning that, if you do something on one side of the planet, you will see results on another side of the planet,' he said.

'If you create something here, it can seem like nothing happens. The result will be seen in a very different place, which can be very far away, in your understanding.

'This planet is a tiny place in the universe. But you can have effects from this miniscule place happening in a different place in the universe.

'That is why this planet needs to be in a better balance, creating better energy—which is not necessarily the same thing as creating a better world for humankind. It's about the planet.'

Nerida nodded. 'If humankind doesn't learn to look after the planet more respectfully, the planet will look after itself without humankind.'

'It will. This planet needs gentler creatures living on it.'

Nerida felt a cry in her chest when he said that. 'So,' she said, 'we're engaged in an endeavour to see if humans can be those gentler creatures or not.'

Outdoors, the dogs took off, thundering across the yard, shaking the house as they passed. They ran like greyhounds around the houses. The smell of the dust seeped in through the vents. Kids ran off excited, the adults calling them back.

With a deep sigh, M'Hoq Toq explained. 'There is a new, almost like a new species, of gentler individuals emerging. There will be more and more of them.

'But you still have these (we would call them) 'classics' around. They're bad.

'They just need to learn quick and leave. So, they can recollect what they've done and come back in a different way. Or not come back at all.'

'Are you talking about a gentler kind of person coming, or are you talking about another animal, like the whales?'

'Everything has to become gentler. Treat each other and other species with the respect that's needed,' M'Hoq Toq said. 'Manmade belief systems don't support this. They teach who is superior to someone else and who's not. They don't teach respect and tolerance.

'They need to defeat others, because they feel superior to them. This is an old problem. It has started many wars— eliminating whole groups of living beings.'

Nerida agreed. 'The people here in the desert have a particular story. Their land was poisoned for thousands of years. Atomic bombs were detonated on it. It happened when I was a child. The people had to move away. They found this place to come and live, far away from others.' Her fingers entwined. She rubbed her thumb against her palm.

Some of her patients were survivors of the British-Australian nuclear bombings ('tests') in the desert nearby in the 1950s and 60s. Everyone there knew someone, most had a family member, affected by the blasts. A couple of her patients were dying of the effects of exposure as children.

After decades of degradation and difficulty, the people chose that place and built the town in a heroic exercise of self-determination. It was remote, almost 700 kilometres from the nearest town. Nerida was used to working with other Aboriginal people in remote places. That was a reason they chose her.

'It is a good place for them,' M'Hoq Toq said. 'Except there are others who want this place.'

Nerida took a moment. *Others want to take control of this land back. No matter how hard they tried to get away from the exploiters, there's no escaping it. The invaders think this whole island belongs to them now, to use as they please. For the mining companies, the people connected to this place are just surface scrub, scree to be bulldozed. Insignificant in their measure of tonnes per vertical metre.* She felt anger and unease for the people.

'They do have a chance to keep it. And to keep the ones away that want it. But some people in this area have to be convinced, to understand that the ones that want it have reasons unrelated to those of the original people. It's not about caring for the place. It's about greed.'

'Yes. And destruction,' she added.

'This one always comes with the other one, no matter where and how,' he agreed.

The donga baked in the mid-afternoon sun. The fridge revved.

'A place of strange noise,' he observed.

'It's the technology we have, I'm sorry. It's the machine for keeping the food cold so it lasts longer.'

'Hmm.'

'So we don't have to hunt every day,' she explained, even if the hunting and gathering that she and Mari did was at the community's single shop.

'We didn't hunt every day,' he said.

'I know. You could dry your meat,' she said.

'Or put it in the snow.'

How lovely it was to think of snow, now. 'Yes,' she said. 'Much quieter!'

M'Hoq Toq made a sharp exhalation of breath. 'I might go for now. I might need to think about medicine.'

'Thank you. It's been a pleasure to see you, as always.'

'I am delighted. Glad I could talk to you. I hope I've been of some help. We'll talk to you again.'

They stayed inside then, under the air-con, until the sun was lower.

They'll call me a crackpot or a crank, barely tolerated, she thought, if she tried to talk to her colleagues about this. But what was the use of all her studies, all her qualifications, if she couldn't speak up? She massaged her forehead, pulled her fingers through her hair. Made a snack to distract herself.

In the golden hour, Mari wanted to go out, taking photos.

Her wife clambered along the roadside, stretching and crouching to find the perfect shot of sun rays through spinifex or a wallaby posing, chewing grass. Nerida walked around the stones and bushes, thinking about the channelled material.

She was excited when M'Hoq Toq talked about the classes of medicines needed to treat Ebola. *Surely, somebody could be encouraged by that information.*

She planned to go to speak at the United Nations in New York next year.

Representing other rainbow people who worked in health, she had the opportunity to speak up for people of diverse sexual orientations and genders, living in places where they were persecuted.

She thought of her gorgeous gay cousin-brother Greg. Or her beloved friend Andy. *Both flamboyant, queenly types. Andy dressed in a silver sequinned ballgown and sang loud cabaret songs at University reviews. Greg looks amazing in kajal and lipstick.*

Men are hanged in Iran just for being like them.

She gazed lovingly at Mari, reaching into the car to change a lens.

Mari lived in the Maldives, where a fundamentalist current of Islam was the legally enforced state religion, for five years in the 90s. She was a diving instructor there. Before the accident.

Mari knew she loved women then. Kept it a heavily guarded secret. Nerida asked her once what would have happened to her if she was outed as a lesbian in the Maldives.

'I would have been deported immediately. It would have shattered my life,' she said. 'But that's nothing compared to what they did to locals. Men were executed. Women were stoned.'

The sun was setting behind a tall sandhill. *See how fast the world turns.*

Mari scrambled, strong on her hands and knees, looking for the best angle to catch the last of its rays. She'd want to stay to see the remnants of cloud in the east light up orange and purple. 'The best comes after the sun's gone,' she always said.

Sometimes they went out on the darkest nights and Mari photographed the stars.

Her paintings are inspired by light. Nerida turned towards the east, where Mari pointed her camera. *The moon's rising. She'll want to stay for that.*

M'Hoq Toq's protocol for treating Ebola. Maybe I could print flyers to encourage people to explore it. Print an extract of the conversation.

He's a Native American Medicine Man who's sending me to the UN with his insights. They don't need to know that he's a disembodied spirit!

She imagined handing flyers out to the delegates at her session. Or leaving them to be read in a humid, coffee-scented cafeteria.

Perhaps she should go to one of New York's progressive research institutes and talk to researchers.

She visited a famous hospital there once when she was a student, visiting the city on a scholarship. The institute had plants, comfortable chairs and tea in the waiting room.

Even a concierge to take people's wet umbrellas. They were opened-minded, open-hearted people there, she thought then. *But would any of them be open to an idea about treatment from an unknown person who was not an established researcher?*

And what about the people she was going to New York to represent? Her colleagues in the Rainbow Coalition? She might endanger their hard-won standing at the UN, if she was reprimanded for distributing occult ideas.

The desert moon was a huge, creamy pearl. In the moonlight Nerida saw the red of the sand, the white and yellow rocks. The rocks had shadows. Mari's photos would show the desert colours as bright as if they were in daylight, but in unusual tones.

She enjoyed painting that way, using her exquisite sense for colour. It was an aspect of the mystical quality her work had, this close and unusual observation. They watched the moon get smaller as it climbed.

She thought of people in West Africa, sharing that moon. *Lives are at stake. Ebola has a fifty percent fatality rate: a violent death, haemorrhaging out of all orifices, with the people who love you unable to be close. And health workers endangered. It is so highly contagious,* she thought. *We have no treatment for Ebola. I'm going to the UN. Can I get his ideas out?*

CHAPTER 8

Newman, Parnpajinya. Palyku Country

Monday January 12, 2015

They stayed in a metal apartment. Miners' boots shook the whole building when they tramped on the outside stairs at shift changes. Mari and Nerida's kitchen window overlooked a carpark with the ash-yellow remains of a mountain in the distance behind. Clouds of red dust, the earth bleeding into the sky, rose from the ruined mountain with each blast at the mine, through the day. The inside of the house smelled like plastic.

They had stayed at better and worse places in their travels. Their house at Mutitjulu, with a stunning view of Uluru, was unforgettable, as were the snakes that got into the house.

On Christmas Island their accommodation was in a site carved out of rainforest. Their apartment was up on stilts, so the annual migration of the red crabs did not go through the house.

Being on the road, going where Nerida was most needed, gave Mari the chance to explore incomparable landscapes. Nerida enjoyed meeting people from Australia's hundreds of diverse countries. As long as they were safe and learning, life was okay.

And they spent the money they made travelling between blocks of work, allowing Nerida some space to recover from the intensity and trauma of witnessing destruction of lives and land through dispossession, the violence of these forces playing themselves out in people's lives in sicknesses and accidents and the abuse she and her colleagues endured, which mainly came from management. She worked in places almost nobody else would, by choice.

In Newman, the sun came up each morning as if flames were switched on in a furnace. The heat-baked earth held the skeletal trees surviving on their deepest heart wood. There were no flowers. Longing for moisture, including fantasies of rain, filled Nerida's being. Some afternoons a wind came from the south, but it was hot and dry.

It took a while to find out one of the traditional, proper names for the place: Parnpajinya. She found it at a local gallery. The town of Newman was carved out of Parnpajinya's stone and dirt in the 1960s to exploit rich deposits of iron ore in the surrounding country. 'The name is a classic, isn't it?' she said to Mari. 'Cold War mining town in one word. The New Man for the industrial Stone Age. They used to call the people from around here, stone aged, ignorant bastards. But these are the people who'll do anything to claw out the dirt.'

By local reports, miners were treated well when the town was built. To bring them to the desert, which even then had an extreme climate, they were sold brand new houses for small mortgage payments. But if the prices were low, the contracts were long. And when the twenty-five years of the mortgage was up, several families now, especially the handful that were still union members, found themselves driven out, with psychological brutality, just before it was time to own their houses outright.

They weren't the only ones thrown out. Nerida met few other Aboriginal people. Few families were from that place, Traditional Owners. She was told many Palyku people had moved away from their country, she was told by a Noongar man. She imagined the destruction of their land, the memories of what was done to it and the ongoing despoilation kept them away. Memories of the waterholes, the rock art galleries, whole mountains destroyed. It was all too recent and too vivid. It was all still happening.

Martu people were out at Jigalong Community and came in to the hospital when they needed to.

Birds and animals looked for their places there, too. Flocks of grey and pink galahs still came to Parnpajinya. And cockatoos that should have been white. They were all coated in the red dust. They weighed down the swaying powerlines: raucous, squawking witnesses to the disaster.

Dr Nerida saw a lot of injuries. Broken backs, hands and feet. Amputated digits. Shattered minds. The first three weeks she saw mainly women. *Was there ever a female doctor in Newman?*

Her clinic manager, an affable, dark-humoured redhead, saw Mari at the local supermarket. Susan told her, 'Your wife's doing a great job. She knows every woman in town now. And I don't mean by their faces.' Mari told her, a little shocked, over dinner.

It was Friday night and there were shouts from the road. People were drunk already, an hour after sunset.

'Susan's got a crude sense of humour. True, I've had my miner's lamp on,' Nerida said.

Mari did a doubletake. 'Do they know you're a lesbian?'

'Most of them do. I don't think there are many secrets in this town. You know, I refer to my wife occasionally.

'But I'm always professional about my work. The women just appreciate being able to get the test done, I think, without me hurting them. It's a mechanical sort of process. You know. There's nothing sexual about it.'

'I guess that's what I was worried about. I mean, does it kill all the nice feelings you have about women's bodies, doing that?' Mari sliced her steak.

'It doesn't kill the nice feelings I have about your body. Because I love you. Do you think an ophthalmologist can still gaze into her lover's eyes and see her soul?' Nerida smiled.

She sighed then. 'Doing all the Pap tests is okay. But women need to talk. It's the psychological work that's hard. There's a lot of anxiety and grief. People work every day for weeks. Some of the FIFO miners think they're lucky because they work every day for six weeks, then get two weeks off.

But in the two weeks they go home they're just maintaining themselves. They go home to their families and sleep. Play video games. Drink. Their marriages die. They totally underestimate the toll the work takes on them.

'They are better off, though, than the workers that fly in from overseas. I looked after a woman from Ireland who worked every day for three months before she came to see me, broken down.

'Another young man from Estonia whose gut burst out of his belly when he lifted a slab of concrete. The company somehow got him flown home with the injury so that their insurance wouldn't have to pay to for his operation. They didn't want to lose their no-claim bonus, so they denied him his only chance to have his surgery paid for.'

Nerida worked two consecutive seventy-hour weeks herself and finally, exhausted, had a single day off.

CHAPTER 9

Newman, Parnpajinya

Nerida rose when the sun was high and avoided looking at a clock. She gazed out the kitchen window at the dirt mountain of mine tailings she could see above the sheoak trees.

When Mari got up, she offered to channel. Nerida grabbed her notepad and tablet. Scrabbled for a pen that worked.

Her wife closed her eyes, straightened her back and squared her feet on the floor. She shook her head slightly, black curls settling on her shoulders.

'See you,' she said with a smile.

'Hello.' He spoke at a lower register than Mari did, even if he used the same vocal cords. 'It has been a long time. What do you do in this place without horses?'

This is M'Hoq Toq. He thinks of horses. She straightened herself up.

'We use machines, but they get very hot,' she said.

'Horses do get hot, too,' he said.

'People have told me that when it was hot here and very dry,' she said, 'people didn't come here much. There was a mountain here they used for ceremony, but they passed through quickly and didn't camp.'

M'Hoq Toq agreed. 'No one stayed here. They came for a short time, for teachings or receiving messages. Very powerful.' He moved Mari's head from side to side slowly, as if sensing the area.

'Very powerful place,' he reiterated. 'Too much power to stay longer.'

She felt the intensity of the place's energy as he spoke.

Good to be here, she thought. She liked powerful places. She and Mari were attracted to them.

'Power creates that thing, infectious things in this case—in the ground,' he said.

Maybe not so good, she thought.

M'Hoq Toq observed, 'You disturb the ground it's in, you create suffering.

'People have been passing through here, to receive messages and teachings. Not only from one another. Because it's so powerful, they could receive teachings from ancestors. But it was too powerful, always, to stay longer than maybe a handful of nights.

'So they stayed, maybe, a handful of nights in one place. Then they moved on. Getting out of here quick. As quick as they were able, back then.

'Humans expose themselves to very powerful bad things here. The ground is disturbed.'

What does he mean? Radiation? Viruses? Nerida saw patients with severe viral illnesses. The health workers called the airplanes that came to Newman petrie dishes. People brought sicknesses from all over the world.

There were mineworkers from northern Europe, China. Many came from New Zealand, where wages had been driven down over the past thirty years.

Many Australian Fly-In-Fly-Out workers lived in Bali or southern Thailand because flights and rent were cheap.

Many paid for sex there, with sex workers who were not well cared for. Sexually transmitted diseases, as well as sickening viruses, were rampant among FIFOs.

But it seemed that M'Hoq Toq was talking about something more than that. *What, worse than HIV?*

Nerida had admitted people to their small hospital with bacterial infections that their antibiotics couldn't touch. Wounds that smelled bad enough to make her gag when the dressing was taken down. One was flown to Perth with sepsis. He was in intensive care, fighting for his life.

M'Hoq Toq seemed to be looking at how the mineworkers could protect themselves. 'They use these machines,' he said. 'Staying within them could help a bit. But most of the humans here are exposed to these things longer than they should be.

'It is a very bad place, that's creating suffering.

'But if you go further, a little to where the sun rises, and a little to the north, it's much worse.'

Nerida tried to recall what was mined to the northeast of Newman. Maybe Jimblebar mine, but they only mined iron ore there, as far as she knew. There was the salt lake the white Australians called Lake Disappointment to the east. *Kumpupirntily, the Martu people call it.*

'The ground is disturbed there as well,' he said, 'not as much as here.

'Not yet, I should say. But the bad seeds there are much more powerful. It is an unexpected mix, that comes with what they want.

'They only look for a few things when they mine, but they get more than they ask for. They haven't found that out so far.'

Nerida felt that familiar burn. She wanted to know. She felt the spirit's love and compassion. She also felt the looming threat of poisoned people, death of the plants and animals, toxic water and air. -

These fears shadowed her, all her life. She could remember being a small child, perhaps four years old, worrying about these things. *Is that why I'm open to the idea that I'm a spirit returned to this planet, already with a history, carrying knowledge? Because I remember observations from being a little one?*

'They are changing the power lines within the earth,' M'Hoq Toq went on.

What does he mean by that? Some kind of energy grid?

He moved Mari's long-fingered hands like a coursing river.

'It makes a detour, because it's interrupted in one place. It goes somewhere else, mixes up with things it was never supposed to mix up with, and then joins where the power line continues.' He paused, seeming to sense her confusion. 'You might call it a magnetic field.'

'Aboriginal people call them songlines,' she suggested.

'They did use songlines for orientation,' he granted. 'It meant looking at a bigger picture for them. But here I am talking about something else.

'Songlines are something people could feel if they listened to the earth. I am talking about something physical, something that's there, you could touch it. You can't touch songlines. You can feel them, you can be guided by them, if your mind is open—and your heart.

'This one is not for guidance. It is about balance, physical balance of the place. You remove it, it makes big disruptions. You put something else where you removed it, it is disturbed.'

Something physical? Does he mean a mineral? The giant bands of iron ore woven through the mountains here?

'It's creating a negative power that causes, what you might call, disease.

'Some disease is not like spots or scales on a skin or cuts on a skin, or a bad stomach. It can cause vibrations that interact with your brain. So your mind will be out of place. The brain needs strong protection.'

Oh no. We're in tinfoil hat territory again. She got agitated when they talked about vibrations. *Where is the science in it?*

When they lived near Uluru, Aedgar used to talk about some kind of radiation coming off the gigantic Rock in the hottest time of the year. Not just the heat, which was enough, on its own, to fry a person's brain. One of her colleagues had measured fifty-eight degrees radiating off the Rock in the summer, on paths people walked.

Aedgar, and the other channeled beings, used to warn her away from it.

Two of the most respected Traditional Owners at the Aboriginal Community near Uluru developed severe cognitive impairment in the years they lived there. Both were accomplished tour guides who taught visitors lessons etched in the Rock. Each was a powerful advocate for their culture and people.

Nerida had come to believe that it was true the Rock didn't want people near it when the heat was extreme. She told patients. She wrote medical certificates for pregnant tour guides or bus drivers to work away from there in summer.

M'Hoq Toq tilted Mari's head slightly. 'They use these little plastic shells, which no one would recommend for this kind of force.'

Their helmets.

'These people think because they can't see it, it's not there. It is building up continuously. It's getting stronger. As it changes the balance, some places get hotter than others.'

If Newman got hotter, humans would not survive there. She saw birds drop dead out of the sky from the heat. Swarms of buzzing blowflies colonised their bodies for moisture.

Nerida had stopped walking to work. She took the car. Mari didn't want the car to go anywhere in the heat of the day anyway. She stayed inside, painting with cool, wet brushes. Washing clothes, linen and floors.

'Increased heat creates these thermal up-streams.' M'Hoq Toq made a spiral like an eagle's ascent with the hands. 'Which create big storms. It can take these things—they are similar to what you call particles—storms will take them to other places.

'That sickness follows the wind and the air. It would follow the water, too, if there was water around.

So, if you disrupt and disturb one place, it will affect lots of places, because once it is out there it is able to locate other possibilities of where to go, just go with the wind. It is very powerful.'

It can locate where it wants to go? What, a germ?

Nerida was reminded of a concept she learned from the Traditional Aboriginal healers.

Her cousin-brother Greg was one of them, even if he would never admit it. He knew about the old sicknesses.

And he knew, now, not to talk about his healing powers, having suffered ostracism when he became excited (and perhaps, he admitted, a little boastful) after his initiation as a healer.

CHAPTER 10
TIME SLIP 3

The people of the Central desert, the Anangu, talked about a bad spirit, a pathogen: a *mamu*.

A mamu blows in with the hot wind from the west, she learned. It makes people sick. When she was in the West, in later years, she would occasionally look over the dusty plains and wonder: *Is this where mamu come from?*

Some Traditional Aboriginal healers she knew were mainly occupied with taking out mamu, hunting them down and pulling them out of peoples' bodies or picking them up from around the camp. Sometimes mamu lived in the dust.

Sometimes people carried them into the Community on (or in) their bodies. She understood that there was variation in the level of the mamu's penetration and connections or attachments it had. But she was no expert.

Mari had survived an encounter with a serious mamu. People there knew then, that mamu were not just an Anangu thing. And that Mari was not like other people.

Nerida had seen mamu herself, slinking away out of the corner of her eye in an unhappy, neglected house. Or lurking as fungating shadows in a person.

She'd taken one or two out of people at work when they lived near Uluru.

That was after years of study and practise, including astral travel. In her spirit body, she searched at night, travelling along the Eastern Australian Great Dividing Range, looking for the place to take mamu she had removed. Dangerous pathogens she could not carry for long or keep with her.

She worked with people with cancer then. Removing a mamu didn't cure them. But maybe they stopped vomiting. Or felt better in themselves.

To bury a mamu, she needed a place where the Earth had the capacity to tolerate the thing, where it could be left undisturbed.

She found, in her astral travels, that fewer and fewer places on the large island were left undisturbed.

Working in the Central Australian desert later, she washed mamu down the clinic sink with the sulphurous bore water, murmuring a prayer of gratitude to the water, requesting the assistance of the earth.

CHAPTER 11

Newman, Parnpajinya

Early afternoon, January 18, 2015

She took a sip of water. Focused.

M'Hoq Toq was still talking about this pathogen, whatever it was they were digging up.

'And it does have, you could call it, consciousness,' he said. 'If people knew about the abilities of these particles (you can't really call it 'particles,' because, as I said, it's got consciousness); if they knew they would stay well away from it.

'They would be scared out of their minds. And they should be. Given that it has some sort of consciousness, it can cause major damage, especially to the ones that cause the disruption.'

Nerida always felt loved and respected when M'Hoq Toq was in the room. There was a lovely openness in her chest and her belly that must be the way she felt as a well-nursed baby. *I won't tell him that.* She felt she must appear as a child to him already sometimes. She trusted him implicitly.

Which makes it even more alarming when he explores darkness, like this idea of a virus with consciousness.

He seemed to step back a little from the suffering he foretold. 'It is something that you can't confine to an area, because it has the ability to move away with the wind, for example, or the water, even along a magnetic grid, underground. In this case, the disruption detours and affects other areas as well.' Again, that snaking movement with the hand.

'So, it is not possible to reverse it.' *With humans exploring the moon and Mars, why should I be surprised that there were unknown pathogens and other strange things on Earth, as well?*

Her breathing tightened.

'You could stop it,' he said, searching for a solution. 'Leave it alone so the flow of these things would slow down eventually.

'But keep on going, digging it up, causing more disruption, this will cause more of it to come out. It will slow down over decades (or

centuries, maybe, even), if it were left alone now. It can't be
reversed because it has been taken out. Even if they try to replace it
with something else, it won't work, because it has damaged the flow
of energy.

'Power. This will cause big headaches for future generation,
literally and in other ways.'

Nerida asked, 'It's not just uranium, that people understand is
radioactive; digging up the iron ore and the gold and the copper is
also causing these problems?'

'Yes.' He paused. 'You like to write down words.'

She felt his attention focus on her behind Mari's closed eyes
and paused with her pen raised over the paper.

'If you think, "That's a nice part. I'll take it out, put it
somewhere else." You take your words out of context, they change
the meaning.

'It's the same with these things. You take it out of its physical
context. And it turns into something else—not only the part that
you take out changes. The part that you leave in there changes as
well.

'They form, we could call it, other relationships, bonds, with
some other things, creating new things you haven't ever heard
about.'

*Is he talking about minerals in the soil now? Or radioactive elements? Or
viruses?*

'You haven't found a way to measure it. It has no name at
your place, so far. There are about 5 of these things that have been
created.'

He held up Mari's hand, showing her palm and five fingers.

'Five of these, where you don't have a name, you can't
measure it, but it's there.

'It will take a few generations perhaps: at least one generation,
to learn about, maybe, two of these things. It might take another
generation or two to learn about the other three.'

'Are they viruses? Are they like viruses or bacteria?' she asked.

'You could call it a virus or bacteria because it can affect you
and animals and plants. But the thing that's different about it, is
that it's got some kind of consciousness.

So, these things, travelling through the atmosphere with the big storms, they cause, say, diseases to develop some kind of consciousness as well.'

'Mari was infected by a disease when we were on an island. We were told that it was like a new kind of virus.'

Mari contracted bird flu when they were on the Cocos-Keeling Islands. The house where they stayed for Nerida's work had chickens and ducks, which mixed with wild birds from Java.

Chicks, ducklings, then the grown chickens, died mysteriously when they were there. Two weeks after they left the islands, Mari, who cleaned up after the birds, became ill.

'Same thing,' he said. 'Developing a kind of consciousness.'

This is very weird, she thought. Then asked, 'Can you negotiate with this kind of consciousness or communicate with it?'

'It hasn't even got a name at your place yet. You can't measure it. There is not anything you would call negotiation at this point.'

He seemed to consult with unseen allies for a moment. 'You might try to get some sort of contact on a basis of something like waves, vibrations—' As he spoke, he held his hands in a prayer-like gesture, moving them out purposely from Mari's third eye, '—with your consciousness. But then, it might see that as an invitation.

'Our friend tried it, being curious about things. She found a way in the end to some sort of negotiation. She won't remember it, but this made it possible to separate from it.'

'She was very sick.' *It's strange that he would call Mari 'curious.'* If she told her wife about this, she was likely to be infuriated by the idea. *They are so far removed from our reality, these spirit beings. Mari was really suffering, then. Don't they have any compassion?*

Mari was desperately ill some nights with the bird flu. With a high fever, struggling to breathe. Nerida wanted to take her to hospital, get her some oxygen. Hardly able to talk, Mari refused with all her strength to go to the hospital again. Nerida was afraid for a few hours then, for her wife's life.

They were treated badly the first time. Doctors refused to believe it could be Avian Influenza, despite their convincing history. They refused to test for it. *I guess they didn't want to be bothered with public health reports, contact tracing.*

The urban GP was the same. He sent tests for Mari's liver function, blood glucose level, kidneys and so on, but refused to test for H1N1. It was frustrating.

Mari said later, 'They didn't respect your judgement. They thought, "What would she know? She's only a bush doctor. She's Aboriginal. She's a lesbian. She's probably hysterical." They think doctors who work in remote places go there because they're not good enough to work in the city. Because they don't know enough.'

M'Hoq Toq continued. 'It's not an easy thing. If others are not as strong, they won't have time to get to that stage or point. There won't be time to think about things.'

'They'll just get sick and die?' she asked.

'You could call it that way. It's a quick experience. It could, kind of, 'catapult' you into a new experience. That's how quickly it can work.'

She didn't understand the mechanics of dying abruptly. Did he mean that a person would suddenly find themselves on the other side? Or reborn into another lifetime? *It is too much. Some unnamable, high-mortality, excavated pathogen that can never be put back in and causes people to lose their minds? Or kills them so quickly, they don't know what hit them? This is like sci-fi.*

She said, 'You're warning of a kind of a plague.'

'Nothing that this planet has ever seen,' he said. 'That which you call The Plague didn't have anything close to a consciousness.

'You were unlucky if you were close to someone that contracted it. But this one will be able to pick individuals.

'It's going to start with the ones that caused the disruption. It begins first amongst them, which could be a blessing, in some way.

'It will follow, then, the mine workers that just did what they thought was their duty, doing what they were told. They were not bright enough to see that this kind of disruption is not what you should do. They just followed an order, like some stupid little soldiers, that just follow the order of someone who's greedy for power. Same thing, almost.

'Many of these 'soldiers' die, wanting to start a different life, all over again, once they realise how bad the result is, or how bad their decision to participate in the disruption was.

'Many of them suffer a long time—for the rest of this lifetime and maybe in a new one as well. Would it be worth it? Most probably not.

'They will get "wealthy"—some of the tokens of wealth in your understanding. But this sort of wealth can't buy you a proper mind, a brain that's been left intact. Or happiness. You can't buy health either. This will be a very bad wake-up for a lot of them.

'You might find some souls here or there, already, who, if you ask them directly, will say: "What have I done? What could I have done differently?

'Could I have passed on information? Things that I saw that are still kept a secret?

'Things I have witnessed—other people suffering from things no one knows about?"

'There will be quite a few that, we could say, have their mind displaced. They're, like, out of their minds.'

CHAPTER 12

Newman Hospital, Parnpajinya

January 15, 2015

Last week, Nerida sent two men to the psych ward in Perth, mad enough to be dangerous to themselves and others.

One had taken an overdose of paracetamol and needed urgent evacuation. She gave him his first dose of N-acetylcysteine, grateful the hospital had it in supply.

'I'll connect you up with somebody kind to talk to down there, write a letter so you don't have to tell the story all over. You've saved yourself from a slow death by irreversible liver failure. Thank you for calling the ambulance in time.'

Two nights later, the other patient frightened the nurses. Nerida came to the ED when she heard shouting. A high-pitched male voice screamed, 'Fuck off! Fuck off!' The female nurse had taken a mattress off one of the ED beds and was using it clumsily as a shield. He wasn't throwing anything. The patient was empty-handed, holding himself.

'That's a funny old technique,' Nerida said. 'Do people still do that?' The nurse, upset, dropped the mattress and ran from the room. In half a minute Sarah appeared, sidling in beside the doorway. Nerida, focused on the young man, nevertheless noticed her composed presence.

The patient stood pressed against a wall, agitated. Nerida approached sidewards, avoiding eye contact, keeping her shoulders down. He could run out the back if he wanted. A willowy young man, *fair-skinned Aboriginal,* she thought.

I don't frighten him. Sometimes I'm glad to be older and small. 'Rough day, sonboy?'

His eyes met hers, startled, from under his black hood. 'I'm not your sonboy.'

'True. I'm an othersider. Goori. This isn't my Country. I'm the doctor here. Just visiting. You're younger than my kids.'

Nerida spoke softly. He started to cry. Said emphatically, 'This is my Country. I'm Palyku. My Country. Nobody knows me, but. I come here for work. Nobody knows me.'

He screwed up his face and swiped his fist half-heartedly against the wall. Then crumpled to the floor, utterly defeated. 'I can't do this. They just ripping it all up.'

Nerida sat alongside, a safe distance from him.

'I know what you mean,' she said.

As they talked Nerida saw how tightly he held his arm. His jacket sleeve was wet. Looking quickly above and behind her, she saw dark blood on the wall where the young man had hit it. Sarah had seen it already.

'You're bleeding!' Nerida said softly. A big drop of dark blood came off his sleeved elbow, landing on the beige floor. 'Have you cut yourself? Will you let me see? Come on up on the bed, eh. Let's have a look at you.'

Sarah already had a kidney dish with saline, antiseptic and sterile plastic tweezers with a pile of gauze squares out on the stainless-steel trolley next to the treatment bed, the one that was still intact.

Wielding scissors with blunted ends, Sarah said, 'We have to cut your jacket up. Don't worry, we'll find you another one in the rag bag.' He released his arm. Her blue-gloved hands got stained with his blood as she carefully lifted the cut sleeve away. 'Let's wash this and see the damage. Lots of cuts, but they look pretty clean. Seems to be venous blood. Think you might want some glue, doctor?'

'Yeah. And a suturing kit. I'll get some local anesthetic first.'

The youth laid down, relieved to be looked after.

'I'll make your arm properly numb so we can wash it and stitch it up, eh? Had stitches before?' Nerida touched his arm gently. The pale, soft skin was laced with scars.

He'd cut himself with a razor straight from a packet, he said. Most of the cuts were shallow enough to put together with glue and steri-strips. He'd missed the arteries. There was a deeper, ragged cut around the side of his arm that needed stitches.

Sarah picked up his bag. Took the razor blade out of his hoodie pocket. He had a couple of battered cigarettes. One for now, one for later on.

He and Nerida went outside so that he could smoke, once his arm was tightly bandaged. She was glad of the night air.

She explained the pros and cons of the antipsychotic medications. To quiet the aggressive voices in his head.

'If the voices are making you feel like shit, you might need medicine to quiet them for a while. I know what those nasty voices are like,' she continued. 'I had them after I took some rubbish drugs, or maybe just too much dope, when I was young.'

'What did you do? How did you get better?'

'An old Aboriginal man told me to start loving myself. He wasn't trying to make money out of me, or bed me, so somehow it got in. I tried to eat better. Go for walks. I went out to sing to the Bush in a made-up language. I didn't have my own Aboriginal language yet, then. I still don't know it.

'They didn't have the antipsychotic drugs they've got now. I wish they'd had Olanzapine.'

He'd accepted an antipsychotic wafer an hour before. It suited him.

'You might be hearing voices because you're sensitive. It can get better. The voices got so loud and mean because your brain's unbalanced by bad things that happened to you. Probably some toxic chemicals, too'

She could see him processing carefully, choosing which thoughts to listen to. Through, past and around the derogatory, abusive voice, lurking in his head like a crocodile. *Gotta learn to live with the crocodile*, she thought. *Till it goes away.*

'You might be a healer. You might have been born to help heal this country. You don't know yet. You're having this experience for a reason. You'll find out in a while why you got sick like this. You'll find better ways to get your pain out than cutting. You have time. Be patient and kind to yourself.'

The Flying Doctor picked him up the next day. She gave him a hug, wishing him good medicine, time in nature and healing.

CHAPTER 13

Newman, Parnpajinya

Afternoon, January 18, 2015

So, is there something they're digging up that actively attacks the brain and mind, targeting the miners?

Listening to the spirit M'Hoq Toq, she felt a burden: to speak up about dangers, help people. The weight of it seemed to change of air pressure in the room. 'What can we do?'

M'Hoq Toq was slow answering. 'It is always good to witness things, pass on knowledge.'

He stopped to let her digest the idea that bearing witness might be enough.

'You and our friend will be safe. Don't talk to the wrong people.'

Keeping safe may be enough, for now. 'Is it like a response of the earth to protect herself, the release of this pathological agent?'

He chose his words carefully.

'You think you are on top of the Evolution. You think you've got consciousness. If you have consciousness, how can you do this? This desecration of the planet?

'So, if you are not able to use what's been given to you in the way it should be, there will be something created that's got, probably, more consciousness than you've ever had.

'And once you are not on top of the evolution anymore, you might change.

'Something had to be put there, or create itself, with the help of the ones who think they are at the top of the evolution, to teach.'

She tried to figure this out. 'It's partly our own creation, then?'

'Yes. But humans created something that has consciousness without greed.'

I don't really know what he means by that. Like, it's like an animal? Innocent?

His voice was deep and dark. 'There is another factor that you should be cautious about, which you would call revenge. The consciousness created there has this power: Its greed is replaced with revenge.'

'So those who are greedy have revenge taken upon them?'

'You could see it that way.'

'It's my simple thought.'

'Thoughts are not bad because they're simple,' he said.

'Changes are happening on this planet. Other people are moving forward, working themselves into powerful positions. It will take a while, thinking in your terms, but it's on its way. Little changes will be made, everywhere at the same time.'

'Some of them might read our book,' she offered. One day she would put his words in a book.

'Sounds interesting,' he said calmly. 'Educational. Every kind of education is good. Every piece of information that will get out there is important.'

Sounds good. But getting people to believe it might be difficult.

Nerida watched Mari's eyelids twitching. Aedgar had been able to open Mari's eyes. He'd said it was a mechanical challenge. Monica said it involved moving consciousness into the tiny muscles around the eyes. To M'Hoq Toq now Nerida said with a smile, 'You might open those eyes soon.'

'I try at times,' he conceded. 'I know some of the others can do it. Not sure if I'll be glad about what I see.

'I can feel disrupted energy.'

They're probably blasting over in the mine she thought. She felt and heard a boom. Then said, 'We've recently been in Kalgoorlie, where there is a gold mine big as a city. They call it the Super Pit. There are earthquakes around there every day, but the mine owners say the earthquakes have nothing to do with the mine'.

He responded. 'Sometimes the earth shakes a little, trying to get things back in place. These little shakes are not enough. At some stage, it might have to shake a little bit harder.'

'It's terrible what they're doing there.' She and Mari were awed and appalled by the extent of the mine. It was like Manhattan Island with all its skyscrapers, as a giant, upside-down, negative, hole. *It is impressive, what people will do when they're determined to get something.*

M'Hoq Toq agreed. 'Yes, but digging big holes is not the only injury. You can't only say that the bigger the destruction, the bigger the impact in the end.

'Sometimes you can, for example, poke a needle, or a knife for that matter, into the skin and then you cut something in there that makes all the blood go away. You cut all the electric information that goes in that body and yet it's still only a tiny hole.'

He indicated a cut across Mari's forearm. 'A little cut on the surface.'

'You mean like fracking?' she asked.

'Disrupting energy. There will be places where they take something out that has been in there for centuries—longer, probably—they take it out. They create something like a bubble.'

He used the hands to show how something taken away under the earth could create a space.

'It's going to collapse. Where it collapses, the energy is interrupted as well. They cause disruption. It's the same as digging a big hole. The result, for the planet, will be the same.

'They will create powerful things that are bad for the "top of the evolution" (as they think of themselves).

'These things…'

I guess he means these pathogens that are dug up.

'—go with the water. Or whatever flows or moves.'

So, the wind, the flooding rains when they come. Dust storms?

'You might have the earth shake there as well. Different layers of it will move.

'If you drill a hole somewhere else where these things have moved to, you might get a mix out of it that no one would ever ask for.' He sounded grim.

So, does he means that if miners drill or frack where these pathogens have flowed to, then they can get out and hurt people? Do they move under the Earth's crust with the magma?

'They are not able to see what is going on in a bigger picture or, given that time doesn't exist, in the long term. They have no idea what they are creating. Because they think they know it all.

'The good ones, the very good ones, still don't know much, but they know it. They understand that there is so much more out there that they don't know. They practice caution.' He put energy behind that last word.

'Because if you have no idea what you're doing, and you combine it with a mind and a brain that thinks "I know it all"— you're gonna create a disaster. This is the direction they're heading to. They're going towards disaster.'

Nerida reflected for a moment. Kalgoorlie, a thousand kilometres to the south, was a gold mining town.

Her Mari was a skilled prospector. With one leg, walking on uneven ground was challenging. She watched and assessed the ground constantly, so she noticed any tiny sparkle. She had picked up a couple of rocks with gold in them in their travels around Kalgoorlie.

She'd found a pretty rock on a pile of scree on the edge of Parnpajinya. It was pyrites, fool's gold.

People were attracted to gold for millennia. Nerida understood. She knew that doctors and scientists were not supposed to believe that rocks held magical powers. But she was Aboriginal. Just because she studied science that didn't mean that rocks stopped talking to her.

Now, she said, 'In Kalgoorlie the gold under the ground was arranged like a deck of cards in layers.' She used her hands to show it, as their tour guide at the mine had done, even if M'Hoq Toq couldn't see in the conventional sense. 'What that gold's power? Before it was mined, I mean? When it was still in the ground in that sort of formation? Did it do something for the earth?'

'The gold was used by the planet to convey energy,' he replied. 'To spread it out evenly. At the same time, it served as a kind of insulation, protection.

'It's like a traffic junction. Everything flowed to there, came up to there. The gold evenly spread the things that needed to be, while being shield at the same time from other things.'

Nerida tried to get her mind around it. 'Shielding living things from energy that was too strong, for example?'

M'Hoq Toq agreed. 'If you think about cards in a pile,' he said, using Mari's hands, 'it goes from one layer to the next, going up this way, going up that way, going up that way, going up this way.'

The layers extended in four directions in stacks parallel to the ground. 'And it didn't originate as the whole thing at once. Cause that would have been too much, too powerful.'

She strained to imagine the geologically slow growth of a network of gold, evolving like an organ of the earth.

He threw up the hands, 'So if you take the gold out, that function is gone. Nothing can be distributed evenly. Nothing is shielded that's below it. Again, you create a bad mixture of power, that creates what you call viruses and bacteria with a consciousness.'

There was a pounding on the metal roof.

Nerida cried to hear it, releasing tension she wasn't aware she carried. 'The rain is here,' she said. 'I'm so grateful. We've been longing for it.'

'Rain. I can sense it. I can sense your gratefulness. It will last for a while,' he said.

They listened for a few moments.

Maybe I should not be participating in all this. She asked herself, as many of her patients did. 'Is it okay for us to continue to visit and stay in these places where people are mining?' she asked then.

M'Hoq Toq nodded. 'You have to be aware that these difficulties people have—there will be more of it—it will become harder to treat their illnesses. They will need someone who understands that.'

I should stay here to look after these people. I'll speak up for them at public meetings, do the research to document the problems here. I have to follow through, to speak up about what I know. I'm afraid of where that path may lead me. People have been killed for speaking up against big companies.

'But we all have a lot of work to do,' M'Hoq Toq said, as if reading her thoughts. 'You know that we go wherever you go. We are trying to give our best wherever we are.

'If a place makes you happy without having too much to do for it, if you feel good in a place, that's the place to stay.

'For example, you have much more work to do than you ever did, you work almost day and night, but you still feel good—it is a good place because it supports you.

'If you are in a place, for example, where it is very quiet, considered beautiful by some people, not much to do in your regular work, but you don't feel good, it's not a good place. Go with your feeling.'

Nerida smiled. 'But I feel good everywhere, M'Hoq Toq.'

'You do. But, as I said, if you work more than ever and you still feel strong, there are no doubts about things, then you are in a good place.

'If you're surrounded by beauty, have a lot of (what they call) free time, but you're not happy, you don't feel good—it's the wrong place. It could be that it's a good place or a perfect place for someone else, but not for you.

'Listen to your feelings, to your intuition. If you don't have to work hard to feel good, it is the right place. If you have to have too many complicated thoughts to work something out, it's the wrong place.'

'If you get sick, you might have asked for it and it can still be a good place. You might have done some experiments. Could still be a good place.'

'People learn by being sick, don't they?' she asked. She was robust. But spent all her days and half her nights tending people who were fighting with their bodies. Or their bodies were fighting with them.

She often asked her patients why they were sick. They usually knew why and told her.

CHAPTER 14

The Western Desert Community

Same time

In the Western desert community, a man was dying of lung disease. He needed oxygen, which he carried on a little cart behind him. Always short of breath, he made an effort. He was determined to keep walking, enjoyed seeing the kids playing, surveying the surrounding country. He'd stop for a chat, even if his part of the conversation was mainly smiling, nodding, softly panting. With skin the colour of dark chocolate, bright brown eyes and healthy teeth, stained by thousands of cups of tea, his silver head was a welcome sight.

Jeep (which was his English-language name) had been to hospital seven times in half a year.

The community had a merry-go-round of doctors who didn't know them.

Almost every time a doctor saw Jeep the doctor got anxious and sent him to hospital. Each admission, Jeep spent a week or two on intravenous antibiotics and steroids.

Each time, Community people feared it would be the last time they'd see him. And every time Jeep travelled the five-hundred-kilometre journey back to their remote Community, he came back weaker, bonier, more weary.

Nerida asked the other health workers, one of whom, Simon, was Jeep's nephew, about what Jeep wanted to do in the last period of his life.

She spent days on the phone. Tracking down the hospital specialists, they acknowledged that Jeep never got better. They had several diagnoses of Jeep's problems. But none of the medicines prescribed ever really worked.

Jeep was being treated for chronic obstructive lung disease. Or asthma. Was it cancer of unknown primary, that wasn't showing on the scans yet? Possibly heart failure. And yes, definitely kidney failure. Medical people assumed he'd been a heavy smoker.

Simon arranged a meeting. Jeep sat with his wife in the warm, red sand in front of their house, the coals of the day's fire still glowing in front of him.

Despite the summer heat, the open fire was their preferred means of making tea and cooking.

His wife sat behind him, small and flexible, listening carefully. Two sons and three daughters came and went from the meeting. Kids came and went too. A four-year-old stayed by her great-grandfather's side, interested and remarkably patient. *She's engaged by people the way other kids are glued to games on phones*, Nerida thought.

Simon and Nerida sat awkwardly, both stiff jointed and plump from too many hours in front of computers.

Bronwyn, the nurse, was the only non-Aboriginal person there. She was like a mouse in a burrow, arms wrapped tightly around her knees, still and small as she could be, trying to blend into the concrete wall of the house the health workers all leaned against. So frightened of showing disrespect or causing offense. Nerida felt for her. *It's hard to be so insensitive to body language that it paralyses you among others who are fluent in it. At least she knows there's a lot she doesn't know.*

With no real diagnosis for Jeep's malady, but aware that it looked likely to kill him soon anyway, Nerida asked, through Simon, what the family and Jeep understood about his sickness.

Jeep's wife spoke up, low-voiced but clear, in her musical Western desert tongue. Simon listened, thought carefully and then interpreted. 'When Jeep was a little boy, that black smoke caught 'im. That black smoke came all over Country! It stayed for a long, long time! People couldn't breathe. A lot of people passed away.'

Simon stopped and listened again, as Jeep's wife went on, using her hands to illustrate what happened.

'He hid in a cave between the rocks,' Simon translated. 'Going in as far as he could. He stayed there till someone pulled him out after. People from that other family came to get him.'

Simon leaned towards his aunt. He paused to process the impact of what she said, then interpreted for Nerida and Bronwyn. 'That mob saw that bright light, you know? They felt it in their bodies.'

'Boom!' Jeep said, clapping his hands. Everyone laughed, despite the grim topic.

It took a few beats for Nerida to understand. 'His lungs were damaged by the radioactive fallout after the nuclear bomb went off…' Horror showed on her face. She recalled what she knew about the nuclear 'tests' in the desert. 'Must have been the early seventies.'

Simon looked up, calculating. 'He would have been about ten, yeah. He was never strong after that. All the family knows that.'

It's a radioactive pneumonitis, Nerida thought. She sat with it for a while. *Nobody asked the family what was wrong with him. All those years he's been sick.*

There probably wasn't any medicine that would have helped. But several of the many medicines Jeep took conscientiously probably weren't helping and might even harm him.

Jeep spoke in Aboriginal English then. 'That black smoke been kill dead a lot of people. That bomb: a lotta people died after that. Long time. More than one bomb, too.'

'*Yuwa,*' everyone agreed, quietly. Except poor Bronwyn, who looked even paler than usual.

CHAPTER 15

Same day

Nerida returned from her recollection. M'Hoq Toq tilted the head slightly. He was talking about what people learn from being sick, responding to her question. 'Yes. Even the not-so-well-educated ones in your profession realise that.

'For example, little children get sick. And then, once they've recovered, they've got a new skill or new words; a different way of attempting to do things.

'It helps. It's a little new start. You take what you need with you, you start new, you make gains, leaving the things you don't want behind.'

Nerida thought of Mari, her bewitching, stubborn wife. 'So, if you're not very good at leaving things behind, being sick could be a way of your spirit encouraging you to let this happen.'

'You could see it that way. It gives the body a way to struggle a bit, a way to fight a bit harder. And you come out on the other side with (you could call it) a new set of skills in some way or the other.

'Some ask for a task that's too much at that point. They must opt out and make a complete, new start. That happens too.'

Souls ask for a task, to learn. He means if they can't handle the lesson, they leave this life and start again.

Even if Nerida was confident that Mari would stay with her—their love was strong as silk—she worried about her.

She asked directly now about that one she loved—still recovering from the bird flu, still with a cough she couldn't shake. The desert dust probably wasn't good for Mari, even though she loved the spectacular stony landscape around Parnpajinya.

She had chronic pain in her neck and back from the strain of years of carrying air tanks and pulling people out of the water as a diving instructor. Then years on crutches and now years as an amputee with a prosthetic leg. 'How is Mari's energy today?'

'It was a little bit difficult coming into this body,' he said. 'I tried to realign some things. There might still be more that has to be done. We can realign energies, but we can't put in things that are missing, because we don't have the physical ability.'

He gestured towards her wife's titanium and silicon foot. 'We can help these energies attract the things they need. So we always try to do our best, but sometimes it just needs that little push more.'

I guess that's why she gets sick, she thought.

'We're going back to the US. I'm attracted to Wyoming—but it's very out of the way.' There was a writer's conference in Wyoming. Nerida wanted to be a writer.

'If you feel attracted to something and it makes you feel good and you don't have to do too much for it, it is good. If it just falls into your lap no matter what you do—you're supposed to go there.

'If you have too much struggle, even if you're attracted, there might be other opportunities. They might lead you to other things you haven't thought about.

'But, if it's too difficult to do it, if you have to have too many complicated thoughts about it, do something else.'

'Mari is taking me to a place you might know in the southwest of America called Antelope Canyon.'

M'Hoq Toq spoke thoughtfully, as one still related to the area. 'We do have a lot of smooth rock places that have been used for teachings, gatherings. We do have soft rocks, in these sorts of colours. I haven't heard of Antelope Canyon before. Soft rocks form quickly. It might not have been there before, or not called a canyon, because it was just, maybe, a waterway somewhere or a crack in the earth.'

A truck's reversing beeper intruded from outside.

M'Hoq Toq turned the head to listen. 'Strange sounds. Not a bird. Trying to imitate a bird. Poorly done. We used whistles to do things like this, but people couldn't tell if it was the bird or us. Not even the bird could tell. It was used for hunting. This one would be hopeless.'

Nerida smiled. They ended the session with salutations of respect.

Mari returned without awareness of who she'd channelled or what they said. She rose, brewed coffee. They exchanged stories from the week over a late lunch of cheese and ham, with buttered bread and tomatoes.

They drove out of town for the sunset.

'Cathedral Gorge takes its name from the colours in the rocks. They are like stained glass. Exquisite! You won't believe it. I went there with Mum and Dad when we came here.' Mari drove, long-lensed camera heavy in her lap.

'With your then-partner, too, right?' Nerida couldn't help being jealous of Mari's ex sometimes. They traveled the world together in the 90s, when Mari was a diving instructor and then a travel agent.

'She didn't see it. She didn't get out of the car.'

They arrived at a roadside path leading up between increasingly bigger rocks of burnt orange, sienna and mauve. Trees offered shade. The air smelled of eucalyptus and acacia.

Mari took photos, then turned back to the climbing path. Nerida admired her agility with her prosthetic leg as she carefully, automatically, chose each flattish place. She never used a stick. They could see rust red mesas rising from the spinifex dotted plains. 'I'm surprised how green this place still is,' said Nerida, gasping a little in the early evening heat.

The light was delicious. Steep rectangular rocks streaked with orange loomed ahead and above.

They came over a rise. The sight ahead astonished them. A dirt road, with piles of dying plants and piles of newly gouged soil on either side of it.

'What the fuck?' said Mari.

A felled tree lay across the path. Twenty metres beyond, a metal sign, held up by freshly turned earth, read: 'Private Property. Trespassers with be Prosecuted.'

'It's the mining company. They've got a lease on it.' Mari called out in frustration, 'Aargh.'

Nerida's voice was steely. 'They don't want people to see how unique and powerful it is. What they will destroy.'

CHAPTER 16

Newman Hospital

January 23, 2015

Newman made Nerida feel how small she was, like a spore from a mushroom compared to those vast mechanical structures, with earth-shaking trucks two stories high.

A few kilometres from the hospital there were bucket wheeled excavators over thirty stories high, digging up over two hundred and forty thousand tonnes of earth every day. They called the dirt without ore 'overburden'. Even these machines were dwarfed by the clouds of desert earth flying off in all directions. *Air travel has tricked us all on scale and distance,* she told herself, *the way television turned time into slices of thirty-minute pie.*

Through clunking exit doors, behind the hospital's rehab ward, she found an outdoor space with a shaded table. It was past three, but Nerida was determined to have her lunch. She sat. Took a long draught from her water bottle.

The narrow yard was dominated by a tree, with ferny leaves, fringing white tufts for flowers and magenta berries. The tree trunk was thick and gnarly. She put her hand on the trunk. Surely this was a tree she'd never seen before. *So, you are flowering when nothing else does, unafraid of heat.*

She was reading *Messages from Michael* again, a book on channelling from the 70s. She first read it in 2006, before she met Mari. She was training with the Traditional Healers then. Her teachers spoke Pitjatjantjara. Nerida didn't.

A diehard materialist who had only begun to consider the idea of a spirit because of her experiences with Andy, her patients and the old desert healers, she searched then for written material to help her understand what it meant to have or to be a spirit, accumulating experience. The book resonated with her and was useful. She read it with different eyes now. She was no longer looking for proof of spirit's existence.

Experience led her to accept what could not be validated, or disproved, by scientific methods.

She didn't want anyone at work, where her work was required to be scientific, to see her with the book.

Of course, somebody came out. 'That looks like an unusual book. What are you reading?'

Ro was a respiratory therapist at the hospital, a thin, white woman with an unconscious air of privilege. 'Having to work with mucous and wheezes,' Ro said, 'what a disgusting job.' Nerida felt sorry for her. She felt the loneliness.

Overtired and pleased to talk about what really mattered to her, Nerida soon found herself explaining Mari's exceptional gift. Ro was invigoratingly open to spiritual ideas. 'She's a full body, deep trance channel,' Nerida said, 'with no awareness of the material she channels. That's rare in the world.'

Ro twisted her hands in front of her. A bead of sweat rolled past the end of an overplucked brow. 'I am desperate for news of my soul mate. I need him now.

'How can I get your wife to come and do a channeling session for me? You must persuade her. I need it so much. I'm going to America to meet him soon. I know I am. I can't miss him,' Ro insisted. 'I won't pay her. But I'll cook a fabulous dinner for both of you. Come on, it'll be great!'

Might be good experience for Mari, Nerida thought. *Her health is better when she channels. And it's always interesting when she channels for a stranger.* They could be sure, then, that Mari knew nothing about the person, even subconsciously. Mari's confidence was boosted by channelling for strangers before.

Ro was boundlessly excited.

It lit a fire in Nerida, too, to be able to talk freely. She told Ro about Aedgar, Bartgrinn and M'Hoq Toq, the three ancient spirits Mari usually channelled.

Then the woman treated her with a kind of distorted reverence. 'But it has to be the Indian who comes to talk to me,' Ro asserted.

Nerida baulked. 'We don't get to control who comes. We can't even guarantee that it'll work. But it usually does,' she said. 'Have you been to a channelling session before?'

'Yes! Thousands. I've had readings with mediums and psychics. Had my cards read. It never works for me, though,' she said plaintively. 'No one ever tells me what I need to know.'

Back on the ward, Sarah, whose purple hair had faded to pink, was freshly arrived on the afternoon shift. In the medication room, Nerida assembled an anti-constipation regime, while Sarah put pills in a plastic box with a different compartment for each day of the week. 'Coming to the football on Saturday?' Sarah asked.

'Appreciate the invitation. Probably not. I'd like to watch but I'll be tired.'

'So, I guess there's no point asking you to come join our touch footy game after work tomorrow?'

Nerida grinned. She pulled packs of a stool-softening powder from the box, labelling them, and putting them in a brown paper bag. 'Sounds like fun. But no, my wife will want me at home.'

'She can come with you.'

'We're not really sporty. I think I inherited the 'too-slow, unco' gene.'

Sarah chuckled. 'What, your family don't play sport?'

'Oh, no. They all do. My sister's good at netball. My brother plays Aussie Rules. My parents are both mad-keen sports fans and fast runners.

'The short-legged gene is double recessive and I'm the lucky one. Mum always said it was sad. "Your Dad's got such nice Aboriginal legs," she'd say.'

'Ah well, the invitation's there if you change your mind.' She finished putting medicines in the dosette box and went to the nurse's station looking for a pen.

At dinner that evening, Nerida tried to convey her excitement about a session with Ro to her wife.

'Why should I do this for some random person? I feel used. You should have asked me first.' Mari said.

They went to Ro's house the following Tuesday evening. The box of wood and fibro that served as staff accommodation still baked from the heat of the day. Ro's apartment was up wooden stairs. She had left the door open for air. Flies, moths and mosquitoes rushed in.

Ro put on a caftan and lit incense to make for a more spiritual setting. And when the guests arrived, swatting biting mozzies on their arms and cheeks, she paced the room anxiously, spraying a dense cloud of insecticide. 'I just got home ten minutes ago. Do you want to eat now?'

'Mari fasts before channelling,' Nerida explained as they sat on the plasticised wood chairs around the plasticised wood table. 'We should have the channeling session now. We can eat later.'

'I want to know why people don't—' Ro began.

'Don't tell me anything.' Mari held up her hand to stop her. 'I don't want to know. I won't be here.'

'Oh,' said Ro. She sat down.

Nerida spoke quietly to Ro as Mari closed her eyes and settled into the chair. 'There are some rules. You don't stare at Mari as she is going into trance.' Ro, who had been staring, turned toward Nerida with a jolt.

'You don't touch Mari when she's in trance because you might knock her out of it. There's no guarantee a spirit will come through. We don't get to ask for who we want.'

Ro looked cranky. Started to object.

'Shh. You treat any being who does come with respect. You listen, right? Let them finish what they want to say. Sometimes there are pauses while they find out more. Then you wait.'

CHAPTER 17

Ro's Place, Newman, Parnpajinya

Tuesday January 27, 2015

After all that it seemed that Mari might not be able to go into trance anyway.

She made the usual movements as she offered herself to it, flexing her neck and relaxing her shoulders, placing her feet flat on the vinyl-covered floor. Ro's tension and frustration filled the air.

After about ten minutes, Nerida was relieved to see Mari's shoulders relax further and her head, poised, straighten her spine. M'hoq Toq spoke, his tone tainted by revulsion.

'Is this a killing field of some kind?'

'Do you mean the history of this land? Were there massacres here?' Nerida asked.

'Here and now. The air is poisoned. We almost did not come at all.' He shocked her by saying that. *None of the channelled beings has ever made such a judgement. It must be bad for him. Do they really care so much about the insects? I guess they care about life in all its forms.*

Ro took it for granted that M'Hoq Toq had come, as she had demanded.

She assumed that he could tell her about her soulmate, who she was determined to meet on an upcoming trip to the United States. 'Indeed, he is there,' M'Hoq Toq confirmed.

But Ro got into an argument then about her new love's form. She was determined that her lover would be a dark, Native American man. Or, at least, Black.

'He is fair. Blue eyes. He comes from somewhere else in the Americas. Near the equator.'

'From Mexico?' Nerida asked. Her knowledge of the geography of Central America was sketchy but she wanted to encourage M'Hoq Toq.

'The name derives from its place on the equator.'

'Equador,' Nerida suggested.

'No, he is not from there,' Ro persisted. 'He is Navajo or something. I know it.'

'He is not Diné.' M'Hoq Toq used the people's proper name, unfamiliar to the Australians.

The session did not get better. When Ro asked M'Hoq Toq why her grown children made her so unhappy, torturing her with their absence from her life, he said, 'You know why they are angry with you. You knew what was going on and you did not help them.'

'I don't know what you mean,' Ro said stiffly.

'You do know. You knew then. You knew for years and years. They were only little children. You were complicit.'

Ro's face was red and wet. *Tears of anger and frustration, perhaps shame*, Nerida thought.

'You can open the door to them by being honest. Only the truth will make a reconciliation possible,' M'Hoq Toq said.

When Mari came out of trance, Ro was tense and miserable. The salad she brought from the kitchen was limp, drenched in a bottled dressing heavy with sugar and food acid.

The sausages were cheap, little more than lamb-flavoured breadcrumbs. Nerida and Mari did not linger.

'What happened?' Mari asked, as soon as they were in the car. 'It's never gone badly before. I'm used to coming back to people being emotional. Sometimes I can see they've been crying. But she was really angry. What did they say to her?'

'She didn't like what M'Hoq Toq told her, that's all. I can't tell you what he said. But she really didn't like it.'

'But I want to help people. That's what I do this for. What's the point of all the stress and losing hours of my life, if he says terrible things?'

'The terrible things were not his responsibility,' Nerida said.

A few days later, Nerida saw Ro in the carpark after work and waved to her under the hot, orange sky.

She avoided eye contact with Nerida. *She doesn't want to talk. I suppose she'll be off to America soon.* Saving what little energy she had for home, Nerida unlocked the oven of her car, turning the aircon on full blast for the seven-minute drive home. Pulling a silk scarf from her bag she used it to handle the steering wheel.

She wasn't comfortable with Ro not liking her. *But I guess somebody has told her, finally, what she needs to know. Maybe she'll appreciate it, five or ten years from now. Interacting with spirit can be painful, but it's always worthwhile.*

CHAPTER 18

A Gallery in the Pilbara

Saturday January 31, 2015

The Aboriginal artist sat on a camp chair at a trestle table on the deck outside the community art gallery. He had thick hair and a grey beard, and a modest, expectant air.

The gallery was built of two dongas, ubiquitous portable accommodation units, joined by a tin roof and a wooden deck.

Nerida wanted to go to the gallery, but was admonished not to buy any paintings, 'Since we don't,' Mari said, 'have a house with any walls to put them on. I'd like to have room to hang some of my work, too, when we eventually have our own house.'

'Okay,' said Nerida. 'Let's show our support by going to see the artists' work. She knew she would spend money.'

Inside the donga, paintings hung like clothes on a rack. Bold, bright canvases showed the astral perspective of landscape central to Aboriginal art. Each artist had a set of colours they felt comfortable using, which was related to the Country they had permission, by inheritance and culture, to paint. Endearing animal sculptures made of *tjanpi*, spinifex grass bound with coloured string, and jewellery made of local seeds and seedcases were laid out neatly on narrow white tables to tempt them. Nerida bought a t-shirt with a design related to bringing rain for Mari and a pair of orange and red seed earrings for herself.

She appreciated being out among healthy people. They had talked about having a house in Newman, as they did almost everywhere they cared to stay. Susan, Nerida's manager, sent them emails of an adorable puppy, the dog they could have if they settled there.

Mari always considered staying in a place where she saw her doctor wife treated with respect. She advocated for any manager who paid them properly and didn't hurt Nerida. And wherever they went, they saw beauty and power in the land. They watched for Dreaming places, animals and beings in the rock formations.

Watched the clouds gather, build and disperse. Listened for eagles calling with the car windows wound down.

The Pilbara's coloured canyons and gorges inspired and nourished them. After years of living in Central Australia, they were thrilled by running creeks and full waterholes. Sometimes they drove out in the evenings, just to see the light on the tall red mesas, their concave slopes studded with bunches of green spinifex and draped with sensuous ghost gums.

'If people knew how magnificent this country is, they would stop the mining,' Nerida said to Mari. She said it to her patients, too. Anyone who'd listen.

On the gallery deck, they introduced themselves to the local artist, attracted to his magnetic energy. He invited them to sit with him. They responded to his air of authority.

'Sickness Place,' he explained. He pointed to the east, Nerida thought. His insistent manner and odd subject matter made her wonder if he was a bit mad.

'My Country's got a Sickness Place. Kumpupirntily. Lake Disappointment, whitefellas call it. Poison in there!'

He learned forward with laser intensity. 'People ne'er used to go there,' he said. 'Bad spirits live there. Anybody who went there got sick. Some mob died.

'I was taught this by my father, my grandfather, my great-grandfather. And on back,' he gestured to show the many generations, 'all the way, you know? This is a true story.'

He pointed with his open hand in the direction of the country. 'Over there. People should stay away! Old people always knew. You leave that place alone!'

His voice rang in the space between the dongas.

'Now,' he paused for impact, 'they dig it up!'

The whites of his eyes were bright against his glossy, brown skin. His bushy, grey-speckled brows shot up in alarm.

'I made a movie about it. Wanna see this movie?'

He picked up a tablet, flecked and imprinted, like his hands, with paint and orange sand.

A bright animation appeared on the screen. Nerida resisted.

She was tired from the fortnight's work. It was scorching hot with no whisper of a breeze. This was her first day off in fifteen days. *How long is this gonna be? I could be back in bed under the air conditioner.*

The old man fixed her with his sparkling eyes. Glanced at Mari. 'Look now,' he said. The video showed rolling red and yellow sand hills marked by olive-green, spikey bushes and black, dead trees.

From the side of the frame an earth mover trundled in—an engaging toy jerking along in stop animation. The earth mover started digging, red sand slipping from the sides of its toothed yellow bucket.

Suddenly, thick, black, snake-like creatures with staring eyes exploded out of the centre of the screen, emerging from the pit the machinery dug. Little men in yellow helmets ran away in fear.

'That's mamu, eh?' Nerida said quietly.

'Cannibal beings,' he responded.

Zombie-like creatures with frightening skeleton grins emerged and started marching across the land from the pit where they had been dug up. They kept coming and coming in horrifying, infinite supply.

The little miners got sick with swollen red heads. Their helmets blasted off. Spiralling eyes, mouths gasping for air. Their heads exploded. They died in heaps. The zombie killers found the corpses. Tore them apart with jagged teeth.

The video was only minutes long.

Rain started on the metal roof. Cold, colossal drops shattered in the sand. Thunder rumbled. The smell of the rain on the hot sand was intoxicating.

'People helped me make this video,' the artist said with pride. 'We bin showing it at festivals. Won prizes, too.'

'Very good,' Nerida said. 'That's a story to think about.'

'So that's what happens when they mine sickness country? You know that?' Mari said. She leaned forward intently.

'*Yuwa,*' he affirmed, yes. 'I know that.'

CHAPTER 19

Friday, March 13, 2015

They walked to the corner of East 42nd and 1st in the dark that morning, heads down, with icy sleet from across the grey Hudson River stinging their faces.

At the corner, waiting for the lights to change, Mari pulled Nerida's collar up and her hat down, kissed her. And turned to go.

Mari was not allowed to come in to support Nerida making her speech. Even if Nerida was allowed to make it, her wife did not have security clearance to come inside. Nerida pulled her scarf up over her face, placed her feet carefully on the icy sidewalk. *Today I make my speech at the United Nations Congress on Marginalized People.*

They had travelled for days. Two days driving out of the desert. A day flying from the regional capital to Sydney. Thirty hours travel from Sydney to Los Angeles.

Then another six hours flight the next day to get to New York. Nerida bought their airfares with her credit card because she wanted to do this.

The UN hall was still empty when Nerida arrived. She was granted access by the plastic tag hung on her neck, given a sticker and a wristband.

The hall smelled of paper dust, fragrant wood and old leather. She was assigned a spot with a red-lit digital clock incorporating a timer and headphones for translation.

Walking down to the imposing dais, she introduced herself to the one other person there and explained her purpose.

The Congress Chair was a woman in her sixties with flat shoes, comfortable beige clothing and strings of wooden beads. She told Nerida that she would do her best to give her a chance to speak.

'I'm from South America. Nobody ever talks about people like us. There or here.'

Their eyes met. They smiled.

'It's a really long meeting though.' She lifted the pages on her clipboard. 'I've got more than fifty speakers on this list. You've only got two minutes.'

'Two minutes! I was told I had five. I've prepared five,' Nerida protested. Her timed speech was a product of collaboration with brilliant colleagues. *Every word must work.*

'Take five, then,' she said, checking that Nerida was on the list. She was number 61. Last.

The hall filled and the meeting started in a roaring hubbub. The Chair hosted an hour-long panel discussion first. An Indigenous panellist from South America who arrived very late was granted speaking time. Her discourse was rambling, and she took fifty-five minutes instead of the ten she was assigned. She had a broad-brimmed hat and a withered arm.

But that's no excuse for not giving a decent speech. She's disabled and Indigenous, so no one has the nerve to shut her up. I wouldn't mind if she spoke powerfully. The meeting Chair is from South America, too, but she's white, so she won't stop her. 'Get off that ride of white guilt!' Nerida felt like calling out. *'She's got no problem using her mouth.'*

She wondered then if she was channelling Mari. And smiled. Shuffled the papers in her hands. Her five-minute speech that she had printed out in sixteen-point type.

The red digital clock at her desk showed over two hours when the delegates began their contributions. Most read notes full of evasion and platitudes. Nerida listened, cultivating patience in her tight yellow dress and unaccustomed pantyhose, grateful to be there. She watched delegates busy with their notes. Or lunch boxes. *I should have brought something to eat.*

There were African women in splendid, curve-enhancing cotton suits. She envied them their tailors. *I would go to Africa for a wardrobe of those dresses*, she thought. *Look how they still wear their jewel colours in the dead of Winter.*

Lesbian colleagues, past presenters at an international women's conference, had warned Nerida that a contingent of African women came to them after they spoke, asking what they meant by "lesbians," or "same-sex attracted" women. They didn't know this word, 'bisexual.' Products of missionary education and colonial homophobia, Nerida supposed, they had no concept. *Will any of those women will give me the time of day after hearing what I came to say?*

Most delegates couched their reports on conditions of women or the disabled in terms of legislation. A couple of delegates mentioned the homeless. The more interesting reports cited statistics.

There was an honest and frightening report on maternal mortality and teenage pregnancy from one of the smaller African nations. Another woman reported on deaths caused by incomplete, illegal abortions in a Caribbean country. Vatican City and Saudi Arabia distinguished themselves by having jaded male delegates present on the great progress women had made within their remit. Sierra Leone's delegate made a mildly interesting presentation about a government-sponsored work for the disabled program.

After four hours the program drew to a close. A Pacific Islands delegate, one of the last on the national delegate list, spoke up about the urgency of the coming submersion of their islands due to global warming. Their whole country was marginalized, as it would cease to exist within a decade or two, she said passionately. Nerida understood.

She and Mari witnessed it at the Cocos-Keeling Islands—a remote Australian Territory in the Indian Ocean. They saw piles of sandbags at the wharf bus stop, which was now underwater, sandbags and all. The crystalline white beaches of the atoll were disappearing under the turquoise waves. People she cared for at CKI were losing their home, too. She applauded the delegate energetically.

Finally, the NGO representatives had their turn. Delegates were tired and hungry as Nerida's neighbour spoke up for migrant women living on the industrial wastelands at Calais in France.

No one had mentioned lesbian, gay, bisexual or trans-gendered people. It was as if the rainbow people did not exist.

It was Nerida's go. She adjusted her microphone. A green light came on and she pushed the button to speak.

'Good Afternoon.' Her voice was clear and bright. She spoke with rolled r's so that ears attuned to American English might understand her better.

'My name is Nerida Green. I'm a medical doctor from Australia. I have a good life. I am beloved and cared for. I have good access to food, shelter and medical care. I am respected, listened to. I feel safe in my home and at work. In short, I live a life of great privilege in the world at this time.'

The part about feeling safe at work isn't always true, but true compared to doctors working in, say, Syria. The crowd was hushed. People didn't usually talk about their privilege at the UN. Her voice rang. She spoke slowly and firmly, taking time for the interpreters who were huddled into their microphones or splayed back in their chairs, bored, in their tinted glass booths.

'As I speak, millions like me live in terror, jailed by a stony prison, or mentally imprisoned by legitimate fear.

'Many face execution, just for being like me.

'Untold numbers have already been executed, judicially or on the streets—shot, poisoned, beheaded, stoned, beaten or tortured to death, for being like me. Untold numbers live in the shadows of their communities, having been psychologically and often physically harassed and tortured—just for being like me.

'I am lesbian, gay, homosexual. This way of being is called many names, some of them derogatory and abusive.

'People like me, attracted to their same gender, loving others of the same gender, that is, homosexual people; or people facing a different reality—experiencing themselves as different genders than whatever a doctor, or the world, judges them to be—'

She took a breath. The clock was already at two minutes. *Don't rush it. Let them learn.*

'—people called transgender or genderqueer; and people who are born without a definitive gender who are called intersex; those who might not discriminate about gender in their attraction to a partner who can be called bisexual...'

She was trying to explain who they were in half a minute. Half a minute already beyond her allowed time.

'All of us and more constitute a rainbow of diversity: diverse sexual orientation and gender identity. All of us suffer to some extent because of the attitudes of some powerful, backward humans to how and who we are.

'I represent an organisation of people with diverse sexual orientations and gender identities. Health workers, including doctors like me, and our partners and supporters.

'Even in such a wealthy country as Australia, same-sex attracted women suffer at least twice the levels of depression, anxiety and suicidal thoughts, reflecting marginalisation, misogyny and hatred of rainbow people.'

Show, don't tell, she thought.

'My wife and I were legally married in New Zealand in 2009 in a civil union ceremony, but this formal relationship is not recognised in Australia, where gay marriage of any kind remains illegal.'

The red timer passed three minutes. People seemed to be listening. She continued, her voice shaking a little.

'We did not invite family and friends to our wedding because we did not want to impose extensive and expensive travel costs upon them. We didn't want to provoke conflict in our families about our wedding either. So, we married quietly on our own, with strangers who became new friends. It was nevertheless a joyous occasion. We are, every day, happy to be together.

'There is now robust evidence that same sex attracted people living in jurisdictions that legally recognise their relationships have significantly better health than those in jurisdictions that do not.

'Many of you are aware that in Australia, the Indigenous peoples are marginalised and deprived, enduring death and sickness at a rate many times that of non-Indigenous people.

'Many people in Australia live in poverty. There is hunger and homelessness. Thousands of refugees remain imprisoned in camps.

'Alongside the economic and social deprivation which is a product of racism and the class system, having different sexual orientation and gender identity is an independent risk factor for poorer physical and mental health.

'And it is some kind of secret that many of the asylum seekers imprisoned in Australia's detention centres—jailed indefinitely— have run for their lives, fleeing oppression because of their sexual orientation or gender identity.

'I was a community doctor on Christmas Island, an Australian Territory in the Indian Ocean used by the government as a place of indefinite detention of thousands of asylum seekers.

'There was a heavy load of grief and trauma there, among the refugees. And in the island's inhabitants, who'd seen people drowned or killed on the volcanic rocks there when boats were wrecked in storms. It is a haunted island.

'One Friday night, my wife and I relaxed at a bar overlooking the ocean with my work colleagues—doctors and nurses. Watching the sunset, having a cool drink, we waited for our dinner.

'Conversation turned to one of our patients. He was from a privileged layer in his country of origin. His mother was a wealthy and highly respected doctor. That man had a terrifying experience coming to Australia seeking asylum. The boat he was on broke up in the open ocean. Twenty-three people drowned.

'The man's health was severely damaged by the experience. "Why would he do that?" asked one of my colleagues.

'The conversation following implied that the man was a fool, perhaps a greedy one.'

The clock approached six minutes. *I can be cut off at any time, now.* She kept her voice steady and clear. Avoided looking at the Chair. The woman from the Pacific island was listening, leaning against a wooden divider.

'My wife spoke up, "I haven't met him, but obviously this man is gay. He lived in a land where gay people face execution. His wealthy and respected mother may have turned him out. She couldn't offer him protection anyway from imprisonment, torture and death. Of course, he would do anything to find a better life." My wife knows Egypt. She has worked there. Homosexuality was outlawed there in 2000.'

The cavernous UN hall was silent. No one moved. None had walked out. *I'll finish. Nobody's stopping me.*

'Hatred toward people like me, hatred of those of us with different sexual orientation and gender identity—this hatred serves the interests of many in power. It is sustained by corrupt churches, by reactionary political leaders, by exploitative capitalists, by those who have their own interests in keeping people backward and divided from each other.

'This hatred, homophobia and transphobia, in despising a minority, keeps the majority repressed and fearful, keeps the majority looking at marginalised individuals as the enemy, keeps the majority alienated and ignorant about the nature of love.

'By opposing such hatred and deliberately dignifying sexual orientation and gender identity minorities in your own heart, mind and consciousness, as well as endorsing affirming laws, you will allow us to live as full citizens, so that we can contribute to creating a better society for all.

'We are all part of the rainbow.'

She spoke for eight minutes without interruption or harassment. People applauded.

Nerida beamed a smile to the chair. The assistant of one of the European delegates came over, presenting her boss's card. She whispered, 'We're like you, too. Thank you.'

As people streamed out for a late lunch, the colourfully dressed African women, like birds of paradise in the florescent winter light, approached.

Here we go.

Greeting Nerida with broad smiles, they congratulated her on the speech. 'Well done,' said a tall woman in purple.

As if they anticipated her concerns, a woman in forest green and gold, with big hands, grabbed hers and said, 'We know what you are talking about. Thank you for speaking up.'

The women dispersed, leaving one behind.

Wearing a drab grey suit, her head and limbs hung in grief.

She ran a support group through her church in South Africa, she said, with tears in her eyes.

Her daughter was remanded in jail at home in Nigeria, facing a sentence of up to fourteen years for lesbianism.

'How many voices does it take?' Nerida asked, smoothing her own hair, her breast, 'and for how long do we need to talk?'

NEW YORKER
WYNDHAM

It was dark already when Nerida walked back to the hotel to be with Mari. *Such short days in these northern winters.* She was exhilarated by her speech. But, approaching the hotel, she felt concerned for Mari, stuck inside all day. And left out.

The building was dark and narrow, with an old elevator with a folding door.

It smelled mouldy. The hallway was decorated with gold flock wallpaper, which must have looked smashing in 1973.

Nerida knocked on the hollow door. They only had one key. Their room was nothing more than a bed, with a television at the foot of it and a barred window looking into a brick light well. A small, bathroom completed the brown and yellow suite.

Mari opened the door. Greeted her with an enveloping hug. 'Did you get to speak? Did it go well?'

Nerida's story bubbled out. She took off her coat and scarf. Unzipped her black ankle boots, not made for snow. Her feet were wet.

'Tell me about your day,' Nerida said, towelling her feet. She braced. *This could be a miserable tale of bad news and bad television.*

'I came here to the hotel room after I left you. I was a bit down, you know?'

Nerida wriggled out of her tights and unzipped her dress, peeling it off.

'It's so cold outside. I can't go anywhere. And my lovely Nerida is speaking to hundreds of people from all over the world, giving her soon-to-be famous speech.' She rubbed Nerida's earlobe affectionately.

'I turned on the television. Fifty-six American channels and nothing to watch. I thought I might as well watch the news on the BBC,' Mari smiled, coming out of their hug.

'Just as I put it on, there was a story from the British Museum. The artists from our Western Desert Community had an exhibition opening there today. Their huge paintings! Their collaboratives. The ones Ryan had to clean the dogs' pawprints off.

'Two of the artists were there, with Ryan and his wife. All four of them on the news from London!

'One of the old men shook hands with that big-eared Royal. You know the one I mean.'

'Charles. That would be Prince Charles,' Nerida said. She felt happiness rising between them.

'The one with the big ears, yes. They both had the catalogue—with my photos of the desert artists—in their hands.'

Nerida stacked pillows behind her, bouncing in her bra and pants as she sat on the squeaky bed.

'Let me get this straight. You're in New York.

'You drop your wife off for her speech at the UN and go back to the hotel...

'Where you happen to see your friends, traditional desert people with their art centre managers—from one of the most remote communities on mainland Australia—on television, shaking hands with royalty in London.

'And all of them with the book, with your photos in it, in their hands.'

'Yes,' Mari replied. Her eyes shone. 'That was quite a moment, that.'

She lay down beside Nerida, glowing.

CHAPTER 20

Airport hotel, Los Angeles

Tuesday, March 17, 2015

Nerida had a dinner date booked with Jim and his wife, Cindy, outside of Los Angeles on their way home from the UN meeting in New York.

'Do you have to go?' Mari said.

'You know I want to. I booked this room an extra night to have a chance to see him.'

'You're hoping for what? That he has an epiphany?'

'I know he won't. But he's still my son. I haven't seen him in years. You could come if you like. You know, at least he's not a criminal anymore.'

'He's a real estate salesman. Are you sure he's not a criminal anymore? He's probably money laundering and evicting people and demolishing neighbourhoods.'

'Oh, stop it, Mari.'

Jim texted his mother at 3.30 that afternoon. 'Hey mum, can't do dinner. Cindy has a prior engagement & committed me 2. You know wives! LOL. Stop by my work 4 coffee? Link 2 address.'

Nerida took a cab. Jim's office was a partitioned desk at the back of the realtor's shop in Compton.

Jim embraced her with his glowing smile. *He still is beautiful, my boy.*

The office had a coffee machine, generating a small mountain of jewel pods mounting out of the bin on the way to landfill. He made them both coffees and they sat on a plastic bench in the small carpark at the back of the shop.

'Sorry about dinner,' he said. 'Cindy and I do a lot of community work, you know? There's a proposal to build a needle exchange around the corner from our church. We have to let the council know that we can't have that.'

'You're going to a demo?'

'Just like you always did.' He smiled. Patted her on the back.

Nerida screwed up her face. 'But Jim, you and Cindy were both injecting drug users when you met. You met at a rehab meeting. Right?'

'That's what makes us so powerful in speaking up against this. We know the type of people we used to be. And how Jesus saved us.'

'But if people don't get saved by Jesus, can't we keep them alive until that happens? Like, keeping them safe from hepatitis and HIV? Don't you think that would be a good thing? There but for the grace of God and all that?'

Jim sighed and shook his head. His face was handsome and tanned. His muscles ticced in his neck and temple. His mother was exasperating sometimes. 'It's always gotta be about politics with you straight away, doesn't it? Always looking for an argument.'

Nerida took a deep breath and sipped her coffee. A pigeon perched on the neighbour's guttering watch them, contented.

'How's work going?'

'It's brilliant. They love me here. We've got a huge project coming up in Bell Gardens. Condominiums. It's going to being high spec. Immaculate. You should see the tiles they're using for the splashbacks. One and a half baths in two-bedroom apartments. You should buy one as an investment.'

'I don't make that kind of money, darling.'

'I'm driving to Vegas again on the weekend. We've got a massive development there, too.'

'I'm surprised you still go to Vegas. You know, with what happened there.'

'I've still got mates in Vegas. Good mates who look after me. I'm not a gambling addict anymore, Mum. Don't worry about me. I'm recovered from that. Cindy and me have a drink or, you know, eight, on a Saturday night.'

He laughed mirthlessly. 'But we always make it to church on Sunday morning. And have church people over for lunch or potluck there at the church. She's teaching Sunday school. And I pay a good tithe. You should be proud of me.'

'I am proud that you're as well as you are, sonboy. I'm grateful you've survived all that you've been through. And that you have a wife and friends here who love and care about you. That's all that matters.'

She touched him tenderly on the cheek. He backed away.

The pigeon cooed. 'Did you see my post about my speech?' Hundreds of her friends had liked her UN speech and sent supportive messages.

'Yeah. That's embarrassing!' His knee bobbed up and down, getting faster. 'It's disgusting, really. I was so angry with you. You always have to advertise what kind of a freak you are, don't you Mum? You never could be discrete.'

'What do you mean?'

'You know what I mean. About your sins. Marching in Mardi Gras when we were kids.'

'You and your sister used to love Mardi Gras.'

'It was child abuse, Mum. Taking us to march with perverts and sickos.'

Nerida took a deep breath. Looked into the distance. 'Listen to the pigeon's coo,' she said. 'He's telling us to calm down.'

'Some things you need to fight about Mum. You taught me that. And Grandma and Grandad. You blackfellas always fought for the wrong things, but.'

'What do you mean?

'Trying to hold onto pagan things. Stopping progress. Hugging trees. Huh! And you still, now, keep going back to those people with backward, heathen ways. If you're not trying to change them, why do you go?'

'There's a lot of value in the Old Ways, my son.'

'Well. It's been great to see you, Mum.' He pecked her on the cheek. Showed his teeth in a smirk that was meant to cover tension as he left.

Nerida's vision was clouded by tears. The traffic fumes felt suffocating as she crossed the road to where Mari had come to pick her up in a rental car. When Jim cancelled dinner, they'd changed their plans. They would drive up into the canyons to visit Dawn and maybe have a channelling session with Monica that evening.

'Oh, my darling,' Mari said. Nerida cried quietly as she got into the car.

Jim climbed into a red Porsche across the road.

'Well, he's got a fancy car,' Mari noticed.

'Probably belongs to the company.' Nerida said as he gunned the engine and sped off.

'I don't think so,' Mari said. 'Did you see the licence plate? MAT 5:44. That's a bible verse. I remember it from school.'

'What is it?'

'I'd have to look it up. From memory, it's something like "Love your enemies and pray for those who persecute you." Why would he use that?'

'He prays for me, then. Somehow, he thinks I abused him, just by being who I am.'

Mari shook her head. 'He's always the victim, Nerida. Haven't you noticed?'

CHAPTER 21

Newman, Parnpajinya Western Australia

Thursday March 26, 2015

Nerida woke in a panic. Pulled on her jeans. Pulled off her nightie, searched for a bra.

Mari snored softly beside her. The red light of the digital clock showed 4am.

Nerida opened the bedroom door, running. *Where is my stethoscope?* Snapped the light on in the kitchen.

'Where are you going?' Mari called wearily.

'To the hospital. The phone rang. I have to go in.'

'The phone didn't ring. Check it.'

Mari was right. There was no call.

'You are never doing on-call again. You're hypervigilant. Fuck this job. Come back to bed.'

Shit, I must have dreamt it. Too early to be up for work. Too scared to sleep. Nerida took her jeans off.

Drank some water. Went to pee. Reproached herself in the mirror. *You've done it now.*

She had no fever. It was nothing she ate. *Maybe I'm still jet-lagged from New York. No, that's not it.*

Her soft skin burned with an irritated itch: on her scalp, her neck and cheek, her vulva, the soles of her feet. She scratched and rubbed herself, picked up a balm from the bathroom vanity, knew there was not much soothing in it. She'd imbibed too much of something drying, liked coffee. Or chili. Or the drug of overwork.

It was being in the desert. It was knowing what she knew.

It was knowledge she couldn't share even with Mari, but that came rising up out of her through the day, maybe shaping words she didn't choose, distorting her way of being in the world. *You'll be sacked. You'll never work as a doctor again. You'll be struck off. You think they'll ever trust you to look after anyone once they know what you do?*

She rolled back into bed. The mattress creaked, Mari stirred and murmured. She put her hand on her wife's blanketed shoulder and murmured back, soothing Mari back to sleep, unable to soothe herself.

Guilt and an overdeveloped sense of responsibility harangued her. *I was given a formula for the treatment of Ebola and did nothing about it.*

CHAPTER 22
TIME SLIP 4: Near Future

Planet Earth afflicted

Thursday July 27, 2028

On another sleepless night, Nerida was desperately overtired. Her mind was active. She was angry with herself. Felt like cutting her head off to shut her brain up.

It was 3.30am the last time she let herself look at the clock. Too tired to get up, too crazy to sleep, she closed her eyes and counted her breaths backwards from one hundred.

As she breathed in for fifty-seven, she felt herself carried through black space, stars shooting at the corners of spirit-body eyes, wind around her. A voice explaining without being a voice.

Miners went to the moon. They made a fundamental mistake, being too sophisticated to pay attention to the basics. Focused on getting to the real money, digging rare earths out of Mars.

There was a detonation on the moon. She saw it, white and purple, blinding her spirit-eyes. An explosion seen from Earth, the voice said. Even places where it was daylight saw the blowout burst in the sky. In the following days and years people burned with rage at the injustice of it.

Now the ocean tides are disrupted. The animals are confused, too. Cows are stressed and don't give milk. Horses won't let people ride them because they don't sleep properly. Plagues of insects eat the crops after the lizards that ate them died.

Birds are unable to navigate to their feeding and nesting grounds.

Pets cry and howl ceaselessly until their owners sedate them or have them euthanised. Whales and dolphins are stranding, dying in their hundreds.

Volcanoes vent lava and hurl rocks. Geologists say the centre of the planet lost its balance. This causes cyclones and storms, tidal waves. Clouds of volcanic ash hang around the earth like an intractable skin disease.

The planet's axis changed abruptly. Some people imagine they felt the lurch. Astronomers see it all until their scopes stop working. The internet evaporates into nothing after the satellites stop. They crash into each other, fall out of orbit into space. Or randomly plunge to earth as space junk, killing anyone.

The banks break. Whether you have debts or savings doesn't matter. Money doesn't matter. You need labour or goods to trade for food or shelter. Navigation systems are gone, so ships and planes are grounded.

Yachts, canoes and surviving whales share hushed seas.

The moon travels on a different course, in a different shape.

One of the singular dependable events in human life, through birth and death, joy and grieving, love and loss—the moon—is gone. It no longer cycles in any way we understand.

Women's menstrual cycles are irregular because their bodies, water in cells interacting with hormones, doesn't know how to adapt. Because the moon has had more than just a part amputated.

One chunk of the blasted-off moonrock is big enough to make another little moon. Astronomers haven't tracked a rhythm in it yet.

It may not develop one. It might crash into the Earth or spin off into space, more debris sending a message of human idiocy into the galaxy.

Several pieces hit the earth as the moon exploded. Hundreds of people were killed, evaporated in the dust of new craters. Scientists say the planet itself could have been knocked off its course into oblivion, all life destroyed.

Others are not sure whether the moon will continue to pull the tides at all in future. The shape is unstable. More could crack and break.

And no one is responsible. 'We were doing everything right.' They saw the representative of the mining company say on the news. 'I have here a copy of our environmental impact statement.'

'You weren't! You fuckers! *Arschlöcher!*' Mari yells. She slams her drink bottle on the table. Leaves the room in fury. Nerida hears things slamming and crashing in the next room.

Nothing was illegal, people say on the news, even if it was all profoundly immoral.

Now when the moon rises, it's a different shape.

'Someone took a bite out of it. I wished they'd choked,' Mari says, when they see it in the sky, misshapen and skewed. Never to heal.

Nerida cries for years. She cannot put her grief into words.

Mari was calling her, touching her gently, jiggling her shoulder. 'It's all right sweetheart. Wake up, darling. Nerida!'

Returning from the nightmare, Nerida pulled herself up. Her feet were cool on the concrete floor. Empty, exhausted by crying and the passage of time she'd experienced. Devastated by fury at the stupidity she'd witnessed. Wounded by the vision.

She went out the front door to the metal staircase where the full moon was setting as the sun rose.

Turning behind, Mari was at the window in her t-shirt and pants. She'd hopped there, pulling herself on the plasterboard walls and cheap furniture. Hands up on the glass, she watched Nerida, concerned.

Nerida saw her own reflection, looking wild-eyed and disturbed. Barefoot and heavy breasted in her nightie.

She stood and watched the moon disappear behind the broken mountain where the miners with their machinery still worked through the night. Making sure that moon was still, then, reliably round.

CHAPTER 23

Return to Linear Time: Recent Past

Byron Bay NSW, Bundjalung Land

Monday 23 September 2019

'If I work only three days a week for better money, I can write books,' Nerida said. 'We can go where people have money, eh?'

'I'm not sure. You might not like it.'

'People say it's a paradise.' She drove on. 'Is it that you still don't want me to write the books?'

'It's gonna make you start fighting if I say what I think. You get all prickly.'

'No, go on.' Nerida was on a freeway, charging up the overtaking lane. Mari sat beside her, watching the traffic and the weather.

She flexed her shoulders, raising her hands above her head. She looked vulnerable, sitting there without her artificial leg. Her stump and phantom limb had been hurting lately. 'I still think you shouldn't come out that way. I still don't see why you can't write it under a fake name. What do you call it?'

'A pen name. A pseudonym. I've told you before why I don't feel like I can.'

'I know. You feel like it's about your integrity as an Indigenous woman and all that.'

'Don't say 'all that.' That's not nothing. Being honest about all aspects of who you are. That's our way.' She overtook two trucks, that felt like they were inches from them, flattening the accelerator up to one hundred and forty kilometres an hour. 'There's power in this being our real, lived experience,' she insisted.

People should understand that channelling is not just weird religious shit. Or a Hollywood gimmick. If people know that you do this, that we really are, all of us, spirits that get reincarnated, that we really have spirit guides. It could make the world a better place. That's the point, isn't it? That this is not just a fairy tale?'

'You think you have to prove the phenomenon scientifically.' Mari sounded irritable, pointed her finger as she spoke.

'Of course, I do. That's what science is about. Observing new phenomena, finding out about them. Learning.'

'And if I am the phenomenon? If I was an alien, would you let them take my body and dissect me?'

'It's not the same. Channelling in public won't kill you.'

'But it would kill your reputation and your ability to do your work as a doctor. I don't see how you can be so ready to give up what you struggled so hard over so many years to achieve.'

'Because the truth is worth everything.'

'You don't even know what the truth is. I don't even know what I do! How can you stake our lives on it?'

Nerida did not reply then. She knew that any argument worth having had no easy solution. And this was one they'd had many times. She drove on. 'Look for a sign,' she said. 'I'd like to stop at the next rest stop if it has a toilet.'

'Okay.' Mari looked out the window.

After a few minutes, Nerida said, 'And I've spent all those years building a platform.'

'Fucking platform.' Mari gestured with frustration, grabbing at the air in front of her. 'You don't believe in that marketing shit anyway. And now you've got this insane fantasy that the crowd at Byron Bay with the tiny balls and the rubber duck lips is gonna love us. Fall in love with your brand! They will never love us!'

'Not everyone there is like that. And not everyone who uses steroids or lip-fillers is a bad person.' She paused. 'Some of the influencers have sold their souls to the devil, I grant you. But not everyone has to love us, anyway. We'll never be for everybody.' Nerida accelerated, overtaking again. Fossils dragging caravans lumbered ahead.

'Well, if you want to be with the ones that aren't like that, don't go there! We could be lost in all that *scheisse*. Don't you see? That crowd could be very bad for us.'

Nerida noticed her tenderness, then. And felt attracted to Mari's protectiveness of their privacy, to her smooth olive neck, the shape of her breasts and her tapered hands. She pushed the feeling aside and said, 'Mari, you don't see the contradictions in people or places. It's always black and white with you.'

A bully, driving even faster than Nerida, came up to the back of their car and threatened them, tailgating at speed. Nerida steered back into the centre lane.

Because Mari was able to criticise but unable to make a better decision, they went to Byron Bay in northern New South Wales. It was a region of powerful rivers, beaches, and forested hills. Many people, on websites and billboards at least, described it as paradise.

We can afford a house with more than three rooms, Nerida thought with satisfaction. They were not far from Nerida's Aboriginal clan's country, and within a day's drive of family further south. Her brother could send her a bottle of his home-brewed beer and have it arrive in one piece.

Mari wasn't ready to move into their house in Narooma. Plenty of Nerida's family lived near there. If she was honest, Nerida wasn't sure about living there, either. Nerida's mother could be passive and needy, her father bossy. A couple of her cousins were drug addicts. Her nephew was a pathological liar, just as bad at avoiding responsibility as Nerida's son. But closer. Nerida was reasonably confident she could say 'No,' as needed. But Mari's trust in Nerida was shaken to its foundations after their time in Germany. Her trust in the world was broken.

Mari wasn't ready for regular interaction with extended family. Nerida wasn't sure she'd ever be. She saw her wife trying to process the realisation that her parents had died. The grim circumstances and gross injustice of their deaths.

And then, her youngest brother had caused so much damage. That family wasn't always a good thing. *Complicated grief, we call it.* Mari still had nightmares, was hyper vigilant, sometimes more than a little paranoid. Woke up sobbing having hallucinations that her mother was calling her.

Nerida told her wife she wanted a house so that she could unpack her things and live with them awhile. But she cared more about giving Mari time with the things she owned and treasured, especially her possessions from Germany: small pieces of furniture—a sewing table with marks from her mother's tailoring scissors, two wooden chairs her grandfather built, a hammer with her father's hand imprinted in the handle—as well as the childhood toys she'd salvaged.

And grown-up pleasures from their life before all that drama and difficulty had happened. Her leather jackets and her jewellery. The photos she'd taken, but not yet processed. The photographic books she'd created. And her unfinished artworks from Central Australia, abandoned when they left abruptly. Nerida hoped that being surrounded by them, instead of having them packed away in a storage container down the coast, might help Mari heal. She who highly valued human creations, objects people made with their knowledge, hands and tools.

So, they looked for a house. Near the coast, Mari insisted. After the desert years, she craved the ocean. She hated the bugs in the hinterland forest, even if rents were more reasonable there.

Back in their hotel room one evening, Nerida exclaimed. 'Oh,' she said to Mari. 'Do you remember Jeep? He's died.'

'That's sad. He was such a friendly, easy-going guy. I remember him from the art shed. He didn't paint much anymore. But he'd sit and watch. Handsome old man.' Mari had an excellent memory, even when she was stressed.

'There's an email here from Bronwyn. He died peacefully at home. Had the medicines he needed, she said.' Nerida licked salt off her fingers. She was snacking on chips before dinner.

'Was he the one you made palliative? You had trouble getting someone the drugs, right? Was that him?' Mari asked. Nerida sometimes told her the outline of a patient's important story after they'd left a place.

'I forgot that. You're right. I got him opiates and benzos so that he could breathe better. Stopped a few of his other tablets. He was pretty happy about that.

'I'm glad Bronwyn was still there. She was very nervous when we had that palliative care meeting. The family wanted Jeep to stay home and not have to go to the hospital every second week. Simon did an excellent job that day.'

Mari had invited Bronwyn for coffee once or twice during their last stay in the western desert. 'Bronwyn said she couldn't believe the doctors had got it so wrong.'

'She told you about Jeep? She breached confidentiality?'

'She didn't tell me his name and I didn't ask. She told me that a patient there was misdiagnosed and mistreated for decades though, because nobody bothered to listen to their family. She was terrified that the family would sue the doctors for not finding out what was wrong with him all those years.'

'I s'pose they'd have a case. I didn't think of that.' Nerida picked up her bowl, washed it and started scouting for dinner.

'Bronwyn thought about medico-legal stuff all the time. I think that's why she didn't like you much. She thought you had no fear.'

'Well, she's wrong about that. Just because I have different boundaries, doesn't mean I have none,' said Nerida.

'Don't you feel angry about what they did to Jeep? It's disgusting.'

Nerida pulled salad vegetables out of the bar fridge. 'Jeep wasn't angry anymore. But he knew what injustice looked like. That mob did sue the government about the bombings, you know. That's how they built their community. They won their court case. Got a few crumbs of compensation.'

'But doctors should know better!' Mari gestured with both hands in frustration. 'They go to work in remote communities. They know nothing of the language, the history. They have no idea where they are. Then, they ask why Aboriginal people don't feel safe going to hospital. And blame them for it.'

'The ones who go to remote communities are usually well-meaning. My colleagues don't see their blind spots.' Nerida washed tomatoes. 'That's how instutionalised racism works. It's gonna take a lot more than our rage or rejection to change their minds about that.'

'So many fucking years.' Mari moved behind her, put a pan on the hotplate, drizzled oil on it from the little bottle they travelled with.

'It didn't occur to the respiratory specialists, the physicians, the cardiologists or any of the GPs that Jeep saw in a lifetime to ask him or his wife what had made him sick?'

Nerida was learning to be more comfortable when Mari was angry. To not try to talk her out of her feelings. *Just because I bottle things up, doesn't mean Mari has to.* 'You're right. It is sickening. They didn't think or care that remote desert people might know more than doctors about their bodies and their illnesses. Okay, they needed an interpreter.'

'But who needs an interpreter when you can just yell at people to make them understand you, right?' Mari almost shouted. She was cutting forcefully with a blunted knife.

She'd been in life and death situations with doctors who did that to people. With her mild European accent, she'd been yelled at as if she was an idiot, too, more than once.

Nerida let it be. Peeled and sliced a cucumber. Mari tossed haloumi into the little pan. The sizzle was consoling.

'I'm glad we got to meet Jeep and his family,' Nerida said. 'I'll always remember him. Oh, I've got one of his paintings. I bought it just before we left.'

'You didn't tell me that.'

'I don't tell you everything I spend money on. And, if I'm honest, I don't remember everything I buy. If we get a house soon, we can put some paintings up.'

So, they kept alive their memories and knowledge of the privations and privileges of the Bush.

On the coast now, each woman noticed the comforts of an urban environment. Food was easy to find, if not within walking distance, then within a short drive. Fuel was less than half the price. Electricity and telephone companies allowed you to pay for their services after you'd used them, unlike remote people, who often had to pay in advance for limited, expensive services.

Fresh seafood was abundant. The lettuce was not wilted before it was purchased. In fact, the array of produce was overwhelming.

Sometimes Nerida spent half of her shopping time gazing at the fruit. The country was dry but there were magnificent, ancient trees, sandy beaches piled with driftwood, rivers still flowing despite years of drought.

Striving to become tenants was a slog, though. Each of their several applications needed a dozen pages of documentation. Conscientious as she was, Nerida's paperwork wasn't sufficient. They'd stayed in community accommodation and with family in past years and travelled broadly. They had no rental record.

'We have to work so hard to be allowed to pay someone else's mortgage. Unbelievable!' Mari slammed the car door as they left another home viewing with a super-cool, supercilious real estate agent.

The women paid a mortgage themselves on a modest house further down the coast that they'd bought when Nerida was just beginning to earn better money in 2010. They became landlords themselves, letting the house when they went to live in the desert in 2011. But the rent their tenant paid was low: about half what they would have to pay to live in Byron Bay. The tenant was an odd, secretive man who worked sometimes in mining, who had told them he expected visits from his grown children occasionally. They'd rented to him after the previous tenants sublet the house and had about twenty people living there.

Mari had taken her visiting parents, proud to show them the house and they were all shocked by the overcrowding. The little children scratched the walls with their scooters and bikes. Cigarette butts were stuffed into cracks in the balcony balustrade.

Their house was at Narooma, a coastal town. They could see the ships go by from their front windows. And whales splashing, in the season, when humpbacks travelled up the coast from Antarctica to mate and breed in the Pacific. Mari loved that. On a hill, the rusty-orange stucco concrete box was protected by forest behind. They talked about going to live there, sometimes with longing, over the years.

But the price of the view was a steep driveway. Mari couldn't walk on it. And evicting the tenant, even if he didn't pay regularly, might be hard. He was an uncommunicative man, becoming worse over the years. Always as late as he could be with his rent. And there were laws against evicting people now that COVID had hit.

After their fourth failed application for a house, Nerida realised that the years the women lived on credit, in crisis, were hurting them now.

Perhaps the real estate agents and landlords didn't like that Nerida was Aboriginal. Or they didn't like lesbians.

Nerida wrote a passionate letter. She successfully advocated for change and action all the time for her patients. Sometimes her voice was enough to overcome prejudice.

But their applications were rejected. Maybe their debt-to-income ratio was just too high. They failed to fit the algorithm.

CHAPTER 24

Byron Bay NSW, Bundjalung Land

Wednesday 25 September 2019

Nevertheless, Nerida was excited about starting her new job at a Byron Bay Integrated Medicine Clinic. 'I'll do more of the medicine I like, listening to people, prescribing herbs, including medicinal cannabis, and acupuncture,' she told her mum on the phone. 'Hmm,' her mother said, trying to refrain from snap judgements about her daughter's career.

So, Nerida studied prescribing medical marijuana in expensive online training courses. She renewed her skills in herbal medicine and updated her acupuncturist's registration.

'It'll be great to work with open-minded, holistic practitioners,' she said. *Mari might even be able to practice there as a channel one day.* 'A lot of people around here believe in channelling.'

'A lot of them are pretending they do,' Mari responded.

Nerida had great hopes. Perhaps she could leave behind the cognitive dissonance, the continual psychic noise of being a scientifically trained professional who listened to channelled spirits.

There was isolation and fracture within their marriage since Mari started channelling. They loved each other; this was given. Neither had known unconditional love and care as adults before. Nerida was sure that she would be with Mari until the end of her life. *And perhaps into the next one or two, as well.*

Mari often spoke of Nerida to family and friends, or even strangers, as 'The love of my life.' She didn't expect to survive Nerida's death, she said sometimes. 'I can't imagine life without you.'

Still, each woman wrestled with demons the other could not appreciate. Nerida was the breadwinner. She needed Mari's support to do the work she did. And they had agreed early in their marriage that she would support them financially so that Mari could be an artist. They earned more working together and had more opportunities when they travelled for medicine and art.

Since 2012 though, Mari was alone with her abilities and all their attendant mysteries.

Nerida was alone with the channelled messages and carried the weighty responsibility of the knowledge she was given. She researched what the spirits told her. Often enough she found a scientific basis, or speculation, a theory at least, supporting what they said.

When what they said contradicted science outright, though, she sometimes kept it to herself.

She didn't feel that she could post such material on Aedgar's website, for fear of brewing a backward, out-of-context version of what the spirits said. The world was full of half-truths, deception, and damned statistics. She would not sow further confusion.

Most days, she worried, too, about Mari's health. Her moods were stormy. Her sensitivity to the suffering she saw in the world, her intense frustration with stupidity—Nerida was afraid that these strong feelings, with the powerlessness she carried since their time in Germany, could hurt her.

There were times, sometimes months-long, when Mari was in pain day after day. Her body hurt when she lay down at night and when she woke up in the morning, when she slept at all. They'd been married long enough now that Nerida recognised the pattern.

By day, Mari abandoned her painting, left her palettes unwashed. Her paint was wasted. Brushes were ruined. That was when Nerida could see that the pain, emotional and physical, was overwhelming her. She tried to care for her with touch, herbs, acupuncture. Sometimes the acupuncture needles were the only thing that helped, when accepting comfort any other way was rejected.

For her part, Mari worried that Nerida liked the spirits more than she loved Mari. 'You're always so relaxed when they've been. You smile when you talk about them with other people.' *It's not true,* Nerida thought. *Sometimes what they tell me makes me sick for days. Sometimes I don't sleep at night trying to figure out what they mean.*

'I smile when I talk about you with other people, too,' Nerida responded with a hug. 'That happens more often. And you know there are not many people I talk to about the spirits. Most wouldn't understand.' A quiet part of her would grieve about losing the transcendence of talking to the spirits if Mari did not channel. But there was no one to talk to about that, either.

Combing conditioner through her hair in the quiet evening, after of visiting dirty, run down, overpriced houses, Nerida thought back to the time she last felt that she understood the world; before all this knowledge had fallen on her.

At Byron Bay they went to the beach for sunset most days. Heaving waves, lifting spray in the evening wind, the salty air restored them.

Sometimes Mari's walking wasn't up to being on sand, or even getting out of the car. Nerida could be impatient with her then, mentally berating her lack of resilience.

Mari responded as if she heard her thoughts, 'How do I say to you, my love, that I'm trying with all my might to keep up with everything you find so effortless to do?'

CHAPTER 25

Nerida wore her écru linen suit with a crisp collared shirt for a series of interviews and training at her new workplace. Mari had washed her shirt and it smelled like rosewater. The earthy aroma of herbs and tinctures greeted her in the clinic waiting area.

She spent the morning meeting the clinic admin workers, nurses, acupuncturists, and herbalists. There was a practitioner who used pretty bottles of coloured fluid to make people feel better. *M'Hoq Toq talked about healing powers of light. Maybe there's something in it. But I thought he was talking about lasers.* One of the nurses was giving a client an intravenous dose of vitamins. *An insanely large dose*, Nerida thought. *But then, what do I know about it?*

Waiting in the staff tearoom later, she was touched to see that the practice owner, Felix, had made a little shrine, with an affirmation wrapped around fragrant tobacco, saying 'Dr Nerida Green Attracts Abundance at Home and Healed Medical Practice.' Nerida was touched by the gesture.

Felix was a naturopath, as well as co-owner. He invited Nerida to sit in with him in a consult, to learn how they might work as a team.

'This place is a dream come true,' she told Felix. 'To work with other healers. It was one of the reasons I studied medicine.'

In the windowless box which would soon be Nerida's consult room, Felix and another doctor reviewed a thick volume of pathology results. The patient and Nerida sat quietly, knees almost touching on their narrow chairs, as the healers looked at numbers, calculating.

They had two hundred printed pages. Some numbers had improved, apparently. There was a formula that the patient should buy and take now to change other numbers. Oh, and another formula. And these minerals. And this vitamin. There'd need to be more pathology tests, expensive ones, to monitor the new numbers while all these were taken.

'I don't know about those pathology tests,' Nerida objected to Felix later. 'I can't sign requests for tests that I don't understand.' A doctor's signature meant government money supported the cost of the tests.

'We all go for training weekends on the Gold Coast,' Felix enthused. His skin was unnaturally smooth, his hair unnaturally dark. 'You'll like it.'

'By the way,' Felix said later, 'that doctor we sat in with is being audited by the government. This is the third time.' He inclined his head sympathetically. 'We're standing by him, trying to help him. Would you be able to supervise him when you come and work here?'

'I'm not sure. I've been a supervisor of junior doctors. But I can't supervise what I don't understand.' Nerida frowned.

'That's all right. No pressure, of course.' Felix's smile was strained. 'We will need you to prescribe more ACE inhibitors and antibiotics and statins, too, for our accreditation. Will that be all right?'

'Sure,' Nerida said. 'I mean, I prescribe those drugs all the time to people who need them.' *But that wasn't what I was hoping to do here.*

Felix laid out plans to market Nerida's arrival at the practice. There would be interviews, they would tell her what to say, for the local radio and advertorials in the paper. The practice would get a banner printed announcing her name to the heavy passing traffic. 'Because we're spending so much money on you at the beginning, your percentage will start low, but it will build up over time,' Felix explained.

A letter from Felix with Nerida's high expected income did the trick to persuade one of the landlords that they would be good tenants. She was obliged to him.

The women successfully rented a 12-year-old project home with cool, white, faux-marble tiles and dark carpets that were once beige. It was probably coming to the end of its planned obsolescence, but the house was just up the road from a natural pond of mauve waterlilies. The wetlands attracted birds.

The house had a pool taking up most of the small backyard.

Nerida felt an eight-year-old inside her, singing, as she signed the lease. They were both girls inside, who always wanted a pool.

The place, a suburb really, south of Byron Bay, was called Lennox Head, after an English Duke. Their house was behind hills, away from the eponymous head and the beaches. Sometimes at night, Nerida thought she could hear the waves. Mari didn't.

Lennox was spawning swatches of project homes built on sometimes swampy subdivided land that used to be mostly dairy farms. The dairy farmers were packing up and selling out since the Chinese didn't want their powdered milk and the EU started selling milk to Australia's former markets.

Up the hill on the other side of the wetlands, new houses were erected daily. A supermarket, carparks and a childcare centre were being assembled from steel beams and concrete slabs. Crashes of steel and the lumbering groans of earth lifters echoed daily in the valley.

A tea tree forest behind the houses looked thin and stunted after years of drought. Up the hill to the east, a little park survived among the new buildings, with three magnificent fig trees, their immense limbs hanging low to the ground. They could see them from the kitchen through over the neighbours' fences. 'Those trees would be a century old,' Nerida told Mari. 'The bats love them. I s'pose the rainforest was still here not so long ago.'

She looked up a quote on her phone. 'Hermann Hesse,' who grew up close to Mari's original home in the Black Forest, 'said: "Whoever has learned how to listen to trees no longer wants to be a tree. He wants to be nothing except what he is. That is home. That is happiness." My home is with you, Mari.'

Nerida relished having a house. The garden had tall palms, red-leafed cordyline and canna lilies. Even limes and a magnolia tree grew in the shadows of the palms.

'Paying rent causes pain,' Mari said.

'But it's possibly cheaper than keeping our goods in storage and staying in cabins or hotels between jobs,' Nerida countered.

'Well, you earn the money. I don't really get to say,' Mari complained.

'We earn the money together and you know it,' Nerida countered.

Those stints were never enough for Nerida to write her books. She'd been promising herself (and others) that she'd write books, including conversations with their spirit friends, for years now.

Mari had projects to finish, too, including a triptych of paintings she'd half-finished before putting them in storage in 2017.

After a month in the new house, they got their goods out of storage, a ten-hour drive away. They raced the removalists up the freeway to the house. Twenty hours of driving left weeks of chronic tiredness on them.

Unpacking took an age.

They unwrapped clothes, dishes and books they'd not seen for ten years, packed away when they first went to work in Outback Australia. Nerida greeted knick-knacks: an incised clay dish a uni friend gave her, incised with a shield pattern like her tattoo, a chiming Tibetan bowl her brother gave her. And paintings she hadn't lived with since she was a student, twenty years ago. 'We need to see how we like living with these things,' she said to Mari. 'I don't want to be held down by things. But I want to see if I like them.'

Mari valued the work and the materials that went into well-made goods. It was emotional for her to unpack treasures they'd shipped from Germany. Everything was in good condition: lead crystal glasses, a red Chinese teapot, her teddy. 'He's more than fifty years old,' she said, massaging his snout into a properly unpacked face.

She made an office in a small front room. Unwrapped and set up the first part of her incomplete triptych of paintings against the wall. It was a swirling pattern of blue, aqua, gold and orange, with fish in the first and middle part, and seabirds in the third. It was great to have walls to prop paintings against and hang things on, she had to admit.

Nerida relished unpacking. Just having closets and drawers. To put things away. To be able to find a pair of scissors. Or open a favourite book. To be able to work in one room, knowing Mari was nearby, without having to be in the same small room or vehicle. *Simple things—space, privacy, quiet—are true luxury.* This was why

Nerida wanted a house. And she wanted to live with the lovely things they owned. To enjoy her books and her jewelry. To see her wife working on projects that inspired her.

Nerida rose early, feeling called outside. She scooped leaves from the pool. She learned how to use the robot vacuum cleaner and swept the surrounding deck, pushing leaves back into the garden mulch, chopping up fallen palm fronds with secateurs she kept in the garden shed.

'You're turning into one of those people who smashes around with a broom at sunrise every morning?' Mari arose after ten, brewed coffee. Nerida smiled, 'Yeah, maybe.'

'We call it *senile Bettflucht.*'

'Senilla what?'

'Bed-flight. Old people who escape their bed at a ridiculous hour of the morning. Then complain all day about how tired they are.' Mari laughed.

Their landlord was supposed to maintain the pool. But after six weeks with no sign of him, Nerida paid a pool man to come and show her how. The bearded, friendly young man took the cover off the skimmer box. Under a handful of brown and black leaves a massive, odious toad pointed its warty snout at them.

'Cane toad? You don't kill them?'

'Nah. Just don't want it blocking your filter up. Messier when they're dead,' he said.

He put his hand in the basket and pulled the giant toad out by the foot, throwing it over the fence in a deft swing. *Hope our new neighbour doesn't see that flying by*, Nerida thought.

Nerida dug her thumbnail into the skin of an orange and made a face at Mari.

'The pathology tests cost thousands of dollars. They barely asked the patient how she was going. I suppose they listened to her another time. They do a lot of talking. But I don't even understand what's supposed to be wrong with her,' Nerida complained.

Mari was heating oil. 'I warned you. Byron Bay is pretentious. It's all about money.' She threw onions into the pan, which crackled.

'It was strange to me. Doctors get unhappy, our jobs are too hard. I get that. But those guys are really not coping. They've all been audited, probably because they're spending government money on these weird, obscure tests no one's ever heard of.'

'You've never been audited.' Mari caramelised chopped onions with smoked paprika. The smell made Nerida's mouth water.

'No. I've got a consistent profile. I've always worked in Aboriginal health, rehab, pall care. Places where long consultations are normal. Even when I've worked in private practice, I've never been a burn-and-churn type.'

'What's that mean?'

'You know, see patients quickly, maximise the profit. Want some orange?' She peeled the pith off a segment and fed it to Mari, who had both hands full, popping it into her mouth.

Nerida paced along the counter, eating the fruit and rearranging things.

'My billing profile's on the extreme end of the bell curve for long consultations. I only see a client or two in an hour sometimes. They do long consultations at Home and Healed, too. But people pay an awful lot for it.'

'People pay for vitamins and formulas, too. New ones every month. I've seen it in Germany,' Mari said.

'The education they get is sales training, really,' Nerida agreed. 'There's even less evidence for the formulas they sell than for dodgy Big Pharma drugs they hate so much,' Nerida complained. 'I don't go to drug company dinners. I don't prescribe medicines I don't understand. Why would they?'

'For the money,' Mari said. She dropped in strips of chicken breast to sauté. 'And they probably do believe in what they do. Some people think that's what naturopathy is. I tried to warn you. Do you want quinoa with this?'

'Yes, please. I didn't think it could be so bad. Some of the clients are really sick. Terribly sick people that medicine can't help. At the end of the road with all the investigations and drugs. Lots of complicated, painful, immune-mediated problems. They diagnose them with metal poisoning or a deficiency of an obscure enzyme.

Maybe they're right. What do I know? I don't know about those things. I'm not an immunologist.

'And then, there's people with very little wrong with them. The thin ones. Some have plastic surgery faces, poor things. They live with a lot of pressures I don't understand. They're looking for perfection. Or immortality.'

'Or maybe they just work in a job where the way you look is everything,' Mari suggested.

Nerida sat down. 'Some of them come every week. They're pathologising life. People who aren't sick at all, having bizarre conversations with their bodies. Spending lots of money on it.

'I'd have to listen to them. I'm not sure I can work in such an extreme and intense place. I was looking for less stress in my work. I didn't expect this in such a famously prosperous place, you know?' She wrestled with the chilli sauce bottle.

'Most people in the remote communities only come to you when they're hurt or sick,' Mari said, undoing the cap with ease and handing it back to her. 'But you get really sick people there, out in the Bush.'

'Of course, we do, yeah. But mob don't expect me to solve all their problems for them. They might need us to arrange a feed for that night, or accommodation at the hostel while they're in town for tests. But that's different.'

'Because they're asking for help for material things they really need? Is that it?' Mari was spooning sauce on their plates, not leaving a drop in the saucepan.

'I guess so. People have their own cultures, their own ways of looking after themselves and each other. They don't expect me to fix them, the way these urban people seem to.'

The sun set as they ate. Afterwards, they went outside to see Mars rise, a red star in the moonless sky. Bats argued noisily in the trees in surrounding gardens.

If Nerida joined the integrative medicine practice, because she was a doctor, she'd end up doing less of the kind of medicine she liked and more that she didn't believe in.

'I'm disappointed,' she said to Mari as they looked at the stars. 'They only want to use me.'

'Well, you would use them to make money. Wasn't that the idea?' Mari asked.

'It's not enough. Making money's good. But if it's the only reason you do something, that never works. What are we doing here?' She leaned her head under Mari's arm.

'We're together,' Mari said, kissing her. 'And we can swim.'

CHAPTER 26

Fitzroy Crossing, The Kimberley, North Western Australia

Tuesday December 3, 2019

They needed money but Nerida refused the job at Byron Bay for the sake of her mental health. They kept the house with its expensive lease. There was always plenty of local work. But Mari was eager to travel again. 'We both love the Kimberley,' she said. 'Can we let it draw us back?'

An eight-hundred-kilometre drive south from home to Sydney airport, went past bushfire-ravaged bush, some still flaming, many blackened trunks smouldering. So began their journey back to Fitzroy Crossing.

The small town in Western Australia was five or six thousand kilometres distant, on the other side of the country.

In 2020 Fitzroy Crossing had a modest supermarket and two pubs. Two caravan parks which showed the marks of flood and fire. Rumour had it that they were all owned, with the post office and the takeaway, by the same person.

Two fuel stations competed for customers on the Great Northern Highway, where a gang of cheeky youth were known to throw rocks at passing trucks.

Fitzroy was a supply stop for grey nomads and truckies. Its fresh food was better than other remote places they'd stayed. The supermarket had little competition, though. Cherries for Christmas were forty-five dollars a kilo, more than twice the price they were in Perth. But mangoes grew on trees all over town.

Fitzroy businesses were mostly staffed by travellers, backpackers, who found the Australian Outback more exotic and interesting than urban Australians did. Their cramped, dirty living conditions, long hours and poor pay could probably only be endured for a limited time, as part of a world-travelling adventure.

The women stayed in a three-roomed house, made of tin and board on a wooden frame. 'I'm grateful we're not paying the power bill,' Nerida said. Mari had the air conditioners on constantly. *Trying to keep geckos and centipedes out by blowing,* Nerida thought.

Keeping the house cool slowed lizards and insects down. It made them easier to catch if Mari asked her to throw one out.

The women kept the house and car locked. Fitzroy Crossing had a reputation for violence and crime. They avoided walking at night.

Some nights, indeed, Mari sat up guarding the front door, with furniture stacked against it and a club ready by her hand. It was usually when the moon was full and young people roamed noisily, looking for drama. Creating some.

It was no worse than other places they'd lived. And there were sea eagles and wallabies to photograph and draw during the day.

Travelling to the clinics around the valley was one of the pleasures of Nerida's job. When they weren't too tired to talk, she yarned with colleagues. Sometimes Nerida drove.

But mostly she enjoyed the privilege of looking out the window at the dry, grassy plains and red, rocky cliffs and mesas. Smoke on the horizon warned of distant fires. Other days she slept, gathering energy for the busy day.

Cherise was in her early twenties, a slim, small woman with hyperalert eyes, the whites bright against her dark skin. She came to the clinic as soon as they opened that morning.

Her forearm was swollen, scratched and probably broken. Her shoulder hurt. She couldn't move the arm much. Her eye on the same side was puffy and blackening. Scratches still bled on her cheek and throat. Her neck was tender. She walked into the nurse's room delicately, protecting her arm, ribs and ankle. As she lay on the exam bench, Nerida noticed that her skin was dull and sallow. She was dehydrated, maybe too dry to cry.

'You take me la women's shelter?' she asked quietly in Kriol.

'Course we will.'

Nerida went to call the shelter while nurse Laney found pain medication for Cherise.

Nerida's relief was like rain falling when Didi, the worker at the other end, told her that there was a bed at the Fitzroy shelter for the battered woman.

Nurse Laney made a plaster cast for Cherise's forearm. 'That's a defensive injury,' Nerida said as Laney wound a bandage. She raised her arm and ducked under it. Cherise nodded.

'Poor thing. You must've been very frightened.'

Cherise nodded again.

'Where is that one who hit you now?' Nerida asked.

'Snorin' his head off. He was really drunk last night.' The room smelled of salt and fear.

'You know I'm supposed to tell the police about this, eh?' Nerida asked. She could lose her job if she didn't. Most people knew that.

'Yeah. Tell 'em. He should go to jail for what he's been doing,' she said.

After more talking and gentle examination, Nerida went to jot her findings on a notepad. She called the hospital and the police.

Laney popped her head in. 'Sleeping now. Tramadol worked. And the plaster helped. Have you spoken to ED?'

'Yeah.' Nerida blinked. 'We'd better get her out of here before he wakes up. My computer won't let me in, anyway. What do you think?'

'Close the clinic, I reckon. And hit the road,' Laney said. She had a warm, pragmatic air that matched her cropped grey hair and friendly, brown eyes. She was of Chinese-Anglo ancestry, descended from the pearl divers of Broome. 'None of the computers are working. We can't access patient records.' She met Nerida's eyes, showing sadness. 'And we've both been in clinics before when these men wake up.'

Nerida turned the computer off and packed her bag. Thinking about being besieged by violence in a clinic made her hand shake. 'Yeah. Let's get out of here.'

Laney put a sign on the door, 'Clinic Closed. Emergency Evacuation.'

They arrived at the Women's Shelter three hours later, emotionally exhausted by the vigilance of driving their client across unsealed roads, watching for dust out the back to be sure they weren't followed and fretting that Cherise was in pain.

Didi, the shelter coordinator, took off her scarf and wrapped it around Cherise, who had been self-contained in the car. But she cried and shivered, safe in Didi's arms as she was ushered inside.

'If you do a handover to the afternoon shift in ED, I'll see if she'll come over,' Didi told Nerida.

Nerida went to the crowded office at the hospital and typed up comprehensive notes. *The police will use these notes to prosecute that man one day.*

She went to talk to Dr Khumalo in their two-bed emergency department, explaining her concerns about Cherise, should she agree to come to hospital. 'It's tricky, you know. She needs to be seen as soon as possible for a forensic exam. But women are afraid of getting men in trouble with the Police.'

Her colleague shrugged his shoulders lightly. 'It's the same in South Africa,' he said. 'Police have a history of racism. People don't trust them.'

'Laney or I will check in on her at the shelter tomorrow if she doesn't come,' Nerida said. 'She might come to the hospital for more pain relief. I'm not sure if what I was able to give her will hold her.'

The sun was low on the horizon when she walked home. Clouds gathered there every afternoon. A breeze came. But rain didn't.

The yellow flowers of the kapok tree fell, leaving tight wooden pods rattling on the tree. Kids still played on the oval. People talked in little groups, walking their dogs.

Mari was full of the news, talking fast and loud as Nerida put her bag down.

'You know there was a factory fire in Sudan that killed more than twenty people last week. And now more than a hundred people were sleeping in another factory and about half of them died, in a fire, in Delhi.'

'Poor Delhi,' Nerida said, filling her drink bottle. She took a draught of water.

'Wuhan in China—'

'Yes, I know Wuhan is in China,' said Nerida.

'It's where they built imitation European buildings, like their own Eiffel Tower. Do you remember?'

'Yeah, like Vegas. The Eiffel Tower wasn't in Wuhan. It's in Hangzhou, next door.' Nerida didn't understand why Mari hated people copying European buildings so much. 'There are plenty of imitation Chinese buildings in every city in the world. There's a Great Wall being built in America as we speak.'

'Not the same thing. Anyway,' Mari said, 'There's a nasty weird virus making lots of people sick there. In Wuhan.'

Nerida put the water jug under the tap to refill it. Water plopped through the filter. She moved out the way so that Mari could drain the beans into the sink.

'There was an announcement from Bangladesh that a leprosy free world is possible. Guess they don't know about the Kimberley, huh?'

Nerida grunted. Reached for a banana.

Mari had been doing this information dump as long as Nerida knew her. It took years to stop her doing it when they went to bed. So hearing all the news when she came home from work was better.

Nerida was political to her bones but was also an empath. She'd grown a thick shell to function in medicine. But she didn't like to watch the news every day, let alone more than once in a day. It could make her cry. Or torture her.

In contrast, Mari watched the news at midday, at dinnertime and then last thing before bed. And flourished on the fire it lit in her.

Nerida tried to dissuade her from the 11pm bulletin.

'You're always disappointed anyway that the news hasn't changed. They don't have enough staff there. This is Australia. It's gonna be the same reports all day. Unless it's 9/11, they won't change it,' Nerida explained.

'I just wanna see the weather,' Mari said, waiting through the same sports reports repeating interviews with inarticulate footballers and cricketers. And then horse races, and the swimmers. *Sport is the one true religion in Australia*, Nerida sometimes thought.

Mari loved the satellite map of clouds over the island of Australia. Clouds swirling into storms, cold fronts coming up from Antarctica, or Monsoon clouds from Indonesia.

She watched the international weather reports for friends in the Pacific and her family in the US and the Black Forest in Germany.

Nerida watched it for her daughter Ruby in South Australia, imagining the cool wind from the sea blowing inland to dry the sweat from Ruby's back as she rowed. The sounds of oars dropping in water was the rhythm of Ruby's days.

At least it was before she got pregnant. Ruby was in her thirties, perfectly matched with Seb, a rangy, athletic man who didn't say much but showed his adoration of Ruby in a thousand ways. He laughed at her jokes, cooked for her after work most nights.

Her daughter was ecstatic to be pregnant for the first time. Nerida was happy, too. She imagined sending Ruby a belt to support her belly, even when she wasn't showing yet. She looked at pregnancy pillows online, pictured her daughter's pleasure if a giant box filled with a body-sized pillow arrived as a surprise gift. The favoured name for the little girl was Jedda.

Nerida checked the weather in Sydney for her parents, who were elderly and well. Her mum was active in her suburban community, organizing Meals on Wheels. Dad had his garden.

And kept an eye out for Los Angeles: her son, Jim. She didn't hear much from Jim, reliant as he was on his devout wife, who didn't care for gay people. He had different politics. But she knew he was okay. Maybe even contented a lot of the time. He did well in his work as an engineer. He had his jazz piano.

Mari's keen interest in the weather went back to her days at the prow of a live-aboard boat in the Maldives, or Sulawesi, watching for a coming storm, protecting her scuba diving clients and their crew.

She had a seafarer's intuition then. She'd turn the boat around from their destination, a popular dive site or a colourful reef, on the strength of an inkling from wisps of cloud on the horizon. She was almost always right. She was comfortable arguing with entitled tourists who tried to insist on sticking to their printed schedule when the wind, rain and waves told Mari to do otherwise.

It was not until after she started consciously channelling though, that Mari began calling the rain.

From 2012, she'd leave their desert house and gesture almost surreptitiously, if Nerida was watching, towards the horizon.

Later, Nerida realised that when she went out with her camera and sketchpad, Mari did call the rain—as well as talking to the animals, she talked to the clouds. Perhaps her movements were more elaborate when no one was there.

Mari believed she could call the rain. 'I imagine the smell of the rain on the dust and the noise of it on the tin roof,' she said.

Weeks went by. Sometimes massive thunderheads massed in the northwest. Lightning lit the clouds purple and started fires. The air smelled of smoke. No rain came.

On December 20, Mari had a wracking, barking cough. 'It hurts,' she gasped, holding her arms across her chest. Her head radiated fever. She was weak with it.

Nerida held a hand against her wife's forehead. 'Have you got a headache?'

'Yes. My throat is burning,' she rasped.

The glands in her neck and under her chin were swollen and her pulse was fast.

There was nothing more frightening to Nerida than touching her wife's fine, sweet skin and knowing how quickly it could be catastrophically taken from her. The edge of the thought released adrenaline.

Nerida took days off work to look after her, fetching Mari drinks, putting a wrapped icepack on her forehead and neck, remembering to the minute when to give her pain relief. The coughing was worst at night. Nerida sometimes put her fingers in her hears to block the sound of Mari's suffering for just a few minutes.

'I feel like the bones in my back are broken.'

She gave her wife acupuncture. Set up a fan with wet rags from the fridge. The house smelled of eucalyptus and lemon myrtle oils. Mari slept when she could for days. Her prosthetic foot sat unused by the bed. As did Nerida's workbag.

When Mari woke, Nerida fed her electrolyte iceblocks, peppermint tea or sips of soup. *That cough is horrible. Sounds like pertussis.* 'Are you coughing till you vomit?' she asked.

Even though they were immunised against it, they knew pertussis, whooping cough. Nerida brought it home from work once and infected Mari. She caught it from a patient at work during the 2010 outbreak in New South Wales. Mari coughed and vomited, day and night, for nearly three months, then. It took another three to get her strength back. For a half-year, the house was stifled by suffering and fear.

In Fitzroy, two days before Christmas, Nerida got the fever too. They were both sick in bed. *This cough is bad enough to crack a rib.* Sometimes Nerida had to sit up in bed or stand and pace, exhausted, to breath.

In her fever she dreaded going home to the house at Lennox. *How many toads will be in the pool?* Toads and disease got mixed up in her delirium. She'd forgotten about geckos and scorpions in Fitzroy.

On Christmas eve, lying down exhausted with the covers kicked off—in the small hours when their coughs were the only sounds—Nerida realised she must go to the hospital to get tested.

If she had pertussis, she was a danger to others. The several pregnant women and the unimmunised new babies she'd looked after that week depended on it. She counted the days, to work out when she would be able to return to work if she started antibiotics tomorrow.

On Christmas morning, then, she dragged herself to the hospital. The young doctor in ED was from China.

'Which part of China?' she asked politely.

'Hangzhou,' he said. He was a full-faced, robust lad. He had the Chinese way of blowing out a candle when he said an H.

Nerida helped him look up the guidelines for possible pertussis. She backed her head against the wall to show him how to take a nasopharyngeal swab.

'Keep going. Keep going. That's right. Ugh.' He hit her nasopharynx with a sharp sting.

She convinced him to give her some codeine so that they might be able to stop coughing for just one or two nights. She told him to prescribe antibiotics, in case it was pertussis. 'If I've had the antibiotics, I can return to work in five days,' she told him.

It took him about half an hour, probably phoning a friend, to come back to her with the antibiotics. She told him what to write on the pathology request form for the PCR swab. She felt better walking home, her first walk out in a week, knowing she'd done the right thing for public health. She could be back at work soon.

On Christmas afternoon, Mari got up and cooked them a better soup.

On Christmas evening and over New Year, they slept and drank, swallowed tablets and ate little. *Two weeks without pay. Happy New Year.* But by the first Monday in 2021 Nerida was indeed well enough to go back to work.

Mari was still weak and coughing badly, spiking fevers in the afternoons. Her lungs were not as robust since she had pneumonia just before she met Nerida in real life, after their online courtship, in 2006. 'That Hong Kong harbour water you inhaled never quite left, it seems,' Nerida said when she listened to her wife's noisy chest. She prescribed her a course of antibiotics, too. Toddled up to the hospital to collect them.

At work, three of the nurses had been sick with the same fever. One, back to work on Tuesday, flew on the plane out to community with Nerida, but was too weak to stand at the end of the workday. Nerida took her to the hospital, where they gave her steroids. The nurse was off work for five weeks. Nerida watched the community for signs of the illness. Blessedly, no one had caught it.

Nerida and Mari were thinner and weaker when they went to the shop the following week.

'You look well.' Nerida smiled at the cashier. The young woman's soft face lit up.

'Thank you. I've been really sick. I'm just getting better now. My friend is still really sick. Fever and everything.'

She gestured to a colleague at the next register, a tall, fair-skinned Australian woman. Her face was red and sweating. Nerida told her to go home to bed. 'It's a bad virus that one. I've had it.

We've had it. You'll make other people sick, being at work. Do you want me to write you a certificate?' she offered kindly.

The young cashier finished packing their goods. 'Where are you from?' Nerida asked.

'China. We are all from China, everyone except my friend there. All of us working here now. We've all been sick.'

'Whereabouts in China? I've been to some places in China.'

'From Wuhan. Do you know Wuhan?'

On January 14, 2020, word came from Sydney and Melbourne of the first COVID-19 cases in Australia. People brought the sickness from Wuhan. Another brought it home from Guangzhou.

Nerida looked up her test results. The hospital had three different record-keeping systems, part of the intolerable, everyday chaos of the place. She obtained a password and permission from IT to access the third system, which she normally didn't use. She called the pathology labs in Broome and in Perth.

Finally, it was clear. There was no entry in the records and no record of a test under her name.

The young locum doctor had made no record of her visit to the hospital. 'He must have thrown that swab out,' she said to Laney.

She spoke to Dr Khumalo in the ED about it. 'I had a nasty infection with a cough and high fever, viral or bacterial. At least four of the nurses and one of our admin workers have had it. I infected my wife and she's still coughing and exhausted. I could have tested that swab for COVID.

'Now, I have no way of knowing what it is because an overwhelmed, undertrained, under-supervised doctor didn't want to know. Where is he? Is he coming back?'

'He's gone back to Hangzhou,' her colleague said.

She smacked her hands on his desk in frustration.

CHAPTER 27

They were due to return to Fitzroy Crossing in February. But news that Mari's Australian citizenship ceremony was scheduled in the second week of March changed their plans. 'You've worked so hard for that. We're not gonna miss it,' Nerida said. 'I want to have some security that we can stay in the same country after what happened to me in Germany.'

In 2017, Nerida was deported from Germany amid caring for her severely disabled, terminally ill mother-in-law. The attack came when a homophobic immigration officer did not accept her marriage to Mari as legal. It was a traumatic time for both.

Mari was conflicted. She had worked hard for her citizenship.

'Fitzroy turns into an island when the river floods. People get stuck. We might not get out in time, even if we take the car. It's starting to rain there now. It'll get stronger.' Mari loved the Kimberley. But was ambivalent about having crocs swimming in the streets around the house.

She's been in Australia more than a decade. Knows the country better than most.

Nerida called her agency. 'Can I work closer to home, just for a week or two before the citizenship ceremony, so we can be sure to get home for it?'

'How about Yulara?' her agent said. 'They're looking for a doctor in February.'

Mari had not been back to Yulara since their abrupt departure to care for Mari's parents in Germany in 2017. That peculiar, remote, resort town, the base for tourists travelling to Uluru, had been their home. Plenty of residents would be happy to see Dr Green again.

It was a privilege to be near Uluru. The massive red Rock, with its projections, gullies and valleys, its tumbled boulders, its microclimates and animals, always engaged their hearts and minds. They were energized by the surrounding red sands and the spectacular array of stars at night.

February was an unpleasant time of year there, though. Hot, with intense lightning storms. No time to walk near the big, red rocks at Uluru or Kata Tjuta.

'You're out in that heat for five minutes and it takes forty-five minutes inside to get over it.' Nerida mentally compared it to living in a polar region in winter. It took preparation, endurance, recovery to venture out. And the reward was splendid isolation and moments of awe-inspiring beauty.

Mari made photos and paintings of lightning on Uluru when they lived at the community of Traditional Owners closer to the Rock years earlier.

'But I'm still looking for that photo of lightning on Kata Tjuta,' she said.

Kata Tjuta, a sacred place of towering domed mountains, was an hour's drive west of Yulara. They were excited to go back to it. But there was a week's work to do first.

Most of their colleagues at the health service had left after they did. Nerida felt comfortable anyway. She knew the plants, the stones, the houses.

The new manager was a decent man, compassionate and direct. And the nurses warmed to her quickly.

Celia, an experienced Remote Area Nurse with spiky mascara on lashes surrounding kind eyes, came to see Nerida at the end of her first day. She moved a wisp of white hair out of her face, sitting down carefully in the patient chair. Her lips were still stained red by the morning's swipe of lipstick.

'We've got some sad news to break to you,' she said. 'Old Viktor, you must have looked after him, was evacuated to Alice Springs hospital last Tuesday night.'

'Is he all right? He's strong for his age. I'm impressed he's still working here after his son died.'

Viktor was a slender, emphatic German, still riding his bike and working in his eighties. He ran the housekeeping department with a level of organisation that made him exceptional in the Northern Territory.

Viktor worked to support his severely disabled son, who needed high level nursing home care after a car accident.

Nerida heard that his son died in 2017, not long after she and Mari left Yulara to go to Germany.

Workmates loved Viktor for his tradesman's skills, his leadership, and his knack for defending repelling management's hare-brained schemes.

He came from the same tribe of the Black Forest as Mari did and shared many of her traits: respect for work, care with money, and a roaring laugh complementing an earthy sense of humour.

They shared books and conversation, swearing and laughing together in their dialect. 'I'm glad he's still here. Mari will love seeing him.' Nerida rarely saw him in the clinic.

Celia nodded. Nerida could feel her holding something important back. *Maybe his prostate cancer took a turn for the worse*, she worried.

'He stayed in Yulara. Somehow, he wasn't going to fit in back home. His daughter had a flatette ready for him in her house.

'Family were all keen to have him home in South Australia. But Viktor didn't go. I think he worked out that after forty years in the desert, he wasn't going to be happy in the suburbs.'

'He's had prostate cancer for years, but it was stable. He was good with it. Didn't have any pain. Still a fearsome fella to cross,' Nerida said. 'What happened?'

'It wasn't the cancer,' Celia said. 'He had pneumonia. Really sudden. He was well at work that day, then after dinner he was so sick he called us at night.

'He had a cough, raging temp. Sats were like, fifty-five percent and crashing. He wasn't getting much oxygen, even if he was still lying there talking to us. Couldn't hear much on his chest. Tachy as hell. Two hundred and forty beats per minute.'

'Jeez. He was working hard,' Nerida said.

'In Alice he went straight to Intensive Care. IV antibiotics and steroids. He was good by Wednesday night. Still needing oxygen but they didn't need to intubate.'

'Did you call to talk to them? How is he now?'

'Yeah, I spoke to the ICU nurse in charge on Thursday. She called me. Because in the small hours of Thursday morning he just died.

Nerida put her head in her hands, rocking against her desk. 'Oh no.' She covered her mouth with her hands.

Celia gave her a moment.

'You should see the x-ray. Can you get his x-ray up?'

Nerida opened the imagining program, typed in Viktor's name with tears welling in her eyes. *This is what we do. Transmute grief into intellectual curiosity.* The chest x-ray that came up was astonishing.

'Complete white out!' She turned to Celia. 'He's bled out into his lungs.'

'Look at the time.' Celia pointed to the screen. 'They took that at 3.15am. They've listed his time of death as 3.30am.'

'Why would he haemorrhage like that?' Nerida asked. 'Did they test him for COVID?'

'He didn't fit the criteria for testing,' Celia replied, wringing her hands.

Nerida got up, tore at her hair, didn't know what to do with herself. Celia, with her kind but uncovered face, moved in for a consoling hug.

'Don't!' Nerida moved away, 'I just...I'm sorry.'

She left the building. Marched home.

Where she couldn't bring herself to tell Mari about Viktor's death until the next day. Because she dreaded the confusion, rage and bitterness sure to be mixed in her wife's grief, reflecting her own.

CHAPTER 28

Yulara, APY Lands Northern Territory

Wednesday February 12, 2020

'So, to clarify: he's had fevers of forty, pain all over his body, lethargy, bouts of difficulty breathing, that started with a cough. And I can't test him for SARS-CoV-2?' Nerida rapped her fingers on the desk, meeting her patient's eyes over her mask as she talked into the landline receiver.

'You know Yulara's busy, right? Half a million people visited last year. Staff here are in and out from all over the country and the world, too. Some local Aboriginal people, from the community, have multiple comorbidities. A Coronavirus outbreak here would be a massive disaster.'

She put the receiver down and hit the speaker button so her patient, Peter, could hear the public health doctor's response, too.

Later, this would haunt her—although there was scarcely time to count the ghosts for those that lived through the early days.

'I've put you on speaker,' Nerida said. 'Peter's been sick in bed for nearly a week. He's been self-isolating, luckily. His story's credible for COVID. Peter's manager came back to work last Monday for a meeting, even though she was so sick she could hardly walk. She felt she was irreplaceable.'

'Some people are so selfish!' said Donna, the public health doctor on the line.

'Peter was sick on Thursday night with the same symptoms. One of his colleagues is sick at home, too, with the same thing, since yesterday. I'll visit him at home this afternoon.'

Peter, a muscular man in his late thirties, coughed into his fist through his surgical mask. He wore a singlet and shorts. Sweat glistened on his skin. Nerida pushed him a bottle of sanitizer.

'The manager has not been to China. But the husband, who made *her* sick, was on the domestic leg of an international flight. He flew from Brisbane to Sydney on a flight that came from Shanghai. A woman was coughing right behind him on the flight.'

'Peter, you haven't been in China yourself?' Donna asked over the phone.

Peter coughed and managed a weak smile. 'No.'

'And you've not been in contact with anyone actually diagnosed with COVID-19?'

Peter wrapped his arms around his midriff and leaned toward the phone. 'I reckon that manager's got it. But it sounds like she won't qualify for testing, from what you and Dr Nerida are saying. So, no.' He pulled his mask down and took a swig from his water bottle.

'And neither would her husband, even if he came to me. Is that right?' Nerida asked.

'No. The husband hasn't been in direct contact with a diagnosed person and hasn't been in Wuhan. So officially, it couldn't be COVID-19,' said Donna.

Nerida exhaled sharply. 'This is ridiculous. What is it about, really? Are the path labs at full capacity before we've even got our first people tested?'

In the city at the end of the phone, Donna sighed. 'Yep. Something like that. I'm getting several calls a day like this. There's some nasty virus around and we have no way of knowing if it's SARS-CoV-2. We just don't have the resources yet.'

'And maybe we don't want to know,' said Nerida.

The call ended, Nerida told Peter, 'You've got some awful virus. But your chest is clear and you're getting plenty of oxygen.' She waved a hand at the oximeter on his finger. 'This may well be COVID, but as you heard, we're not allowed to test you to tell. You're doing the right thing. Keep it up. Stay at home. I'll write you a certificate. Have you got any sick leave?'

'Plenty,' he said.

'Good. Drink plenty of water, regular paracetamol. Call the nurses if you're frightened. After a week you might be past the worst of it already. You're normally pretty strong, right?'

Peter nodded. 'Have you ever seen it before, doc?'

'My wife and I were sick in Fitzroy Crossing at the end of December. Just like you. Very high fevers, sore throat, pain all through the body, horrible paroxysmal cough. You cough like you're going to vomit, yeah?

'The community store there was staffed by workers from Wuhan. They had also been sick. We could hardly move out of bed at Christmas. So, we might have had COVID-19.

'A man here in Yulara was sent with the flying doctor to hospital a week ago. Had pneumonia. He might have had COVID-19. As long as the testing criteria are so restricted, we can't know.'

She got up, washed her hands thoroughly. Wiped her desk and the phone with alcohol. Picked up a fresh mask.

'Come on. I'll drive you home. Show me where your workmate lives. I'll check on him.' She put a couple of sleeves of paracetamol in her bag. Grabbed a paper gown and safety glasses. Cleaned her stethoscope with alcohol and packed that too.

'That's gonna freak him out if you're dressed in that,' Peter said. He pointed his chin to the paper gown.

'He's not gonna be that surprised, though, is he?' she said, opening the door for him.

Her home visit was with Simon.

His colleague Peter texted to warn him that Dr Nerida was arriving in PPE. In response, Simon put a plastic pot on his head and overalls. He opened the door and said, 'We Are Devo.'

She laughed, 'Diva, more like.' Theatrical music was playing, loud in Simon's small unit.

He was feverish and slightly manic with it. He reminded her of Andy, her close friend from medical school. *He would've been forty this year*, she thought in a flash.

'Don't make a me a cup of tea. Come and sit down and let me look after you a bit,' she said. She put her gloved hand on his forehead. 'You're burning up.'

'Is it COVID? Do you think?'

She listened to his chest. *Diminished breath sounds in the left lower lobe.* 'It's probably some kind of nasty virus with a high fever like that. I think you've got pneumonia. Have you ever had it before? Do you smoke.'

He shook his head. 'I live on gym and smoothies. Like Peter, even if I'm not as buffed.' He coughed painfully.

She put her sats probe on his finger. He wasn't getting as much oxygen as he should. Looked into his brown eyes. 'What do you think about a trip to hospital?' she asked.

'In the plane?'

'That's right. Special trip for you, darling, in the plane. You stay here and rest. I'll go and organise it. They'll all be suited up like me. You might have to sing Devo songs to yourself.'

'I like this one!' Simon sang along with the swelling music.

It was the theme from *The Phantom of the Opera*. 'A good friend of mine was in the Sydney production. He used to sing that quite often. But his voice was bigger than yours.'

Everything about Andy was big. He was over two metres tall, with broad shoulders and a round, friendly face. He was noisy. He played timpani in the orchestra. He would sing phrases from operas and musicals in his booming voice with theatrical gestures just for fun.

He shaved messages in his hair and dyed them when he ran for student council. Nerida was grateful he didn't win. It was hard enough to get any time with him. Andy had the gift of giving hundreds of people the feeling that each was his special friend. Walking from a lecture theatre to a lab with him, they would be interrupted five or six times.

On the student centre verandah one afternoon, Andy smoked without inhaling, discussing a biochemistry pathway that could help people stay slim. They were interrupted by sirens. Up the road in the distance, Nerida saw a kerfuffle at the hospital laundry dock. Police cars pulled up there.

'The police are pushing a man!' she called into the student lounge. 'He's cuffed behind his back.'

The small group of law students and two office staff came outside. They saw a policeman push the man to the ground, kicking him when he was down.

Watching, scared for his life, they felt powerless and frightened.

The man was still moving when he was dragged into an ambulance. 'He's still alive,' Andy said.

They'd all been counselled the next day, which meant the police came to the centre to make sure none of them were going to complain about it.

It's amazing how music triggers memories.

Simon's song finished. He rested on the lounge, looking exhausted.

'The music takes you away, doesn't it, Doc?'

Nerida smiled behind her mask and looked into his eyes. She grabbed his hand in her gloved one. 'I'll ask Celia to come and help you. She'll bring some oxygen. She can help you pack a bag for hospital, too.'

CHAPTER 29

Tuesday March 3, 2020

Back in the forested hills and damp soils of Lennox, by a churning gray sea still warm and ash-laden from summer's fires, Nerida worked to get the pool into shape. The landlord came with his pH tester and bags of salt. Within days, the water was clear and bright.

Tempted by the water, one afternoon she sat with her legs in the water for a few minutes before getting in. Sliding in, then, was invigorating. Nerida stroked the water with her arms, enjoyed her buoyancy, fanned her toes. Kicked. The garden was transformed from the level of the water, with palms and lilies towering over her framing the dense blue sky.

She took a job at a local hospital two days a week. On the other days she applied for writing jobs, working from home.

Nerida worried about Mari. Her chronic neck pain was worse again, disturbing her sleep. She refused to take the cannabis oil prescribed to her because she wouldn't give up driving. Driving under the influence of prescribed cannabis was still a crime in New South Wales.

'Come on,' Nerida said. 'I really felt like I got you back when you took that. It's the first thing we found that really helped you.' Pain changed people. Nerida knew. She occasionally wondered how their lives together might be different without the incessant grinding pain caused by Mari's lifetime of medical maltreatment. *What relieves her pain? Escape from gravity. Hard to find in this material life. She's only truly free in the sea with a mask and snorkel. Such a strong woman, choosing to come to desert places with me.* When they met and fell in love, Mari used to say she would follow her to Timbuktu.

Nerida accepted an offer to edit a medical journal. And a doctor friend wanted to write a training manual with her. It was about a small organisation named Pick Up, who helped prisoners rebuild their lives when they were released. Most of the prisoners were Aboriginal men with complicated trauma, some of them from her clan. Pick Up gave people a chance to build a life outside of an institution. As she learned more, any fear of the ex-convicts faded. *It's not hard to end up in jail*, she realized. Her respect for the Pick Up team grew. *The jobs fell in my lap, as M'Hoq Toq would say.*

Before the summer passed, Mari got into the pool with her a couple of times, delighting Nerida. Who climbed on her back or wrapped herself around the front of her, enjoying the touch of Mari's skin; relishing her wife's confidence in the water.

Hugging her on land, Nerida was always aware that she might push Mari over if she caught her off balance. In the pool, Mari was in her element, whichever way Nerida grabbed her. *You really are like an orca or a dolphin*, Nerida thought, admiring her curvy wife, diving, laughing.

Once they were getting paid again, Mari bought a rose gold bracelet with a baroque pearl in it, online from a shop they'd visited in the Kimberley. 'It was half price,' she said.

Mari hardly ever spends the money I put in her account to buy whatever she wants.

'It's beautiful. Look at how it shines!' When Mari opened the box, Nerida saw red and green light glinting from the small vase-shaped pearl. 'I love baroque pearls. So much more interesting than a perfectly round one.'

'I thought Ruby should have a present after the baby's born. Do you think she'll like it?' Mari said.

'She'll love it. Mothers should have presents.'

Nerida had bought Mari a gift, too. Ten days later she gave her the silk scarf. It had an Aboriginal design of patterns from the sea in royal blue, aqua and coral pink, to wear to her citizenship ceremony.

Getting dressed up to celebrate was a refreshing change from wearing at-home clothes to work on the computer, or scrubs for work.

Mari wore a shirt with a design made of sunset colours, contrasting with her new scarf. Gold jewellery, from her Romany mother, glowed against her brown skin. She looked crisp and confident. Nerida put on makeup, her sparkling painted lips and dark-rimmed eyes shone above her embroidered lace dress.

The ceremony was conducted in a small, wood-panelled room. The mayor who led the new Australians in their oath-taking was a short man, with red hair sticking out like light on a plasma ball. His friendly blue eyes met Mari's as he awarded her citizenship.

She'd already passed the knowledge test. 'One hundred percent on questions many Australians couldn't answer,' Nerida had said.

At the reception afterwards they were served sausage rolls and pies, lamingtons and fairy bread, all with little paper flags on them.

While they were mingling, Nerida asked one of the council workers about traps for the cane toads. A neighbour had suggested that Council might provide them. When they lived in the desert, rangers set traps for feral cats in people's yards.

But this Ballina council worker shook his head. 'Freezing them is the best way to kill them,' he said authoritatively. Nerida repressed the impulse to say what she knew about the reanimation of frozen cane toads. *Surely nobody wants to put these toxic things in a freezer? With their food?*

'I got a golf club from the tip shop,' she told him. 'It works well.' He looked shocked. This small, sweet-looking woman with her grey-streaked hair. 'I know that sounds cruel, but I'm pretty good at it now. It only takes a well-aimed blow, or two. I can be sure they're dead.' He nodded politely and moved away to talk to other people.

Arm in arm, Mari and Nerida had their photo taken with the Aboriginal flag in the Council chamber. There was a large, artistic photograph of Ballina's tourist attraction, a ten-metre-high metal prawn.

'It's very Australian,' Mari said.

'It makes sense to me to worship food animals.' Nerida laughed. She was fond of animals but had an Indigenous attitude to the practical use of their bodies to sustain humans. She'd eaten plenty of kangaroo, possum and fish. Even snake and crocodile meat. Being urban, she thought she might have trouble eating turtle or koala.

They were endangered for other reasons. People that hunted and ate them always looked after the animals, leaving them if their numbers were low in a hard season, protecting the young and creatures of breeding age. As they looked after humans, before the machine age.

Cane toads were the only animals Nerida ever killed by necessity, unless you counted flies, roaches and mosquitoes.

She had learned to guide even those out of her house or car after talking to Aedgar, who implied that spirit could occupy even insects. He called them by endearing names.

They never had a feral cat trap in the desert. Neither could bear the thought of it then, even though they knew each feral cat killed hundreds of native animals a year.

Cane toads also caused the decline and extinction of many native animals.

And they didn't seem to mind that Nerida killed them. They just sat, waiting for their poison to kill any enemy. She paid them respect before she clubbed them. *You were brought to the wrong place. I know it's not your fault. But you have to leave this life now.*

They celebrated Mari's citizenship at the beach, sharing sparkling wine in plastic goblets Mari brought them when she came to live in Australia, to be with the love of her life. As the sun set behind the inland hills, blue-grey clouds piled in mountains on the horizon. Huge container ships looked like black metal toys out at sea, as the edges of the clouds lit orange.

It was the last Citizenship Ceremony held for a long time, as Coronavirus restrictions closed in. A different man-made plague, with greater consequences than a toad.

All staff were given donning and doffing lessons to refresh their memory on how to use PPE. Masks and thermometers reappeared in public for the first time in Australia since polio. People refused to touch the post, or parcels. They left them outside to weather, just in case. It was anywhere fear could be.

After twelve years of marriage, it still took discipline to wait to hug and kiss until Nerida had showered and changed when she came home from work.

Nerida did her best to stay relaxed and happy, but the virus imposed itself into the most natural and normal parts of their lives. She was too tired to communicate when she came home from her shift and Mari had learned to wait, days or weeks, to hear about work.

Maybe they'd had Coronavirus infections already in Fitzroy Crossing. Antibody testing was not available, so there was no way to know. Mari had bouts of exhaustion and coughing fits, sometimes bad enough to keep her up at night, which Nerida attributed to that viral attack, whatever it was. Nerida quietly hoped that they had some immunity to SARS-CoV-2. It helped her feel safe to think they might.

She brought home two different kinds of inhaled medicines for Mari to try, to help with the cough and wheeze.

She didn't want to talk about the hospital. Most days the place was bed-blocked.

Patients waited with agitated ambulance officers, who knew they were needed elsewhere, in the hospital carpark. Or lay on trolleys, moaning, crying or stoic, in the corridors. Nerida was grateful to be there only three days a week but was under constant pressure to do more.

People in the Emergency Department that needed admission couldn't be moved into the wards. They often couldn't be moved to larger hospitals, either. Nerida spent four hours of a shift pushing for a bed for a man who needed to be in Intensive Care.

At the less acute end of the scale, people who might have found shelter in the ED years ago, homeless people with complex psychiatric and other health issues, were pushed back out onto the street to make space for those who were ill in a more manageable way. The hospital was a miserable place, as the staff coped with and recovered from shouted abuse, thrown chairs, a violent patient moving to pick up a needle or a scalpel. It smelled of vomit, shit, alcohol, fear and disinfectant. Six days in a row they had a Code Black—a violent or threatening patient or family member in the unit.

SARS-CoV-2 was a psychic undertow they all swam around.

Nerida was good at talking down crazy people. Her small but sturdy body and her loving acceptance of every human put people at ease. She told the truth and disarmed frightened people by speaking Aboriginal or working-class English, as they did. She understood how it felt to be hurt and paranoid. She became less threatening when she encountered frightened and insecure people. Some people are good with horses. Nerida was good with drug-fucked schizophrenics.

Her gift was the ability to look for the person's soul and almost always connect. So, she was often needed in dangerous situations when she worked in Emergency. While she was there, the patients were okay.

Dealing with the trauma and upset in her colleagues when they debriefed, especially about what happened when she was not there, was a heavier load. Caring for her colleagues was a priority. She would not stop doing that.

Not everyone at the hospital was honest about their situation. The registrars, those junior doctors coming to the end of their training, argued with her as if she was an idiot. Maybe they were taught by their consultants (who already had long lists of people to care for). 'Speak to the hand,' one of the registrars used to say, holding his hand up in a stop sign, as if that was witty.

Maybe they were born that way. They pretended her patients weren't really as sick as she said they were. That she was incapable of making a correct diagnosis if that diagnosis involved the need for hospital admission. The patient's misery and incapacity counted for nothing without numbers to prove it.

She argued for a heavily pregnant woman with the flu.

'We'll need to get a D-dimer first,' the registrar said.

'That's not useful test in the third trimester of pregnancy. The false positive rate is too high. She's sick. She needs admission for observation. She's going to need to stay. And we can't keep her in the ED.'

It was seven minutes to midnight and Nerida was due to leave. Her client travelled one hundred and seventy kilometres on potholed roads to get to the hospital. She was too sick to be out in town. Her husband was out of his depth trying to care for her at home.

'She's at risk of premature rupture of membranes, and she lives in the bush far from care. And, I know it's low risk, but it could be COVID-19.'

The phone went dead. 'He hung up on me!' she protested to the noisy department. Nobody was listening. Down the hall, she

saw her client, belly a mountain under the sheet, her head turned
to the wall.

The man in mask and gown stroking his wife's head, looking
to Nerida. They didn't even have a separate room in the ED to
accommodate her. The triage nurse had pretended that the fever
couldn't be COVID because they hadn't been in contact with a
diagnosed case.

'There's no community transmission here,' she said to Nerida.

'Well, there won't be if we are not the ones who find it. It's our
job to watch for it,' Nerida said. The nurse turned her back and
walked away, back to the lonely cubicle where she was supposed to
isolate people for Coronavirus testing.

This sort of medical 'culture' kills me.

Nerida tried not to bring the frustration home.

Mari picked up the tension anyway, tried to disperse it by
scrubbing, sweeping and chopping. She shouted at the politicians
on the news, 'Why don't you stop lying?'

She argued with the television about the criteria for COVID-
19 testing. About the people left on cruise-ships. Or allowed to
leave them without testing or quarantine. About the homeless being
told to stay at home. 'Where are they supposed to go?' She was
wounded by reports of people missing their visitors, or getting sick
or dying, in nursing homes.

In Victoria, to the south the Premier announced a state of
emergency. South Australia, where Nerida's daughter Ruby lived
with her de-facto husband, their 'son-outlaw,' Seb, was inaccessible
by road.

The pandemic cast a shadow over the joy and expectation
they felt over Ruby's much-wanted pregnancy. Seb was not
allowed in when Ruby went for her ultrasound. 'I was thinking of
them when I had a pregnant woman with a fever at work today.'

Mari grated parmesan over the risotto.

'I wonder if we'll be able to go to South Australia to be with
Ruby for the birth.' Nerida used the food to distract herself from
worry. 'This is delicious.'

'It sounds like the other interstate borders might be closed any
day,' Mari said.

She had been waking at 2 or 3am, worrying about people she'd seen at hospital, sometimes calling the nurses in the middle of the night to check that someone had been prescribed a medicine or that the medicine she'd prescribed had worked.

'Your patient is sleeping well, Dr Green. You should be, too. Go back to bed. We'll see you at 7am,' the night nurse said.

Watching television after dinner, Nerida ate to keep herself awake. Mari gave her a look as she opened a packet of potato chips.

Nerida crunched. 'You know what? I think I'll give up the hospital shifts. I've been wanting to write from home for a long time. I added the numbers up. We can make enough money from my writing to pay the rent.'

'Will they let you leave, with COVID and everything?' Mari asked.

'They don't get to say. Maybe they'll draft me into the hospital another time. They're still pretending COVID doesn't exist.

'Nobody's wearing PPE except the nurse who's supposed to see people with respiratory symptoms. I don't think it's safe for me to be there. I'm as concerned about my mental health as I am about COVID. I feel bad because more of us will leave acute care and it will get worse. But I think I have to leave for now.'

Sunday morning was already hot when Nerida rose. She had a cool shower, threw on a cheap cotton dress to pull the net through the pool water in the small yard.

They both loved swimming and never had a pool before. They dreamed of a pool over years of living in the desert. It was a major reason to take the house. The light on the water made rainbows.

Nerida caught leaves and bits of stick, insects and dirt, each morning. She cut fallen palm fronds into pieces for the compost bin, admiring the strong material, thinking of houses, dishes and mats you could make of it. She swept leaves from the deck.

There were articles to subedit and flats to proof, waiting in her inbox.

She was grateful to have writing work and a home fit to stay in. Tomorrow would do for that Monday kind of work.

CHAPTER 30

Sunday March 15, 2020

Over morning coffee, Mari said, 'I'll try to channel later today. I want to spend a few hours on the blue painting. The middle one of my triptych. I want to get the yellow pattern right.'

They sat down at their chipboard table when shadows stretched in the yard outside the kitchen window. A neighbour cut grass with a moaning, high-pitched machine. Seated across from Mari, Nerida drew little boxes like apartments in her notebook.

Mari closed her eyes and her breathing changed.

Nerida had a deep swallow at the thought of what new responsibility might be coming through. The adrenaline in the moment of change, Mari's slump of shoulders, set her anxiety to flight.

She imagined Mari diving into the deep blue ocean. It was the image her wife used to transport her spirit away when she went into trance. Nerida drew spirals and leaves. Quietly observing.

Mari shook herself irritably a couple of times. After long minutes, she seemed to go into a deep trance. Nerida saw familiar spirits pass through Mari's relaxed face, having a visit, as it were.

Finally, someone settled in and spoke softly, in a deep tone, with a rounded, well-enunciated accent.

'Hello,' he said. Nerida felt an openness in her chest and head. She made a little sigh. All would be well. Mari's eyes remained closed, and the slackness of her cheeks and jaw gave her face an altered appearance. Relaxed shoulders made her neck seem longer. Nerida recognised Bartgrinn by such subtle cues.

'S been a while, hasn't it?' he said.

'I've missed you,' she said softly.

Moving Mari's head gently from side to side, he tilted it toward her right shoulder, as if listening. 'Different place,' he commented.

'This is our new home,' she said.

'Hmm. Not as bad as other places you have been to,' he
granted. 'Not perfect. Better than many other places.'

'It is.'

After a few quiet moments, he moved Mari's head toward the
east side of the house and said, 'Something going on over there.
Water. Water going below.'

'Oh yes. Below the house.' Mari was sensitive to mould in that
side of the house. She'd posited that there was water in the soil
underneath. Nerida thought her wife exaggerated.

Always highly critical when they moved into a new place, as
they often did, it was a camp-securing instinct from her Romany
ancestors, Nerida reckoned. After a few weeks of sunlight and open
windows, absorbent chemicals and dishes of tea tree and eucalyptus
oils, the room and the house smelled better, and Nerida had
forgotten the issue.

'Not supposed to happen,' Bartgrinn commented.

She agreed. But did Bartgrinn mean that the soil was damp?
Or was he describing a river running under the house?

'So, the house is yours?' he asked.

'No.'

'You don't need to worry then.'

'No. We won't buy it,' she confirmed. It was enough to earn
the rent each week.

'Good,' he said. 'We would strongly advise against buying.'

'Thank you,' she said. Mari had been channelling for about
eight years now. Nerida was past being surprised that the spirit of a
Druid from the first century in Britain should give them real estate
advice.

Bartgrinn was absorbed in the geography, as if he felt it. 'Like
a reservoir of water, could be a natural well, underneath there. Like
that bubble of water that sometimes you have in these atolls, that
freshwater thing?'

'A lens,' said Nerida. She and Mari had stayed in places that
depended on a freshwater lens for survival. She drew a lens-shape
on her notepad, sketched palm trees. A lens is a bubble of fresh
water that sits under a sandy place.

'Yes,' he agreed. 'Probably one and a half metres below.'

'A silly place to build a house then?' she asked. They were close to wetlands. That little lake full of birds—Mari called it a swamp—just down the road.

'Yes. Plenty of these lenses and bubbles. Quite a few over that way,' he said, indicating the south-west. 'Yes.'

She visualised collections of fresh water beneath the suburban houses and out under the tea tree forest. 'At least we were safe from the fires,' she said with a rueful smile.

Vast areas of bushland were consumed by wildfires earlier that year in Australia. She and Mari were grateful for their damp-prone rental then.

He agreed, then paused, drawing up Mari's spine into an erect posture, as if preparing. 'What can we do for you, my dear?'

Nerida reflected. 'Well,' she said, 'I'm curious to hear your opinions about the sickness that's got everybody talking—and some people suffering greatly.'

He took his time to answer and spoke in measured tone. 'Well, it is not like when we talked before about "The planet shaking these irritations off—" like natural disasters affecting the humans. Not like an earthquake or a volcanic eruption or a flood.'

Nerida murmured encouragement, concentrating on the meaning of his words.

'This is different,' he said.

'Yes?' she asked.

'Vicious plan!' he hissed.

Nerida took a deep breath to stay calm. This was not what she expected. She put her pen down.

Bartgrinn gave a small sigh; took a long pause. Each word was carefully chosen. 'It was an act of deliberation, done by a force that most of humanity on the planet would consider incapable.'

Nerida held her breath, even as the world tipped inside her. *The virus, a product of biological warfare?*

'Very poor place that.' He sighed. 'Very poor. No, what you call, no resources. Those resources that should not be taken out anyway, even if you have them. But they don't have any, even if they wanted them.'

Sounds like a riddle. 'You mean like weapons?'

'Resources in the ground,' he clarified. 'The place doesn't have them. Poor, and known to be poor by the rest of the world. They were a bit like, "We're going to teach them."'

He made a small, sharp exhalation and commented, 'There was a bit of a miscalculation.

'They planned it to be slower. Slower and,' he sighed again '— more dangerous. This was not how it was intended to go. This was supposed to be a small test.'

'Hmm?' queried Nerida. She felt as though she was in a spy movie.

'It worked so quickly, they wanted to see if it worked at the same speed in other areas with different climates. They were delighted.

'They still feel very smart and clever because they think no one will ever know. And if others find out, they will be like "We're all such poor people. We would not have the capacity to do such things."'

'Hmm,' said Nerida. Something in Bartgrinn's energy made the rage these ideas should provoke seem safely distant. His calm approach. She was spellbound.

'It will take a while to find out. We see a blame game happening, with the big ones trying to blame each other. Once it's discovered that that thing was created, they will be blaming each other.

'Very, very poor place with a big population, considering the size of the land,' he finally observed.

'Okay,' said Nerida. The scientist in her was fascinated. 'What was the motivation for using this weapon?'

'To show others how it's gonna feel to have nothing.'

'Whoa. And they intended to kill thousands or millions of people?' she asked, trying to process the enormity of what he was saying.

'If that's what it takes, yes,' he said.

Nerida murmured understanding but felt, *What? Resignation plastering over heartbreak and rage.*

Bartgrinn said: 'It's a bit like, "The rest of the world does not care about us. Why should we care about the rest of the world?"'

'It's a kind of terrorist attack then?' she interjected.

'"Claiming respect." That's what they call it.' Bartgrinn said, ignoring her. *These spirits inspect humanity's darkest places*, she thought.

But she said, 'Okay.'

Bartgrinn observed a moment more and said dryly, 'We would suggest that's the wrong way of doing so.'

He held back, as if waiting for her to recover, then said, 'They did not think it could kill people that quickly. It's a problem for people who have other ailments, you know—which is something they don't really have themselves.'

'Right.' Nerida reflected sadly on all the places where people did not live long enough to be troubled by the chronic diseases of middle age.

She had a strong desire to learn which government or party was responsible for this heinous crime, but she wanted the spirit to be able to say what he needed to say. Perhaps he was a better judge of what she needed to hear now.

'Is that because their population tends to die younger from infectious diseases?'

'Yes,' Bartgrinn agreed, pensively. 'Missing hygiene. Sometimes not enough food. If you don't have enough water to drink, you don't consider hygiene.'

'That's right,' she said. *Too true*, she thought.

After a lull, Bartgrinn made small forceful exhalations. She felt as if he had stepped aside, and was perhaps consulting with, or listening to, others: a non-physical being responding to unseen stimuli.

Perhaps some kind of Council of Spirit advised him, what did she know? The kitchen clock ticked. Eventually, he spoke, 'They have a small coastline. Small—but there is not much fishing anymore.'

'Right,' she said. Fishermen pulling empty nets from the planet's depleted seas. *So, this country is near an area of pollution or overfishing.*

CHAPTER 31

TIME SLIP 5: Past

Andy came back to uni after a year at home with his Mum, adapting to the loss of his ability to walk.

It began in 1998 with loss of feeling in his feet. At the cafeteria he shuffled his feet under the table. 'See what I mean? My shoes have come off and I didn't feel it. I don't understand what's going on with my feet. I'm not diabetic. But I've lost feeling in them. They're numb.'

A few weeks later, Andy failed to come to a study date. She rang, ready to growl at him.

'I'm so glad you called, sis. I'm not there because I'm having trouble walking. You know I can't dial out on this phone because we don't pay the bill often enough.'

She went to retrieve him, holding his hand and arm to keep him steady. He walked like someone in flippers, unable to feel or control his feet.

'People are going to think we're on together,' Andy said, when they walked past the Med Lawn. She gave him her energy, somehow supporting his weight. They moved together, bound by her firm, fluid grip. 'I don't care what they think,' she said. Nerida took him to the hospital.

That walk was his last.

He came back to study in a wheelchair. With verve and audacity, fighting his way into suitable accommodation, creating access to his studies.

His mind was laser sharp. He could teach her neuroanatomy, physiology. He worked on a program to recruit more Aboriginal and Torres Strait Islander people into medicine. Extracted the cooperation of the Chemistry, Biochem and Biology departments with his irresistible, wheelchair-spinning charm. 'I'll tell you something more important,' he confided over coffee. 'I'm getting good at telephone sex.' He grinned.

'You have a lovely voice. You'll do well in that.' Nerida rubbed his shoulder. 'Could be a marketable skill. I think the pay's probably better than being an intern.'

Andy complained of waves of paralysis creeping up his body at night. 'Sometimes I can't breathe. I just wait for it to pass.'

She, the scientist, the medical student, was imbued with skepticism—thought he was having night terrors. Hoped so. 'You'd better see the neurologist,' she said. 'Or the psychiatrist.'

Nerida was at Andy's place at night, a month or two later, with Keira. She was a bright, soft-skinned woman, only a year or so out of high school. She was from Java, of Chinese ethnicity. She brought Nerida and Andy study resources from her other study groups.

Keira's Chinese name was Kun, a word Nerida recognised from the *I Ching*, the Chinese fortune telling book. It meant earth, yin, receptivity, the ability to tolerate and carry all. When she asked Keira about the name, she'd told Nerida that Australian men were rude about 'Kun.'

'So, you took your English name from the actress? You're small like her,' Nerida asked. Keira was tiny, with a waist Andy could probably have put his hands around and touched fingers.

'No,' Keira said. 'I first went to University in Australia in Wollongong. A beautiful mountain named Keira overlooks the campus. I thought that meaning was close to what my parents had in mind when they named me.'

At Andy's wheelchair-adapted home, the three had been eating pizza, studying biochemistry. They poured over an impressive chart Keira brought, showing the biochemical pathways of energy production in a cell.

When Andy dropped his slice of pizza. 'I've lost power in my hands and arms. You see, it's coming up me now. That feeling. I can't move my hands now. I haven't had it when I'm awake, sitting up, before.' His head flopped onto his chest. Nerida's arm ached as she held Andy's heavy head up to keep his airway open while Keira phoned the ambulance.

That night turned into months in the hospital. Doctors investigated and experimented, washing Andy's blood in machines, giving him massive infusions of steroids and immunosuppressant drugs, unable to diagnose or treat his devastating malady.

He used to ask her to hold his hand, try to pull energy into it. At first she could feel something, little sparks like the embers of a dying fire. She tried. But his hand was like a soft, empty mitten. And he couldn't feel her touch.

Andy put the Aboriginal flag on the wall over his bed and had a friend come in to play didgeridoo. Elders smoked the place with a dish of lemon myrtle and eucalyptus. Nerida and his other friends—he had so many—made a roster to visit and care for him.

When she visited, with another friend, they wheeled Andy's bed downstairs like escapees. Waiting to get a hoist and help to put him in a wheelchair took too long. They trucked his bed to a grassy corner in front of the hospital where Andy smoked spliffs and ate lemon chicken from the Chinese across the road.

In his room alone together, one day when storm clouds gathered out the window, Andy said, 'They hid my razor away where I can't reach it. Won't you help me finish all this, Nerida?'

'No, Andy. I can't do that.' She hugged him then, missing the days when he embraced her in his arms. She cried with her friend. He didn't ask her to feel his hand anymore.

Now, in the summer of 99, doctors had given up on restoring the function of his limbs. Andy was in a rehabilitation ward near the ocean. Learning.

It was a place of vivid and painful memories. 'My children's father, Sam, was brought here and stayed for months after his accident,' she told him. 'They had an intensive care ward here then.' The old hospital perched on sandstone cliffs. Originally built for TB patients, salt spray was in the air. Sea birds wheeled and bright pink pig face grew among the rocks.

'They're gonna close it down,' he said. Always looking for a fight.

'I know. The real estate developers will get it. Can't have such a magnificent place stay public land.' She breathed the salt air. 'I like your new chair. It's impressive.'

Andy's wheelchair had a motor strong enough to carry his weight up the pot-holed road to the grassy spot where they saw the silver blue ocean. There was a delicious breeze to make the strong sun bearable.

'I got this movement back in my fingers to drive it, see? I can use the computer the uni bought me with these fingers. Sometimes I use a stick on my head. It's a bit like a dildo.'

'What?'

'It's a bondage thing, I think. A dildo strapped to your forehead. Haven't you seen it?'

Nerida laughed. 'Not that one, no.'

'You're bisexual. You should know about these things.'

She might have looked a bit gobsmacked. His laugh faded.

But his eyes were bright. 'I'm finding all this important information, Nerida. They've given me a diagnosis: an immune-mediated central and peripheral neuropathy.'

'It sounds more like a description of what happened to you than a diagnosis.'

He was able to nod his head slightly. 'There are only about a dozen cases in the world. I've also been researching the crustacean protein they injected me with. It had only been used in vitro before.

'They shouldna done that, injected that into you.' She felt guilty for not stopping him from going to the experiment that day. 'Didn't they ask about your medical history? Did you write to them for your record?'

'I did. I wrote to the Dean, asking for the protocol and results of the trial I was part of. I got a letter back from the University lawyers. A hard, nasty, shut-the-fuck-up letter. It was only a simple request. I didn't expect that.'

They watched an albatross fly in from the sea over the hospital buildings and circle back out to sea.

Andy went on, 'The crustaceans have different physiology. They don't have an immune system the way we do. They have special blood cells that respond to attacks.

'I think the viral coat got the foreign proteins into my DNA in a way that programmed my immune system to destroy me.

'That's what they say, you know, that my immune system's been destroying my nerves. You saw the MRI of my spinal column. Something has destroyed it.

Nerida squeezed his hand. She had seen the images, with cavernous gaps where most of his spinal cord used to be.

'I've got all the material saved on a separate hard drive. I'm putting it all together. Might end up with a doctorate.

'I keep the drives in a locked cabinet, Nerida. Every day when I finish work, I watch one of the nurses lock it away. The key is around my neck, see?'

She felt two of his fingers twitch under hers, recalling the way Andy used his hands to talk before this catastrophe. Saw the key and wondered if Andy was being overly dramatic.

'They say I've got to go to a nursing home, sis. You know, I need the hoist to transfer. It takes two people. Mum can't have me at home. She's not well herself.

'I'm looking at what I would need to live independently. There's technology coming where you can make a sound to turn the lights on and off, even open a door. You can clap your hands. Maybe I can get back enough power to clap my hands. Or shout.' His voice was not strong anymore. She hadn't heard him sing in a long time.

Nerida was frightened for him. She felt exhausted, powerless.

'It would cost about three hundred thousand dollars. I worked it out. I'd need to get public housing and adapt it.

'The medical students could have a ball to raise it. Don't you think?

'You know I was on the waiting list for ten years for public housing, so that I could afford to study medicine.' *This is not the kind of money you raise with cake stalls and raffles.*

'So, you know people who work in the public housing office. That'll help,' he said.

She didn't visit again for weeks. She didn't feel she could cope and kidded herself that he didn't need her. Guilt became the dominant emotion she felt when she thought of Andy. Guilt over grief.

She had distractions that got in the way of visiting Andy. She worked a couple jobs, went to political meetings and rallies.

Her son Jim got his first job and went happily to work in a shiny, crisp outfit of black-and-whites his grandmother bought him.

But he was held up at knife point on his way to work by local gang members. 'Must've thought you look rich, my love,' she said, hugging him, worried for him. Jim went to the job.

But it took a fight alongside the union to get the employer to pay him and other students employed that Summer.

Nerida thought they would have to move house. Go somewhere safer. Couldn't imagine how they would afford it. She might need to take more time off her studies, go back to working fulltime.

It was the end of February already when the phone rang at 11pm.

It was Andy's stepdad. 'Andy's died, love. They want you to go and identify him.' His voice broke. 'He had this attack where he couldn't breathe.

'They called the ambulance and the ambos put a tube in his throat and did CPR. They say they've gotta leave all that stuff on 'im, the tube and cannulas and all that because of the coroner. Can you go?'

At the funeral, Andy's mum, a shell of herself in the bustling, weeping crowd, took Nerida aside.

His computer hard drive, his paper notes and his discs and external drives had been removed already when they went to the hospital the morning after he died, to get his things.

'The screen and the keyboard were there. And his head-stick he used to joke about. His chair, his shells, his flag, everything else.

'But the hard drive had been taken out of his computer.

'And the key to his drawer, where he kept all his papers, was gone from around his neck.'

Someone didn't want anyone to know what Andy knew.

CHAPTER 32
Return to Linear Time

Lennox Head

Sunday March 15, 2020

Bartgrinn was looking or listening. He sighed. Looked some more. 'Hmm,' he said. 'It thrives in water.'

She kept quiet to encourage him. The light was golden on Mari's face.

'It does not survive boiling. So, boiling would make it die quickly—you don't have to do it for a long time.'

Steam cleaning might work well, she reflected.

'But it survives freezing.'

'Yes.' She thought of the deep snows in South Korea, Canada, with their penetrating chill. Imagined the snows full of deadly virus.

'It survives being dried,' he said, then took another breathing space. 'If it gets in the ground it subsists there. It's very contagious. If it gets in the dust and the wind blows it, it spreads because it survives the dry.

'If you have a dog or a cat that goes outside, it stays in their fur. It stays in the feathers of birds if they're exposed.'

'Uhuh.' Nerida imagined a sandstorm full of disease, fearing for people in its path. She imagined people holding their pets and even the birds carrying the deadly virus and shuddered.

'It does not like saltwater. It does not like radiation either,' he continued. 'It is not very dangerous to most of the people, but it has the potential to evolve over the years. You can develop immunity to it. But it's a different kind of immunity. It does not stop you from being affected again.'

'Mhmm.'

'But it will get milder over time—until it evolves and modifies itself over some years, then you might get the full brunt again.

'Oh,' said Nerida, disappointed. She was relieved for some immunity conferred. She remembered the hospital now and asked, 'How about the chemicals we use? These strong-smelling chemicals to kill germs. Do they help at all?' Years ago, she asked M'Hoq Toq a similar question about Ebola. Bartgrinn's answer now was different.

'To some extent,' he conceded. 'It does not like alcohol,' he added thoughtfully. 'But it needs to be a high concentration. If you use pure alcohol, that will do. That will kill it.'

'Mhmm.' They would make a hand sanitiser out of the cheap vodka in the pantry. Or use it to wash down benches. She had read that fifty to seventy percent alcohol killed the virus, not one hundred percent. *Who knows what a first century Druid thinks of as pure alcohol, anyway?*

Bartgrinn was still contemplating the virus. 'It is so bad in some areas because it survives freezing. A very cold climate doesn't affect it.' She was queasy in her stomach. *People I love live in cold places.*

'Hot and dry is better than hot and humid,' he said.

'Because it likes the water so much?'

'Yes. Water that's not saltwater.'

'Mmm.' Her parents lived in Sydney, a hot and humid city. She wished to sweep them all up and take them out to the desert. But then she remembered the dust storms. *Is anywhere safe?*

'It does not survive boiling, even for a short period, but in these really humid areas, it does not get hot enough to boil it away. Which is fortunate for humans, of course.'

'That would kill us, as well,' she said. *Sometimes he does seem to be from another planet.*

'Yes.'

'So, it needs boiling,' she prompted. She wanted to understand how to manage this virus. How would she function as a doctor and avoid getting sick or spreading the disease?

He responded as if he read her mind. 'Yes. When you get back from an area that might be affected, wash with strong soap and put your clothes into hot water—wash them in hot water. This is for people like you.'

'Yes,' she said.

'Yes.

'If you work in an area like you do, and you must have contact with these infected people, you'll need a suit that's completely sealed off.' Bartgrinn used Mari's hands to indicate the area to be protected—the mouth, the torso, the closed, almond-shaped eyes.

'In these little masks, these little suits and these other kinds of masks they use over the eyes—you sweat. It's humid in there.'

Just talking about the protective equipment made Nerida feel hot and sweaty.

'That thing goes through the pores of the skin that's exposed,' he said, indicating the temple. She felt a jolt of alarm.

'You don't need to breathe it in. It can be skin contact. It goes through the pores of the skin,' he continued. A sense of doom loomed over Nerida. In a moment, she was terrified.

'Your eyes are moist. It goes through the tear duct.' He pointed delicately to the inner canthus of Mari's left eye.

'Somebody sneezing or coughing? Of course, it's a source. But it's not the only one.' He paused, measuring her response. 'You understand?'

Nerida felt an underlying buzz of fear. 'I think so. It can be conveyed by touch?'

'Yes.'

'It can be on objects?' she checked.

'Yes.'

She brushed her face, as if wiping away that stinging sweat under her work goggles and mask. Itchy heat at the crown of her head felt like being under a paper hood. 'The virus can be in any kind of body fluid, I guess?' she asked.

'Yes. We would not want to go into detail about the other ones—'

'Yes.'

'—but, yes. People sweat. They lean onto things. People have a fever when they come to you. They sweat. They touch something. It goes there.' He moved the hands as if grasping metal hospital bed railings. She sensed she was there, with a desperate patient: burning up, trying to suck more oxygen out of the mask on their face.

'Then you touch it. It goes through the pores of your skin if you don't wear full protection.'

Nerida's hands closed into fists.

'Wearing gloves helps,' he added.

She breathed out. Outside the window, a compact black and white bird, a peewee, fussed and chirped, chasing a beetle among the pot plants.

At work there was a shortage of everything. She had small hands, like many of the nurses. Small gloves ran out first. 'Yes,' she said. 'Would it be effective to clean the rails of a bed, for example, with salt water?'

'You need to have a high concentration of salt,' he said.

'Uhuh.' *Of course*, she thought. *You can't keep a hospital clean with seawater.* Sweat didn't kill the virus.

'Alcohol. Pure alcohol.'

'Yes.'

'As we said, it does not like saltwater,' he added, seeming to catch up with her. 'You will not need any alcohol if there's a higher concentration of salt in the water. Like, a lot higher than the body liquids.' She flashed on the salty taste of blood as he spoke.

'More than seawater, then?'

'Just above, yes.'

'So poorer places could use seawater with extra salt added as a disinfectant?' she asked.

'To clean, yes,' he corrected.

She liked that idea. India and Bangladesh had seawater and salt. Desert places had salty bore water.

Now she was ready to ask more. 'Has this virus been released in several places in the world, or was it released in China and then it spread from China?'

'It was released in different places,' he replied. 'There was one place they tried first. They thought, "We need to try some other places, to see." It was about seven places. They did it on each continent.'

She wondered about Australia, sometimes called a continent.

He responded to her thoughts. 'On this island, here—it did not happen. No industry, low population, undesirable climate— which turned out to be an advantage in this case. But there is no industry.'

'So, the cases that are here in Australia have come from contagion, from other places?'

'Yes,' he said. 'Yes. The ones that did it consider that digging things out of the ground—which the ones of low intelligence here consider their best export—a dirty industry. And not really an industry.'

'Mm,' she said. *The great, filthy mines.* 'Well, they have a point.'

'They do have some ethics,' he said, 'these poor people. They consider the place here as a few people getting very rich; most people don't. Unless they made a fortune somewhere else and then came to settle here. It's not a desirable place for them because of an undesirable climate. And no industry. You understand?'

'I do.' Australia was unbearably hot in summer. *And there is no industry here anymore.*

'So, it was not worth considering,' he said.

She tried to process the information. *About six places across the continents. Take out Australia and Antarctica.* 'Does that mean more of these poisonous seeds were sown in the Americas?' she asked.

'Yes.'

Nerida took a deep breath. 'It's going to get worse there?'

'Yes. It might spread to the southern part of the Americas, where they have some industry, because there might be interaction. But it wasn't put there. It was put in the northern part of the Americas,' he said.

'Is it true that it kills mainly the older people? Or the people who've been sick before?' she asked.

'No. It's not true. It depends on the circumstances and how long you've been exposed to it.'

'Oh,' she said. She liked the idea that the length of exposure time made a difference. One of the most frightening ideas was that you could catch Sars-CoV-2 from a brief, casual encounter, a person who brushed by you in the street.

'If you have someone who is transmitting it, who has it, who stays with you for a long time, you will get it, too. And it does not matter how old you are.' But then he said, 'Children are not very susceptible.' He paused again, looking.

'It was not intended to spare children,' he said.

Oh, these people are cold! They don't care if the children get sick? How can Bartgrinn say they have any ethics?

'It is just that their system—how should I put it?' he asked, still focused on the children.

'It's a bit like it goes right through them because it's not recognised as a germ, a virus or a bacterium.'

He made a breezy gesture with Mari's hand. 'Hmmm. We don't know how to explain it. People will not understand. It's too difficult,' he said.

Try me, thought Nerida. *I have two science degrees.*

He persevered, 'The mitochondria of children are different.' He enunciated the word carefully, as if he was reading, or just learning it. *What would a Druid know about mitochondria?* she thought.

'They're not fully developed,' he went on. 'They are mitochondria, but they have a—hmmm—there is some deviation from the adult one—which helps in this case.'

It was a long time since she studied mitochondria, minuscule factories, her lecturer called them.

They were organs within cells—organelles—that produced energy. She picked up her pen doodled the looping shapes of one.

Bartgrinn continued, 'Children are more susceptible to blood diseases like leukaemia because their mitochondria are a tiny bit different.

'You have not found this difference yet, on this planet.'

Nerida wondered briefly whether beings on other planets had mitochondria, too.

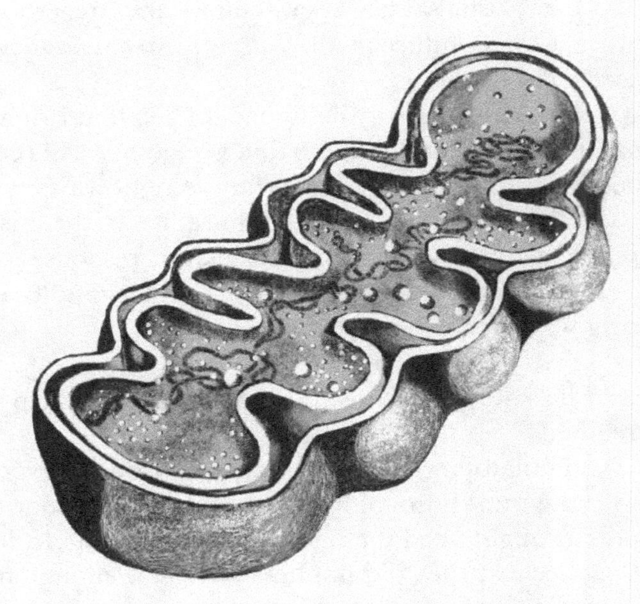

'That's why this would be hard to understand,' he continued.
'There are some tiny tweaks that make a huge difference.

'It might take another ten or twelve years to find that tiny link,'
he reflected with some satisfaction. 'It would help children not to
get so many blood diseases, attacking the red blood cells, for
example. The diseases arise from an imbalance, in the end.'

'Okay.'

'So, there is this difference that helps keep, for example, the
blood cells in balance. And that's something that comes from the
mitochondria.'

Nerida's mind flashed on a blood film and a white cell
differential: pathology tests she used every day. She considered
children in the cancer wards. Recalling a chemical chain in the
mitochondria from her medical studies, she asked, 'Is it related to
the process of oxidative phosphorylation?'

'Something similar,' he agreed. 'Yes, there might be a bright
kid who will find this out in ten or twelve years.'

'Okay,' she said, also grateful for the suggestion of a brighter future. Or any future at all. *Talking about this helps me recover from the shock of it all.*

Bartgrinn's energy lightened. 'Then that bright kid will be mature enough to link these things together. All the information is there. It's just not put together in the right way yet,' he said.

'Okay,' Nerida said, ready to return to the crisis at hand. 'Do you have any advice for prioritising our response as health workers in caring for those with this virus? I understand that we need airtight, protective clothing.'

'Yes.'

She said, 'We've been using machines to help very sick people breathe.'

Ventilators were the crunch-point. Each hospital only had a few—the rural hospital where she worked had one—and very sick patients might need them for weeks to survive. In Italy, many were dying because they did not have access to enough machines.

'The sick people would need a very strong immune system because in these machines—that you said would help people breathe—there is humidity. The humidity is the problem,' he said.

'Hmm,' Nerida murmured. But she protested inside. *No! How can reality be so cruel?*

Bartgrinn was relentless. 'It might help them to breathe, and it helps that thing to breed. You understand?'

'Mmm. I do,' she said. *Can't stand it*, she thought. *It breeds in ventilator tubing?* She refused to believe it.

'If they would—hmm—you would not like this. But it would need to be filtered, dry air because the humidity that builds up in that machine breeds that thing.'

'Mmm,' she said, irritated by the idea. 'I have a personal question then.'

'Yes?'

'I have a machine that uses humid air to help me breathe at night.'

'Yes,' he said, unfazed by her sudden focus on herself. 'Keep it clean. Keep it as clean as possible.' He paused as if surveying the house again. 'There's some other issue here like spores?' he asked.

'Yes. There's mould here,' she said.

'Yes. So, keep it clean.

'Keep that machine as clean as you can. You should almost find something like they use to boil a baby bottle. Maybe you get one of these little machines to sanitise it. And you don't leave it uncovered in the room at all.'

'Okay.'

'You take it out of the cleaning machine, you turn it on. You understand?'

'I do. I'll sleep without it until I can clean it better.'

'You have these spores here.' He moved Mari's head, sensing around him. 'You do. You don't have that other thing moving around here, as far as we can tell.'

'Good,' she said, reassured. *No virus in the house.*

'You risk getting this from people visiting from outside the area. It's brought in from outside. This is not an industrial area. You understand?'

'I do. Thank you,' she said. *Not an industrial area, not targeted for the virus.* They were safe-ish.

She was almost ready to return to the atrocious idea that the hospital ventilators were teeming with the virus.

'There's a reason I don't like it when you say the air needs to be dry and filtered. We don't even have enough machines, as they are, to be able to look after the numbers of sick people, in most countries. Asking any more of these broken systems...'

Bartgrinn lifted an eyebrow and said, 'They used to have a machine to help breathe paralysed people. Those machines have no tubes, no humidity. They have nothing going into the lungs. It was like a mechanical thing that worked from the outside with a vacuum. Do you recall?'

'Yes. They called it an iron lung.' Nerida remembered adults talking about such a machine when she was a child. 'It was used for people with polio or high-level spinal injuries.'

'Yes.'

'So, places that still have those should get them out and use them?' She could not imagine suggesting the use of such archaic technology.

Perhaps there were still such things in hospitals in poorer countries, where nobody wanted to throw anything out. *An iron lung would be practically a museum piece, not used since last century.*

But Bartgrinn was determined. 'Yes,' he said. 'Because the humidity won't go in there and so can't breed. But surfaces have to be very clean,' he added.

'Yes.'

'There are other ways, then, to help the people breathe. If you have something like this respirator that you use now, it will be almost impossible to clean.

'A lot of people that are put on these machines to help them breathe will die. And they will die because of this machine.'

'Right,' said Nerida through clenched teeth.

That was all the world needed, families objecting to their loved ones being put on a respirator. *How am I supposed to talk about this in the scientific community?* Sometimes she hated the things Mari channelled. A conflict roared at the core of her.

If Bartgrinn was right, she had to tell other doctors.

Her colleagues would say that this whole idea of meeting with Spirit was a delusion, *a folie à deux.* She would be considered psychiatrically ill and dangerous for promulgating these ideas.

'This machine can be helpful,' he reiterated, 'but only for someone who is young, with a very temporary problem and a very strong immune system.'

Nerida nodded reluctantly, her resistance dropping away.

Something loving in his energy allowed her to let go and listen.

'I understand. So, it's almost impossible for us to make those machines clean enough to be safe to use at the moment?' she asked.

'You would need completely new equipment for each person: every single tube, every single filter, everything has to be changed,' he said.

'It's not gonna happen, is it?' she surmised, glumly.

'We think that the effort is too much,' he said.

'That's right. It is.' She relaxed with Bartgrinn. Her bone-deep exhaustion persisted, underneath, like the mould beneath the house.

At work, eyes above masked faces revealed deep-set weariness. Many colleagues walked sadly already, even before the virus had hit, with depleted postures and flat voices.

Nerida herself often worked twelve- or fourteen-hour days.

She saw, in her mind's eye, an overworked nurse bringing a respirator to the side of a patient's bed, setting the dials, setting up the tubing with professional, almost automatic movements.

'It should not be! If that's the only solution they have, it's unethical that they don't make the effort to clean it properly. But it's like, "You've got the machine. You should be glad. We do the best we can." Which in this case is not good enough!' he judged.

'Yes,' she said and paused, feeling the weight of what he told her on her chest. *People die when health workers don't do their job properly.* 'Should I publish that information at this stage?'

'You will be told you're a fool.'

CHAPTER 33

Lennox Head

Same day

'We know you're not,' he said softly. 'We are not sure you will be ready for it. If you do publish this material, people will say you're a complete idiot.

'And then, in about a year from now—that's how long it probably takes—people will say, 'I've seen that before. I know I have seen that somewhere.' And then your reputation will be restored.

'But can you handle the time in between? For something that you don't need to do?'

Nerida was compelled to share the information given. She felt it in her bones, her waters, her spirit.

What benefit to the world, though, to reveal that she'd been told these things by a non-physical spirit that periodically used her wife's body to communicate? It was outlandish. If she was not happy to accept the sales pitch at Home and Healed Medical Centre, she could hardly promote the spirit's suggestions, ideas apparently out of thin air.

'Well, the problem is,' she said, 'My employers or colleagues won't act on it anyway. They're not going to change their management.'

That was always the test question in her practical profession. *Will knowing this result or doing this investigation change the way we manage the patient's illness?* In this case, she knew it would not. *Even good, rational science has little or no effect on management decisions at my hospital.* She felt defeated.

But she also saw a glimmer of relief that she might avoid this responsibility. And instantly felt guilty for wanting that. She might continue to keep quiet about what she knew from the spirit.

Bartgrinn sighed. 'Well, they don't know better. They refer to the plague and the 'flu. That was a long time ago. These are the things they have to read about and to learn from. And they will say,

"Everyone's so much better off now because there was so much progress." But still, they use the old rules and practices to apply their new knowledge. Means there is no real progress.

'Back then, an awful lot of people died, even without the craziness of moving around that you have right now.'

She and Mari travelled tens of thousands of kilometres a year, crisscrossing the island and the planet. He was right. It was mad.

Bartgrinn said, 'One of the few things they did have back then was to separate the ones that were sick from the others. And for some of the sick ones, all they had was keeping things clean, trying to. There wasn't much medication.

'So, for example, washing your hands, even for a long time, using the wrong foaming stuff and fresh water, is not gonna help. You can wash them for hours.'

Nerida felt demoralisation edging in again.

'Use saltwater and special soap or soapy stuff that still works in saltwater.'

She rallied. 'Okay.' *There'll be a run on saltwater camping soap if anyone believes that. I should buy shares.*

'That would be better because it does not like the saltwater,' he restated. She wondered for the thousandth time at how spirits, like the old people they'd been more than once, had no problem repeating themselves. He said, 'You need a lot of harsher additives to clean with the freshwater because that's what it likes.

'And you will expose the pores of your skin, the back of your hands, the palms, working where you are.'

She held her scrubbed hands together against her belly.

'You should wear gloves. When you leave the room, you leave the gloves there and then wash your hands or use alcohol. Then go outside in a different area and wash them again.'

Following him, she saw herself taking gloves off in the patient's room, then cleaning her hands twice.

'Taking it outside on your skin and then washing hands, or washing your hands in the same room and picking it up again as you go outside the room—you don't do this. You understand?'

'Yes.'

'It's complicated.'

'It takes practice,' she offered.

'Yes.'

'And thought.'

'Yes,' he agreed. 'People are used to seeing quick results. "I want it all. All of it—and I want it right now!" You know?'

'Yes.' She was chastised by Bartgrinn for impatience more than once before.

'Everyone's like that,' he said, kindly.

But then his voice hardened: 'Even those of low intelligence who believe they are above everyone else. They put something out there. They want results right now. If it doesn't work, they go onto something else.'

He continued, 'Keep doing it. Keep doing it thoroughly. Don't think, "Oh that does not work. We'll just go on to something else because that has proven not to function, it's no good, it's not sufficient."

'This contagion is something that you can't stop just from one minute to the next. The problem is you can start it from one minute to the next, but you can't stop it from one minute to the next.'

There was something pushing up in Nerida's mind, like a seed sprouting in soil. She asked: 'Do the people who created it have a remedy?'

Bartgrinn paused, then said evenly, 'We think they were clever enough to have one.' He took a moment, then gave a clue to the other question uppermost in her mind. Which group or nation committed this crime? 'Just look at a poor country or country considered poor,' he said, 'that does not have it or is only minimally affected by it.' She remained puzzled. But she wasn't sure if she was ready to hear exactly who it was. She didn't want to start the third world war.

He went on, 'But there will first be that blame game, and some will even be saying, "Well, could have been our idea—not such a bad one, after all." They get distracted. They stop searching for the one that did it.'

Returning to the point, he said, 'They do have the remedy. It's an easy one. It's like a food supplement.'

'Really?'

'Yes.' He made a sphere with Mari's right hand as if literally trying to grasp the name of it. 'Like an orangey colour,' he said slowly, '—it's got like an orangey-yellow colour.'

'Is it Vitamin C?' Nerida interrupted, impatiently.

'This can help to support your immune system if you don't have it,' he conceded. 'It's not a remedy if you do have it.

'It's a chemical thing. It's related to sulphur... Orangey-yellow.'

'Does it come from a plant?' she asked, searching her memory and intuition.

'It's derived from a plant,' he said. 'The root of a plant.'

There was a long pause.

Orange root flashed in her brain. 'Turmeric?' she asked.

'No. No. It's very poisonous if you get too much of it.' He waited again, still looking. Even the birds outside seemed to quieten. 'It's from the mountainous regions.'

Ten seconds more passed. She gasped. 'Oh, ginseng? No.' She dismissed her idea immediately. *Ginseng is dusty brown.*

After a minute or two more of intense concentration, Bartgrinn let go. 'I can't tell you more at the moment. Mountainous regions, roots, orangey-yellow.'

But Nerida wouldn't release him. *If I can't get the name, I need more clues.* 'Which mountains? Asia? Europe? South America?'

'The more temperate climates,' he said. 'It's in the places where it gets cold in the winter and not too hot in the summer.' He exhaled a short, sharp breath. 'You'll find it on more than one continent.'

'Good,' she said. 'Is it a common herb?'

'It's from a mountainous region, that's why it's not so common. People make tinctures.'

'So, they use it for medicine already?' she asked.

'They use it for medicine,' he confirmed. 'Some have the idea it enhances fertility... and the drive to procreate. It's from a root. Small plant, small.' He showed a height of about ten or twelve centimetres.

'Does it have a flower?'

'Not always. There is a male and a female plant.'

'It's not ashwagandha, is it?' she asked.

'What is it?'

'Ashwagandha.' The root's not orange. *It's another dusty brown one*, she thought.

'We don't know this name,' Bartgrinn said.

He's not omniscient, even if he seems so. 'Okay. We'll do some research,' she said.

Bartgrinn was sounding weary now. 'We have to get back and study the names of things.' They always did have a problem with names. The spirits said names were not important where they were. She groaned with a wave of frustration.

'Yes, this one could be very helpful,' she said.

In the hiatus Bartgrinn sighed.

Nerida's brain searched for a yellow-orange plant. 'It's not saffron?' Again, she spoke without thinking. 'No!' she chided herself. 'Saffron is the stamen of the flower—'

Bartgrinn spoke over her with renewed force. 'Yes,' he said, astonishing her. 'It's poisonous when you have too much.'

'It's the root of the saffron?' she queried.

'It's the root. We would think it's closely related to saffron. Comes from flowers—the root of flowers. Not all of these plants have flowers. Blue—if it has a flower it's blue.

'People make tinctures with alcohol or oil,' he concluded.

'Okay,' Nerida said, breathing out. She had a mind full of irises, then. Something about orris root powder. But irises were not small plants and you couldn't eat them. And the orris root was the wrong colour.

He said again, to be clear, 'It's not called saffron. We think it could be the root of a related plant.'

At least we might know the genus. 'Yes, thank you,' she said.

'They have it in the mountainous regions of Italy, the Swiss mountains, Austria, France,' he continued, surveying. 'They have similar ones in the mountainous region of what you call California now. Even further north.'

'Canada?'

Bartgrinn ignored her interruption again, musing, 'A lot of the places affected, where the sickness was spread, the remedy grows there.'

Nerida asked, 'Does it grow in the mountains in Iran?'

'Yes.'

She was encouraged. 'Okay. Should it be used for people who are very sick, this root?'

'Not the ones who are only a little sick, because it will pass,' he replied.

'Yes.'

'It's for the ones that have more exposure. It's not an age thing—it's the exposure,' he repeated.

'Okay,' she said, beginning to understand. 'So, a tincture, an alcohol-based tincture taken orally?'

'Under the tongue,' he agreed, curling the tongue. 'Yes. Or it could be used on the inside part of the wrist as an oil.' He gently stroked the pale skin of Mari's narrow wrist. 'Places here or on the upper arm where the skin is quite thin. And this area of the neck.' He indicated the side of the neck, just above the collarbone.

He continued, 'The number of drops under the tongue depends on the concentration. In the right concentration, you need just one drop. Possibly twice a day. No longer than a week.'

'It will probably take less.'

She breathed slowly with a quiet, swelling hope.

He responded: 'If you tell the world, my dear, they will call you a witch.'

'Yes,' she acceded.

'They might not burn you at the stake, but they won't be pleased with you.'

'Yes.'

'I know this sounds strange coming from us—'

'Yes?'

Bartgrinn cleared the throat 'Maybe you should wait 'til they're a bit more desperate. It depends on how strong you are. There could be bad attacks on you personally. We are not sure you would be strong enough to tolerate it.'

Nerida wasn't sure that she was strong enough to take it, either. She'd worked so hard to be the first doctor in her family. After a beat, she said, 'My concern is that I need to be able to earn money for Mari and me to live. If my livelihood's taken from me that gets much more difficult.'

'We see.' There was a hush. He said softly, 'Maybe you should write it as a fairy tale. Or some friend told you this story and you just thought it was so mad and crazy, you might share it so other people can laugh as much as you did.'

'I could say it was a dream,' she suggested.

He was severe. 'No. Do not use this.'

Her eyes widened.

'Make it clear it was a conscious decision that you made to put it out there. And it's not coming from you!

'It was just so ridiculous that you thought it might be a big joke to tell everybody else.

'This *was not* a dream. This did not come from your head. This did not come from *anyone* you know closely!'

'Mmm.'

'You understand?'

'Uhuh.'

He made a sharp exhalation of breath. 'No dreams. People in your profession don't dream.'

Nerida suppressed an outburst of laughter. She loved the spirit's perspective on medical culture.

Bartgrinn was earnest: 'They don't dream up solutions and treatments to serious problems. You'll be called a witch. Worse. This is not what you need.'

'Yes. You have experience with this,' she said.

Bartgrinn lived during times of war and persecution. He'd been alive during the Viking and Roman invasions of Britain. He'd alluded to torture and abuse of healers before.

'Yes. And it's not good,' he said simply.

'We have to protect ourselves,' she said.

'Yeah.'

'Okay.'

'Some people put information out,' he said, 'as jokes. That can work.'

'Hmm,' said Nerida. *Perhaps I should train in stand-up comedy?*

'People laugh,' Bartgrinn continued. 'And some people start to think.

'That's all you want.

'You don't need attacks!'

'Mhmm. That's true.' *Life is hard enough*, she thought. But how could she not share this with the world, if she sincerely believed it was true? The scientist in her wrestled with the spiritual seeker.

Bartgrinn recalled, from his time on Earth as a Druid healer, 'I had to protect myself. I used herbs, helping people to cross in an easy way.'

'You had to keep that secret,' she said. She imagined him caring for the dying: wiping the sweat from a brow, giving a powder or tincture to relieve their pain, palliating them discretely in times and places where these things were not discussed.

He agreed, 'People decide you've got too much power. They get afraid. And then they tell all sorts of lies and stories about you.'

He clicked the fingers. 'If the stories are bad enough, you can live somewhere in quiet and peace. Because once your reputation is gone, you can do whatever you like,' he said with a half-smile.

'It's true.' *How peaceful and lovely to not care about anyone's opinion.*

'But you are not in a position to be that way at the moment because you need to provide for yourself and your family.'

'That's right,' she said.

'You can say "It was the biggest joke I've ever heard." This is fine with us.'

She winced at the idea of being so disrespectful about this sublime, transcendent process. It was such a privilege to be able to talk to the spirit. Gratitude for Mari and Bartgrinn swelled in her chest. She felt tears in her eyes. 'That's very kind.'

'We are trying to help, not to get you in trouble, my friend.'

'Yes.' She relaxed, but asked, 'What about the fact that the germ was intentionally placed? Is that something that can be shared in the context—'

'—of a joke?'

'Of a joke?' She could hardly imagine it.

'Yeah. Like: "This person told me a weird story. What should I read into that? Isn't it strange what people come up with if they have no idea what's going on?" These are things you can say.'

'So, I shouldn't put this on the regular web page when I quote you and Aedgar and M'Hoq Toq? You think I shouldn't?' she asked.

'Well, they consider us weird, anyway.'

'Yes.'

'But don't post it or put it out there where your colleagues are. You don't.'

'That's right. Some separation—'

'You need it!' he interjected.

'—between my self and the material.' *Would it be enough?* Could she keep these encounters secret and still share the content of the conversations with the world?

'You need it now more than ever,' he advised.

Softly, she said, 'Thank you.' She felt loved and cared for.

Quietly, he said, 'You're welcome.'

'I appreciate your wisdom and your protection.' Nerida had tears in her eyes. The intensity of the subject, the responsibility thrust on her and Bartgrinn's understanding brought on strong emotions. She had been wrenched and exhausted but now reconnected with her own soul. A seed of enthusiasm, a hope of healing, was in her. Tears spilled over, trickled down her face.

'Hold it close to your heart, my friend,' he said tenderly.

What if she didn't need to sacrifice her livelihood and reputation to be able to share this information with the world?

How could she mock it? But how could she not share it?

What the spirits told her resonated, including with her scientific understanding, an integral part of her. Most of what she didn't understand now would be confirmed to her in future, she had learned from experience. She had developed an almost unshakeable faith in what the spirits told her.

Mari had been in trance for over an hour. She'd be tired from sitting on the hard kitchen chair. But there was one more thing Nerida wanted to acknowledge. A couple of months earlier, Mari seemed to slip into a trance, sitting beside her, when they were travelling.

Now, Nerida said to Bartgrinn, 'We owe you thanks—you and Aedgar and our other spirit friends—for intervening in a dangerous flight. Mari and I were over the desert a little while ago. No one could tell if the pilot would land the plane safely—'

Their pilot made three attempts to land.

They finally hit the ground with a frightening thud, the metal joints of the machine shuddering. They alighted, with other passengers for the desert town, into a strong smell of burned rubber and oil.

The plane took off to continue its trans-Australian flight from the inland. But they found out later the pilot made a forced landing only halfway to the intended destination on the coast because of a mechanical problem with the plane.

Bartgrinn smiled. She felt a rush of mischievous energy. 'That was our friend! That was Aedgar.'

'Aedgar did that?'

'Yes.'

'Thank you. Thank him.'

'He likes to do things like that,' Bartgrinn almost chuckled.

'He's good at it!' she gushed with relief.

'He thinks he's good at it,' Bartgrinn replied.

Nerida laughed. 'Well. I think he's saved us a couple of times now.'

Breezily, he said, 'He likes to interfere in things that he's got no idea about.'

She chortled.

'And then he will go, "Told you so. Fixed it!"'

'Yes?'

'It was just so easy.' Bartgrinn spoke in an urbane tone, imitating his comrade spirit.

'Uhuh.' Nerida smiled.

'Yes.'

There was a lull. The clock ticked. 'We think we might go.'

She responded. 'The body is tired,' she said. Bartgrinn was moving away already.

'Yes. It's very difficult for us to talk.' Mari's mouth was dry.

She must be thirsty. Their friends had never learned to sip water while in Mari's body the way that Monica did when Dawn channeled her.

Nerida suggested a drink of water to Aedgar once or twice. He declined. If opening the eyes was complicated for a spirit in someone else's body, swallowing water must be even more so. *He and Bartgrinn probably prefer beer to water, anyway.* Aedgar said as much when they first met in 2012. Mari herself tended to say that water was for washing in.

'Thank you so much for your efforts,' Nerida said. She didn't understand what challenges or energy were encountered to allow them to come into this denser, physical reality and speak to her, but acknowledged it.

'You're welcome, my friend,' he said. 'So, we'll talk another time.'

'Yes, please.'

With precision, but already sounding further away, he said, 'Take care, my friend.'

Nerida got up and turned on the air-conditioning. She filled the kettle. Orange-tinted clouds outside signalled approaching night.

Mari slumped. She looked asleep sitting up. She opened her eyes slowly.

'Hello, my love,' said Nerida, kissing her soft cheek. She rubbed her wife's broad, relaxed shoulders. *I'm so grateful she always comes back.*

Mari murmured, put her arms on the table and rested her head on them, as Nerida wandered back to the kitchen and began pulling vegetables out for their evening meal.

Two days later, Nerida interrupted her morning's writing. 'We need fruit. Let's go out.'

Driving to the supermarket, Nerida explained a few of the ideas Mari had channelled. She spoke in general terms—Mari hated hearing what she had channelled. She explained that Bartgrinn said the virus was created by humans. It was not naturally occurring.

'I thought that,' Mari said, to Nerida's relief. Sometimes Mari was evidently given insight into the content the spirits wanted to share. This was a recent development. She'd only been open to listening to them, Nerida supposed, for the last year or so.

Mari never wanted to hear the details of what she'd channelled, but Nerida sometimes needed to tell her the broad strokes. Especially if she was apprehensive about the social impact of the material on a client, on the world or on them. *If I'm going to put that outrageous idea in a book, Mari had better know about it.*

They treasured their private, peaceful life together.

'I thought it was germ warfare, you know,' said Mari. Then after a pause. 'What if it really is just me talking and not spirits at all?'

So, she still doubts herself, even after all this time. Nerida looked ahead at the road. 'Do you know what you say when you're in trance?' she asked Mari.

Mari's black curls bounced as she turned her head toward her.

'No. You know I don't. I knew it was Bartgrinn because he always comes in through here.' She patted the side of her head. 'But I don't hear what they say.'

I'm still alone then, with my grim speculation about which despot, which impoverished country, used it as a weapon. Nerida suppressed a sigh. Sunlight sparkled on the estuary as they crossed a bridge into town. Squinting, she saw pelicans and ducks bobbing on the water.

'So, how's your knowledge of oxidative phosphorylation?' Nerida asked, smiling.

'What?'

'In the mitochondria,' Nerida asked.

'I don't know what that means,' Mari looked out the passenger-side window.

'Then it's not you,' Nerida said, caressing Mari's knee. She turned on the indicator and pulled into the shopping centre carpark. 'What do we need at the shop?'

'I'd like to get some Vitamin C,' said Mari. 'I've got a feeling it'd be good to take some.'

'Great idea. I'm going to look at a baby-bottle steriliser,' Nerida replied as she parked the car.

'What do you want that for?' asked Mari.

Keeping their distance from strangers, they pulled on their masks. And chatted as they ambled into the mall. *Her eyes are so lovely.* 'You look good in a mask.'

'Hides the wrinkles,' Mari laughed.

CHAPTER 34

Kempsey NSW. Dhanggati Country

Saturday April 25, 2020

Nerida felt it when they came onto Dhanggati land. Something changed in her body. It felt lighter, more a part of everything around here. Even driving at one hundred and ten kilometres an hour. She felt herself get out of her own way.

In the east, the creeks were dry. Even the mighty rivers were stagnant, with algae brewing along their banks. They breathed smoke.

She and Mari booked a room at a small motel outside of Sydney, unlikely to have been used for quarantine. The five-hour flight to Perth the next day might be a chance to sleep. But first there was the long drive.

Pulling into a roadside rest spot, the tyres crunched on gravel. Nerida eased her stiff limbs out of the car. Stretched.

Mari went to the corrugated iron bathroom while Nerida read the tourist information.

Delighted, she saw stories from the tribe she'd never heard, written on metal signs near the picnic area. *Dhanggati people are coming forward.* As cars sped by on the expressway, she became absorbed in the story of the blue wren.

Shooing flies, she pulled her hat down to shade her eyes. And read about the blue wren that compensated for its tiny size with cleverness.

The first non-physical being who spoke English that Mari channelled, Aedgar, sometimes visited the women by inhabiting a blue wren. They thought of him whenever they saw the opalescent bird.

Other times Aedgar came into a willy wagtail, a cheeky black and white wren that swung its tail. As she read the story then, a wagtail chirruped at her, greeting her from the dried grass. She smiled.

Black and white birds were the totem of women in Nerida's clan, so she was good at listening to them.

Nerida climbed up into the car and leaned back, holding the seat belt off her neck. Mari took a turn driving. Nerida felt high from the story, happy to put her feet on country, even for a few minutes on a grassy traffic island. In a little while she noticed the colours.

Rainbow colours, brilliant as oil broken on a sunlit puddle, came into the front of her vision. She thought it was light breaking up between the trees, or reflections of roadside water. But there was no water. Country was drought-stricken.

'I'm seeing amazing colours,' she said to Mari. 'Do you see the rainbows?'

She enjoyed the gorgeous iridescence. The colours were bright and translucent or reflective, like scales of a giant fish body. Or sequins.

When she closed her eyes and the colours were still there, the doctor in her was concerned. This wasn't just an effect of the light.

She remembered stories Andy told about auras. Andy was epileptic, following a head injury in a car rollover when he was a teen. He was the first person Nerida met who had epilepsy with auras, coloured lights and shapes signalling an impending seizure. He described impressive psychedelic patterns of wonder.

'Like you're s'posed to see on acid,' she said to him then.

'Did you ever see them on acid?' Andy asked her.

'No. When I took acid I mainly cried a lot. I always felt frightened and degraded, somehow. Could never properly relax.

'My boyfriends promised me a good time, but I never went there. The last time I took something that was supposed to be acid, there was something toxic in it. I kept seeing these octagonal or hexagonal kind of tunnels everywhere. So I had visual hallucinations. You know, what you're s'posed to find so amazing. Well, they were amazing.

'Only they didn't go away when the acid wore off. The worst was that I could hear people talking about me or bossing me around in my head. Saying nasty, disapproving things about me. It felt like there was no distance, no walls to houses. Like I had no skin.'

'Like the Talking Heads song. *Where is the protection that I needed?*' Andy sang in his clear, light upper register.

'Exactly,' said Nerida.

Now, in the car, she started to wonder whether the pretty colours might be a bad thing. Especially since they persisted when she closed her eyes. *Am I having a seizure? Or a stroke?* It was the kind of exquisite, transcendent experience Andy described.

I have worked away about thirty kilos of weight in the past year.

Do I have an electrolyte imbalance? Is my blood pressure too low? Reaching through the rainbows into the glovebox, she found electrolyte tablets. She plopped one into her water bottle. It fizzed prettily, making an upside-down rain of rainbow bubbles in the clear plastic bottle. She dropped another in. The salted water tasted good. *Probably a sign that I need it.*

'I'm a bit worried about this now,' she said to Mari. 'We might have to go to the hospital at Newcastle.'

'The hospital? Really?' Newcastle was two hours away. 'Do you want me to stop at Taree?'

'If I've got a problem, Taree'll send me to Newcastle anyway. We may as well be driving. I haven't got a headache or anything. You know, I've been getting dizzy at home...This is so pretty though. I wish you could see it. Don't you see it?'

She put the seat back and snuggled against it. Thought: *If I'm dying or part of my brain is, I may as well enjoy the charm of it.* 'I'm tired now,' she said. Mari glanced at her, dark brows creasing her forehead. Her shoulders were tense. She gripped the wheel.

'I'll go to sleep now,' Nerida said, 'so I don't get anxious. If I've still got this when we get to Newcastle, we'll have to go to Emergency.'

When she awoke, they were driving over the grey-green expanse of the Hunter River, just north of Newcastle. She opened the window to feel the breeze in her hair. The place smelled of mud.

'There's the big mosquito,' Mari said, as they passed a metal sculpture of the local insect.

It was hard not to smile at the concept of a giant mosquito as a tourist attraction. 'How are you feeling?'

Nerida sat up and rolled her shoulders a little. 'I'm good,' she said. 'Colours are gone. That was sublime. But I did get scared.

'Are you right to drive us to Sydney?'

'Yep. I'm enjoying the drive.' Mari smiled, patted her on the knee. 'Drink your water.'

CHAPTER 35

Perth, Western Australia, Whadjuk Country

Sunday April 26, 2020

Mari was keen to return to the Kimberley, attracted to the land and animals there. She was already painting from photos she took on their last trip. Brolgas were her current fascination, giant blue-grey birds that honked and danced in devoted couples. Their red legs hung down for landing.

Nerida loved the people there. Five different tribes in more than 40 communities across about two hundred kilometres of the sinuous river, expansive flood plains, mesas, and hills they called the Fitzroy Valley. She loved their stories, their languages. Relished feeling that she could really help.

Travel between the Australian states was forbidden to stop the spread of Coronavirus. Dr Nerida qualified for an exemption. They applied to the state's Chief of Police for Mari to come with her. 'I'm not going anywhere without you,' she said to Mari.

She called Harriet, the nurse in charge at the service. 'The last doctor's wife was turned back from Perth airport. They flew from Tasmania and then they wouldn't let her in. He worked six weeks alone,' Harriet told her.

'Ms Mari Wildeburg is essential to the doctor's mental and physical health in challenging, demanding circumstances,' Nerida wrote on the form. Fitzroy Crossing had a rough reputation. The police wanted doctors there for social control more than for the people's wellbeing, she suspected. She didn't care. She knew she was a force for good in her work.

But before work there was quarantine in Perth.

Police in gas masks interviewed them at the airport. They were forced to isolate for two weeks because they came from New South Wales, where the virus was transmitted in the community, to Western Australia, where it wasn't (yet).

Online, Nerida had found them a modest house with a garden. It was a great improvement on the sterile hotel room her employers had offered and cost no more. She was glad of the yard because they were not allowed to leave the house for food or exercise. They were not allowed to leave for any reason, barring a medical emergency. Nerida imagined the ambos arriving in full PPE if one of them got sick.

They had internet though and could order groceries. Mari was frustrated when it took four days, (and three orders) to get a loaf of bread in their food delivery. The supermarket workers packed home orders at the end of the day and kept ticking the box that said bread was 'unavailable,' because it was all gone by then.

Mari was also cranky from being cold at night—the only heater was in the living room. The house was old, wooden. Nerida liked the history in it. But icy drafts came in under the doors, and from under the floor.

Nerida could do her work. Mari was restless. She sketched, sometimes coloured with pastels, but was dissatisfied. She had the television on for hours. The news featured a story about a celebrity barista, Skete Parlour, who was fined for selling a 'light entrancer,' a machine with coloured lights meant to treat COVID, among other things, for thousands of dollars.

He looked agitated and paranoid on television.

Nerida was confident that she would never be a charlatan.

She would never be so blasé about money that she tried to take large sums from people. *I couldn't even get myself to charge people big money to change their pathology numbers, bio-hacking, at that clinic at Byron Bay. I'll never be that celebrity doctor.* She could see the attraction.

She wanted to be famous when she was a child. Money for nothing. Unearned, uncritical approval from the world and love everywhere she went. That's what she thought fame meant then. But she was not that child anymore.

She monitored her mental health. She knew what it was to be mentally ill and would never go there again.

The way Skete Parlour was treated disquieted her, though. He was a long-time campaigner against vaccinations and a celebrity on social media. His wealth and fame came from television work: ads for coffees, baking competitions.

The establishment was delighted to have an excuse to prosecute him. In the interview she watched with Mari, Skete hinted that he might be killed for the disruptive information he had. No doubt the program was edited to maximise the appearance of his anxiety. He was not an influencer in control of his image anymore.

'I think he's manic. He's probably got bipolar disorder,' she said to Mari. 'I reckon he needs medication. Literally. He probably really believed in that carnival machine someone put him up to selling. Now he's shattered because suddenly money matters. And he's wondering what he did to create this.'

'Do you think so?' Mari asked.

'I'm sure of it.' Nerida said.

'Believing in Law of Attraction can make a person so miserable,' Mari commented. 'If you've got no insight or control of your mind. Like me. I hate it.'

Over in Canberra, a politician from the agribusiness party believed that a cheap, anti-parasitic medicine was an effective treatment for COVID-19. People were trying to get him fired for that. Nerida used that medicine a lot. Bad infestations of headlice and scabies, sometimes years-long, were sadly common in some places she worked.

They were parasites of poverty, especially attracted to people in poor, overcrowded housing. She'd had scabies herself, maybe ten times, from when she lived in low-quality housing that let all sorts of bugs into the gaps between the floor and walls. And when she became a doctor, from holding infected babies or kids.

'Some people we know would be well off if ivermectin turns out to protect them from Coronavirus,' she said to Mari. But she saw no evidence that it worked as an anti-viral in humans. It worked in dishes in the lab.

Her experience with Andy taught her that what was harmless and effective in the lab could act the opposite way in a human body.

And, meanwhile, the politician who believed in it was lampooned, belittled and humiliated. *Is that what they will do to me if I speak up about a herb that can treat COVID-19? You bet.*

An African president who endorsed a herbal treatment as a cure died of COVID. But maybe there was corruption involved. Or maybe he was just ignorant.

She understood that if she spoke up about what the spirits told her, to the extent she had any influence she would be reviled, put in a box with other misguided, anti-scientific and sometimes malign people. Especially when people found out that Mari was a channel.

Nerida had been living with Mari's channelling for about seven years and the conflict was not new to her. *But this is the sharp point of it*, she felt.

Nerida kept moving, getting into her work, which distracted and satisfied her. She made progress on the book about Pick Up. Transcribing the stories of the Pick Up staff, and telephone interviews with the ex-prisoners they helped, giving them voices in the world, was interesting and fulfilling.

She wrote about five or six hours a day, finding ways to manage the inflammation in her arms from so much sitting and typing. She did yoga in the mornings. Kept her mind well with meditation when needed. Gave Mari plenty of hugs and smiles. Occasionally cooked.

Nerida discovered she loved writing. Finding the right word or turn of phrase was as good as tasting a delicious food.

The daily pressure in her head to write books of the material Mari channelled took a different turn as she finally began to practice the work of being a writer.

She felt her path opening before her, even as she was not allowed to leave the front gate.

CHAPTER 36

Perth, Western Australia, Whadjuk Country

Monday April 27, 2020

After a productive morning, Nerida returned to her little desk after lunch, flexing her back against the cheap office chair. She had a footrest, a spongy crocodile to squeeze when she rested her hands, and a window crowded by bushes. She could see the sky in the top of the window, and she felt called outside sometimes to see the clouds.

Nerida was absorbed in her writing, though, when Ruby called.

'I'm sorry to call you with bad news,' she said. Then cried so hard she could hardly talk.

'The baby died. I started bleeding two days ago. Bleeding too much! They kept me in hospital. They did an ultrasound. The man said, 'She looks perfect but there is no heartbeat.'

'Oh, my darling daughter. I'm so sorry,' Tears stung her eyes and spilled onto her face. Her breathing stuttered.

Sobs broke up Ruby's voice. 'How can she look perfect? They couldn't tell me why Jedda died.'

'I don't know what to say…'

'They wouldn't let Seb in because of COVID.'

Nerida bridled. *That was cruel and unnecessary. I must get out of here. I have to go to her.*

'I don't know why she died,' Ruby choked.

Nerida imagined her daughter, sturdy and soft-edged, alone in a hospital bed cramping and bleeding. The drip in her arm pumping oxytocin, pushing her body to expel a part of herself that was to be someone else. That tiny beloved child to be. Her gaze drifted to the window of the small office. Rose petals were crushed by the afternoon wind. 'They wouldn't let Seb in?'

'They tested him for Coronavirus and they wouldn't let him in till the results came in, eight hours later. Why did it have to take so long?

'I went into theatre on Saturday morning.'

In her mind's eye, Nerida saw her wan daughter, tears exhausted, her spikey hair under a blue cap, on the cold trolley under a stiff paper sheet. Glimpsing Seb as he pressed against glass.

'I had to labour to push her out. It hurt a lot, Mum. She was pale. I just saw the white shape of her in all the blood. There was a lot of blood. I didn't get to hold her.

'They put me to sleep after she was born because I was bleeding so much. I think I had four bags of blood. I never saw her. I don't know what they said about her. I don't know what she looked like.'

The weeping started up again.

'They burned her body in a fire.' Ruby started keening as she wept.

Nerida's tears ran down her neck, wetting her chest. She could feel her daughter rocking at the end of the phone.

'One of the nurses said she was beautiful. She said the baby had the sweetest face. All her fingers and toes. She held my hand.' Ruby sobbed. 'Was really kind.'

Mother and daughter cried on the phone, three and a half thousand kilometres apart.

After a few minutes, Ruby spoke in her low, grown-up voice. 'I'm all right now. Seb was at the hospital with me as long as he could be, and just brought me home now.

'He's here, coming and going while I talk to you. I am weak. Kinda shaky. They gave me medicine to stop me vomiting yesterday. I guess I'll feel a bit shit till the drugs are out my system.'

Ruby took a big breath. 'This happens to a lot of women in the world, right? Seb says there'll be support groups we can join... This happened to you, Mama, didn't it?'

'Yeah. It was the biggest thing that happened to me before you were born.' She thought about how lonely it had been. 'Aunty Hannah and my cousin Judy had babies that died. All of us had other children.

'But I know you never will forget your Jedda.'

Afterwards, Nerida went to Mari and cried in her arms. 'I was so looking forward to being with that baby. I loved her already. My poor Ruby. My darling daughtergirl. Can I go to her? I want to go to her.'

Mari hated to see Nerida cry. 'We can try,' she said.

Later, she approached Nerida gently. 'What will we do for money, if you have to fly back East and then start your quarantine again when you get back? We've spent what little we saved on rent. And what will your patients in the Fitzroy Valley do without a doctor?'

CHAPTER 37

Perth, Whadjuk WA

Thursday April 30, 2020

The compressor on the fridge started up as Mari went into trance. The loud vibrating buzz of it—normally unnoticed background noise—dominated the space.

It was their fourth day of quarantine. Mari's eyes were closed, her face and shoulders relaxed. Nerida couldn't say how it was that her face changed gender before her eyes, but there it was, the aquiline austerity and erect posture of the Native American healer: M'Hoq Toq.

She jumped with enthusiasm. 'Hello!' Pulling herself back, she thanked him for coming.

He spoke quietly, almost in a whisper. 'You're welcome. What can we do for you?'

'We're in this little house. We're not allowed to leave the house for fourteen days—'

'What bad did you do?' he asked earnestly.

She laughed. 'We didn't do anything bad. It's because of the sickness that's out in the world.'

'The sickness—'

'Yes?'

'—is a tool.'

'A tool?'

'Yes.' He inclined the head.

'Tell me more.'

'It was not invented as a tool. It was created to do harm. It does a lot of harm. But you should see it as a tool to help you see what is important.

'This is the quiet before the storm.

'In some areas it is easing, *a bit*. Most of the people have not changed their minds. They think about the wrong things.

'This tool, if you see it as one, is very powerful.

'The planet is taking a breath.

'The world won't end.

'But humanity has time to think what is important in life.'

Nerida wondered, 'What is important in life?'

'Learning. To progress, to evolve. There are some things that support it: love, a kind of common sense, sensitivity to the world around you. You should feel the energy of others around you, trying to balance.

Humanity should share the same goal: making this planet a better place.'

She felt power in his words. Asked, 'When you say I should feel the energy of others around me, trying to balance—'

'Yes.'

'Do you mean beings, non-physical beings?'

'All of it. Physical and non-physical.'

'Including all of life—'

'Yes,' he said.

'—and even the Earth which is not conventionally considered to be alive, but—'

'It's got consciousness. You differentiate between alive and non-alive. It's really about consciousness. Everything that's got consciousness has to be considered,' he said.

'And all strives for balance,' she said.

'Yeah. Humanity, in many parts, is driven by the wrong ideas. These ideas need to shift. Aim to make it a better place for every thing that's got consciousness.

'Paper with the numbers on it doesn't have consciousness. Why would you go for this? Why would anyone think this is important?

'It's used to take things from one part of the planet to another one in an exchange. Very valid things are transported to the other side of the planet or even just next door. And all you get is a paper with numbers on it. How can this be important?

'Someone was dreaming up a system. It has not worked in the past. People think it is convenient because it represents a value. And you can take a lot of it with you to go to other places and it won't slow you down.

'Humanity needs to slow down.

'It's not about more, bigger and better: these things don't go together. It's about balance.

'Why should it be better if it goes faster or makes more? In the end it's supposed to be better. It is not.'

There was a moment as he reflected sadly. 'We had disease brought to our lives by other humans, coming from other places.'

'Yes,' she whispered.

'It almost killed us all.'

'Yes.'

'It was even more devastating than the guns and weapons they used because, as you understand now, it was invisible. It would hang around, impalpable, and then it came to get you when you least expected it.

'What you're dealing with now is the same. It's not visible.

'The problems it causes in humans and animals are visible. The thing itself is not.

'Problem with this one is you could consider it *a shape-shifter.*'

'Ah. It mutates.'

'Yeah. It was created to be that simple thing. And then it got that kind of consciousness. You would say it is alive. We just say its got consciousness.'

'You can't see it. You can't smell it. You can't feel it, the moment it attacks you.

You can only see and feel these things afterwards: the result of what it does to a body.'

Bushy leaves brushed the kitchen window. The afternoon wind arrived.

'Too many think they have to chase the paper with the numbers on it. They get desperate because they're chasing something that's not integral to being human.

Being human means being able to negotiate living together, interacting, teaching each other. Sometimes it even means participation in things that are not so bright—but something is happening. There's *interaction*. It's expanding your energy, as long as you learn.'

This is the meaning of life. This is why we come to this planet.

'Some humans had this idea,' he continued. '"We're going to make them all chase the same thing." There are some that are better—maybe *trickier*—in their abilities to chase it, compared to others.

'We would say that a lot of the not-so-intelligent ones are the tricky ones, good at chasing it. They have no ability to create things that they could exchange, so they exploit others who do. Craftspeople, farmers: they exploit them.

'This will always leave the ones with better abilities below. It's what the others need to create their wealth.

'Life here would be about learning, creating, producing, learning together. Respecting culture.'

'You know, groups of human beings have their specials ways to do things.

'You can't tell everybody that they have to do every thing in the same way. If every group thinks the way they do it is the only way, you can't learn. You won't be open to learning.

'This affects every aspect of life.

'Some groups, driven by greed, exploit others. They're not better. They're just richer—in their own way of thinking. You know, in their own minds what they consider to be 'rich'.

'Paper with numbers on it? Go ahead and burn it.

'You have these plastic things? Someone could demolish it. Burn them too.

'So what would you be left with?'

'Nothing,' she said.

'So then,' he said, 'those ones would need to go to the others that have a craft: to exploit them again, to get an advantage. But there will come the time when this is not happening anymore.

'It's a time you might call an awakening.

'We don't like that term very much. It was misused in religious ceremonies, 'Awakening' to things. We don't like the expression, but the experience is similar.

'The craftspeople will realise how much more power they have.'

A plane flew overhead, an unusual sound in those days.

'The truly educated ones,' she reflected.

'Yes. You can't provide your own food? You are nothing. Because you can't eat the paper with the numbers on it. You can't eat the plastic things, either.

'People say there is an exchange of value. But that has no value at all.

'You type into your stupid little machines. You gonna suck on the cables? Or on the device itself? You would be very disappointed.

'Won't be satisfying at all.'

Nerida felt a frisson of defensiveness. *Let it go.* 'No nourishment there,' she said.

'No. People planning to exploit others make them go to certain places where they like to live.'

The filthy cities.

'By doing so, they all go to the same areas. As more and more are attracted to it, they start living in little boxes. You can't take care of food or provide for yourself or your family or your community if there is no space to grow it.

'Yes.' Sydney and Melbourne overflowed with expensive, shoddy apartment buildings.

'So, more people are attracted to a specific place. That someone decides is a good place to live because you might get 'rich'. That makes them more dependent on the ones that exploit them. They try to chase that paper with numbers on it.'

'I understand.' *The beings so often avoid using using that word 'money'.*

'And they get more and more dependent on those tricky exploiters. It's not quite legal, the way the exploiters act. But they are so high up. They feel very safe because they think no one will ever know. "This is how it is done." "I was born for this."'

'Not true. Nobody is born for that.'

Nerida tilted her head. 'You have to be tricky to be able to stay alive without actually working?'

'Yes. It passes for intelligence. You're not intelligent. You're just tricky.

'You might have been a pickpocket in a former life and in this one—you see how far you can take it.

'Taking humans, attracting them to specific place in large numbers, is a recipe to create poverty.'

'Yes.' Nerida mused. 'It's the worst kind of poverty because if you have no land to grow food and your neighbour has none—'

'Yes.'

'—that's desperate poverty.'

'Yes. People will start killing each other if they don't earn. Driven by hunger. The one who's stronger—or trickier for that matter—is going to survive.

'If it continues like this.'

Nerida felt sick with anxiety.

'There is always hope,' he said.

There was a bird chirping in the yard, calling her mate.

She chose her words. 'What kind of thoughts do we need to make humanity stronger, more loving, respectful?'

M'Hoq Toq replied, 'Families or groups of people, (related or not), used to live together and support each other. Everyone had a gift to make the community, or the family, thrive.

'Now, you put them in one house. They don't know what to do with each other.

'They get violent. They get bored. Because they don't know how to talk anymore. They don't know how to interact or how to work together.

'They sit, waiting for it to go back to the same as before. Even if, deep inside they know, it was not what they wanted.

'This thing will be around for awhile. It will go a bit dormant. It will come and go. Shape-shifting. It's got consciousness.

'Sometimes people create something and then it turns out to develop a mind of its own.'

'Mmm.' Nerida thought of Mary Shelley and Frankenstein's monster. *But does it have to be so extremely evil? Are there different levels of consciousness that we need to learn about? Frankenstein's monster was not inherently evil. He only seemed that way to the frightened villagers. Even if his origins were revolting.*

'People should know that happens,' he said. 'People do, you know, create children. They map it all out. "This is how it's gonna be."

'And very early on, those little beings have their own mind.

'That's a bit like this thing, this tool that's out there.'

Now he's comparing children to the virus. Great. She sighed.

'It was created to be something different,' he reflected, seeming to go deep within.

'It was created as a weapon?' she asked.

'A demonstration of power: that's how we would put it.'

'Yes,' she whispered.

After a beat, he asked, 'Is there anything else you would like to know?'

'I've so many questions it's hard to know where to start.' *Do I really want to know? This is grim.*

Mildly, he said, 'Oh, just one after another.'

'So, do we need to keep our distance from each other for a long time?

'It would be advisable. But the ones that consider only how to 'prosper' in a wrong way—'

'Yes.'

'—will eventually tell you that it's all fine.'

'They're doing it already,' she said.

'It is not,' he said. 'We would think—we are not very good with time—but some time from now it will go dormant. Not completely, but mostly. That's why we said it's the quiet before the storm here. Others are still in it: the first little storm.'

206

'There's worse coming?'

'Yeah. It could be worse, what's coming. It's still about the state of humanity wanting to go back to where they came from.'

'Ah.'

'Once that changes, people could see improvement in many places on this planet. For now, they choose to ignore the improvements. They look at other things.'

Nerida suggested, 'So many things have improved. The air is cleaner, the ocean is quieter.'

'This is not what they want to put out in this world. You understand? They will lose control. "You start talking about all the good developments and all the good things that come out of this situation, you're going to lose your grip on power." So they show the world nothing but bad things.

'And it will be constant, everywhere, for a long time. It has been already. They will always find that point, that area where it is the worst. They want you to be afraid of what's coming.

'They're telling you. "We are the ones keeping you safe, taking care of you. We have everything under control."

'It has always been like that.'

'Yes,' she said.

'There will be a lot of blame pushed back and forth.'

Cars whooshed by outside.

'But it's not the right ones, where it's being pushed back and forth.'

The smell of orange blossom and jasmine wafted in from the back garden. The wind outside pushed perfume through the cracks.

'Someone else is sitting in a corner giggling while others fight,' he said quietly. 'Many say "Attack is the best defence." So they attack each other. They are afraid of each other. They wanna take advantage of the moment.

'Everybody wants to take advantage of something. Somehow, of course, they know that they all think the same way. So, where's it gonna start? Where will it end? If everybody wants the advantage? I want an advantage and you want an advantage. We attack each other. While someone else is doing things quietly.

Nerida sat quietly. She wasn't sure she wanted to know about this possible terrorist. She asked, 'Are they releasing more of that disease in the world? Or have they stopped?'

'We would say there was another incident not that long ago. They might do it again. At the moment they are kinda scared. They're still watching from a distance. Because it was not confined to the areas where they wanted it to go.

'Those people don't get around very much. So, they don't quite understand how far and how quickly it can be taken to other places. They had some idea but they did not get the full picture.'

'Do they have any conscience about how many people have died?' She asked bitterly.

'They don't care. They are a little scared that someone might find out. That's all.

'They don't care. They think that the rest of the world doesn't care what happens to them. So why should they care for the rest of the world?'

'But even their own people are going to get hurt,' she bridled.

'Yes.'

'They don't care about their own people either?'

M'Hoq Toq sighed. 'Somehow, they do. But somehow they're kept in a different state of mind.'

'They think they're not part of this planet with the rest of us?'

'They feel excluded,' he explained. 'They have been going hungry for decades.'

'Yes.'

'The world did not care.

'People had an idea? They got killed. The world didn't care.

'You understand?'

'I do.' She had an inkling about the people he might be implicating. She didn't want to follow the thought.

'So why should they care for anyone else?' He continued. 'They've been trained in the mindset of 'the survival of the fittest.' You understand? That's how they think of their own people, too.'

Nerida nodded. 'That's how starving people think.'

'Yes.' He looked into it. 'They think people who are not able to produce—or fight, when they have to—don't deserve the food.

They eat the food that someone else could eat—someone more productive. Do you understand?'

'I do. Is there anything else that you'd like to tell me now?'

'This is not the end of the world,' he said. 'There is hope. There is always hope, otherwise we would not come to talk to you.

'We just try to give you little ideas: a little bit of turning your heads so you can look into a slightly different direction.'

He gestured gently. 'Understand that most things you see are the results of something else. People say, "seeing is believing". That's wrong. Because you see what you want to see or what you are meant to see, to make you believe that what you see is true.'

Nerida lived in a country with the world's most concentrated media ownership. Eleven of the twelve major newspapers and outlets were owned by two mind-bogglingly wealthy families. 'Yes.'

'This is the bigger picture,' he said. 'Open your eyes. Try to see the real cause of things.'

'The seeds, so to speak.' *The seeds of trouble or the seeds of something better?*

'Yes.'

'The roots.' *Both.*

'Yes.'

The wind was wild now. Branches scratched and banged on the wooden walls and the metal roof.

'A couple of personal questions now, if I may. I'm having trouble with dizziness.' Sometimes she felt like she'd tip over. It had started in the damp house and persisted. She'd checked her blood pressure.

'Dizzyness?'

'Yes.'

He looked into it. She felt like a pool of clear water as he did so. 'You should eat more substantial food.'

'Like starchy foods?'

'Yes.'

'I felt better after some potatoes today.'

'It's the balance of things. Too much of anything you can think of can turn into poison. Cutting something out is not a solution. You can reduce it but you don't stop it. You need a little bit of everything to keep the balance.'

He looked a little more. She felt his energy flow gently through her.

'There might be some mechanical issue,' he said.

'I should keep working on my back and my neck, then?'

'On this level,' he said, gesturing to chest height with both hands. 'And this.' He moved the hands down over Mari's belly.

'Is it something that's happened since I lost weight? It changed the balance of my body?'

'You're missing part of you.'

'Oh.'

'You did not want to admit that you're missing it.

'You need to be stronger. You made a decision. You made the decision to feel better. You need to adapt to the decision you made.

'You have to realise you're still a complete person. You can keep yourself safe.'

That hits the spot. She had been heavier since her teenage years to keep herself safe. Her fat was about protection. *Now I can protect myself without it. I will trust myself to do so.*

'If your shape has changed, it is still you. You are still the same being.'

Appreciating his tenderness, she thanked him softly.

'You might have issues with one of your arms at times, as well. Somewhere here.' He drew the hand along Mari's right forearm.

Nerida had not told Mari about the inflammation in her arm from typing.

'Same issue. It's kind of a heaviness. We can sense some sort of a heaviness. Not pain.

'But the food you eat should be more healthy.'

'I've been avoiding white flour and sugar. I can fill up with it cheaply. It's hard for me to control my intake of it, though. It doesn't satisfy my hunger. It doesn't help me.

'You can eat things that are grown in a good way, with less treatment. Treating food to look nicer or last longer takes the value out of it. More natural will be a lot better.

210

'You should not go back to these very white things. You can have the natural grains, ground. The end result does not look so nice but it's still good for you.

'Again, it's about the balance. Too much of things are not good for you. If you replace something you have been eating—maybe not even that much—with a big volume of a different kind of food, you'll still be out of balance because you've replaced that lot with another lot.

'If you have a pair of scales: you take a weight off here and put something else there, then you still have imbalance.'

'Thank you. That makes sense. My last question is for my daughter, Ruby and my son-in-law Seb.'

'Yes.'

'I wonder if you have any advice for them. They're having a hard time.' She felt the emptiness of grief in her belly. Had a lump in her throat.

He took a moment, then said, 'It will come back.'

Nerida sighed. 'That's lovely.'

'It was not a good time. This is the quiet before the storm. It would have arrived, that soul, just at the beginning of the big storm. So, it was like, "I'm not doing this."

"I am very eager to come back."'

"Eager to come back?" She took a deep breath.

'Yes. That's what we got.'

'Good.'

'It might not be in the same form. Undecided.'

'About gender?'

'Yes. The gender is undecided. That's why we say 'it'. But the same soul, the same spirit will come back.'

'Good.'

"Can't wait to come back," he conveyed.

Nerida let the light, joyous feeling of that sink in.

'But this is not upon those two. You understand? It's the circumstances.'

'Oh. So, they shouldn't feel like they've done anything wrong?'

'No. They didn't. It was like,' he flung up the hands, '"I'm out of here. This is not a good time."'

'If this larger situation had ended now, they would have stayed. But it's the quiet before the storm. Do you understand?'

'I do. Thank you. That's reassuring.' *Sort of.*

'It will come back. Gender's not important at the moment.'

A small bird landed, bouncing on the branch outside the window. Looked in. Flew off again.

'She would have loved to meet them. But it does not matter because it will come back. Same one.'

'I'm looking forward to seeing that one, too.' She would have been Nerida and Mari's first grandchild.

'It left before it happened,' he said. 'You understand?'

'No.' *Left where? What happened?*

'The soul left before it happened—' he said.

'The soul left before the little body died?'

'—before the physical thing happened,' he agreed. 'The soul left.'

'Aah. So, they didn't suffer.'

'We are not very good with time. Say about one day before, maybe even two days. She might have felt a bit funny.'

'Mhmm.' She thought a moment. 'I had an interesting experience.'

'Yes?'

'I had a pattern in my eyes. I could see rainbows in it. I thought it was coming from my brain because it was in both my eyes, whether I opened them or not. It stayed for quite a while.'

'You had a visit.'

'I thought maybe—'

'You had a visit.'

'Was it Andy?'

'Yeah.'

'Oh.'

'He was trying to tell you that the soul had come.'

'The soul had come to him?'

'Yes. There were a few others around.'

'Oh.' *The little one's spirit was greeted and cared for on the other side.* Tears pricked her eyes and her chest felt tight.

'But you didn't know,' M'Hoq Toq said.

'I wasn't good enough at listening.' *Fear got in the way.*

'He was trying to tell you. Those rainbow colours—that's a sign of hope.'

'It was so pretty. I felt Andy with me. I wasn't afraid when it was happening. But afterwards I was.'

M'Hoq Toq made a beckoning gesture with the smallest finger of Mari's right hand. 'That's what he gave me, with this little finger.'

'Oh? Sweet.'

'We dunno if it's sweet. We just got that.'

Nerida laughed.

'Instead of this,' he beckoned with the index finger, 'he's using that,' beckoning with the pinky. "You don't need to be tall to be powerful." I think that was the message for you.

'So we assume you are not tall.'

'I'm not tall at all, no.' She grinned.

'Yes.' He waited. 'Is there anything else?'

'My sincere gratitude to see you and to be able to talk to you. Thank you so much.'

'You're welcome.'

'I can't tell you how you enrich our lives, all of us.'

'We come to help. I'm not sure if you could call it "enriching."'

'You know what I mean.'

'We don't like to talk about rich and poor. It's like *awakening*.'

The house was quiet. Mari returned slowly from trance with a deep sigh.

'Come back to me, my love,' Nerida said.

CHAPTER 38

Sunday May 3, 2020

After the first week in quarantine Nerida stopped flinching if she started to think 'When I go out,' or 'I'd like to go to—' She looked at her wallet on the dressing table. They weren't going anywhere except to the garden.

The garden was fenced, so Nerida could see the sky without anyone seeing her.

A shady lillipilli dropped hot pink fruits on the artificial grass, creating a mushy feast for flies.

Nerida picked a few fruits each morning, nevertheless, enjoying their tangy taste.

A winding path made the most of blowsy roses and heady jasmine. There was coriander near the back fence, which she plucked for cooking. The mint and parsley died in the drought, burnt by the sun in spite of the early morning sprinklers. A native peppertree, with flowering spikes of darkening berries, reminded her of the hot pink berries on the invasive, beautiful pepper tree she saw in the hospital yard at Newman years ago.

Mari didn't go out. She couldn't cope with the droning flies. And, even if she didn't say so, she was anxious about getting in trouble for being outside. Her taller head would be visible over the fence.

'I wish you would sit out in the sun just a few minutes,' Nerida said. 'You need the vitamin D.' She massaged her wife's tense shoulders, but only hurt her.

On Sunday, Nerida was surprised and grateful when Mari wanted to channel again.

When the spirit came, he spoke softly. 'Hello. Mm. What can we do for you, my friend?'

'Thank you for coming through. I'm afraid it was quite an effort for you.'

'We had it easier at times.'

'Yes.'

Nerida didn't know where to begin.

'We are here now, so—' he said.

'Well, thank you. So, our friend M'Hoq Toq said—'

'Me?'

'Ah. Greetings.'

'You did not recognise us. How come?'

'I'm so easily confused. I have rubbish my head.'

A truck shifted gears outside the front of the house.

'You should work on your attitude,' he said sternly. 'No one has rubbish in their head. That's misguided. You might have less ability to use what you've been given at times. It has nothing to do with, what you call, rubbish.

'Give yourself a little bit more respect.'

'Thank you,' said Nerida softly.

'You're welcome.'

'We were talking about the *awakening*.' She was not entirely convinced about the word, given its use as the newsletter title of one of the evangelical religions. She did her best to connect with the meaning behind it.

'Yes. We do remember all we talked about.'

'Can we talk about that a little more?'

'Which aspect of it?'

'Well, I love the possibility, the hope of us being more connected to each other and to the animals and the Earth'. She still felt flustered about the rubbish in the head gaffe.

'Some of humanity will change the way they think. It follows that they change the way they act, once they understand what is important.'

That's what we're all working towards, change our minds, actions will follow, she thought.

'Others will just vanish,' M'Hoq Toq said, 'somehow.

'It is the quiet before the storm. When there is more of this coming the ones that got stuck in old patterns will be almost shaken to wake up.' He clenched Mari's fists as if shaking a drunkard by the shoulders.

'A lot of them don't want to listen. They don't want to wake up. They are in a dream of what was their former reality: which is something that won't come back. They don't want to wake up from their reality. They consider it to be normal.

'We don't like the word 'normal'. That implies there is a norm to such things. It's not like that.

'They think and see as they used to, which is, to use your modern word, counterproductive.

'They have the wrong goals in their vision. These are 'goals' that won't come back. They will get distressed because they are chasing what they think normality is, what the 'norms' are. But this is changing.

'You've got a break now: to rethink, to, almost, readjust.

He paused, looking into it. She heard cars like the sound of the wind, zooming by outside.

'It has not been long enough. It has not been painful enough to bring a real change.'

Nerida reflected on the pain of those who lost their beloved people in horrible, torturous conditions.

As if he heard her thought, or read her feeling, M'Hoq Toq said, 'It is enough for some: the ones that did not go too far into that way of thinking.

'That way of thinking is all about paper with numbers on it, plastic cards.' He articulated each word with acuity.

'Or that big bubble that they pretend has money in it.

'It's virtual.

'It's a virtual money box, where they take money out that's not really money anymore: papers with numbers.

'We do understand. They are chasing—we can't say in general wrong things. Because for them it seems to be the right thing. It seems to be the one thing that makes everything better.

'In the bigger picture, they should look somewhere else: how can you live better with fellow humans?

'They don't know how to. A lot of them can't even live with the people that are close to them.

'If there's a small problem, they don't try to solve it. They feel attacked. So, they run off in different directions.

'They don't change.

'They don't put effort into things.

'They chase that: what they call 'wealth' because there is a misunderstanding of what true wealth is. They chase it.

'When it does not work out, they don't work on solving problems. They chase something else.

'It needs to be quick, quick, quick! Fast! More!

'And they think they deserve it.

'What they get in return is separation from other humans. Separation from humans that should be close to them, like family, friends. They get separation and it becomes loneliness. They have not learned, or they've forgotten, what it means to work together, to work things out or make it work.

'They don't.

'And when it doesn't work out? They move quickly onto something else—but only if there is no one else to blame.

'Otherwise, they stay on that singular path that they're on and they blame everybody around them. And everybody who's in that field does the same. So, they blame those people, but the other people blame them.

'Mhm.' Nerida felt tenderness and compassion behind his judgement. But the energy in the room was charged as if there was an electrical storm, instead of the bland blue sky, outside.

'It's a wrong kind of 'give and take.' It has nothing to do with compassion, with understanding, with care. Nothing.

'"This is me. I am there in front." He gestured in front of Mari's open chest, her broad shoulders relaxed in contrast to his intensity. "No one else should be there." "Oh, something's not working out. Well, it's their fault over there! Not mine."

'They tell the story of the victim. It's never their fault. And then, they try to change. Like, jumping onto a different train that they think goes faster, in a similar direction.' He shot the hand forward. 'And they are desperate for anything.

'Their ticket to get on that train is: "I have done nothing wrong. All these people around failed me. So, now I'm here to rescue you, to make your train go faster."'

'Mmm.' *I know the type.*

'Which won't happen because this is still the same person with the same goals and the same ideas. They have not learned a thing.

'You understand?'

'I do.'

'And now, it's getting down to pure survival. As we said before, there'll be a point when they realise that you can't eat things in a virtual account. And, even if you have, physically, the paper with the numbers on it, you can't eat it. And people won't swap it—for food, for example—with you. Because it will be useless.

'A lot of water on this planet is not clean anymore. They have done things to it and poisoned it for the future, for the long term—for some short-term gain or paper with numbers it.'

What is the role of the Coronavirus in all this?

'So, to return to that thing that's around at the moment, that tool to learn and understand—' he said, reading her thought. 'It will stay for quite a while. You need to learn to live with it.

'You will never be able to fight it.

'You can find things to lessen the impact. But you can't eradicate it by fighting it. Because it's got a consciousness. It's shifting shape.

'You understand?'

'I do.' *Viruses mutate.*

'But it is possible—'

'To live in a world—' she suggested.

'—alongside that thing.'

'Yes.'

'It takes something like mutual respect,' he explained. '"If I do this or that in the wrong way, it can get me. There is a border I should not step over." But it will go dormant. That's why you can live alongside it. If you step over these boundaries, if you do wrong things, it just comes back again. Because of the consciousness.'

Nerida wondered what those boundaries were. *Surely, he doesn't mean we have to keep apart from each other forever? If our thoughts create reality, is there some kind of moral boundary we cross, some kind of harmful attitude that the virus intersects?*

She tried to imagine how a post-pandemic world would work. 'If we don't have money, we need a more local economy, more local travel. We need a much more local way of living, if we're going to be bartering, without money.'

218

'Look,' he said, 'it will always be possible to travel again.

'But it won't be: "I'm jumping on that airplane. I'm flying—I don't know how many hours—for three days of pure fun, and then returning."

'You will have to select what is important. "What do I want to do there? Is it worth money, time, effort? Is it worth all of this?" Then, it is important.

'Do you understand?'

'I do.'

'So, you will still be able to travel but it will be to a different extent.'

She nodded. 'It needs to be prioritised.' *Perhaps this is the end of tourism, or at least the worst aspects of it: misuse of resources with stubborn ignorance of local cultures. Being sealed off from the experience of the local people for the sake of your own indulgence.*

'Yes.'

'Travel for a purpose. For humane, sustaining values,' she said. Nerida travelled around Asia, from Bangkok to Sumatra and from Kathmandu to Laddakh, as a young woman. It was a formative experience.

'Yes.' M'Hoq Toq said.

'So, travelling to learn, to love, to do good work will still be possible?'

'Yes.'

'Okay. That sounds like a great world, to me.'

M'Hoq Toq explained, 'Some people jump on means of transportation to go somewhere and spend a long time, let's say, numbing their brain with substances. We don't think this way of travelling, no matter the means of transportation, will be valuable to these people anymore.'

'Uhuh.' She thought of tourists on alcoholic binges in Bali now. British youth in Spain.

Her own attempts to numb her brain during adolescent drug experimentation only served to increase awareness of her brain's power in making her miserable when it was unbalanced.

The lovers she had then, including Sam, who became her children's father, were interested in opening the doors of perception, they said. Maybe it was true. Nerida was trying to make herself numb then. She felt too much for the world. And she was bisexual. And Aboriginal. She didn't know how to be in the world. She didn't know anyone like her, yet.

M'Hoq Toq was still looking at the broader human cultures. 'It will become difficult to convince others that traveling for self-obliteration is necessary.

'So, it will be more difficult to do these things. They'll feel like it's not worth the effort.

'Because if you want to numb your mind, your thoughts, your brain with some substances; or even just to numb the body and its feelings—they might as well do it where they are.

'There is no need to go from one side of the world to another for things like this.

'People think about going somewhere else to get their skin burned—will it be worth the effort? Probably not.'

'Good. I was wondering today if we might be living in the end of the period of cruise ships.' She and Mari had watched, appalled, when the *Diamond Princess* was kept docked in Japan, laden with disease as it spread through the ship's ventilation (or was it the catering?) in February.

Then the *Ruby Princess* discharged its passengers, some of them infected, directly into Sydney in March.

'Means of transportation?' he asked.

'Yes. Ships that are as big as an island; sometimes bigger than the islands they visit.'

M'Hoq Toq observed with a distance that made Nerida wondered whether he had looked at cruise ships before. 'They made it so big to pack more people onto it. And it reduced the paper with numbers they had to bring to be part of the experience.

'Some things like that will still be happening, but on a much smaller scale. There will be associated difficulties.

'So, you want to go on this big box to numb yourself and your environment down. Floating around for that? Probably not.

'You wanna go to a place, interact with the people there, learn from them?

'What plants do they have? How do they harvest them? How do they live? Get more insight than comes from snapping a picture—to put on a screen. That will be a valuable thing to do.

'Understand: Why do I want to go there? What can I learn? What can I achieve? And more importantly: What can I bring to those people? And we are not talking about paper with numbers on it.

'We're talking true exchange.'

Nerida nodded. 'Sharing.'

'It should be mutual,' he said.

'Yes.'

'You go there. They come here. No matter where you are.'

'Yes.' Nerida thought of friends in the Pacific. Years before, she and Mari helped Kenneth, a healer from a mountain tribe, travel to a conference with other Aboriginal healers and doctors. The cost and bureaucratic difficulty was enormous.

Pacific brothers and sisters were stuck in their islands, visited by cruise ships but unable to travel to the places they came from. No number of cultural tours, showing his plant medicines, would ever have paid an airfare for Kenneth to travel to one of the wealthier countries on the Pacific Rim.

'There needs to be sense behind what you do,' M'Hoq Toq concluded.

But now she reflected on all the senseless death SARS-CoV-2 brought. Nerida heard in spiritual circles that there were no senseless deaths, that each soul has a say about how and when they leave this life.

She tried reading *The Individual and Mass Events*, Jane Roberts' book of channelled material from Seth. Her understanding was limited. She was living and working in the Cocos-Keeling Islands in the Indian Ocean then.

Maybe he said that souls agree to a certain kind of death, sometimes in a 'mass event,' like an earthquake or bombing, for their own reasons. Usually, they were old souls who wanted to teach. That was her impression. She didn't finish the book. She found the concepts too abstract, too removed from human suffering. She couldn't accept the ideas there. She put the book aside and went fishing instead.

Now she struggled to ask M'Hoq Toq about it. She cried every day reading the news from Italy, Spain, New York.

New York's first case was in March. Over 20,000 people died by mid-April. They were digging mass graves in the parks. Brazil had its first case in February. Now over 6,000 people were dead, many of them Indigenous.

'There've been…more than a hundred and fifty thousand of people have died, already, from the virus,' she said.

'I have the impression that some of those who die are going because their life has reached a kind of a dead end. I guess you can't really generalise, though.' *Do I really think that, or is that a psychological defence?* She felt loss.

'You mean literally?' asked the non-physical being.

'I meant spiritually, that they're not learning anymore and so they leave the planet because they're not evolving.'

He seemed to survey an ocean of spirit. *How does he do that? Is he feeling the vibrations of those hundreds of thousands of souls?*

'Some of them have reached that point,' he said. 'They think, "I need to start somewhere else, again." Or "I've had enough."

'Those are the ones that say, "I'm out of here."

'But then there are others where someone else makes this decision.

'Do you understand?'

She didn't. *Someone else makes a decision about a person's passing? What does he mean?*

'They say, "You don't look like you're still learning." "You don't look like you still have something to contribute." "I feel like you should not be around. You are a burden to others."

'There are those groups. There are two groups. You might find out, further down the track, so to say: if and what happened.

'Not everyone makes their own decision.'

Two groups? Those who decide themselves and those who have others assess whether they live or die?

She asked, 'When you talk about the second group, are you talking about the judgement of those who support them spiritually?' *Does he mean Spirit Guides?* 'They make a decision?'

'No.'

'Oh,' it dawned on her, 'you're talking about people in my profession, doctors?'

'Well, in your profession, similar professions,' he said. 'Look, the mindset is "Are you of worth for the environment?"'

'We would call it "environment." They call it "economy." "So, you don't contribute? Maybe you reached the end of your path in your job?"'

There was a clatter on the wooden verandah and the doorbell rang. It would be their groceries delivered. Nerida ignored it. M'Hoq Toq seemed not to notice.

'Then there are the people considered unable to think by themselves. But they still teach compassion.' There was power in his voice, as if he put his energy behind it.

Footsteps left across the verandah and the front gate clunked closed.

The abuse and neglect of disabled people, using COVID-19 as an excuse. Nerida felt her face wet with tears. 'Yes.'

'They bring understanding and insight into what is important in life. They still teach.' She felt his tender consideration in the insistence.

'For some, that is an inconvenient thing to watch, and it will always be an inconvenient truth.

'Some of these deaths are accidents because there is still no understanding of how this thing works.

'It has consciousness. That's one thing that they don't understand. It is alive.'

She felt him changing the subject. Curiosity lifted her away from grief.

'Instead of going, "Yeah, that's how these kinds of things usually work."' He gestured as if he had a book or computer in front of him.

'They should look in all directions—not the usual one. This usual scientific framework is part of it, but it's a small part of it.

'For healing, you mean?' She was having trouble following.

'No, the way it spreads, the way it reproduces, the way it moves around. Where it tries to 'hide'. We can't really say it's hiding. It doesn't have to because you can't see it.

'But it has favourite spots.

'And they don't understand. This is unusual. This is not what they have been dealing with before. They don't know a thing.'

'Mhm.' *Here we go again. Decimation of scientific certainty. It still irritated her, how the spirits dismissed hard-won knowledge like that.*

But M'Hoq Toq insisted. 'They know a tiny part. And they think they understand it all because "We are the specialists. We are the professionals. We know how it works. We're gonna tell you." You could say they have not done their homework.

'They have to look in all directions available. Look at it with open minds. "Oh, no. It can't be. No, that's the usual path. We stay close to that."' He used the hands to indicate a narrow path, a blinkered approach.

'That thing works in different ways. Not only that one way. And you could say it operates on different levels. It causes different problems: they have not found out what they are yet. There are big surprises coming up.'

'Mmm.' *Sounds dreadful* she thought. But she felt stronger now. 'I had news from colleagues in Italy weeks ago—'

'Yes?'

'At their hospital, anybody over sixty-five, anyone who had a different medical condition, even younger people—they were not treated. They were left to die. They were—'

'That's the problem in your society. People look at numbers.'

'Yeah.'

'If they're printed on paper, if the numbers are in these columns on the paper?

'They should stop this! These sick people, you know, they have professions, they have skills, they can teach others. It is not about a number.'

Of course, he's right. 'Well, the numbers are about this machine, the respirator,' she went on.

'Dangerous.'

'Yes, Bartgrinn told us about that.'

'Yes.'

Nerida persisted. 'But they have the idea that the respirator is the only effective treatment. And because they have a limited number of these machines—'

'They rely too much on machines.'

'Yes. I'm sure of that.'

'The machines are good for a small number of humans,' he said quietly. 'For the majority they are not.

'Your colleagues are helpless, like headless chickens running around. They think the machine is a solution. Or, they think, "We put that information out there, so the rest of humanity won't realise that we have nothing to offer."'

'Yes.' She recognised that. Nerida found herself apologising for the human fallibility of her profession to Mari at times.

Mari would not hear it. She had experience with lying doctors.

The doctor who mangled her foot after her accident was a drug addict and an alcoholic who ran the orthopaedic department at a major European hospital.

It took Mari fifteen years to successfully sue him for the loss of her foot. She sued him, too, for the other people whose lives were destroyed by his lies and deception.

One of the nurses had told her that they used to strap the surgeon into a chair to operate because his intoxication was so severe.

In the pandemic, though, it was not only her colleagues who used half-truths and platitudes. She and her wife saw a lot of alteration and limitation of information—government-run lying.

Watching the news with Mari was exhausting. She raged at the prevarication and cover-ups.

The half-baked public health responses made them argue. 'What's the use of that?' Mari snapped when a football game was shifted to a different city, releasing contaminated sportsmen out of a shutdown.

She refused to accept that entertainment and distraction were government priorities.

That month, Mari's obsession was with the idea that the virus could be spread through air-conditioning systems, when they witnessed transmission in the blighted cruise ships.

'It was in the drinking and washing water, too. The ships pick it up from the same ports,' she also insisted. 'That's not Aedgar's opinion, that's mine.'

Now she stared at the yellow lettering on a red cereal box on the bench. 'Natural energy,' it said. *Focus.*

She wanted to know more about effective treatment. 'Some of the doctors in New York lie the patients down on their bellies. Is that helpful?'

'It's a desperate measure,' M'Hoq Toq said. 'Again, it helps some. For others, they won't even have the time to turn them on that side because it can be so quick.'

'Yes. My colleagues dealing with this illness are overflowing with grief and trauma.'

'They should be. They should be.'

Nerida put her head in her hands. Tiny orange ants made a track on the metal edge of the table.

M'Hoq Toq's fire surged. He spoke emphatically. 'You have learned about healing people. You don't take orders from someone who has not learned how to heal people, who says, "You are a god now. You make the decision."

'Your colleagues should have said, "We don't." "This is not our job."

'A lot of humans would have died anyway, but there would be less, what you call trauma, amongst those people.'

'Yes.'

'This trauma was put on them by people who have no idea, sitting up there saying, "You make the decision because I don't want to."

'It's like sending people off to war. The damage that was done to your colleagues will last longer because they were trained to heal. They're not trained to neglect and kill.'

'Yes.' Tears wet her face again.

'If someone is sent off to war, they are not trained to heal.

'They know what they're getting into. They still have trauma. There is a lot of it. A lot of them have this awakening once they're in the middle of it, like: "What am I doing here? I am taking lives. And I have to expect that someone else takes my life."

'Those colleagues of yours are trained to heal, to make people better.

'Or, to support people, if they want to leave the planet, to do it in dignity. It did not happen. It still doesn't happen. There is still a lot of it and there is more to come.'

Nerida wept. She got up and pulled a box of tissues to the table.

'How can you tolerate a position where you have to make such terrible decisions?' he asked. 'They make a comparison: "Oh, this is what we do when we go to war." This is not a war! Do your job.

'You understand?'

'I do.' Military triage, they called it. She'd been trained in it. *Coloured cards on disaster victims to mark how much effort should go into saving them. A black card means that you're not expected to survive.*

'You don't take orders. You are a healer. You are not a soldier.'

She took a deep breath. He continued.

'There could have been, at least, kindness. By giving people some herbs, for example, or medicines, that reduce suffering. That relieve misery. You still have an obligation to heal. Or try to heal.

'If that is not possible, support them. Help them. You're there to help, not to destroy.

'Letting people slip away in this unkind way—this is not helping. This is refusing to help because you've taken orders from someone who has no idea about your profession and what it is about.'

'Yes.' *It's cruel. People dying from COVID alone, often without medicines that could help them feel better. They don't have palliative care training in the ED or ICU. Might be a nurse or a doctor holding the person's hand, if they're able. If they're not trying to save someone else.*

She sought a healing thought. 'Have the oceans become quieter for the whales?'

'A bit, yes. A bit.'

'Something to be grateful for,' she said.

'Yes, some things in Nature have improved.'

'The air got cleaner in China for a while.' They saw satellite pictures of Beijing emerging from the clouds and dust of brown coal.

'It won't last long because they think they have to make up for what they've lost. They have not learned a thing.

'In the ocean, for example, there is less noise. But there are still points where there is poison released into the ocean. Every day, every night, it's continuing. No one talks about it. No one.'

He's talking about Fukushima. Or nuclear waste from North Korea, she thought.

M'Hoq Toq acknowledged, 'Some people see, "Oh yeah, there is that problem!"

'Then those who have no idea about anything but seem to make big decisions, they say, "We have other problems now to handle."

'For them, the virus is not a tool to learn, it's an excuse: "We don't do anything about that poison now. We're busy with other things." Which is not true. Tricky people are in these positions. They do what they like. They try to get the maximum out of it while it is going.'

'Yes.'

'But it will come back. It will get some of those ones. It has already gotten some. But it will get a lot more of them.'

Does he mean that the consciousness of the disease is that of a worthy avenger? That can't be so.

'Can I clarify: this virus was not something that the Earth or that Spirit on a higher level, some people call it God, has planned to make things better or to make a breakthrough?'

M'Hoq Toq sighed. 'You can't say a god or God. People following religions will misunderstand this.'

'Yes.'

'It will be denied. They will hate anyone who says that.'

'Yes.' *Fair enough*, she thought. *Gods are supposed to be good to the people who believe in them.*

M'Hoq Toq explained. 'It's the collective rise of the energy. A lot of people, especially young people, decided, kept saying, "It can't go on like this."

'Then some stupid human, a group of humans, did create this thing. They released it. It was not supposed to go that far. They lost control. It developed consciousness.

'But the energy level had risen. The people's feelings were, "There needs to be change. It can't continue like this." So, there is some sort of—hmm—thought that "You might as well use part of that vessel to change things."'

Nerida raised her eyebrows. She spoke slowly, 'The release of the virus intersected energy that was on the rise already—'

'Yes.'

'—and we face what was created out of—'

'Yes.'

'The intersection of those separate situations. They came together and that's what happened.'

'That's the part that gave it consciousness,' he said.

'So, even though it seems like a devil, there's not really any devil, is there?'

'No.'

'In a way, it's part of Nature,' she said.

'Yeah, it's the collected energy of all the ones that want a change. But they will not understand, you know?'

'I don't—'

'It will be like, "No. I did not want to kill all these people."

Is he talking about the ones who longed for change? Of course, they would feel that way.

'A lot of the people died of neglect. They did not die of the disease.'

'Yes.' She stopped then. The sadness of the deaths and deprivation in the nursing homes crept up again. The crushing loneliness.

M'Hoq Toq said, 'All these young ones fighting for a better world, for a future, for cleaner air, cleaner oceans, all of that—'

'Mhmm.'

'—no one hears about them now. The only things you see or hear at the moment are little things that amuse people. Or that tool out there.'

It was true. There was no news except about the Coronavirus. And kitten videos had thirty million views.

'Someone picks what they want people to hear about. It's the same everywhere,' he continued. 'People still think and care about the environment. But you're not told. Because these tricky ones—of low intelligence, as our friend says—are clearing a path for all the ones that don't care about the environment at all.

'Everyone is busy—and distracted. They use that situation as an excuse, "We don't do anything else at the moment. We have other problems." They feed to everyone else the idea that there is nothing going on but that tool. Many people believe that, while the tricky ones are doing other things behind closed doors.

'The effect of what they do spreads out like—you don't like the wildfire in this country—like wildfire. Under cover of that tool.'

While SARS-CoV-2 destroyed people's lives, the South Australian premier approved sonic testing for mining. Sonic booms would kill fish and torture the cetaceans. Thousands of square kilometres throughout the Spencer Gulf were to be seismically pounded for undersea mining of gold and uranium. The prospect of it drove Mari to distraction.

She scowled. 'Fuckers. These low-lifes have no idea what they're doing. It's all about the money they're gonna make now. They don't care about the future. They think they're not gonna be there.

'They have the special cuttlefish that come there every year, you know.

'I guess they wanna kill off all the white sharks and tunas and all that disgusting sea-life. So then, all the marine life's gone. None of those yucky fish. "We can use it as a dump. Out of sight, out of mind, you know?" Like they used to do in the Maldives when they tied up all the rubbish with rocks and threw it out to sea. And then when the plastic broke down a bit it all floated up again.

'Only these ones will have more sophisticated poisons. Like nuclear waste to dump in the ocean.'

Nerida understood her pain. Mari was more comfortable underwater than she was on dry land. It amazed and delighted her, how comfortable her wife was in the sea.

'There's so much we don't know about it,' Mari said. 'Food and medicines there, too. It makes my blood boil that they think it doesn't matter if they destroy it.'

Mari noticed coal mines begun or reopened, and coal-fuelled power stations, due to be closed, given new leases by Federal politicians.

'Everything they ever wanted to do, to get away with, they do it now,' she railed.

The Prime Minister mooted a 'gas-led recovery,' determined to drain every last drop of gas from under the earth and the seas around Australia.

And from East Timor to the northeast, where an Australian fossil-fuel company stole a million dollars a day from the poorest country in the world.

In America, the president was opening doors to massive exploration and mining of decomposed plants and animals as fuel. Mari noticed. And made sure her wife was aware, too.

Sometimes Mari's tirades drove Nerida to a frenzy of irritation, 'What do you want me to do about it? How do you think I could fix that up?' She knew it was unfair. *Too exhausted looking after sick people. Too burnt out to be a reasonable human being. I've gotta get an easier job*, she thought.

M'Hoq Toq went on. 'Once there is a break, when it's gone dormant, people will say, "Oh, what happens here?" They will be told, "It's too late now. We did this a long time ago."'

'They've removed controls on polluters,' Nerida concluded.

'Yes.'

'They've opened the way for heavier use of fossil fuels.'

M'Hoq Toq nodded slightly, made a small sigh. 'Yes. At the moment no one wants it. No one needs it. It's not worth anything.

'There are some that buy a lot of it and put it somewhere. They think, "We'll get back to that point where it will all be the same again." They don't know that it will never happen.

'Oh.'

'Not the way they know it.'

Nerida thought of the tanks of oil stored at the coast. She would rather it stayed in the ground because it probably had a purpose there. *But if it was never burned that would be great.* 'That's a consolation.'

'Yeah.'

She felt better.

'They do think, "Yeah, we've got it all. And when people need it again, we'll change the value of it. That's how we get back what we invested." They have squandered what humanity paid to them for *good* uses,' he said darkly.

'That's right. They're not doing useful things with it.' She thought of all the working people who made things, maintained them, grew them. The fruits of their labour and the taxes they paid being wasted by insatiable, greedy gamblers.

'No. They're short-sighted,' he said. 'They think it's going back to what it was. They will try. It wakes up again.

'There is either a waking up of humanity, of the majority, or it's the waking up of the tool that's about at the moment. It will go like this.

'You still haven't learned enough? Here we go again.'

Nerida tried to process the idea that there could be some kind of justice in the world.

'Do you understand?' he asked.

'I'm beginning to understand. Thank you.'

'Good.'

Nerida shifted on her wooden chair. 'I'm planning to put these conversations in a little book.' *I have to share this*, she thought.

'You have to be careful. You can put it out there. You can. Don't say, "This is the truth." We are at a point where we can say, "This is what's gonna happen." But there are different aspects to the situation. It can develop into something not quite like it. It will be similar.

'Yes.'

'We can't say exactly what's gonna happen. But we can give you the direction it is moving towards.'

'I understand. You look at the seeds. You describe the tendency.'

Nerida consulted the *I Ching—the Chinese Book of Changes*. She'd done it since she was twenty.

Her father gave her a copy of the book when she was mentally ill from taking too many experimental chemicals. She still smoked bongs then. She'd get stoned, throw the coins and accept the judgement of the ancient book.

The book was good at saying no, and some its Confucian ideas about women were obnoxious. She argued with it. Threw the coins again until she could accept the answer.

It was a way of studying when her concentration was poor. She and Sam had no money then, either. No television. Little food.

Thirty years later, she still threw the coins and drew the hexagrams, consulting the book sometimes to help untangle a knotty problem.

She understood the concept. 'And that's because nothing is preordained. We always have a choice about how we respond to things.'

'Yes. That's right. You have a choice. Your colleagues should have used their choice. So, make sure you are very careful. Your colleagues will hate you if you are not careful.

'I understand.' She took a deep sigh.

'Is there anything else you'd like to say?' she asked.

'What would you like to know?'

'Do you have any advice for Mari and me going back up to the Kimberley, to work in the valleys around the river?'

'Geographically, we think it's a good place to be in these times,' he said. 'You have to be careful with some of the people around.'

'There are some rough people there,' she agreed.

'Yes. They will not harm you. But some of them can be very…testing.'

Nerida laughed. 'Yes.'

'You need to be sure that they don't think you come from somewhere that you've got everything they need.'

'Mhmm.'

'Make sure you don't give anyone any ideas about what you might have or what you don't have.'

'What do you mean?'

'Don't show what you have. Don't give anyone ideas of what you have by saying, "Oh, I don't have this or this." They will assume you have everything else: "You need those five things? So, you must have the twenty other things that we want." "If that's all you're looking for, I can get what I need from your other things."

'If someone says, "I don't have cheese or fresh fruit," you could say, "Oh, yeah, wouldn't it be good to have it? I don't have it, either." You understand?'

'I do.'

'If you say, for example, "I wish I had wine and cake and jewellery," you know? Then they will think, "Ah. She's got meat and flour and new shoes," and other things.

'Mhmm.'

"Because she's asking for something that we could never afford in the first place."

'Yes. Thank you. We'll keep ourselves grounded. People are materially very poor in that area.'

'Yes. It's always good to say, "I don't drink. I don't smoke."'

'Mhmm.' That was easy because it was true.

'"And I'm eating cheap food because I can't afford anything else." You know? "But there are days when it's not enough." Because that's the same level that they are living on.'

'And I understand. I have lived that way, certainly.'

She lived for years with limited, cheap food for herself and her kids. She remembered days at university when an apple and crackers in her bag were all she had to eat.

'Yes. But it's not something you would tell them. "Oh, I've lived that way, too." Because that would imply that you don't…'

'It will give them the feeling of jealousy or envy: Don't.'

'Yes, thank you.'

There was a lull. One of the neighbours was moving bins in from the kerb. She heard the banging around.

'Is there anything else we can do?' He asked gracefully.

'I'm afraid I need to let you go.' Mari would be ready for her dinner and tiring from the hard kitchen chair.

'Oh.'

'Thank you so much for coming and for all your teaching.'

'So, we'll talk to you another time, then.'

'I look forward to it.'

'You might recognise us,' he said with the trace of a smile.

'I hope so.'

There was a long deep quiet then. Mari's head looked heavy. Her chin fell onto her chest. She returned with a sharp intake of breath.

'Hello darling.' Nerida said softly.

'Hey.'

'Well done.'

Mari sighed, as if relieved that the channeling must have worked.

'You must be very hungry.' Nerida touched her shoulder. Her wife had nothing but coffee all day.

'Nope.'

'Come and have some dinner, anyway. I need to take a Vitamin C.'

'Yep. Good idea,' Mari said.

CHAPTER 39

Fitzroy Valley Hospital, WA

Monday May 25, 2020

The hospital doctors were having their morning meetings outdoors, a concession to the threat of the virus. No one was wearing masks, though, unless they were in the Coronavirus testing rooms, because every patient with respiratory symptoms was sent there.

Which worked, until it didn't. On her first day, working in town, Nerida was asked to see a lady about her chronic disease script. The woman came in sweating and coughing.

Nerida, not sure what to do, left the room to find the protocol for a patient with obvious viral symptoms. By the time she returned the patient had left. The woman had entered the hospital by stepping around security at the front entrance when another patient was collapsed there, and the security guard and triage nurse were distracted.

Dr Khumalo was just back from South Africa, where, the nurses said, one (or more) of his relatives had died of COVID-19. Nobody had expected him to come back to Fitzroy Crossing. Nerida was delighted to see him. He wouldn't touch elbows with her, though. 'I don't do that,' he said. 'I'll shake hands or nothing at all.'

Nerida figured her colleagues were just like her. Traumatised and anxious. All trying their best to figure out how to respond to the threat of the pandemic. To care for people, keep them safe and not get sick themselves.

Dr Nerida worked long days at the community clinics around the valley throughout the week. It was satisfying to help people feel better, but it was emotionally exhausting. Mari kept her going, buying and preparing food and washing fine red dust from their linen and the floors every day. On the weekends they drove out to see the country. Mari took photos to inspire her drawings and paintings.

That Monday evening Nerida came back from work through the laundry door. She peeled off her clinic clothes. She scoured herself. Even her watch and earrings. She washed her hair every night. The towel and bathmat went into the machine with her scrubs. Only then, she embraced her wife, smiling into her chest, relishing Mari's strong embrace.

That night it rained.

Frogs sprouted in the puddles outside their small metal house. She heard them up the shower drain.

'They keep croaking, "Greg, greg, greg," that's all I heard,' Mari said. Nerida's cousin-brother Greg was gorgeous, with eyes as dark green as malachite. Eyes the wrong colour for the desert, skin dark enough to draw attention in the city. She looked at Mari with tenderness. To see her imagining something supportive in her environment was as refreshing as the rain.

'Where is he lately? Do you think the frogs mean he'll come and see us?' Mari asked.

'Last I heard, he was still in northern Queensland. But you know Greg. He could be in Nepal. Or Costa Rica.'

Mari was cooking pork ribs. She opened the oven bag to allow them to crisp up. A wave of aromatic heat filled the room. 'Do you want beans with the pork? Or do you want me to make a salad?'

'I don't know. Just do what you want to. I'll enjoy whatever you make.' Nerida had no decision-making juices left.

'France found out that their first COVID-19 case was infected in December, so it was there months before they thought it was,' Mari reported.

'Hmm. That's interesting.' Nerida was clicking through the channels on the tv. She settled on a game show where people answered multiple choice questions for a chance to make a machine push coin-shaped tokens over a step to win money. She sat and stared at it.

'So it was already around in December. And Kim Jong-Un sent a message to that Chinese bastard—'

'Xi,' said Nerida.

'Yeah. Sent him a message congratulating him on what a great job they did on COVID.'

'As if it was him that did any of the work,' Nerida said. A contestant just missed pushing the star token, worth ten thousand pounds, over the step.

'Those assholes crucified that Chinese doctor who blew the whistle.'

'The one who died in February, yeah.' Another contestant jumped for joy as the star token dropped.

'I marinated that chicken. We'll have it on Wednesday.'

'Thanks.'

'Rwanda has been given robots to screen for Coronavirus. They take people's temperature and video them coughing.' Mari put potatoes into the oven around the ribs. The house filled with a steamy cloud.

'Smells delicious in here,' Nerida said.

'There are five robots. They can give medicine or bring food to people with COVID, too,' Mari said.

'That sounds horrible. And ridiculous.' Nerida muted the television. She couldn't stand the shouting on the ads.

The smells and sounds of Mari's cooking cheered her, though. So what if they stayed in a house less than ten square metres? It was up off the ground. Snakes didn't come in. It had electricity and a cooler, food in the fridge and a television that worked when it wasn't too stormy.

North-western Australia's Kimberley region was a dramatic landscape of sinuous rivers, grassy plains and towering red cliffs, buttes and mesas. Mari went out with her tripod and camera when she got restless. Suddenly she was patient, out on the savannah or at the gorge. Still. Waiting for the light to change, murmuring to the birds and kangaroos.

Nerida saw the country and animals travelling to different clinics in the Valley every weekday. Sometimes she and the nurses drove for hours to get to and from a clinic. Other days they flew in a small plane. She saw the cracks in the grey planes, the reduced, muddied waterholes with animals trying to drink from them.

'The puddles will be dried and gone by the morning. The clouds are scattered,' she said. 'I saw the rain coming down in patches on the horizon.'

Mari finished making a salad, covered the bowl. 'The pork will need another hour or so. I'll put it on low. I could channel now if you like.'

CHAPTER 40

Monday May 25, 2020

An offer to channel on a Monday was rare.

Nerida set up her recorder and found her notebook.

She felt a rush of energy as Aedgar spoke up, sounding chipper. 'Hello.'

Nerida grinned. 'Hello.'

'Oh,' he said, as if surprised. He seemed to take in where they were. 'What can we do for you, my dear?'

'Thank you for coming.'

'You're welcome. Wasn't as easy as we wish it would be.' He kept the eyes closed, she noticed.

Mari's eyes must be dry. 'Our friend is tired,' she said.

'Yes. It's a bit difficult to get in. Something in the neck—' he gestured, 'out of balance.'

Nerida spoke now of what kept her awake at night. 'Our friend Bartgrinn said that children were not so susceptible to COVID-19 because of their mitochondria—that the virus could pretty much pass through them without affecting them.'

'Well, it affects some of them,' Aedgar conceded. 'But calling it a passing through…' Mari's long fingers moved like a breeze, 'is a wonderful description. Sometimes, in passing through, it gets stuck in problem zones within that body.

'Otherwise, it does pass through, pushing the sickness on to other people.'

She heard the smack of a ball on the road, the thud of a kick, excited shouting in one of the local Aboriginal languages. Children played in the early evening while tea was being cooked.

'These perfect little vessels,' Aedgar mused. 'Everybody likes to touch them.'

Nerida felt the glow of a little child's sweetness.

'And hug them,' he said. 'We would say, not advisable.'

Nerida crossed her arms over her chest. Her forearms felt damp under her warm hands.

'If you have your own group of germs,' Aedgar said, 'and you live with that specific group—it's kind of alright. You might call it 'family,' we can call it 'group of germs'.

Nerida blinked.

'If the children go outside and mingle with others, they come back and pass the virus on. You can stay within your germ group. Not much happens. But that could change drastically if you make those little things expose you to other germ groups. The little ones won't know. They're fine. They don't show it that much.

'It affects them in a different way.

'Some of them who have issues in their little bodies—it will attach to those. And then it can get rapidly worse: first a little bad and then rapidly worse. And some of them won't recover.'

'Yes.' Nerida's shoulders tensed. 'We've had reports from India and New York. A few children have died. Some children have been born with the virus.'

Aedgar inclined the head. 'Yes. Some get it passed on through the mother. It depends on how long she was exposed to it.'

'You could call it a conglomerate of viruses,' he said.

The scientist in her was intrigued.

'They're in groups, clusters. It's not a single one—there are a few of them, with little tweaks, that have evolved in a different direction. It can be fatal quickly, depending on the combination of those.'

'Yes.' Now Nerida felt sick in her stomach. But her anxiety drove her to know about the mutations.

'Your peers are looking for one,' he said. 'They are related—it came from that same germ cluster, or family. But they evolved. They got tweaked in different directions.

'The base is still the same.' He reached out Mari's hands. 'But the "little hands" that touch it to others, on the outside, go in different directions.'

'Hmm. The receptors on the virus are changing?' she asked.

'Yes.'

Nerida reflected. 'That changes a lot. That changes the way it's transmitted. It can change who is susceptible to it. It could change the effects of it.'

'Yes. Yes. And it depends on the host. Their predispositions determine how it will turn up.

'If someone has kidney problems, it will make that a lot worse. They don't get that cough. They don't get the lung problems at all. It just attaches to the weak parts in your body.'

Nerida feared for her clients with kidney disease. Feared for herself, too. *I'm going to miss it. Someone could die because I don't recognise it.*

But even if she recognised COVID, what could she do? They had no treatment. *The hospital doctors didn't diagnose Viktor with it, even if he had all the symptoms.*

Like her other seriously ill patients at Yulara back in February, he didn't fit the criteria for testing, then. He hadn't returned from China, hadn't been in contact with someone else diagnosed with COVID-19.

If she thought that one of her renal patients might have SARS-CoV-2, she could hardly tell the emergency doctors that it could present that way… because a spirit told her so.

'It can sit inside the body for quite a while,' Aedgar continued, 'without being detected. If you have a small load within a body, you can't detect it. You can only detect it once it's replicated and changed already.'

'Oh, really?' *A mutation needs to build up to be discoverable?*

'Yes. That's what happens in the so-called "silent spreaders." They have no issues. They have the so-called base model within them, which spreads, of course.

'But because of the very low load of the virus within the body and the blood—the things that can be tested—or on the mucous membranes, you know, you can put that test in, and you could go next to it.' The spirit's precise articulation seemed to mock the precision she aspired to when taking a swab.

'Because it could just be on the other side of the throat, or wherever, and the test will show you it's not there at all.'

He paused a moment, letting her take that in. *There are false positive results from the PCR test we're using for COVID. People could not have the virus and test positive.*

But her colleague, an infectious diseases nurse, had told her the PCR was a very good test. *Here's Aedgar directly contradicting the current science. Again. Like when he said the virus can penetrate the skin. There's no evidence of that.* She hated the image he gave her of the virus nesting in the pharynx a millimetre away from the tip of her swab.

'It's got consciousness. We wouldn't go so far as to say it's hiding.' Aedgar lifted an eyebrow. 'But it's a bit like that. It's keeping a low profile, you might say. It's sitting there, waiting for a chance.'

That feels sinister, the way he says it, she thought.

She changed the topic. 'People are more concerned about the economy. At least, the ruling class is more concerned about the economy now than the sickness.'

Aedgar's energy felt intense. He said, 'They better be concerned. They better be. It's gonna turn into a major problem, this economy. But the values of the majority of humankind turned into a wrong direction—'

'Yes.'

'—quite a while ago. Long time ago.'

'You can't continue like this. The planet will shake you off like little parasites.

CHAPTER 41

Same Place

Still Monday Night

'People could have realised that—looking at Nature and the environment around you—you are not needed.

'You are—hmm—tolerated, rather.'

Superfluous was the word in Nerida's mind.

'So, you're tolerated. You push it too far, you'll get shaken off,' he continued. 'There will be a lot of combinations of natural events, we might call them, coming up.'

Through tight lips, she accepted this. 'Yes.'

He makes 'combinations' of disasters sound almost poetic. He's so far from the suffering of people smothered in mudslides or scorched by bushfire. Or the poor buggers that have to drag them out.

The spirit went on. 'And it will be a combination because humankind needs a lot more than these little viruses to see what they have done, to be able to change the way they think.'

Nerida felt apprehensive. Deep inside, she felt he was right. *Is there such a thing as karma?* She'd asked Aedgar that before. He had said, 'Not really.' *This is not the Spanish Flu and it's not the Spanish Inquisition either*, she reminded herself.

'You have to adapt.'

'Yes.'

'Humankind has to learn to adapt to a fresh way of living—'

She felt hope rising. 'Mhmm?'

'—which is an old way.'

'Yes.'

'We can put it like that.'

'Yes.' She sighed softly.

'It won't go back to the caveman.'

'Uhuh.' She was relieved.

'But it's a different way. Accepting Nature and not trying to mould Nature. Stop trying to push Nature into that mould, you know? Because you are just tolerated. You're not the master of

Nature, or this planet, or the Universe. You're not. This needs to be understood.'

Sometimes Nerida wanted to ask Mari, *How do you wake up to this, as I did so many years ago? Believing you are one singular entity—then sliding, like a manta ray in the water, into this understanding of 'we' and 'ours.' An awareness so many have to journey through death to experience.*

We two she thought, *are like a thumb and an index finger on the one hand, always a whole other structure standing close by, part of us, and between us.*

She was ashamed sometimes, of her hard edges, stuck in time, in her vessel. Jealous too of the frictionless ease the channel had— the shrugging off of body and everything that continuity brought. *We have never discussed who has the most demanding of the visions. I always say, 'It's not a competition.'*

The frogs had stopped croaking outside. Wind rattled the metal walls of their hut. She could smell rain in the dust blowing under the door. 'There's a big storm heading to this part of the island,' she said.

'Yes, we can feel the ions. It will do quite a bit of damage,' Aedgar agreed.

'It's done a lot of damage already, that storm—' She saw it on the weather reports Mari insisted on watching.

'Yes.'

'In India and Bangladesh.'

'That's a different one,' he corrected.

'I beg your pardon.' She respected his authority on questions about global weather.

'It's different. Well, they are related. It's a kind of teamwork, you might call it.'

'Okay. Between the storms?'

Aedgar nodded. 'They originated in the same part of the ocean.'

'Uhuh. Do storms have consciousness?'

'Yes.'

'Can you tell me what their consciousness is like?'

'Usually, storm consciousness was that of moving rain into an area where it was needed.

'But humankind has done a lot of damage to the planet. So, it's a bit like: "Where do we go first? There is rain needed in all these areas." The storm feels: "Maybe we make it a little bigger, stronger." But then, sometimes the measure taken is not quite right.

'You have changed the magnetic field of this planet already.'

'Humans have?' Nerida felt her throat tighten.

'Yes. This is part of what's going on. Ions in the storm—the way they move and where they're supposed to go—those things have been changed. How do we put it?'

He sighed. Considered. 'You used to have storms and winds generated over the equator?'

'Yes.'

'They went all the way around.' He made a sweeping circle with Mari's right hand. 'There was a rhythm to it.'

Nerida knew the magnificent monsoon. Built by the sky-piercing Himalaya, pouring down through the flooding valleys, filling the Indian rivers and drenching the steaming plains. Then overland to Bangladesh and Myanmar. And sweeping across the sea to Malaysia and Indonesia, filling the rice paddies with jumping ice-water, bending and lifting the leaves of the dark green tropical plants. In the Pacific, too—they had lived there—bending the coconut palms, battering the bats in the breadfruit tree.

'Yes,' she said.

'Tampering with the magnetic field has interrupted that rhythm,' he said. 'You have gaps where nothing happens.'

There in northwest Australia—*there was no rainy season last year. The plains were fissured and ashen before the rains finally came, late.*

Aedgar continued, 'And then you have, behind the gap, something building up a lot stronger and a lot faster and then going along… People have times when there is no wind and then it's followed by a tremendous storm.'

There were floods across the plains and in the valleys when the rains finally came.

Aedgar almost whispered, 'It's—hmm. We don't know how to put it.'

Nerida waited with a quiet mind, as she'd learned to do.

Eventually, he said gently. 'We don't think that humankind is ready to understand this.'

'Okay,' she whispered.

'Not yet.'

'Okay.' She sighed.

Aedgar seemed to resume his thought about the magnetic field. 'If we can put it in a way that's not scientific—'

Nerida smiled at the non-physical being occupying her wife's body who apologised for story telling or myth-making. As an Aboriginal woman, she understood that science often lay within the old stories.

Aedgar gently straightened the spine. 'Change to the field interferes with what you call climate. It interferes with a lot more things, too. There are 'cracks' in the Earth: above the surface, below the surface and below the ocean.'

Hang on. There are cracks above the Earth? In the atmosphere? It could be true. Holes in the ozone layer. She knew about the rifts, the chasms and volcanoes deep in the sea where the vents gave life to strange, blind creatures.

'With the rhythm of the movement changed,' he said, 'these cracks move. With changes in temperature. They get wider. They get narrower again. You have to see it as *breathing*.'

Nerida sensed his compassion for the blue planet. No matter what dreadful calamities he described, or how angry he was, she felt his love. *For what? For All That Is.* 'Yes,' she said.

'When that crack opens under the sea, the ground widens, then it pushes back together again, which forces an enormous wave up. And the ground comes up from both sides, making the interference even worse—the interference with that rhythm that used to be there.

So the changes in climate cause changes in geology, that create earthquakes and tsunami and disturb the climate further, she thought. Nerida felt giddy. 'Can I ask a question?'

'Yes.'

'The rains come once a year here. They didn't come last year. When Mari and I were here earlier this year, the rains did finally come. There were some floods. After they abated, the country greened up. The animals got fatter. Everything felt better. Is it that monsoon rain that's being delayed or missed? Is that an example of upsetting the rhythm?'

'The gaps. That's the gaps,' he said. 'When the rains don't come at all. The rain goes all the way around the planet.' The hands flew in a circle.

'And it used to be in that rhythm. But now you have bigger gaps.

'And after that gap you have the buildup. That could mean that nothing happens for (as you call it) one year, two years.'

Nerida murmured, understanding. The buildup, waiting for the rain in Northern Australia, was a hot and tense, humid and stagnant, time. People hurt each other. The suicide rate went up. There were too many serious car accidents. Too many funerals.

'And when that longer buildup finishes and the water finally comes, it's so much stronger than the soil and the animals and plants. They can't handle it.' He spoke tenderly.

'Yes.'

'They're not strong enough. They get washed away.'

She saw it in her mind's eye: cattle corpses swept down the flooded river; bloated bodies of roos; ancient trees uprooted and tumbling.

Aedgar said, 'And they were weakened already because they were missing out.'

Nerida softly agreed. The drought caused skeletal, drought-stricken livestock. Birds on the roads looked for dew in the roadside ditches.

'And then this huge load comes,' he continued. 'When that storm comes, gigantic trees will go like tiny twigs. The rain and the wind push. Even if the rain is deep, the ground is too dry to let it through. It washes the soil that would be fertile away. It will take a long time to rebuild that soil.'

Nerida sighed.

'We would say you just have to live with bigger storms, more interruptions. It would take many, many lifetimes to make subtle changes.

'You don't want to continue the way you did. I'm talking about humankind.'

Nerida agreed, feeling deflated. But it gratified a stronger part of her. *What he says is true. We couldn't go on the way we'd been.*

'The thing is,' he pushed on, 'there is that thought: "We will go back to what we think is normal."'

Nerida took a deep breath.

'You won't.' He said simply. 'Individuals talk about "a new normal." But they talk within their own understanding of what they call "the new normal." Which is *more control.* More control and interfering with particular groups of people.

'Interfering with Nature—trying to. You can't control Nature; you can just interfere. Mostly in a harmful way.

'If something gets a little better, they think, "Oh yeah, we can go back to what we've done before." This is not how it works. Move forward.

'Change the way you live. Change the way you do things. Think ahead. Think differently.'

Nerida heard cockies and crows calling and cawing outside, agitated by the coming storm.

'If people did things two hundred years ago, and it's still taught in a similar way, at what you call a University, then you can't learn new things,' Aedgar said. 'They should encourage innovative ways of thinking. Think about solutions to problems. You have to *begin solving problems.*

'Humankind created these problems.

'Now, you must take a few steps back—quite a few—to think differently. Because now the time that you could have used to learn new things to solve old problems—'

Is lost? Nerida wondered. *Could time be lost?* It certainly felt like it.

'Problems don't go away because it's a different year, it's a different government, it's a different whatever. The problems will still be there until people sit and talk together and try to find solutions, together.

'If everybody, in every corner of the world, thinks "This is not my problem," well, think again. Because it is.

'It's not right to think, "Never mind. That's far away." Problems created on the other side of the planet will affect you. If they have flooding there, you might not get the floods. You might get the earthquakes that are related to that.' He showed the planet as an imaginary ball between the hands, proposing a connection between trouble in, say, the Amazon Basin, and a corresponding but different disaster in the Philippines on the other side.

'You might not get all the storms. You might get a tsunami that's created by this storm on the other side of the planet. Which was generated, in its turn, by the earthquake over there.

'Everybody's suffering. Everybody suffers differently.

'But it's all related to the same problems.

'Humankind: you have created it.

'Solve it.

'Work on it.

'It's quite late down the track.

'You've been hurtling down that track. More is not better. Less is more. Less and better quality.'

CHAPTER 42

Same Place with a Storm Coming

That Night

Nerida got up and opened one of the small windows. She breathed in the smell of ozone from the lightning around. 'May I ask a question?'

Aedgar sounded weary, but said, 'Yes, please.'

'How did it come to pass that we have moved the magnetic field? How did we create a change in the Earth's magnetic field?'

'By digging up things—'

'Ah.'

'—that are not supposed, were never supposed, to be dug up.'

'Oh.'

'You also change the magnetic field by the electromagnetic rays you put up there. You put up satellites. You call them "satellites," but a real satellite has an attachment to something. These buzz around like a swarm of locusts. Creating signals which interrupt what was naturally there.

'It's not completely interrupted, but they *interfere*. So, the magnetic field is shifting. It has shifted before. But not at that speed.'

'Right.' Nerida leaned forward. Her chair creaked.

'There was always a little movement. We would call it adjustment. Because the Earth was not always at the same angle, as you know. The magnetic field helped with the adjustment. But you interfered with it. You might call that a very negative adjustment.' His tone was acerbic.

'Mmm. So, that's happened recently?'

'Yes.'

'In the last hundred years?'

'Yes.'

Nerida imagined Sputnik, the first space satellite, launched by the Soviet Union eleven years before she was born.

Aedgar said, 'Less than that. We might put it at the last forty.
There was quite an impact in the last forty to fifty years.

'We are not good with time, as you know.

'How can you be good at something that does not exist?'

'I have another question about time,' she said.

'Time. Yes. What would that be?'

'Einstein talked about a relationship between time and space and matter.'

'Yes.'

'Which implies that Time has dimension. But I understand that Time exists, but it has several dimensions to it, in the same way as space does.' She carefully watched a documentary about Einstein's work that week and wanted to compare what she understood to what Aedgar had told her before.

'Yes. It's infinite. You tried to measure it and made it finite.'

'Oh.'

'Because you need to have everything measured to have control. You can't control things. You can participate. Control is out of this equation.'

Nerida smiled ruefully. 'Mmm.'

'It's a multidimensional thing. We don't call it Time. Because for you, time is what it takes from here to there.' He gestured a line, chopped at each end.

'Uhuh.'

'But really, it is what it takes from here to here—' he held one hand up at an angle, above Mari's head '—to here, to there, to there and there, everywhere.' He extended the hands in every direction. *It reminds me of the way we check a person's visual fields, whether they can see in every corner* she thought.

'You haven't found a way to measure these things,' Aedgar said, 'It will not happen for quite a while because you have to take part in other things.'

Nerida understood him to mean that there were important lessons to learn before humans were ready to understand time.

'You should have other priorities,' he said.

'Yes,' she said, determined not to feel abashed for trying to expand her knowledge of metaphysics.

She felt ready to resume learning about the grim reality of the work in clinics and hospitals. *What does Aedgar offer that might save lives or suffering?* 'So, speaking of other priorities…'

'Yes.'

'—we've talked about using the iron lung machine to help people with COVID to breathe.'

'It would have been a more sensible way,' he said.

He sounds regretful. If I had found a safe way to get that idea about, it might have saved lives.

'We talked about a flower with a root that could help to fight the virus,' she said.

'Yes.'

'Are there any other aspects of the care of people with COVID, individually, that you'd like to share?'

Aedgar paused, as if to consult or consider. 'Well, by "the care," you mean the care of people who are really caught up with it?'

'Yes.'

'The best care you could think of is not to get in contact with it in the first place. This sounds difficult, we know.'

He seemed to take a moment to consider what he, or they, wished to convey. 'It stays within the body. It goes to sleep. Comes back. And it can survive for a very long time. We would say it's a bit like what you call the Zoster.'

'Ah, yes, er,' said Nerida. *Horrible herpes. That sleeps in a nerve for years, then bursts out into blistering shingles or genitals from hell.*

Aedgar said, 'You either have it or you don't. But you don't get rid of it. You live with it. You make friends with it. You acknowledge that it's there and have a different attitude.'

You make friends with it. Nerida thought of her Indonesian-Chinese friend Keira, from her biochemistry class at University. She and Andy had wondered why Keira wanted to be around them. Then life, or Keira's fate, made sense of their friendship.

A devout Christian, Keira contracted HIV the first time she had sex. It must have been rough, unprotected sex, but her friend seemed to have no regrets when she talked to Nerida about it. She still smiled. 'He was handsome. Wild. I wish we'd used a condom, of course. But sex opened the world for me in so many ways. Not just getting sick,' she said. 'I mean, don't get me wrong. I cried a lot. I thought it was a punishment. But with the loving support of wise counsellors, the frightening experience of having contracted HIV did not defeat me.'

No longer welcome in her regular church, she extended the forgiveness she had been taught there to herself and to the Universe or God, 'if there is one.' Recovered and recovering from the trauma, caring for herself, Keira had an annual celebration of living with HIV, which she called Iris the Virus. Nerida smiled. *Cheers Keira.*

Outside the window a raven was cawing reflectively.

'Now, if this one hits you and you have other problems, you might not have the time for much care,' Aedgar suggested.

Nerida ducked her head. *So many thousands of deaths daily.* They watched the news from Europe and the US most days. More than twenty-five thousand people had died in Spain and the UK. More than sixty thousand were dead in the US.

The scale of it was incomprehensible.

They saw an interview with a nurse from New Mexico, where people sick and dying with COVID-19 overwhelmed the hospitals.

Nerida and Mari were there in 2014, when they sat to hear stories, bought jewellery and a juniper-scented pot that sat on her bookcase, shared fried bread. There were reports that COVID could hit hard at the Hopi and the Diné. She took a deep breath, told herself not to cry again.

'So, hmm.' He considered. 'Well, if people get a temperature, that can help. You could try to make it higher—'

'Oh?' Nerida was worried. *Is Aedgar suggesting some kind of medieval torture as therapy?*

'—but you would need to control this.'

'Of course.'

'Oxygen is a good thing,' he said. 'But don't put any tubes inside the body. Because that will distract the immune system. Oxygen is helpful.

'It could be useful, as well, to use a way of thinning the blood—'

She agreed with the latter. It was easy to love oxygen as a therapy, and blood thinners seemed entirely appropriate at some stage of COVID treatment, since so many people died of disseminated clots. But you couldn't have people bleeding out. She thought of poor Viktor and his lungs full of blood.

'Thin the blood temporarily, very temporarily,' Aedgar said, as if reading her mind.

'And try to heat the body, raise the temperature,' he explained. 'Just to a level that's tolerable. A moderate temperature is not strong enough. The body needs to reach a higher temperature to fight it. That's the response you want.

'If you put someone on a machine, one that pumps oxygen or air into the body via a tube, the tube distracts the immune system because that's a foreign body within the person's body.'

He had to repeat that, didn't he?

She had dreadful flashes of terrified family members begging harried intensive care doctors not to intubate their love ones. The doctors wouldn't understand. They'd treat them like Adventists, refusing blood transfusion.

Mari's brown eyes were warm, with that strange alertness they had when she channelled. Aedgar didn't look directly into Nerida's eyes. He'd done that once and she'd gasped. It felt as if she'd been physically knocked back into her chair.

'The first thing your colleagues do is try to lower the temperature; trying to control it. Don't lower it or eliminate the fever,' the spirit reiterated.

She knew this from traditional Aboriginal medicine. 'Let it run its course,' her grandmother would say.

Aedgar explained. 'People will feel a bit better if you lower their temperature, but then the sickness comes back, stronger than before—because the body has not quite dealt with it.

'Lowering the temperature within the body, getting the fever down, encourages the virus to stay there.

'That fever's the body's response. It fights it. It creates antibodies. If the first thing you say is: "This person has a temperature. We need to lower it—" Don't. Now, that will sound unfeasible to many of your colleagues, my dear. But—'

Nerida was breathing calmly now.

'—lowering the temperature makes it very comfortable for that virus within its host, so it will replicate instead of going to sleep.'

'Hmm.' *Scary. I need to get my mind out of the Intensive Care Unit now.*
'The medicine that we talked about earlier, the root of the flower—
'

'Yes.'

'Is it meadow saffron? Is that a common English name for it?'
A couple of Aedgar's European readers, one a herbalist, and Lottie,
Mari's sister in Europe, wrote to Nerida to suggest meadow saffron
after she posted what Bartgrinn said.

From what she could see online, meadow saffron had purplish
flowers (not usually blue). But it was related to saffron. The root
was medically usable but highly toxic. It was from the plant family
Colchicaceae.

'Not quite,' he said. 'It is related.'

'Is the medicine colchicine? We use it for gout.' That meadow
saffron was the source of a drug just made her confused, because
she felt like she'd discovered something, but still missed something.
She desperately wanted to know. But also worried about what she
would do with the information of which herb could help people
with COVID-19 if the Beings gave it to her.

Colchicine was derived from meadow saffron. It was a cheap,
common drug. Earlier in Nerida's career, people with gout took
enough colchicine to make them sick with diarrhoea, effectively
poisoned. That was considered the right dose, then. It was a brutal
treatment. Meadow saffron itself, she found out, could be as
poisonous as arsenic, and there was no known antidote.

'It's related,' he said.

'Okay. But the treatment we're searching for is a food
supplement? It's not a drug?' She persevered. There was no way
you could call meadow saffron root a food supplement.

'It's very potent,' he said, soberly. 'It's very potent if you have
the original medicine from the plant. You have to condense it and
use alcohol to make some sort of tincture.'

'Mhmm. But we have to identify it first.' She tapped her loose
fist on the table.

'Yes.'

'A challenge.'

Aedgar took a beat to reply. His tone was kind. 'Some people
of humankind will know the description. They will know.'

This was reassuring. Someone else would figure it out, if she could only get the material out into the world. 'So, we need to get the book out.'

'Yes. Could be helpful.'

Nerida sighed deeply. How could she write and publish a book of conversations with Aedgar and the other spirits when she needed to work to support herself and Mari? *How will I make a living if I publish a book suggesting that intubation of people needing oxygen is bad for their immune system?*

She would be deregistered, mocked. Never again to be allowed to work as a doctor and scientist. She and Mari were in the middle of their lives. They didn't want to live on rice and beans, breaking their bodies with physical labour. Enough of her relatives (Mari's, too) did that. Many died young.

And yet, if what Aedgar said was true, publishing the channelled material could save lives. Deep inside, she trusted him. *He was right about the way the rulers lied about and misused the virus. Maybe he's right about treatment for the virus, too.*

Shouldn't I make any sacrifice for the truth to come out? Nerida had a strong sense of integrity. In Indigenous cultures, a person is known and respected for honesty in all aspects of their lives. An Elder becomes so because they are an example of more than survival. An Elder embodies history and healing through learning from experience, with a willingness to share what they knew. Nerida was growing into a baby Elder. At least, she wanted to be.

But who was she to destroy her career, that had so much potential to help others?

An Aboriginal single mum didn't get through her science degree and medical school without the dedication, love and financial support of many good people. How could she let them down? *And if I save one life, like I do every week here in Fitzroy Crossing, who am I to risk that usefulness, that power and privilege, only on the strength of my spiritual beliefs and feelings?*

'Anything else, my dear?' he asked.

'Well, some personal questions.' She felt the burden of debt, money she still owed for her education, even if she graduated fifteen years ago. They had a mortgage. Her chest felt tight as she took a deep breath.

'Yes.'

'We're considering coming back to work in the Fitzroy Valley longer. I like the people. They accept me. We love the country. And we need to build up some paper with the numbers on it.'

How could he understand? Aedgar, who was the Lord of the manor in his most recent lives. And now has no body to feed, clothe and shelter at all.

'So that I can pay our debts,' she went on, 'and we can secure accommodation for ourselves, that's paid for.'

'Yes.'

'That's a reasonable thing to do?' She was asking his permission. *Please let us live long enough to secure safe housing. Please help me stay in this lifetime long enough to write the books.* She knew the spirits weren't gods. But they could seem that way sometimes.

'Yes. We are not fond of the paper with the numbers on it,' he said.

'Yes.'

'But we do understand. It's a means of sorting things out for you.'

Nerida's chest opened. She heaved a sigh. *That's a good way to put it. A means of sorting things out.*

She was looking for a safe place for them to settle. 'Today I've been considering buying some land within travelling distance of my daughter and her partner. They live on a river in a town in South Australia. The river there is struggling. The land struggles, too. But I'm hoping we could find land that would appreciate our care and nourish us.'

Aedgar paused. She imagined him consulting a map. 'The aim is to be self-sufficient,' he asserted.

'Yes.'

'Try to catch as many rain waters as you can. We are aware there is not much rain. You would have to do something about it.'

Mari makes it rain wherever she goes.

'There is some toxicity—'

'Yes?'

'That affects the water.'

Oh no. Flint, Michigan. People poisoned by river water there.

'Make sure you stay away from dense groves of trees.'

This took her aback. She loved the smell of a forest, the company of trees. 'Really?'

'Forest-like areas. Keep enough distance. If there are one or two or three trees around, it won't be an issue. But stay away from bigger groups.

'Stay away from that river, directly. Because of the issues we told you before, there might be severe flooding from time to time. And make sure you can collect rainwater.'

'Should we head to the hills? It's very cold there. That's the problem for Mari.'

There was another moment of quiet. Aedgar seemed confused. 'I don't understand what you mean when you say, "very cold."'

He used to live in Bristol, in England. Relatively speaking, 'very cold' hardly existed in Australia. 'There's a wind up from Antarctica. Sometimes it sleets or snows,' she explained. 'She doesn't like ice and snow.'

'Oh yeah. We could sense that.'

'Uhuh.' No surprise that he could feel her wife's dislike of the cold in her body.

He considered. 'We don't think she would mind, our friend, if you're not forced to go out every day. We know there was an issue with being forced to go out while it was still dark.'

Nerida thought of little Mari heading out to school in the black European mornings. She had difficulty walking before and after surgeries as a child. And then again as an adult, after the accident, before and after the amputation of her foot.

Aedgar could see it, too. 'With slippery slopes everywhere. And using this stupid means of transportation, never made for these surfaces…'

Teenaged Mari drove to work in the dark, spinning wheels on invisible black ice, in the Black Forest. She worked in a car factory as an industrial designer. Everyone in her village worked there.

Even when she was a baby, less than two, Mari amused her parents' friends by identifying cars by the sound of their engines.

She loved cars. She still flinched sometimes if Nerida used Aedgar's expression for them, 'stupid means of transportation.'

Aedgar was still looking at land in the region, assessing its suitability. 'If you have the power to stay inside when you need to, that could make a big difference. If you find a shelter that's appropriate for that climate, it should not be an issue,' Aedgar said.

'We're talking about building a place out of rammed earth.'

With a small smile, he said, 'We like the sound of it. We wouldn't like to call it 'rammed'. It's a bit violent. But built out of earth sounds very good. Yes.'

'Thank you.'

'Just don't go too close to that river. Don't use the groundwater. If there's a different source somewhere—maybe. But not the groundwater. It's toxic. It's from fertilisers and all sorts of things that went into the groundwater.'

'Are people using the groundwater to wash themselves and even drink, in my daughter's town?'

'They do. They shouldn't.

'There are two unique sources. One is related to the river. And there is another source coming for somewhere else. They are on two different levels.

'We know it sounds not quite right, but it's the water source that's deep down should be avoided. Because it has been tampered with, far away from there.'

'Ah.'

'There would be mercury and other things—chemicals and other things that are not supposed to be in there.'

'Is that from a foam that the military used?' Nerida knew a chemical foam used as a fire retardant got into the groundwater and poisoned it in several places around the country.

'It could be part of it. But there are some other issues as well, that come from further north.'

'Yeah?'

'Further north and to the east of there are issues. People trying to wash out stuff between the layers of the earth. Chemicals there went through cracks and into the groundwater.'

'Is it fracking?'

It was as if he saw the substances arrayed before him. 'Nitrates, sulphur, uranium, mercury, cadmium. It's all there. It's not healthy.'

'No! Very toxic.' It appalled her. *My Ruby and Seb are drinking this?*

'The concentration and the combination of those fluctuates.'

'Right. Are you talking about fracking?' she asked again.

'Pardon?'

Maybe he doesn't know this word. Strange. Mari does. 'Where they break the rock to extract gas and put chemicals in, mixed with water? Between the rocks?'

He nodded. 'That's part of it.'

'Okay.'

'But they're digging out other things, as well. It's a combination of all of this. Because of the cracks in the rocks, the poison goes down into the water, all of it.'

'Is the water that my daughter is using and drinking safe?'

'I would use filters. You can probably get filters for the pipes. They should have filters.'

'Right. Okay.' She would buy the filters for them.

'It could be one issue with that other thing that happened.'

The miscarriage. 'Yes. Thank you.'

'Anything else, my dear?'

She let go a soft sigh. 'I'm satisfied for now. Thank you for coming—'

'One being inquisitive should never be satisfied.'

'I knew you were gonna say something like that.' Nerida sighed again. 'Can you suggest then,' she asked sadly, 'a way of helping people heal who have been through terror and trauma because of this sickness, this virus?'

Now Aedgar exhaled sharply. 'We can only say, identify your mistakes, learn from them. Make sure you do it differently next time.

'We could say it caught you on the wrong foot. They said, "Yeah, it will happen one day. We are prepared." You know?'

She thought of her colleagues working in Public Health. Some had cherished delusions. Now, trying to catch up with COVID was killing them.

'And then it did happen,' he said. 'And they realised they're not prepared at all. Because these things happen rapidly. It's not like, "Oh, I can see it coming. Let's work on my projects—on how to handle it." That's too late.

'It's provided a bit of an insight into their systems, how quickly this moved.

'You think you have a solution to everything. It's not true. Continue working. Thinking in new ways, building on your knowledge.

'Be bold enough to abandon some old knowledge.

'This is not the Spanish Flu. It's not.

'You think you're so advanced. Think again.

'Work through these things: identify the mistakes, acknowledge the mistakes, try to learn as much as possible from them. Build on what you've learned from that. This will give you the satisfaction… to get over it.

'There is no way of "Look out the window, enjoy the blue sky. And everything you've done, or you haven't done, will be fine." This is not how it works. It won't.'

Sounds like a tough slog, thought Nerida.

He paused, contemplating. 'You could give people drugs to expand their minds.'

Nerida grinned. Aedgar and the other beings discussed psychedelic plants for healing before.

'We know some won't like it. But for others it's helpful to get a broader picture of the planet and of the environment you live in— to expand their mind.' He smiled. 'They might get it blown.'

'But this is the work that needs to be done.

'Work through things—evolve.

'Grow your wisdom. Raise the energy around you and evolve.

'You keep doing the same things that have not worked before. They still don't work. Be bold enough to abandon it.

'And don't listen to those individuals who say: "We have always done it that way."

'Because it never worked that way, holding onto the past. Rules someone made because they were not bold enough to go forward. Such people should not be in decision-making positions.'

'Yes. Especially not for other people.' Nerida agreed.

'No. People have to make decisions within their field of expertise.

'Don't decide about things that you have no idea about: how it works, where it comes from, how it evolves, nothing. Don't be that one and make decisions. Because the decisions you make won't work.

'Get the people who have the wisdom and knowledge about what is happening. Sometimes their solutions are quite unconventional. And this is what the ones that hold on to old rules will never accept. They say, "This is not how we've done it back then."

'Well, look up. You're not stuck "back then." And, if you are, get out. Make space for someone who's bold enough to go in a different direction.'

'Yes.'

'You understand?'

'I understand very well. Thank you.'

There was a lull. Nerida pulled her arms into a cardigan she had draped over the back of the chair.

'We have a young leader in some islands across the ocean from here,' she said. 'Her name's Jacinda.'

'Pretty name. Like a flower,' said Aedgar.

'Yes. People are finding her more open-minded. More open to new ideas—'

Aedgar interrupted suddenly with a smile. 'Indigo girl!'

'Oh, is she now?'

'Yes.'

'How lovely!' Nerida exclaimed. 'An Indigo girl made it into the ruling class and is using the power of the role.'

'Well, she has enemies. Enemies that work on the same level that she does,' he cautioned.

'Yes?'

'We mean in the realm of what people see, or think they see. Don't misunderstand. She is on a whole different level.' He sounded proud.

'She's got most of the people behind her. They can feel something different going on.

'She's an Indigo girl. She can give people advice about things, even if she knows they won't like it. They can accept it from her. Because she's got that aura. Most people can't see it. They just know there is something different. And we will at least try.'

Does he mean Spirit Guides will try to work with her? Nerida wondered.

'Many people like what she says,' Aedgar said. 'Of course, she will say things that are not so popular. But she will always find a way to make people understand: showing them there could be a new way out of this.'

Outside, Nerida heard mothers calling their children into the house. It grew cold. Shadows lengthened. She couldn't see the sky from within their hut—the windows looked out on the walls of other huts. But the daylight was fading.

'We might talk to her one day.' Nerida liked to think of travel, of introducing Aedgar to other people.

'Possible,' he agreed. 'She's in a delightful place, from the energy.'

'Yes. Perhaps we'll live there one day.'

She paused as she felt his energy take a step back.

'I'm afraid I should leave you, Aedgar. I think Mari will be tired,' she said.

He spoke softly now. 'Okay. So, we'll talk to you another time, then?'

'Yes, please. Thank you.'

'Thank you for your questions.'

'I have plenty.'

'Good,' he said, and she felt him leaving. Nerida realised the room was full of smoke and went to turn off the oven.

Mari murmured, shook and stretched as if waking up.

'Hello, darling.' Nerida kissed her cheek. 'The pork's very well done.'

'Is it?' Mari said. They were hungry enough not to mind.

CHAPTER 43

Fitzroy Crossing

Monday May 25, 2020

The smoke inside the house was not the only ash in the air that night. The storm arrived, snapping and roaring in a rainless fury of wind and lightning. Thunder rolled and boomed. Fires sprung up in the dried grasses.

When Nerida took the bins out, she saw a delicate crescent moon glowing orange in the breaking clouds.

In the house, the television picture reformed into coherent pixels after the storm moved on.

The women watched the dire news from Detroit. Policeman Derek Chauvin pushed his body weight onto George Floyd's carotid artery and windpipe. The Black man's death took a hellish eternity.

'They're murdering him! Those evil fuckers!' Mari roared.

Nerida felt familiar, sickening grief. Her breath felt like acid, her throat tightened, and her vision blurred with tears.

She recalled Aedgar's words earlier that evening. Their 'new normal' was about more control. 'More control and interfering with particular groups of people.'

I know what he means. I know who those "particular groups" of people are. All my people, she thought. She put her arms around Mari, held on for comfort.

After the storm, an ancient tree-trunk, long-dead, silvered and hard, fell with a loud crack across the road to the river.

It took a dozen people with ropes, a truck and an earthmover to move it the next day. Then it lay by the side of the road, half-tumbled into a dry creek bed. Ravens and kites came to inspect the fallen tree. Offered it consolation in its altered form. Tried the perspective of perching on it.

The land smelt of dust and smoke. The low fires burned, frightening the wild horses and the cattle. The boabs, storing water, were unperturbed.

The next day at work, Nerida saw a child with a fever. She only had her mask on, no face shield, safety glasses or other protection. She tried to smile with her eyes, to be slow and gentle in her movements.

The eight-year-old was not buying it. He let her put the swab at the entrance of his nose. But he'd seen this on telly: the balks and screwed-up faces when the swab went all the way in.

In the end, a nurse and his mum had to hold the poor child down to take the COVID test. His mum's face showed fear. Her child could bring the virus into the small, remote community. It was impossible for her to isolate him from others in her small, crowded home.

Nerida had a lingering dread. *It's only a matter of time before it shows up here.*

After all the tears and shouting, all her sweat and tenderness, touching the boy's fevered cheek to soothe him, *I'll have the virus if he does.*

There it was, in a plastic bag, in a chilled foam box, the cotton swab that could turn their lives around. Loaded into the front of the single-engine Cessna.

It took three days to get pathology results. PCR tests for Coronavirus had to travel twenty-five hundred kilometres to the lab in Perth.

In her inbox that afternoon was news of an American doctor who escorted a respected elderly client to the car park and contracted the virus. They died.

At dinner that evening, Nerida asked Mari, 'What did your Oma teach you about fevers? Do you try to cool a fever?'

Mari took a pinch of salt. 'No, you only try to lower a fever if it runs too hot for too long. Otherwise, you let it run its course. Why?'

'There was a child at the clinic with a fever today.'

'Was it Coronavirus?'

'I don't think so. I had all my PPE on, anyway,' she lied.

Mari didn't have to know every detail of the risks she took at work.

'Poor boy. It was like trying to get a hook out of a fish's mouth. His mother had to hold him down.'

'Fever makes people wild, too,' Mari said, buttering the carrots.

If I get it and give it to her, it could kill my darling, Nerida thought.

And then tried to block out the unthinkable. *My work has made her sick at least three times before. This place is low risk, so far. I don't know how long I should expose her to this risk.*

'You think that's why people with coronavirus have so many contacts?' Nerida asked.

'It always seems to be people who've been to seven cafes, two sports clubs and a brothel in two days.'

'I guess the virus is looking for someone who'll show it a good time,' Mari said.

A conscious virus, looking for a good time. How much does she know of what she channels, really? Nerida chewed on a forkful of beans, looking deeply in her wife's eyes.

CHAPTER 44

Narooma NSW. Yuin Country

Wednesday August 12, 2020

After they came home to New South Wales, the women slept a lot for most of a week. It was warm enough to swim in the pool at the Lennox Head house. They enjoyed afternoon swims.

After a few weeks of working from home at Lennox, they travelled south to visit the house they finally owned after years of mortgage payments. 'We better go see that orange house. We might be asking that fella to leave,' Nerida said.

They called it the orange house for the rust-coloured stucco on its concrete walls.

The house was on a hilltop. Accompanied by a high-heeled woman from the property management, they climbed the hill carefully. Nerida watched Mari closely.

She resisted reaching out for her until the steepest part of the climb, when she took her hand.

The front door was weathered and warped by the horizontal rain that blew against it from the ocean. The property carried the weight of paranoia: cameras surveilled, super-bright lights studded the walls, both looked down from the roof.

They knocked and were ushered in. The house was clean and mostly empty. It seemed that the tenant's family didn't visit as he'd hoped.

'He's glued the downstairs windows shut,' Nerida said quietly to Mari as they followed the agent around.

Another ground-floor window was permanently propped open to admit electrical leads to three of the security cameras. The wooden window frame and the wall around it were rotted from rain getting in.

Tiles were cracked in the bathroom and jets in the spa bath had been filled with glue, so that they no longer functioned. 'That's mysterious,' Nerida murmured. 'Why would anyone do that?'

The tenant had installed a gun safe in the garage downstairs. On the living level a home office was set up to monitor his security system, Mari noticed. 'The computer has nothing but his camera input on it. There's another gun case there under the desk.'

And they saw another weapons case in the small studio upstairs, where the view of the town below, with the lake and the ocean beyond, was spectacular. They breathed out, restored by the sea air.

The man sat perched on a bar stool in the open kitchen while they proceeded with their quiet, respectful inspection. 'Wild kids have been climbing on the roof,' he said. 'Maybe I should put up a sign that the fence is electrified.' He smirked, as if it was a joke.

Matching his tone, Mari said, 'Why not electrify it? Or just shoot them.' She met his gaze levelly. 'I've got a compound bow. I can hit a person's ear from fifty metres.' She bent her ear for emphasis. 'And the best thing is—it's silent.'

Where do you come up with that macho shit? Nerida thought. *Why?*

But maybe Mari's posturing made it easier for the tenant to leave when they evicted him three months later. *Maybe it was a protective impulse from her Romany DNA.*

The property manager feared the departing tenant, so he got most of his bond, despite the glued windows and the ruined bath. Everyone was relieved that he left without a fight.

The women came to stay in the orange house in the New Year.

Li-An, an elderly Vietnamese lady from one of the neighbouring houses held Mari's hands with tears in her eyes to welcome them home.

'Thank you so much for coming back,' she said. 'He was a horrible man.'

Another neighbour told them, 'He was making drugs.' He said that the tenant had shouted racist abuse at the Li-An when he saw her in the yard. 'He told me I should go back to where I came from, too,' the neighbour said. 'I yelled out, "What, go back to Wollongong Hospital?" Fuck, he was an arsehole.'

After they'd been there a week, another, younger, neighbour met Nerida at the letterbox as she prepared herself for the steep climb back up the driveway.

The young woman had been into the orange house once, to review the tenant's recording of the street in front of the house. Her car had been broken into and she was looking for evidence. 'I was shocked,' she said. 'He could hear every word down on the street as clear as me talking to you now.'

They had the house tested for methamphetamine contamination.

Mari and Nerida slept on a blow-up bed, with a couple of camp chairs and a fold-up table.

The place was profoundly peaceful. The suburban setting was belied by the huge sky. Mari loved watching the weather coming. 'Clouds piling up. They'll come in from the sea.'

They saw the moon rise over the ocean.

Mari noted problems in the house. The steps were too many and too steep. Window frames and doors were rotted by the horizontal rain that came with the ocean storms.

'Maybe we should live here in the house, though,' she said. They brought home samples from the tiler, looked at new baths online, thought about a new roof and guttering problems.

The meth test came back negative.

Slowly, they began to trust that they could live there for the connection with friends and family. And the ocean.

They lived for years in Narooma before they went to live and work remotely. Driving around was easy, without having to consult a map. Nerida's parents were two hours away. Ruby and Seb only a day or so's drive.

'It's deeply quiet and private here. I feel good here,' Nerida said.

'Maybe we could put in a lift for you, get these the windows and roof fixed. A new bath.' She put her arms around Mari's waist, spoke into her shoulder as they admired the view together. 'What do you reckon? Should we put down the anchor?'

CHAPTER 45

Fitzroy Crossing, Western Australia

Wednesday September 2, 2020

By Spring, they were back in Fitzroy. On entering Western Australia, they had to quarantine in a Kununurra caravan park. The cabin had an outlook anyone would call beautiful, overlooking the man-made lake. To Nerida, it was drowned country. She was always aware of what lay beneath. The crocs eyes shone at night.

The internet hardly worked, neither did the television.

It took about a week to realise that the welts on their bodies were not mosquito bites. And the strange smell in the bedroom was not disinfectant. Nerida spotted bedbugs crawling on her clothes. The smell was insecticide, which had subdued the biting beetles for the first week.

It was a difficult second week.

Getting out, they were relieved to be back on the road to Halls Creek and winding through the mesas and hills to the little metal house at Fitzroy Crossing. After her first day at work, Nerida felt at home.

A pleasure in being there was learning about the cultures of the tribes in the valleys and plains around the Crossing. Nerida envied the Fitzroy Valley people their languages. Hearing them speak and sing in language strengthened her spirit.

She did not learn her Aboriginal language as a child. Her father was forbidden to learn it, on pain of being removed from his family. It was the era of the Assimilation Act, which used the language of equality. But meant in practice that Aboriginal cultures were to be subsumed and disappear in a White Australian hegemony.

So, she heard little of her Native language from her parents or grandparents. When she went looking to learn her language in her teens, she was told, 'Don't bother. Only a few old people speak it. They'll die soon. The language will die. Forget about it.'

She carried guilt with her then, for not dedicating herself to trying to save the language. She should have gone to sit with those old people, made recordings, written it up. Even if she knew she did useful work, the loss of the language was a sadness that never left her. The satisfaction she took in learning other Aboriginal languages as she travelled was made especially poignant by not being able to learn her own.

She talked to Mari about this over a late breakfast. In the early afternoon they went to the shop together.

There was a huge, long-legged dog tied up with a red lead outside. He barked at cars, people and a peewee, falling over his own feet with fuss.

'He's just a puppy,' Mari laughed. 'He doesn't know what to do with his legs.'

The man who approached them outside the shop was an artist, selling carved boab nuts. His work was detailed. The people and animals carved into the velvety brown seed case were lively and well-proportioned.

Nerida didn't get to see his work. She was too quick to dismiss him. She thought he was begging. It was a professional hazard, judging people by appearance. One she tried to avoid. By the time she realized her mistake, he was gone.

Mari and Nerida wore masks at the shop. No one else did. None of the patients Nerida swabbed had been positive for SARS-CoV-2. *It's probably our internationalist perspective that keeps us aware of it. Most people don't even watch the news.* She mused as she examined the tomatoes. Maybe she knew more about Coronavirus in Italy than she did about the artist selling carved boab nuts in the carpark.

Didi was there, dressed in a scanty, brightly patterned frock, considering the cabbages. Nerida introduced her to Mari. They smiled politely, kept their physical distance. Didi's brow furrowed.

'I'm stressed,' she confessed. She looked at Mari. 'My mum is sick in Wangaratta, in Victoria. My son is making his life hard, too. I could go there, but I'm not sure when I could get back into WA, even if I quarantine for two weeks. I feel torn between my family and my job.'

'Aren't you an essential worker?' Nerida asked. She explained to Mari, 'Didi coordinates the Women's Shelter.'

'Not really. There's no guarantee they'll let me back in to the state.'

Mari was choosing apples. She met Didi's eyes from under black curls. 'Have you ever heard of channelling? Like, spiritual channelling, I mean. Not plumbing or irrigation.'

Didi grinned. 'Of course.'

'Maybe you'd like to talk to one of our non-physical friends. I can channel for you.'

Didi opened her mouth but didn't say anything.

'Talk to Nerida about what time. She organises all that sort of thing.'

Nerida bought the local paper, a slim, over-priced tabloid. 'They're still waiting for the supermarket to be rebuilt in Tennant Creek,' she read to Mari while they waited at the checkout. 'Did you hear about that?'

'Yeah. That was two years ago. Young, bored shitheads did a stupid thing. That was Tennant Creek's only supermarket.'

'You're buying those?' Nerida asked.

Mari had a bag of ground hazelnut and two big slabs of dark chocolate in her basket. 'I'll make cakes for me and your colleagues.'

As Mari packed the groceries into the car, Didi came to Nerida. 'Wow, that's exciting! You didn't tell me Mari could channel. How soon can we do it?' The gangly dog dragged on his red lead. Didi laughed. 'He's trying to take me for a walk. He keeps my arms strong.'

Didi was a bright, attractive woman in her mid-thirties. Descended from the Aboriginal people of the southwest coast on her mother's side, her father was from India.

'Why did you offer a session to Didi, when you don't know her at all?' Nerida asked Mari.

Mari fixed her with her dark brown eyes, as if she was impatient with her. 'It's intuition. She will do well with the knowledge she gains. It might sound strange to say, but I can feel she deserves it.' Mari's voice was loud. 'Other people, I can look at, even just see them from behind, and know that they'll mock it. They can have their epiphany on the last day of their life.

'Didi is one who will appreciate it and use what she learns to grow.'

It daunted Nerida, how firm Mari was in her judgement of people. But she'd learned to respect it.

CHAPTER 46

Fitzroy Crossing

Didi knocked on their door a few minutes early when she joined them for her first experience of a channeling session that Saturday.

The air conditioner and the refrigerator hummed. The dinky house was cool in the early afternoon heat. 'There are a few rules,' Nerida whispered as Mari closed her eyes to go into trance. 'You don't touch Mari when she's in trance because it can startle her out of it. And you don't stare at her when she's going into trance.'

'In case I look really weird,' Mari said with a half-smile, before closing her eyes again. They felt her energy moving away from them. Didi closed her eyes and went into a meditative state quickly herself.

Nerida watched her wife's face change as her trance deepened. The spirits were there.

She whispered to Didi. 'It's okay to look now.'

Eyes closed, Mari's head shifted gently from side to side in a gentle waggle. There was the hint of a smile on her lips. Her relaxed cheeks and jaw were belied by an alert, erect posture and her eyes moving under their lids.

With a characteristic turn of the head, lifting the eyelids as if by strings, Aedgar arrived. The eyes looked at a spot behind them, avoiding direct contact.

'Hello,' said Aedgar softly.

The women responded: Nerida warmly, Didi sounding confident and happy.

Nerida introduced them.

'Oh, we've got company! Welcome,' Aedgar exclaimed. 'Is there anything we can help you with, my dear?' He turned his head and chest towards Didi, who consulted her list of questions. She brushed her hair behind her shoulders, focusing her attention ahead of her.

'We like questions. This is our favourite thing.'

'Okay.' Her paper crackled as she straightened it. 'How can I be of best service to humanity and the environment?'

There was a pause. 'It's a difficult question, my dear. Yet it's quite easy to answer. All of you came with a special set of skills. So, if you feel that something is wrong, do something about it. Don't wait for others to do something. Be yourself.'

'So, I am on the right path?'

'Yes. We have to say, you do veer off your path at times.'

Didi nodded, laughing nervously.

'You have been. And, we're afraid to say, you will veer off in future, as well. You have one—we're not calling it a flaw, you know? You get easily distracted.'

'This is true,' Didi said.

'You have the ability, during these distractions, to learn. You're good at that. But you need to remember that this is not the path you should be on—this distraction. Sometimes it takes you a while to get back to where you're supposed to be.'

'Yes,' Didi said. 'Very much one of my traits.'

Aedgar drew a breath. 'You have an intersection.' He made a crossroad above the table with Mari's hands.

'We are not good at time. (How can you be good at something that doesn't really exist?) But we would say it's coming up soon.

'You will be forced to make a decision that you're not presently prepared for. Somehow, there was an arrangement before you came here that if your spirit thinks that you're ready, they might bring this decision up earlier than your body would choose. You understand?'

'Yes.'

'Your spirit is always with you, but sometimes a little ahead of you. Trying to help you, give you guidance, if there are too many distractions just ahead of that intersection. So, don't worry. You are supported. You're not alone. Spirit will guide you.'

Didi breathed heavily through her nose.

'Just don't listen to all that noise of things going on around you. There will be a lot of it. Pretend you don't hear it and go for what you really want.'

Nerida thought about Didi's busy work place, full of drama and conflict. *Is work the crossroads she has ahead?*

'Go with what you feel you should do. We think it could be something about teaching.'

There was a pause. 'You understand?'

Didi murmured.

'Because you know what it means to get lots of distractions, you can help others to avoid them.'

Didi read from her small piece of notepaper. 'How do I connect myself with spirit?'

'By not trying so hard.

'It's there. It's always there. Don't try to connect with something that's already there. Listen to what you feel. If you feel you should do something and it comes to you easily, without trying too hard, then it will be the right thing.

'Spirit tried to tell you before. You were a bit ignorant about it.'

'Was that when I had my car accident?'

'We know a few people in here that did the same thing,' the spirit said quietly. Nerida smiled fondly. Mari's accident, back in the nineties, was a long, hard path of learning.

'And they are not very pleased,' Aedgar continued, 'to be reminded of these issues. You understand? Don't try too hard. The connection is there.'

Is it painful for spirit guides to see people go through intense suffering to learn? Do they watch such events unfold with regret? Nerida gazed at Mari's face, occupied by this unfathomable being.

'In hindsight I can see I was on the wrong path, in the wrong place, when I had that crash. I almost stepped on a giant brown snake when I was running. I had a fall. Things kept breaking. Nothing went right. I ignored it all. Kept on working at a job I hated in a place I was unhappy.' Didi shook her head. 'But now I feel like I can sit and allow things to unfold.'

'It has started already, and you know it,' he said.

'Can I ask—'

'There might be some unexpected things coming,' Aedgar continued. 'Accept these as a gift from the Universe. Your spirit is trying to provide for you—not only guidance.'

I wonder what that means? Nerida thought. *Are there other strong learning experiences coming up for Didi?*

Didi held her palms up and open in front of her. The aquamarine in her necklace caught light through the blinds. 'I feel ready for my companion. How can I open up to receive them?'

'It's the same. Don't try too hard. Just be yourself. They're not far away. It is going to happen. See it as a gift—someone to support you on your path. Trying to help you to stay on it.'

'Hmm,' Didi smiled but her jaw was tight.

'Might look a bit different than the picture you've got in your head. Go for the feeling, not for the looks.'

Didi laughed, took a deep breath.

Aedgar looked into it. 'It's a person who's not from this area,' he said. 'Quite spiritual. But you'd not think so, to see the person. So, don't go for looks. Go for how it feels. It will feel right. You understand?'

'Yes'

Softly, he said, 'Have a little bit of patience.'

There was a moment. Didi turned to her paper.

'Um, my mother is very unwell at the moment. And I'm unable to get home. Is there a way I can spend time with my family?'

'She has the support she needs. She does not want you to be too close at the moment.'

Didi exhaled.

It's not what she expected to hear, but somewhere inside she is relieved, Nerida thought.

'This is not rejection. This is protection,' Aedgar said.

There was a pause. 'She's protecting you,' Nerida said to Didi. She knew Didi's mother had been selfish in the past and wanted to clarify this, sensing Didi's mother's love. Aedgar would correct her if she was wrong.

'She knows what she's in for,' he said. 'We know it doesn't sound good, but she has been preparing for this, quite a while. She had an issue prior to this, that she ignored a long time. She thought, "This can't happen now. And it should just go away." So she believed anyone who'd tell her, "It's not a big deal. Just handle it." Which is what she did. But it evolved into something else.

'She knew deep inside that it was coming.

'She was like, "Oh, but I didn't ask for that much of it." But she knows it. It is not easy for you to hear, but whatever the outcome, it will be fine for her.

CHAPTER 47

Same place

Time Flowing

There was a moment while that idea soaked in.

Ravens cawed outside. A reminder, for Nerida, of their protection on a journey.

'Yes,' Didi said softly.

'Not necessarily okay for you. But it will be fine for her. Your mother's trying to protect you. Do you understand?'

'Yeah.' She let out a groan.

'It will get better, briefly.'

Tears rolled down Didi's face. Nerida reached for a box of tissues.

'But you will be strong. You will be able to handle it.' He spoke gently. 'Do you understand?'

'Yes.'

'Good. Spirituality will help you. But don't ask for it because it's there. Don't search for it because you found it already.'

She spoke very softly, composing herself. 'Yes. Yeah.'

'Is there anything else we can help you with?'

Didi surprised Nerida by asking, 'Is there a message that Australians and the human race need to hear for this time?'

Aedgar released a small sigh. 'They have misused information and emotions. Like, "Everyone is in this together." And "Everyone will get through this." If you hear this many times, almost all the time, it loses its meaning.

'It is true: everyone is in it. It is true that the Universe is trying, spirits are trying, to help humankind.

'The best thing that could happen is that the virus is kind of partnering up with another one. Scientists might call it a mutation, like a severe mutation. So, it is going to look for a different host— something other than human beings.

'We always come. And we enjoy talking to people. And we always come because there is hope—hope in the real sense of hope, meaning this will get better. Not 'hope' as an excuse: like doing something wrong and then 'hoping' the problem will solve itself.

'This thing was created and released, by fellow human beings, on this planet.

'It did not come by itself. Like a "miracle" from heaven.' He oozed sarcasm.

'So, immunity won't happen. There might be some form of treatment with strong herbs, that can be used to soften the impact of it. But it won't be a medicine that you give to someone and then that person will be saved: this is not going to happen.

'You are asking the Universe, you're activating your spirits, to make sure the Universe knows that it has to mutate, to evolve from the form it is in right now into something different.

'Yes. Okay.'

'Because, so far, nothing has changed since it first occurred. It is spread more widely. You understand?'

'People haven't got the message yet,' Didi reflected.

'No. More people need to understand what this means.

'Staying well is not only about physical separation—we're talking about geographic separation. You have to take precautions to keep from catching it. These things don't see. They don't care about geographic borders or lines.

'The climate that you're in makes you more or less susceptible. It prefers the cold over the heat. It lasts a very long time on cold surfaces, no matter what that surface is. It can travel in the cold. It can travel as frozen water, for example. It does not like the salt water in the ocean. So things that, for example, you would eat, need to be cooked. Or you remove the skin of what you eat if you can't cook it.

'At the moment, it is not in the soil. But that can come anytime.

'Society needs to be careful now how they use the water. You understand? It enjoys being in humid areas.

'Does not like the heat, though. So humidity combined with heat is safer than a humid, cooler place.

'The problem is that if you tell this to fellow human beings, they'll say, "This is not scientific. You are out of your mind." But it's them that are not in their right minds. They're playing the game of blaming each other. No one wants to be responsible.'

Nerida asked, 'How about a vaccine?'

'We told you about that immunity,' said Aedgar.

'Hmm. It's not gonna work?'

'If you can't become immune to something, what would be the point of triggering the immune system? They will try. It will weaken the recipients of it. And it will have some effects later on that they did not see coming.

'Keeping things clean, staying away from very busy places: these are the only things you can do at the moment. And asking spirit to convince that thing, as we do, to find another host, by marrying that friendly other thing that's out there, waiting for it.

The women looked at each other and laughed.

'You're tempting it with romance?' Nerida was incredulous.

'If that's what works, we'll try.'

'Thank you. We appreciate the efforts. You say it's the only possible answer we have right now?'

'Many of you humans (or animals), try to make sure you find another one you like well enough. These things are not so different. They've got consciousness.

'Which, on the other hand, enables them, also, to find the "right" victims. Some of these people said, "I've had enough of this world. I don't wanna be here anymore. I can't watch this any longer, how they're going to destroy themselves and the planet." Do you understand?'

'Yes.' Nerida stroked her cheeks and neck.

'Good. You are one of the few, you know. There's not many out there that would understand that.

'There were some young ones. But now they're scared. They feel a bit guilty. "We were talking about pollution and climate and this thing is so much bigger." But these events can actually support them.'

'The climate?' Didi asked.

'Yes. It helps.'

'We needed to stop,' she mused.

Aedgar nodded. 'Yes. So, that thing that's happening now is part of it. This was not how it was planned. It was not planned to be around to help solve the problems of the planet. It was created to kill in specific areas where it would be released.'

'At the moment everyone is looking at the model of the Spanish Flu.

'There were very different ways of travel and distribution then. Here, they did not understand how much more rapid the spread of it would be. It goes on one person. It goes to the other side of the world. And suddenly, it's everywhere.

'It's not good to miss an important element like that. How can that be called scientific? Scientists are not the brightest ones on the planet. They have a few in each group pointed in one direction, interrogating one tiny thing.

'If it goes a little to the right or the left, you know, they say, "That's not my specialty. I've done my part. Someone else has to do these other parts."

'Losing the view of the whole picture, how can that be scientific?

'You're an idiot that focuses on one special, tiny thing.

'And the more they are specialised—I'm not sure if I should put it in a basic way like this—but the more you specialise, the dumber you are. Because you can't see anything that's going on around your specialty.

'So, use caution if someone tells you, "But I am a specialist on exactly that thing." Because they would not be able to see anything to the side or all around their 'fact', even things that touch and influence it majorly. They can't see it. They have not trained to see the bigger picture. You understand?'

Didi listened quietly, taking it all in.

'Is there anything else?'

CHAPTER 48

The Little Metal House

Time Flexes

Nerida stepped into the lull. 'So, are we from the same soul group? Me and Didi?' She felt an affinity with the younger woman.

'Almost. Not quite.'

'Neighbouring planets?'

'Yes. Close enough to understand each other,' he agreed.

I'm curious. 'And have we worked together in other lifetimes?' she asked Aedgar.

'Once,' the spirit confirmed. 'On this island. You were in the same tribe. Teaching. Teaching about plants. About plants, but not in a medicinal way: how to make the ground more fertile.'

Nerida murmured to Didi, 'Your obsession.' Mari, the channel, did not know about Didi's passion for sustainable agriculture. But Aedgar did.

He spoke as if he was there, observing them in Australia in that long ago lifetime. 'You have to make sure the seeding coincides with the phase of the moon, during the right season, to get a better outcome. Better things than that rotten dried meat.

'It was about making food easier to digest—that kind of use of plants as well. So food was easier for the body to use it, but not in a medicinal way. It was made to preserve things, as well as making it easier to digest.

'Not yourselves, but loved ones, had issues with digesting the available food. You used plants to make everyone feel better, even if they were not sick.

'It was a big job because you were not settled in a certain area.

'You'd plant things in the right season in different areas, then you'd revisit. In your travels you went from one area to the next and the produce would be ready, when you revisit, to harvest. This involved a lot of planning.'

He turned towards Didi. 'This could be one of the important trades, my dear. You still have some of it. If you dig deep inside your mind, you might find it.'

'I don't need to dig deep there. I feel a real affinity with regenerative agriculture.'

'There you go,' the spirit replied. 'This is the way of the future: having the right things, for the right climate, and the best quality you can get. If the quality is very good from a nutritional point of view, you don't need the quantity to compensate.

'You always had this idea of rotating things. Planting the right foods for the place. You can't go to the desert and plant things that need a lot of water. That won't work. You knew this seven hundred years ago, my dear.'

They heard birds calling outside, gathering to go to the nesting trees.

'So, you were same tribe, travelling around. And you told her what to do. "Get those weeds out"'

'Even then!' Nerida blurted. Didi was good at organizing her when needed. 'It's all right,' she chuckled. 'I'll get the weeds out.'

'She's still not very good at it,' Aedgar confided to Didi. 'We have to give it to her. She tries hard.'

'Yes,' Didi said playfully. 'Very.'

'I'm curious about which part of the island we were on,' Nerida said. She imagined their travels between the different eco-systems as Aedgar described them.

'You were moving around in the cooler area. Not coastal. South. Big forest, back then.' His voice saddened, 'There is no forest there now. We can't give you a specific place for this because you had a nomadic lifestyle.'

'Southeast,' Nerida contemplated.

'Ya,' Aedgar said. 'More in the area where the sun rises. Rivers.'

'Rivers?'

Aedgar nodded. 'Forest. And rocky outcrops.'

Didi curled her body over the table. 'Are we still supposed to be teaching people these ways of growing food?'

'Yes. A lot of them never learned it. Some tried to learn but they never understood. Just not enough in the head to understand.

'And a lot of those you knew in previous times have now gone somewhere else.' He paused a beat. 'Some came back, like you. Same place, same island.

Some of our agriculturist mates did not come back to Earth. I wonder why. But others are still around here. People to connect with, Nerida mused. She felt a sense of belonging.

'It needs to be taught.' Aedgar pressed the palms together firmly. 'It is important, more than ever.'

Didi asked. 'Is it possible for us to return to the old ways of caring for the land?'

'Yeah,' Aedgar said. 'People will be biting kicking and screaming if you try to get them back there. Because they think they are so advanced in their technology. Which is poor technology.

'There have been—' he made a short, sharp exhalation, '—human existences that were far more evolved in their technology. The issue is always that they reach a certain point where they think, "We are the crown jewels of the population of this planet." This is always when it goes bad.

'You're not there yet. But getting closer. The more some people think they understand, the more they think how evolved they are, the more power they want, the more ignorant they get. And then they can't accept any ideas other than their own. Which is the doom of that civilisation.'

He paused. 'Those kids made little fights and demonstrations. Their fights and demonstrations got bigger and bigger, (to the surprise of those that have it all). The young ones need to be reactivated. They are needed. The way they think, their mindset, needs to be supported.

'You don't have to go back and live in a cave. But you have resources that you need to hold onto tightly. Use them sparingly.

'There are religions out there that say, "There's plenty. It's all there just for you. Use it all up." What sense does that make? ""It's there for you to use it all up?"" Because that says it already: use it all up and it's gone. Where should it come from, the replenishment?

'It makes no sense to take all those "resources" out of the earth and then send them somewhere else. You won't get them back.

They won't grow back. You have to find other ways, other resources to use.

'It needs the mindset of those young ones, growing up now. They'll find ways to have different transportation, to create different energies. It will be sufficient for everyone on the planet. We had these discussions a lot with our dear friend.' He nodded gently toward Nerida.

'People always going from one place to another because the grass is always greener on the other side: this needs to stop,' he continued.

'And then,' he said, 'to damage this planet so badly that they need to go to a different planet! They still don't understand. You can't just always leave a mess behind and then go somewhere else.

'That's the ignorance that comes with too much power. "I know it all," they say. Ignorance breeds. And then they become incapable of realising how much they don't know. So many things they don't know.'

There was a deep quiet.

'You understand?'

Didi nodded. 'Yes.'

CHAPTER 49

The House Feels Protected

Time is Not What We Think

'Is it true,' Nerida asked, 'that if we're creating in our lives, it's best not to think about how to get where we want, but to go for the feeling of it? Like, if I want to teach people about soil, I imagine myself growing things, content in my garden, talking to others. But trying to plan how it's going to happen, where the money's coming from, where it will be—that could get in the way. Is that correct?'

'Yes,' Aedgar said.

He paused. 'You have to be careful if you use that term "truth." Because true means something different for everyone. But your idea is feasible. If you do something and you believe in it—I am not talking about religion—you believe in what you do, you might experiment. Because only failures teach you how to evolve.

'While you make these things that turn out to be failures you evolve and learn to do things differently if you're intelligent. People will see, "Oh, this person got wonderful crops, plants, fruits." They will come and ask, "How did you do this?" You can tell them. They might fail, too. They try something different. So the knowledge evolves. It's gonna be shared. This is how teaching should go.

'If you go to someone and say, "This is how you do it and there is no other way," do you think anyone would listen?'

'Nah,' said Didi.

'That's your problem in sending your children to school.

'Someone makes rules from someone else who thought, "We know everything. This is what they must learn. This is how it works." If a child has a different idea, they'll give them bad marks that make sure they won't get anywhere. They'll be treated as revolutionaries, you know? As if they could become very bad people.

'But those children might have much better ideas. And even though they're younger, of a younger 'age' in this setting, they might be much more evolved than that person who said, "Here are the rules, this is what you do. Because we know it all."

'It's ignorance. The higher you get up in those systems, the more ignorant you become.

'Do you understand?'

'Yes, thank you,' Nerida said. Didi concurred.

Aedgar continued, 'Teaching means inviting others to have an experience, take the part they need or they want from that experience and then take their learning further.

'This might get them completely out of the rule book, far from the context of what was taught in the first place, but it can evolve to something beautiful. This is what this system of education does not understand.'

He reflected. 'Are we having a rant? Again?'

Children were laughing outside the house.

'Not at all. Lovely to hear you talking on this theme.'

'It's a never-ending story—' he said.

'It's an important story,' Nerida concurred.

'—because it's not changing.'

'No,' Didi agreed.

'We told you, how long ago? You should not have fifty students and one teacher. You should have one student with fifty different teachers. They're all specialists. You need to be informed of the broader concepts, so when you get all these little bits from someone else, you can get the whole picture.'

'Indeed.' Nerida acknowledged. 'Eight years ago, I think, was the last time we had that conversation on this theme.'

'Oh, right,' Didi said.

'And it hasn't changed,' Nerida said.

'Dire prospects,' said Aedgar darkly.

'Ah. More children are at home with their parents because of the virus.' Nerida thought that could be a good thing.

'Yeah, some of these parents do well. We told you that before.

'Some parents don't. They should have never had their 'offspring' in the first place. You know, we had that talk: this is created out of love. And then that thing out of love, has own ideas.'

Nerida murmured agreement.

'And then it's like, "Oh, it's not like me. You take care of that one." And the partner says, "Nah, it's not me either. Let's just send it somewhere else." Like the schools where they come home once a year. Taught by one teacher and a group of thirty, fifty.

'Mhmm. Sad.'

'And then they're all strangers. Why would you listen to a stranger telling you things you don't wanna hear?

'Some so-called parents have a different attitude. They are the ones where the children do well (you could say). The ones that said, "Look, I can afford five of them. I'll show that to the world. They're all dressed nicely." They all have bad attitudes because that's what they learn at home. And at the places they get shipped off to.

'They take a photo and display it. "Isn't that a wonderful family?" It's a group of strangers. That don't get on or go on with each other.

'As soon as they're old enough (or think they're old enough), that offspring, they think, "I can't live with these people." And they go away. And because they have been educated in a different way, in a stupid way, they don't know what to do. They don't know how to create food, how to get a roof over their head, how to grow something. Or even how to talk to people.'

'It's true.' Nerida recognised elements of her own childhood and upbringing.

'Then the children create a problem in society. It's not their fault. It's the parents that have created those problems. But you can't tell the parents. They'll say, "But they got everything they wanted. They were always dressed nicely. And look at that wonderful family photo."

'For a split second, they were all made to smile. And then it's there on a piece of paper for decades.

'And yet it was such an unhappy and ill-suited bunch of human beings.

'You understand?'

'Yes, we do, very well,' Nerida said.

'Is there anything else?'

'Aedgar, where are you from?' Didi asked in her light voice.

'Me?'

'Yeah.' Didi smiled warmly.

'I have been on this planet, maybe, eight times. And then I'd seen enough.

'You know, you can live as a rock in a river and watch things go by. You can be a tree. And you can still have more feeling than a human being.

'We are a spirit that came back, trying to teach. We have been waiting for decades.

'We searched for a shell that we might be able to use.'

It's a romantic story, Nerida thought. She was jealous of Aedgar's intimacy with Mari when he first came through in 2012. Boundaries in their relationships were clearer now. And she didn't mind, as she did earlier, hearing her wife's body referred to as a shell. *Shells are beautiful.*

'The brain is not as advanced as we thought,' he said dryly.

Nerida chortled. 'We won't tell Mari that.'

'We were trying to assist her through the lifetime, to get as much different education into it as we could. This individual has done well. We wish this individual, our friend, or host, would have paid more attention to the things you call science. We could be more eloquent in the way we talk and try to explain, if we could find the words in those dusty drawers up in that brain.

We found a perfect match for us. But sometimes we are quite limited in the way we're able to express ourselves. We have chosen this shell, or vessel, a very long time ago. And we had to convince that one, several times, to stay on this planet.

It's a great opportunity to have, to be able to talk to human beings.

So we go somewhere else, you could say into the Universe, if we're not here, talking. We shift some things around at times, up there. We've always got important things to do.

We are working together so this planet does not get damaged even further, by all the junk that humankind has put up there. Sometimes we have to create a different path for other things in the Universe that fly past. Sometimes we come in to protect our shell. We have done it on airplanes.

But usually we reside in the so-called Universe. It's not a Universe because it's so much bigger than you think. 'Multiverse' gets closer, but still doesn't cover it.

Nerida turned the air conditioner off. All was quiet.

She asked, 'You were involved in the creation of this planet?'

'Yes. We do spheres and other things.' His tone was casual. *For such a formal being, addressing such a grand domain of action,* Nerida thought.

'Aboriginal Dreamtime stories talk about Creator Beings shaping the mountains, forming the rivers. Is there some truth in those stories from your perspective?'

'It is very hard to explain how this happens, to human beings. It is the way human beings should work or function a bit more themselves: You feel what you want. You feel and you think what you want. We're not sitting up there with a piece of clay. We've got no body. We have no hands. We feel.

'So the creation is different than, you know, take a rib from someone, use a bit of clay and make someone else. That's an entertaining story. It is not quite how it happened.

'It's a fusion of feelings of many beings that creates things.

'And yes, you're not alone. And no, you're not the most intelligent out there. That's all we say at the moment.'

Didi smiled, 'I don't think we had any doubts about that.'

Aedgar raised an eyebrow. 'There are plenty of human beings around who have the sincerest doubt. They are confident that they are the most intelligent, not only for their species. They take that illusion very personally. Unfortunately, it can be the ones with least intelligence that go to the top, trying to control things. It should not be that way.'

'Can't we persuade the Coronavirus to have a tendency to go for those that are caught in a dead-end, refusing to learn anything, and having lots of greed and power?' Nerida asked. 'It might be helpful. I know I sound like a terrorist if I say things like that. I'm not a terrorist.'

'That's what you say,' Aedgar said with a half-smile. 'You see, they have their own experiences to make. They have to endure their own failures.

'They create horrible things. As we told you—how many times?—if you think about the idea that you will come back, that you're born again—'

Nerida bobbed her head.

'—you will be the one that has to endure what you've created before. People say, "We have to save the planet for the children and the grandchildren." Actually, you have to save it for yourself.

'As long as humans here don't understand that—and this is not a good thing—it will take a long time. They have to go through it all again: being born again, growing up again, not being able to clean themselves, talk, walk. The whole experience.

'Just to realise, "Oh, what kind of thing have I chosen to come back to?"'

'Congratulations. You helped to create that mess. Deal with it.'

Nerida turned to Didi. 'Do you have any more questions you'd like to ask? You're welcome to ask about your health or past lives, relationships or anything.'

'I have a silly question.'

'Questions are never silly,' Aedgar said.

'It's about my dog.'

Nerida remembered the giant pup biting his paws and barking at the supermarket.

'I feel that the spirit of my dog was the spirit of my cat who passed.'

'Yes. They do these things, yes.'

'Very similar…'

'The spirit has chosen to come back as a dog because cats are not supposed to be in this area.'

'Oh.'

'That's a clever spirit,' Nerida said. Each feral cat killed hundreds native birds and animals a year. Pet cats were banned in Fitzroy Crossing. Too many people left them behind.

Aedgar pressed on. 'Yes. Spirit was sure you would recognise it. Not in the first second. Maybe in the fifth, so to speak. You know we are not good at time. You experienced moments when you thought, "Ooh, I've seen that look before."

'You can see it in the eyes. It was not quite sure at the beginning if it would wanna stay in that clumsy body. It was used to moving in a more sophisticated way.

'Being in that other animal it felt quite free.

'Dogs are more prone to serve you. They wanna make you happy.

'The other animal was more like, "I don't care. I'm around. This is my space. And what you want from me? I don't care."

'Dogs are happy to serve. So the spirit had a little trouble adapting to that. But spirit says it was worth it, 'cause it wants to be back with you.'

'Yep, I know,' Didi said softly.

'It will always come back, that one. Keen to have new experiences.

'Is there anything else we can talk about?'

Didi nibbled her fingernails.

'Tell me about my son. He's had lots of issues.'

Didi tore her paper list into tiny petals.

'Well, he knew when he came into this life. He has chosen the way he is. It was a bit like, "You take care of me because you can't take me for granted. I am precious. I could go any minute."

Aedgar's tone was tender. 'He won't. Each human being could go any minute, if they decide to. But that was the idea. He thought it would be an easier life. "I've had these strong experiences before. I will have an easier one, this time around."

'He might need to get something fixed. Soonish.'

He investigated her son's energy more closely.

'Well, he wanted to have an easier life this time around. He did not realise that having it easier in some ways can create trouble in other ways. You might think you have an easier way of living by not working so hard physically. Doesn't spare you pain. "I've been working so hard. My body aches. I don't wanna have this anymore. I wanna have it easier." You might, then, have to deal with other sorts of pain and suffering. He did not quite consider that when he was coming into this life.

'We can see there is an issue. It's not a big one. But it would need fixing. He might want to keep an eye on that. It's not very obvious at the moment, but it's there.'

There was a long pause. Didi finished tearing the paper and lay her hands flat on the table.

When she was ready, Didi asked, 'Have I learnt the lessons I needed to, through my traumatic relationships, to be ready for this companion?'

'You have learnt quite a bit. You could stop now.' A smile passed over the lips.

'But it is up to you. Do you want to have another lesson? "I truly learned this. I don't need another one." It's as straightforward as that. You're getting in the way of yourself.'

'Yes.'

'But then, that companion is quite close.' He was still a few moments. Then advised, 'Don't go for the looks. Go for the feeling.

'There is one that would match the looks you have in your head. He could be another lesson.

'These two are showing up around the same time. Go for the feeling. It's like, "This one feels right. And this one, nah, he can't be that bad because he looks so nice and friendly."

'Don't fall for it. Go for the one that feels right.'

'You might think, "Ooh, he's got stubble." He rubbed Mari's strong chin. "This other one is so nicely groomed. He behaves so well." But the stubbly one feels like the right thing.

'This is just an example, okay? The one that's right might not have stubble. He might not even be cross-eyed, you know?'

'Good to know.' Nerida smiled.

'They do exist,' Aedgar said. 'It does not make them bad people.

'Well, you can get crossed-eyed people that are bad. You get them everywhere, right? But if a cross-eyed person was bad, you would feel it.

'Go for the feeling.'

Didi took a deep breath.

'We don't mean, "Oh, that guy over there. I'm in love already." That's not the feeling we talk about. You understand?'

Didi smiled, looked down shyly. 'Yes.'

Aedgar went on. 'You talk to someone and you feel you've got something in common. It feels right.

'If you look somewhere and a hundred metres away is that guy or person that's like, "Oh my god. I'm so in love already." This would be a trophy partner: "I like the looks."

'You send out signals to others. If you go for the looks, you will attract someone who's going for exactly the same thing.'

Nerida watched Didi closely. She was pretty. She'd worked as a model when she was younger. *She has that look people might want to own.*

'And then you might like the look of each other but there is not much else that's a match,' Aedgar concluded.

'You have to be aware that it's the signal you're sending. So, go for the feeling.'

The room was quiet again. Children were chasing each other in the driveway outside. Their footsteps smacked the concrete. The metal fence clanged as one of them ran into it.

'Is there anything else? We could be of service.'

'No. I'm feeling very content,' Didi said.

'We don't hear this very often,' he said. He lifted the eyebrows. 'We talk to very demanding people.'

'I've enjoyed the movement of energy in your gestures today very much.' Nerida said.

'We're not quite aware of it.'

'Well, it's beautiful to see, have you seen Mari's pictures of Gorgeous Greg? Do you remember Gorgeous Greg?' She reached across the table where Mari's vibrant sketches shone off the page.

'Yeah, we spoke to him. Looks like us.'

'We thought so,' Nerida smiled. Greg did look remarkably like the image of Aedgar they had from Monica's description when she introduced him back in 2012.

'We have to make ourselves known somehow,' Aedgar said.

'That's right. But Greg is not you. He's part of your audience. He's still learning from you, even if he's a superhero.'

She turned to Didi. 'Greg is a Traditional Aboriginal Healer. But he has different skills than herbs and bone setting. You know, he astral travels. He visits sick people far away, sometimes at night.

Mob think of him as a superhero and he kinda is one. Aedgar advised him on finding his partner, just between us. Helped him learn to disregard the package.'

'That's nice.' Didi held the drawing.

'I don't think Greg would mind me telling you that. He's very open about everything, including his love life. Isn't he gorgeous?'

Didi grinned.

To Aedgar, Nerida said, 'Thank you. You may have given Mari a little nudge there. And me, a boot——'

'Sometimes we do.'

'——up the bum.'

Nerida had taken Mari's refreshing drawings, so unexpected they seemed to be channelled, as a hint to get on with writing her books. It was the first time Mari had drawn people for years. In one of them, Greg wore a superhero costume, complete with a cape blowing in the wind.

'Sometimes we do. It's not always appreciated or listened to,' he said ruefully.

'Thank you. We do our best. Still learning. Perhaps Greg should be in our books.'

'Yes.'

'I hope you come back again soon and help us learn more.'

'We will always come back if we're asked to.'

'Thank you,' said Didi. 'I hope we get to speak again.'

'Oh, this is not up to us. So, we'll talk to you another time, then.'

'Thank you.'

'A pleasure, my dears.'

He left.

Nerida grabbed Didi by the hand.

Didi bubbled, 'I got a lot more——'

'——than you bargained for!' Nerida laughed. 'It's always like that.

'Here she comes. Here's my girl. Hello!' She stroked Mari's arm.

'Hey. Did it work?' Mari asked, blinking.

'Yeah, it worked.' Nerida smiled proudly. 'It worked very well. Good session. Wonderful.'

Mari pulled her hair up off her neck. 'It's a bit hot.'

'Oh, yeah the fan was just so noisy.' Nerida turned the aircon on with a beep.

Mari frowned. 'It's off. There's no light on.'

'Oh, this stupid controller. You press the fan button and it turns off.'

'I hope you get it to work again,' Mari said.

'There,' Didi said. 'It's just a bit slow.'

'It's got a wire crossed. How are you?' Nerida looked into her wife's brown eyes, joyful to see her in them.

'I might need another coffee.'

Nerida went to the kitchen and opened a tin, releasing the fragrance of dark chocolate mixed with apricot and hazelnut. 'How about a slice of this amazing cake you made?'

CHAPTER 50

On the Road, Mainland Australia

Saturday November 2, 2020

After filling up with diesel, Nerida made a detour to the Fitzroy supermarket carpark on the morning of their departure, looking for the artist who carved the boab nuts.

He had two small nuts carved with brolgas and roos. She bought them, paying the tourist price, firstly because she was a doctor and secondly because she wanted to make amends for being a schmuck the first time she saw him there, three months earlier.

The women took about five weeks to drive the three thousand kilometres from Fitzroy Crossing in a roundabout way home to Lennox Head. They visited coastal towns in Western Australia, places they were thinking about buying a house. Nerida had spent hours, it was almost an addiction, reading about places and houses online.

They'd have to sell their New South Wales place, the orange house, to buy elsewhere. 'But you get so much more for your money here,' Nerida said. There was land with the houses, something their townhouse in the east had little of. Privacy and the chance to grow food made buying something bigger, better. She was giddy with the thought of being able to buy trees, as well as a house. *How can a person purchase the privilege of exclusive access to a tree?*

They drove two thousand kilometres down the West Australian coast to Green Head, a little fishing village with small, rocky beaches. They stayed for week, resting and getting a feel for the place. They went to see a couple of houses they'd been dreaming about online.

One was built of rammed earth. It smelt good and was cool. The other had a well-loved garden and a well-organised workshop around a solid brick house. If they sold the orange house and bought one of those, they might have enough money left over to live on for a year, or three.

The people were relaxed and friendly. The local pharmacist offered to go with Nerida to help her negotiate a good rate of pay to work there. Sunsets over the Indian ocean lifted their spirits and meals of fresh lobster nourished their bodies.

Ten days later, they went to see land up in the sand hills at Greenough. The air was freshened by a howling wind that came there every afternoon. The sea was visible over the top of the sheltering sandhill. The ancient sandhills were well-covered with vegetation. They walked around the land for sale. Mari hands on hips, smiled out at the sea and said, '*Schee.*' Beautiful.

Greenough had a bad reputation, though. There was a jail. And the terrible murder of a family happened in a farmhouse there in the 80s. The name had irredeemable bad associations for people who lived in Western Australia. But the women were not from there.

'That makes it affordable for us,' Mari said.

'There's no place in Australia without bloody violence in its soil,' Nerida agreed. They had a friend to visit in Greenough who would be happy to see them, a stylish and sweet-natured Aboriginal person. The country felt good, as long as they stayed away from the convict ruins. Trees bent by the ocean wind modelled resilience. Growth in beauty despite adversity. *Maybe we should live here,* she thought.

When they went inland, though, the peace of a local canyon, a sacred place, was disturbed by racist graffiti, threatening murder.

They saw filth by the same hand at several places as they travelled up and down the coast: on wrecked cars, a sea wall, sprayed on an abandoned farmhouse.

In the 80s in the Kimberley white supremacists dressed up as Ku Klux Klansmen and burned crosses to terrorize local people. 'Racism has a bolder face in the West and the North,' she told Mari. 'In the East and the South, it fucks with your mind more.'

From Greenough on the Indian Ocean in central WA, they planned to return to the East Coast by travelling through Central Australian deserts, visiting friends in Western desert communities and near Uluru. They'd go travel into South Australia then, to see Ruby and Seb. Nerida longed to hug her daughter.

It was an ambitious drive, needing jerry cans of water and fuel, a box of food, blankets. Mari bought an EPIRB in Geraldton, an emergency radio beacon for remote travel along outback roads.

But on the eve of their departure South Australia shut its borders in response to a new Coronavirus outbreak in the East. All roads into South Australia were closed.

Nerida would have to wait longer to see Ruby and comfort her in real life.

They had to drive north again, then, via the Kimberley, the Territory and western Queensland, to get home.

Mari expected big rains soon. 'If the rains come before we're through, we'll get stuck,' she said.

Weather maps showed the Monsoon clouds gathering over Sumatra and Java. Some days there were storm clouds on the horizon as the sun set behind them. Some nights there were spattering showers on tin roofs. Nothing to wet the ground.

So, driving north, they visited Kalbarri, an isolated clifftop town Mari loved. Nerida was aware that when fires came to the National Park surrounding it, they would be cut off.

There wasn't a lot of rain there, either. But there was abundant beauty. And the service station had fresh local eggs. 'I'd still have to bring in soil, though. I can't grow veggies in sand,' Nerida said.

'Ah, but I'd love to see the dolphins every day,' Mari replied. They saw beauty in nature, as they travelled, every day.

They had dinner with Didi up in Broome. She was happily settled there. She cooked them a fresh-caught fish and had a fella there to meet them. 'I went for the feeling,' she whispered in Nerida's ear. 'It's working.'

But houses they looked at around Broome were neglected, smelling of tropical mould and mildew. The one place they saw that was well kept—it had mango trees with pendulous green fruit and a sparkling bore-water pool—was too expensive.

'I don't think we should live again in the tropics.' Nerida sighed. 'It's too hot.'

'Too many crocodiles, large and small,' Mari concurred, as a gecko tut-tutted in the hotel ceiling.

They drove out from Broome and were about to leave Fitzroy Crossing for the second time, after convivial coffee with colleagues, when Nerida's phone rang.

She didn't recognise the number.

CHAPTER 51

Danggu Gorge, near Fitzroy Crossing

Tuesday November 12, 2020

It was a man's voice with a deep timbre, her cousin-brother Greg. The cheeky healer.

'You're in Fitzroy Crossing, eh, sis? I'm in Kununurra, on my way down to Newman. Thought I might visit.'

'When did you get to Kununurra?'

'Yesterday. Come from Darwin. There's a family need me down at Jigalong. One of the Elders had a stroke. Been treating it remotely. Now I need to go there.'

'I hope it's no one I know.' Nerida looked around the tin hut they stayed in. 'We can't put you up. Aren't you supposed to be in quarantine, anyway?'

'Not from the Territory. No COVID in the Territory, they say.'

'I don't believe it. I saw two people with it when I was in Yulara in January. One of my older people died from it. I wasn't allowed to test for it.'

Greg was silent at the end of the line. Showing respect for his sister's experience.

They met at Danggu Gorge. The canyon walls of orange and white clay glowed in the afternoon light. Deep purple shadow crept up the wall. Birds and fish splashed.

Wallabies woke up as the hottest part of the day passed, observing them from the other side of the river. A boab tree reached its arms up to the fading sky, its swollen body mocking the square picnic table.

Greg arrived in a hot pink Holden Monaro. A car that used to be a sleek shark of macho, made sweet by a girly paint job.

They didn't hug. But gave each other wide, toothy grins. Nerida jumped up and down in her excitement to see him, like her totem peewee. They shared a barbecue chicken, chips and coleslaw. Mari made a bottle of Pepsi hiss, peeling off the lid.

Greg said he won the car at cards. Off Eric.

'Eric's still around?' Nerida's jaw tightened. She knew Eric from when they lived at Mutitjulu.

'He's working at one of the land councils. I dunno how he gets people to employ him.'

'Bullies them into it. The shithead,' said Mari.

'He reckons he's good at cards when he's just drunk enough. Not so good when he's had one too many.' Greg was gleeful.

Nerida turned to look at the car. 'Is he gonna let you keep it?'

He laughed. 'He sat on the step of the house I was staying in and moaned and cried about losing it all night. I suppose he gets it. Even someone as stupid as Eric has to understand when the whole

Community's talking about it. Kids laughing and pointing, teasing him. You shoulda been there, sis.'

'He's a terrible person. Last I heard he'd been banned from the casino for threatening to bash an old lady,' Nerida said.

'Yeah, the car likes being with me better. We're gettin' on all right.'

'What year is it? Must be from the 70s,' Mari said.

'It is 1970, yeah. It's older than me. Belonged to a cow cocky who looked after it pretty well. Family gave it to one of the stockmen who looked after it after he passed. It's had a new engine in it a few years ago.'

'So, how'd Eric get it?'

'Won it at cards himself. Probably cheating.'

'You don't cheat though.' Nerida smiled.

'I don't have to.' He acknowledged a kite watching them from the high branches of a gum tree. 'I can read the people's energy.'

'Yeah, Andy used to do that. He counted the cards, too, knew what was left in the pack. He went the casino and played blackjack whenever he had a bill to pay. Until they banned him.'

'He went back once he was in the wheelchair, though, eh.' Greg grinned.

'You knew Andy?' Mari was surprised.

'Everybody knows Andy. *Dhitiyn bayiratikal marrung.* He's a good singer.' He smiled at Nerida. 'That's your language, sis. Did you know they're teaching it now?'

'It's alive?'

'Sure is. People did the work. Dedicated. Took the recordings. Wrote it all down. Thirty years. Now there's a dictionary. They're putting together learning units for a course. You can start learning.'

'Oh, my darling brutha. You brought me good news today.'

A pair of silver brolgas lifted off the river. Nerida could hear the wind of their huge wings. Mari stepped aside, took a photo of the two of them, physically distanced, vibrationally matched.

'How do you say hello?' Nerida asked her cousin-brother.

'*Yuwayi,*' he said.

She whispered it after him. 'And "thank you"?'

'*Murrungbu.*'

It made her glow deep inside to hear the language her father and grandmother were forbidden to teach her.

'You're amazing with languages,' she said. Greg had Bundjalung and Pitjatjantjara himself, which meant he could make himself understood in many dialects. She'd seen him speak German and Swabian with Mari, too.

'One of my many gifts,' he said with a smile.

'You gonna keep that moustache?'

'I might. I like curling the ends of it. It's a bit wicked, don't you reckon?'

After they'd eaten, Mari took the cups and dishes to the tap to wash them.

'Andy's mum called me a few years ago,' Nerida confided to Greg. 'Do you remember Carleen?'

Greg nodded. 'She got very sick herself after Andy's death, didn't she? I remember both of us tried to reach her, to help her. Her spirit was stuck in a kind of hell. Poor thing.'

'I still think of her. Two university professors met with her, with lawyers. I dunno if you remember, I didn't, but Andy had given one of them Power of Attorney to act for him in his interactions with the Uni.

'Carleen reckons he was the one who came and took all of Andy's documents the next day after he died.

'Anyway, this meeting came after years of Carleen calling for investigations everywhere she could think of.

'They apologized. Admitted Andy should not have been injected with that shellfish protein. She said they were defensive, though. They'll keep using the stuff. Something about that it works for over eighty percent of people.'

'So do the other twenty percent end up like Andy?'

'Yeah, that's what Carleen said. But she reckons Andy was murdered. That one of them injected air into his vein.'

'Wouldn't be the first time a helpless, young Aboriginal man was put down like a dog.' Greg's eyes flashed. 'Where's the justice, sis?'

'Keep working on your powers, my brother. I'll keep working on mine. Let's make time our instrument.'

CHAPTER 52

On the Road, Mainland Australia

Thursday November 14, 2020

Mari and Nerida sped through the Northern Territory, which required quarantine and a permit if they wanted to stay. Even so, they stopped for coffee and cake with a friend in Tennant Creek.

He was happy with how well the town was doing. The burned-down supermarket had been rebuilt. The place was a glorious tribute to the powers of the road trains—full of produce.

In Queensland they spent a week at Winton, a peaceful town in sheep country. 'Far from Good and Bad,' Mari described it. It was over a thousand kilometres from the coast, an arid place, totally dependent on bore water.

The barren-looking lands concealed treasure. In the hard yellow ground at Winton there were dinosaur bones. Local sheep and cattle farmers found fossilised skeletons of marine reptiles and sauropods there in the 80s and 90s. People built a remarkable museum on top of a mesa there.

Nerida fell for the place. She liked the hardiness of the people, their acceptance of the smelly water and drought. The splendid open sky and the vibe of treasure in the ground.

The stocky, sturdy wallabies hiding amongst rocks and the red, leggy roos, panting in the shade at midday. 'I would come and stay in a donga up at that museum and learn to brush off the dinosaur bones. I'd like that,' she said.

Mari was enchanted in her own way, too. They purchased a fossicking license and went looking for opals. She found stones with flashes of blue, green and red in them. 'This might be fire opal,' she showed Nerida. It was a soapy stone the colour of a peach's blush.

They stayed in a historic hotel, colourfully furnished by an Aboriginal man Nerida presumed to be gay. *You have no idea how much you would love me*, Nerida thought, whenever he was prickly.

'You're not always right about people being gay,' Mari chastised her.

'I know. But it's polite to assume people are not heterosexual or cis-gendered, until you have evidence to the contrary,' she replied. 'They'll always tell you soon enough. Most heterosexual people can't resist telling you, somehow, within two minutes of meeting them. I guess it gives them a sense of belonging.'

Mari raised an eyebrow. 'Two minutes?'

'Yep. Someone did the research.'

After weeks on the road and months away, arriving home was bliss. Nerida settled quickly into enjoying the space and ease of a whole, proper house. She'd been home two hours before she felt the need to go out to the bright, blue pool.

They'd been away for months but friends had looked after the place up until a fortnight ago. She hung onto the fact that one of her friends was a pool attendant. *Maybe it won't be too bad.* Slipped on outdoor shoes.

There were twenty-eight toads in the pool. In all sizes, from small broken dead toads to a mother bigger than Nerida's hand. She killed the living and buried them all.

Mari greeted her with a rueful smile once she was showered and changed. 'My hero,' Mari said, wrapping her in a soft hug.

The strong smell of the toads followed Nerida for days.

She avoided the yard. It was a fishy, dank, reptilian odour. Like an ill-kept crocodile farm.

She doubted that she'd ever swim in the pool again.

They watched a documentary from Queensland where people on the reef islands hung a cane toad near a turtle nest. The smell protected the eggs from being eaten by goannas.

A genuinely positive use of them. But I feel sorry for the baby turtles. Run, little turtles, run to the sea. Get away from the horrible, smelly toad-ridden world.

CHAPTER 53

Lennox Head, Bundjalung Country

Wednesday November 20, 2020

There was no sign of rain in the week they stayed in Winton. It was disappointing. Nerida saw her wife talking to wisps of cloud on the horizon in the mornings and again at sunset. Saw Mari's fingers pulling and coaxing water vapour as they drove over parched plains. Still, it never came.

Within a week of arriving in Lennox Head, they woke at night to pounding on the roof. 'It's raining! Yes, it's raining,' they whispered to each other. It was a proper drenching.

And it didn't stop. Rain fell day and night. Wild winds came with it, pushing the rain against the windows and doors, stretching the trees..

Nerida went out to the pool to clear the drain of leaves and toads every day. An awkward umbrella kept her head dry. After the soil was saturated, Mari stayed up some nights watching that the pool stayed in its concrete box. The damp side of the house filled with the smell of mould and became unusable for Mari. She shut the doors. The spores made her cough and wheeze. They kept plugs in sinks, covered drainage holes with buckets.

Tired from broken sleep, Mari was frustrated. She hardly used her foot some days, *schlürfen* around, as she said, in a woolly slipper. 'That means shuffling,' she explained to Nerida. 'Not hopping.'

Out in the yard, Nerida pushed herself against the palm trees, telling them to stay standing in the gale. When palm fronds crashed on the roof, she was grateful the trees still stood. She imagined how the roof would split, their bed suddenly soaked, if a big tree fell on the house.

Nevertheless, the wetness was wonderful. Writing, remaining inside, came easily.

After eleven weeks of rain Nerida's routine as a writer was well established. The women enjoyed their days together, relished knowing that the next day would be spent together alone.

Venturing to the letterbox to grab the wet mail before snails ate it, the postman's bike had made a six-inch-deep furrow of chocolate mud in the lawn. Nerida was excited to see a different person then and smiled at the neighbour. Called, 'Isn't the rain beautiful? I feel like I'm living in England!'

Even she was beginning to tire, though, of the closed-in white-grey sky. Coronavirus was around, only one or two cases. Enough, with the weather, to make them feel closed in, in the suburban house.

They missed the stars. Nerida didn't know the phase of the moon.

Nearby, rivers swelled and broke their banks. Floodplains filled. People experienced the immense delta that the Northern Rivers region really was.

Houses were swept off their foundations. Places were flooded with foul-smelling waters full of char from the fires of early 2020. Cattle were stranded. Lifesavers pulled a cow out of the surf at the mouth of the Manning River in Biripi country.

Nerida felt selfish in her enjoyment of the rain then.

'Maybe I asked for too much?' Mari asked. It was a once-in-a-hundred-years flooding event, the weather bureau said.

On a Saturday afternoon when the storms were sufficiently cleared that the phone worked, Nerida spoke to Laney, the nurse in Fitzroy Crossing. 'Just opening a bottle of vino,' she said. 'My house is an island. It's so peaceful. Only the sound of the water rushing all around. Haven't seen any crocs near the house. Yet.'

Behind the house in Lennox, the tea tree forest drank and grew metres taller in days. The wetlands filled with white and mauve lilies. Wading birds walking on lime-green lilypads never wet their long red toes.

On the hill, fig trees lifted their immense arms from the ground.

Mari was amazed. 'Look how the branches rise up.' She held Nerida from behind in the kitchen.

Pushing buttressed roots through the sodden hill, the trees connected with each other, discussed strength and resilience.

People in the surrounding subdivision, meanwhile, discovered where their new houses dripped and leaked and were sodden. Mould grew along brand-new skirting boards, and into white plasterboard walls.

Later, at their place, Mari intercepted travelling nests of ants and spiders climbing the doorframes and walls, seeking shelter. Then she was angry again.

'I hate this house, this *Drecksloch*.' She was still coughing. She sprayed insecticide into gaps between the tiles. 'I never liked it. I never wanted to live here. It's nothing but a stopping off point.'

'You're right. It was always meant to be a transition. To work out where we want to set up our home. But it's the stopping off point where I began writing regularly. It's been good for me,' Nerida responded. Nerida felt that familiar guilt. *We'll have to move soon.* She was all right, but Mari was not. It had happened before, in other places.

The December damp heat was unrelenting.

One evening, Nerida found Mari in the kitchen, rocking.

She grasped the table with her right hand, held the other over her eye. 'It's hurting. There's all this lightning, white light flashing.'

'Follow my finger,' Nerida said. 'Look at me. Does it hurt when you look over here?'

'It hurts just the same whatever I do.'

'Don't turn your head. Follow my finger with your eyes.'

'But if I don't turn my head, I don't see your finger when you hold it there.'

'Come on. We're going. This is an emergency.' Nerida picked up bottles of water, her wallet with their plastic cards for insurance.

She levered Mari, still in her shuffling slipper, into the car. Eyes squeezed shut in pain, she strapped on her leg. Nerida drove them, up over the forested hills, to the hospital.

CHAPTER 54

Friday December 25, 2020

On Christmas Eve, they stayed up past midnight, chatting with Mari's cousin Lottie, who sent a loving glow down the phone.

That morning they ate a lazy brunch of cheeses, homemade salad and prawns from the local fishing co-op. With lemons and guavas fresh from the garden and, for the prawns, a wasabi-flavoured mayonnaise Mari whipped up. Mangoes for dessert. Nerida called her parents, her daughter. *I'll call my son later tonight when they might be home from Church in Los Angeles.*

They went back to bed then, for the mutual, pagan celebration of touch and energy the high Summer warranted.

'I'm so glad we don't go to Church. This is the way to celebrate the old Winter Solstice,' Nerida said afterwards, chuffed. She ran her fingers over Mari's damp skin, sated.

'Holidays are confusing here. Watermelon at Christmas. Just not right,' Mari said. She pulled on her leg and trousers. Ambled to the kitchen. Where she pulled a red crescent of the fruit from the fridge.

Lately, Nerida wrote every day. Mari's eye didn't hurt so much, and she could see more. They had money from the work at Fitzroy. The cupboards and the fridge were full. The air-conditioner was clean and working and skies were blue.

All that was is well. All that is, is well. All that will be, will be well. Doing lazy yoga after sex, Nerida stretched into an asana. 'The naughty dog,' Mari called it. Nerida felt physically strong and balanced; trusted and trustworthy. Mari cut watermelon for a snack.

Later, post-afternoon coffee, Mari offered to channel. Nerida sat with her tablet, ready to record. And Aedgar came.

'It's been a while,' he said. 'Talking in your terms. For us, it's not the same, as you know. What can we do for you, my dear?'

'I hope you are able to work with Mari's throat.' The voice
was dry and croaky.

'Oh, we will always find a way.'

'We've had some drama this past week—'

'Drama?'

'—with her eyes. She lost vision in one of her eyes and it was
painful.'

'Yeah. We realised it's all a bit 'rusty'. Stuck, compressed.' He
waved the hand over Mari's left eye, touching the side of her head
and her temple delicately. The eyes were closed.

'We are worried about the circulation in this body. One of
our—we would not like to call it a concern—one area we would
like to put our thoughts into is down here.' He indicated the stump
of Mari's leg which was swollen and bruised-looking.

Nerida waited while they investigated the area.

'This area is compressed and stagnant, as well.' Aedgar said,
moving Mari's hands around the lower leg. 'Like rusty. This
produces problems in the circulation of nourishing liquids. Fluid
gets stuck in the area. The space is taken up by liquid that has
been, you know, reduced of its useful stuff.'

Deprived of oxygen, she thought.

'And it's unable to get out. So, the new, nourishing liquid is
stuck above and can't go there freely. It's a very basic way of
explaining it. We are sure you know much better—'

'I'm not so sure.'

'—in theory.'

'In theory, perhaps.'

'Yes.'

'That's why the leg gets discoloured,' she said.

'Yeah. It's what you would call the blood flow. But there is also
the other liquid that can't be transported out. You might call it the
lymphatic system.'

'Yes.'

'It's compromised. That's the main thing that is causing the
blood system to be compromised, as well. It's putting pressure on
it.'

She waited again, doodling flowing water on her notepad.

'Then there's the area up here.' He indicated Mari's left occiput, mastoid, the side of her skull. 'This area.' He brushed the fingers over the area, not quite touching.

'Same issue. Circulation needs to happen more. Area here needs to be strengthened to support better circulation in those areas.' He moved the hands across her chest.

'You mean the lungs and the heart, the cardio-thoracic region?'

'Yes. Spending more time in temperate, nice, fresh air will not cure it but it could support the body. We get a sense,' he sighed, 'of impatience, of being held back. From moving to a different place.'

'Yes.'

'What is the issue? What is slowing you down, my dear?'

'We planned to visit the house we're moving back into. But we couldn't visit that area because of the Coronavirus—that the virus was around Sydney. The timing was not right for us to go down there.'

'It was a good move to stay away. We did support that notion a bit. Because you were quite determined, my dear.'

'Yes.' *I wanted to see my family in the week before Christmas.*

Aedgar spoke with sharp consonants. 'We have to throw a lot of sticks into your path. Just to stop you. To make you less impatient to do something. You are here, we can sense, in a safe place.

'Which should not be misunderstood as a good place.' He took a beat for her to process that. 'So, you are going to go away from here?'

'We are.'

'We are glad to hear it. Is there anything we can help you with?'

'There's a lot in the news, and a lot of hope in some people, about the vaccines being offered. Our friends in America are, some of them, being given access to two of them.'

'At the moment, this serves as a distraction. That's all it does. There could be harm from it. It's not the solution they're waiting for. Or hoping for. Do you understand?'

Nerida had a sinking feeling. 'I do.'

'It serves as a distraction for many groups out there.'

'Yes.' *But that can't be all! What about the placebo effect? Even Law of Attraction?* 'But doesn't it give people positive intention or energy or something to get the needle in their arm?' *Doesn't our belief in it help it work?* She was clutching at straws.

Aedgar was sombre. 'It is a distraction from the real problem. From the things those people don't tell you. So, they say, "We put a vaccine out there. It's gonna be the solution. Make people focus on that."

'There are basic requirements to call something a vaccine, like that it acts as a protection from something. It does not protect you.

'Nor does it heal you. People'll still carry the virus around. Passing it on to other people. And not necessarily only to other people who did not get that so-called vaccine.

'There will be this big relief. It will give people a sense of relaxing. It will give them a better mood.

'Until they see what it is capable of (and what it's not). So. It is a temporary relief. A break. To start catching up with your breath again.'

That's a start. Maybe.

'There'll be a lot of people who are sick. But they don't put stress on people like you because they will stay at home. Or, as they used to, continue going to work. "Because it can't be the virus. I was vaccinated." It will spread more freely.'

Nerida drew a deep breath. 'This false sense of security will lead to an even greater surge in sickness?'

'The thing is, you will probably not hear about it,' he said. 'It will, you know, increase the number of people who catch it from thoughtless others.

'They will protect themselves less. They won't stay away from others. Because "Hey, we got that needle. We're all fine now."

'The ones that use it as a distraction and an excuse now won't tell you about that. They won't. They want it to go quiet. They will still have their numbers somewhere. You understand?'

'Yeah, I do.'

CHAPTER 55

Friday December 25, 2020

There were statistics only doctors and scientists saw.
Maybe politicians, too.
She read results of vaccine studies that the companies themselves ran and paid for. Nerida had been trained to consider such research inherently biased. There was further information, but only a few of her profession could access it.
'Their numbers are not made for everyone to hear about or to read about,' he confirmed.
'Hmm.'
'And those devices that people have, give them free access to wherever the people are. This won't be taken back.'
They'll keep access to our movements through our phones. For what? Marketing? Surveillance?
'Even if the virus decides to mutate into a different direction at some stage,' he said. 'We think we got it moving towards mutating further. At the moment, it evolved a way of being where it spreads faster. After that it will look for something else. It will attach itself to something else.'
Nerida felt humbled by the efforts of spirits to make things right again for humans. 'Thank you.'
'We want to tell you, too, more about the issue with our friend.'
'Yeah?'

'It's an area here that needs attention. Right here on the edge of the skull, where it comes down towards the neck.'
'The occiput?'
'No. It's to the side. You'd probably call it lateral.'
'Yes.'
'Yes. There's a triangle.'

The posterior cervical triangle. 'Something stuck there?' *Please god not a tumour.*

'Yes. There's compression. Restriction of movement. Then you can get pressure in areas where you don't want it. Needs to be flowing freely.'

'So it's not just the muscle on the scalp? It's actually the brain?' she asked.

'No. We can't see an issue with the brain.'

Relief flooded her.

'It's the supply and exchange of liquids, that can't nourish, for example, the nerves. Keeps them trapped. If something can't be transported away it tends to expand. Which makes the surroundings put pressure on it.'

'Yes. Would swimming help her?' *Maybe if I could get the pool usable. Mari's happy in the water.*

'It could. But it's less about the movement. It's getting these parts stretched out again—which sounds a bit wrong if you're talking about the neck.'

She flashed briefly on what neck-stretching meant in Tudor England.

'You need to relax those muscles. Get the pressure off so that everything can flow freely again.

'So what she needs is more like floating around than swimming. Concentrate on expanding the area.'

I could do that with acupuncture, she thought.

'There might be some mechanical issues, as well. After it's relaxed and freed up you might need to strengthen the muscles so that they are able to hold it in a better place. Which is quite, um, tricky. If you strengthen the wrong muscles, you'll make it worse.

'So you might need to the help of someone who is very good at balancing that. Anything else?'

'She had a vision. A violent vision.'

Mari woke Nerida, calling out in the early hours of the morning. When Nerida touched her arm, it was trembling and wet with sweat.

Nerida put the light on and sat her up.

'I can't tell you how horrible it was,' Mari said. She looked pale. 'I was murdering people, hacking them to bits. I was a serial killer.' Her dark eyes were wide. 'It was a battlefield, I think.'

Nerida wondered if it was a flashback to a past lifetimes. Aedgar told them years ago that she and Mari were brothers in arms in a notoriously brutal army.

Later, in 2015, Bartgrinn said that Mari and one of their friends were battlefield 'surgeons', in a past life, rescuing soldiers that could be saved and swiftly disposing of those that could not, terrible work across fields of carnage. Their friend was a work colleague in this life. Mari worked as an ambulance driver with him then.

Aedgar took a few moments. 'It was violent. We can tell you it did not have anything to do with this life or any other lives. It was more like the imagination putting things and places that were familiar together with horrible things. It had to do with some tweaking of the brain. Could there be drugs?'

'Yes, she's had some drugs.' *She's been taking antihistamines to help her sleep, with all her rashes and bug bites.*

'There was pressure on the nerve. And then, a drug opened the way for an explosion of imagination.'

Nerida heaved a sigh.

'We see it was vivid. The only thing we could say is: Stay away from drugs. That was a tiny warning.

'There are beneficial drugs. And there are drugs that are not.

'There was an unfavourable mix up of drugs. It has to do with the overlap. There was still a residue, hidden in some corner.'

'Aah,' said Nerida. *It's promethazine. The little blue pill that reduces the histamine in the body. And then she took an Endone to help with the pain.*

'That's an opiate,' she said. 'You know what an opiate is.' He must have used extracts of the opium poppy as a healer during his past lifetimes.

'There was something like a toxin left over in the body that reacted in an unfortunate way,' he said. 'The drug itself would not cause a 'vision' like that. The toxin would cause it by itself. The drug mixed with that toxin and kind of freed it up. To make imagination explode. If you were in a sad or bad mood already, that's the way it goes.

'If you were very happy, you might not be able to help yourself out of that endless happiness. But our friend is not in that state at the moment.

'There is too much coming in from everywhere. If we say everywhere, we don't mean that little pond you've got here. Not even that island you're sitting on.'

'That's right.' *So, Mari is picking up distressed vibes again, like she did when we lived in other disturbed places. Only this time, the vibrations come from the world. Poor darling.*

She said, 'That's reassuring, thank you. I can tell her that she was not a serial killer. At least as far as we know.'

'With that kind of vision,' he said, 'anybody would think that. Very vivid. Pushed over the limits. Extreme violence. There are some around that would have liked that. They would have gotten happiness out of it at the end. But our friend is not like that. Neither are you.'

'No.'

'We appreciate that.'

Nerida smiled a little. *No channelling with axe murders, then.*

CHAPTER 56

Lennox Head NSW, Bundjalung Country

Friday December 25, 2020

The world, then, here and now, demanded her attention. 'Can you tell me about what's happening in America? The descendants of the enslaved are infected and dying disproportionately. The Native American people are hit particularly hard too, like the descendants of the Spanish, and the Native people of middle America. It's a very, very hard time.'

Aedgar sighed deeply. For once, she sensed momentary resistance.

'Where to start?

'So, those people of Black colour were brought to a place against their will. They were used. They still are used. It has not changed. They let some of them have a fantastic career, while keeping the others going and running in that hamster wheel.

'It's still the same thing happening. They're not in a place they were supposed to be. They're in a place where they were made to be. They are trying to make the best of it.

'Others think they are superior because they got a different colour. They will have to learn from this same experience. Probably from people who have different eyes.'

Nerida made an encouraging noise. But thought, *What?*

'They will have this experience to understand what they have done to the ones of Black colour.'

People with different eyes will teach the so-called superior ones about oppression? The hoary fear of Chinese invasion of America will come true?

Oh, no Aedgar. This is too much.

'Oh,' she said. Appalled. 'This is a very big picture idea.'

'Very big. And we're talking about the longer term. This is not just around the corner.'

'Yes.' She grabbed that thought.

'This conflict has been going for centuries. So, you can't expect it to be fixed in what you call a year, or two. Or four, as might be more appropriate, over there.'

'Yeah.' *The election results are still being contested. And what could anyone fix in four years of being a figurehead for the bourgeoisie, anyway? "If voting changed anything, they'd make it illegal," Emma Goldman said.*

'Then there are the Spanish people,' Aedgar continued. 'They are not where they are supposed to be, either. They invaded, mainly, the southern part, where they pushed out the locals, making them go further north. Then some white people came and chose a border freely.

'They fought heavy fights to expand those borders, taking up the space, again, that those who were pushed north were living in.

'So, the people, or the descendants of the people, that actually are supposed to be in that place are scattered all over. It's theirs. Yet they are still largely ignored, even by the ones of Black skin. For them, it's like, "But at least you're in the place where you belong. We were brought here. We have to function in a place that we were forced into. We were forced to make it ours. We did not want that."'

'Yes.' Conversely, she'd heard Native American friends say that at least African Americans had Africa or somewhere else to go home to. *As if they could or should.*

'They feel, "So, we have priority to be helped by those people." They call those people "without colour." Because it's not white, is it?'

Nerida smiled. She never liked the term 'White.' Her mother was pink, not white, she insisted to people as a child. *'Without colour' is pretty good, though, for people like Mum, who don't know where they're from or how what happened to their ancestors that still shapes them.*

'Them fighting for equal rights makes the original people miss out even more,' he said.

Nerida murmured. She could not agree. *Could Blacks fighting for their rights disadvantage Native Americans?*

'The people of Black colour will still fight the people who were always there. Do you understand? This is in the nature of human beings.'

Nerida was unimpressed. This scenario, Black people fighting Native Americans, made her furious. 'Right,' she said. *Are humans so terrible?*

And yet, she'd seen oppressed people hammer at each other. In the 90s she went to Townsville in North Queensland after people said that police drowned an Aboriginal man in the river. The erudition of the Indigenous people there astonished her. And the violence they reported rocked her. A girl was raped by white supremacists with a broken bottle, a nurse told her.

She stood on a picket line, then, with striking abattoir workers defending a senior Aboriginal man, run out by a racist boss. She went there to do that.

After her second week, a respected Aboriginal Elder took her aside to tell Nerida the secret to Aboriginal oppression. 'It's the Torres Strait Islanders,' she said. 'They take all the funding.'

They called it lateral violence in the 90s, oppressed people hating and destroying each other.

Nerida felt disgust and pity when she realized that this woman of substance had fallen into the trap laid for her: believing her oppression was created by other dispossessed Black and Brown people, who came from the Torres Strait. Her people and theirs both needing to recover from the past two centuries of calamity.

'Nah, look to the common enemy, Aunt,' she said then. 'It's a class of people that takes from us, not an ethnicity.'

We go forward together or fall back separately.

Her parents and grandparents taught her.

Except for Nana, who hated Japanese people with a passion born of wartime propaganda. She wondered sometimes how Nana would have accepted her wife, a German of Romany ancestry.

CHAPTER 57

'And all this will go on for a very long time.' Aedgar hammered.

'Other people will come in who think that they're superior to all of them. The ones of Black colour will support them coming in because they're fighting the ones with no colour. Those that spent centuries showing them "their place" in this particular area of the planet.

'And then the Black and brown people realise the new ones coming have different colour and different eyes to them. And they will be next.'

This is a dismal bloody picture.

'The ones that are always missing out are the ones who were always there,' he said.

Indigenous peoples' deprivation goes on and on, yes. That sounds sickly familiar.

'They can't see beyond the horizon. "This happened to us. That was done to us. And that's just because we have a different colour." You know?'

'We're talking about the African-American people now?'

'Yes. And then, the white ones will say, "You've done all this to us because we have a different colour, too," (that will be later). "And different eyes." So, the people with Black colour will support the ones with different eyes. This is an example. You can take it literally or not. It's not meant to be taken that way, but if that's how you get something out of it…anyway.

'So, they will gang up with the ones with different eyes. To fight the ones with no colour, until they have them on a very low level of power. Then the ones with different eyes will fight the ones with the black colour.

'And all the ones who miss out on everything, they are keen on missing out on the fights, you know? But they will miss out on everything else. The ones who were always there.'

'Yeah.' Nerida sat in a chasm of confusion and despair.

'Native,' he said, to clarify.

'Yes.'

'So,' Aedgar concluded, 'It will all go on like this unless those Native people are recognised by all of them: you the invaders, you who were brought against your will, you who were victims put there.

'—And they still fight the original people because they find them easiest to fight. "I get hit by those people without colour all the time. I dump it on those other people." Do you understand? It's not something you can solve like this.' He snapped Mari's fingers, as if to wake her from her misery.

'Does this mean we're doomed to centuries of racist warfare and abuse and oppression?' she asked.

'Yes. Unless they all recognise those who haven't done anything to them.'

Recognition of the Indigenous Peoples and understanding them is the source of healing. Makes sense. Indigenous peoples have survived to keep the knowledge and teach others what's needed for humankind to survive and flourish. We need to remind each other of this.

Aedgar stopped, as if he sensed her desperation. 'This would be the path they're on, if people don't feel: "We should stop, think differently. And then we can act differently."

'Just going somewhere and saying something doesn't change anything,' he added.

She agreed with that, too. *Fine words don't butter my parsnips.*

'Racists don't realise that they are racists, you know, until they are discriminated against by someone else. "Oh my god, that's how it feels. I had no idea!" Welcome to a different world.'

But does the whole human experience have to be shaped by racists? Isn't there another way? Nerida bit her lip.

Aedgar's tone mellowed. 'Some people have had different lives in different colours, with different eye shapes. They are sitting in positions where they are trying to change the way people think.

Only when they change the way people think, will they act differently. There are still not enough of them. You understand?'

Nerida sputtered, 'Ya, I mean—'

'There are more and more of those experienced souls coming. But it can't all happen within what you call a year. You need to make a beginning,' he said gently. 'You need to start. And it starts by listening.'

Offered a road out of this uncoiling disaster, she stroked her chin, deep in thought.

'Not going on: complaining, complaining, complaining, complaining. "I am a victim, a victim, a victim." That's not working.

'If you are a victim, if you don't like the way you're treated, then don't treat others the way you are treated. And try to change the way those others think. You take action.'

A magpie trilled in the tree outside. Nerida understood. As a young woman she felt victimhood was integral to her Aboriginal identity. If people asked, 'How are you?' she'd always talk about something bad. 'Struggling,' she'd say. Or, 'Doing it hard.' If she was happy, she'd say, 'Not too bad, in spite of everything.'

To say that she was well seemed like a betrayal of the history she knew. Suffering was a way of paying respect and identifying with her ancestry.

It was good to hear a spirit challenge that notion. She outgrew it. She knew now that her ancestors wanted her to be happy, strong and proud.

But she'd seen many of her people, including in her own family, succumb to stubborn perseverance in victimhood. *My troubled sonboy.* Jim's addiction had already destroyed two marriages (each to poorly chosen partners, in his mother's quiet opinion).

His addiction led him to steal from Nerida. He smashed up Mari's car and pretended someone else had done it. He moved to the States after his mother went to work in the Bush. Where his gambling habit lost him a house with his second marriage. All before he was thirty-five.

Despite small excursions into rehab programs, usually Court-ordered, it was all, always, somebody else's fault. If it wasn't white people or Democrats or the Chinese, it was his parents who were the root cause of Jim's problems. He never seemed to learn. *He's always looking outside himself for someone to blame, with no concept of taking responsibility for his own healing.*

Aedgar waited. Then said mildly, 'We're talking about the place you asked us about,' he said.

'Yes. Thank you.' She felt subdued. The trajectory he saw for the United States was almost unbearable to contemplate. And her son lived there.

People had to change their minds.

If I put Aedgar's words in a book, could that help change people's minds? Who would read such a weird book?

Jim will hate it.

'See, they have this one guy,' Aedgar was saying, his awareness still Stateside. 'You can't call this guy a villain. He's got a brain like a child. And he thinks he's grown up. He's a big man now. He's in a very high position. But that doesn't change the brain that he's got.'

'Yeah.'

'He acts and thinks like a child. He was not capable. He had good intentions, we have to say. But he was incapable of doing anything at all. He did not try hard enough. He couldn't.'

'Mhmm.' Nerida thought of politicians and moguls. She had her own idea who he was talking about.

'When he thinks of himself, he's wise. That doesn't work.

'You are wise if other people talk about you that way. This is something you don't call yourself.'

'Mhmm.' *It's like being a healer or shaman. It's only real if other people decide to acknowledge it. Greg learned that the hard way.*

'You know,' Aedgar said, 'cohorts of people say, "I am an Old Soul." No, you're not. You don't act like one. You say you are wise? No. No one can see it. You don't act like you've inherited wisdom from other lifetimes. You don't.

'You understand?'

'I do.'

'A lot of humans don't.

'We have to break it to you somehow.

'Sometimes it's interesting to watch. Painful, too. How far they will go before they get up and say, "Something has to change, and we'll start doing it differently. Right now." We're still waiting.

'There is always hope.'

'There needs to be.' Her tone was bitter.

She gazed out the window. The magnolia tree had a blossom in bud, like a giant white chilli.

'Yes. There is always hope amongst all the distraction. The whole distraction thing.'

Nerida reflected on what Aedgar meant by 'the whole distraction thing.' *Hours spent numbing out on rubbish television, eating too much. Fantasizing about fashion on the internet. Or spending all your money on the horses. Or porn. Or any of the other addictive behaviours that amount to wishing your life away. We're all so good at that.*

'This burden that came over the world—it was bred, created and put out there. It was not an accident.'

'Yes.' Her lips were pressed.

'What's happening now is what we would consider an accident. It's the distraction of having something that seems to deal with it.'

Oh, he means the vaccine. Does he call it an accident because some people are going to be hurt by it?

She still had trouble accepting the idea that all of the anti-COVID vaccines could be bad. The media was thick with news of the 'vaccine rollout.' News from America seemed to indicate that the number of deaths was decreasing as vaccination increased. It was confusing. She trusted Aedgar. But she was not opposed to vaccines.

In 1992 she saw a ten-day-old baby dead of *tetanus neonatorum* in Indonesia. His mother had no immunity from being immunised against tetanus. The bacterium got into his umbilical stump. The little one suffocated after hours of seizures, fever and bloody diarrhoea. Local herbalists and nurses were unable to effectively treat him. She would never forget the grief of the baby's parents. She was a scientist then. The experience solidified her decision to study medicine.

Now, as a doctor, whenever Nerida injected her injured patients with Tet-Tox she felt a prayer of gratitude. Especially in

Northern Australia, so close to Indonesia, she thought, *People just across the water can't get this. Use the strength we share to make things better for all.*

Nerida was born ten years after the peak of the polio epidemic.

She grew up with people around her talking about it. Remembered the safety she felt as a kindergartener getting the sweet pink syrup of the Sabin vaccine. Appreciation for vaccination was in her bones.

She tolerated the non-physical beings' objections to the anti-COVID vaccines, though, partly because she had no evidence to firmly contradict them.

And they've been right so many times before.

Or am I displaying cognitive bias? Observer bias? Of course, I am. You are deep in trouble now, Dr Nerida, she told herself.

Aedgar may have sensed her conflict. He said, 'People could do a lot more with simple things.'

'Yes.'

'Like face-covering.'

'Yes.'

'Staying away from large groups, you know?'

'Yes.'

'People think, they will think, "It's all good, now." And it's not. Some of your good colleagues say: "It is not over. Keep doing what we told you." There is a reason for it.

'But their voice is not strong or loud enough, even if they were in the position to be influential. They are intimidated by others.

'It's like, "I wanna have this miracle out there. I wanted it to happen. So, I made it happen." No, you didn't. They didn't.

'It's still a game, a very big game, of greed. Even if the pharmaceutical companies don't charge now (or not as much as they would like), it will be like, "We made this great thing. And the world owes us one."

'Or two. Or ten. "And everyone is going to make it happen so we can earn ourselves stupid." That's the continuum you always had. It has to be broken at some stage.'

CHAPTER 58

Shifting the Energy in a Place

Flowing on, kindly

'We know you are talking to us,' he acknowledged.

She felt recognised. Relaxed in the connection.

'There are plenty, plenty of people that still don't understand. We think it's a very important fact. You don't do your farming properly—you will have nothing to eat.

'You get greedy, you want it to grow faster, to grow bigger, so you can get more money out of it? Wrong move.

'We always say, it's not quantity, it's quality.

'Stick with that dictum. It enhances your quality of life.

'You have one glass of wine—it enhances the quality of your life. You have more than that? You're destroying it.

'You have one chocolate bar? It makes you happy for a while. You have ten in one day (or even five)? It's gonna destroy your life if you keep doing it.

'With every thing: quantity is not what you go for.

'A tiny amount of poison? You will be fine. If it's a big amount, your life is done.

'Maybe you should see it with the poison version. If the wine and the chocolate doesn't make you understand, choose the 'poison' version of the story. If you have a tiny amount you can get help. You can be fixed. You will be fine. Huge amount? You're out of there.'

Nerida agreed. 'And anything can be a poison if there's too much of it.'

'You've seen it. You've got too much water? You're dead.'

'I have seen it.' She treated tourists in the desert who drank too much water and put themselves in danger of 'coning'—the base of the brain pulled into the spinal canal causing death. Their body salt was too dilute.

'You get too much salt, you're dead,' he continued.

'Yes.' *Aboriginal people of the desert know that. Where water is scarce, salt can kill.*

Aedgar said, 'You take too much camomile tea? You're dead. This concept won't get into the heads of the so-called health gurus out there.

'Having more of something does not make it better. Think of that.

'One vitamin tablet can help you a lot.

'Taking them over a long period, taking more than one?' he asked. 'Your life changes. And not in a good way. Quality matters. Quantity takes the benefit from you.

'It's the same with the planet: take what you need, you'll be fine. Nature will replenish it.

'Taking as much as you can, will deplete it. It can't fill itself up again.

'And we don't know where to start, talking about people taking things out of the earth, depleting it and sending it somewhere else.'

'They take all of it out. They don't need a hundredth or a thousandth of it. They sell it off to someone else. For paper with numbers on it that they can't eat.

'Where did the evolution go? It stopped somewhere, quite a while ago.

'And then,' he said, 'they talk about future generations. "We can't destroy this planet because of future generations." You will come back! You will be the one that has to deal with it. If you don't understand this one concept—

'They think, "I get it all out. I take it all. Because then I die and it's all over. I had a wonderful life with all the paper with the numbers on it I could ever think of. The fastest cars, the biggest houses, the most expensive jewelry. I only ate at the finest restaurants."

'And then, you'll come back into a new life and experience famine. Poverty. And you're the one that created it. Maybe not single-handed. But you were part of it.

'It doesn't make it less stupid if everybody else does it. "I'm just doing it because all these others do."

'Don't you wanna be the one that's different? Wouldn't you like to be that one? Ten years later, people say, "This is a wise person."

'Or, "He's got the brain of a child. Can't help it. There's lots of them around there."

'You understand?'

'I do.' She was downcast.

'We have to say, over and over again, you need to change because there is still hope out there. You have to nourish that tiny plant of hope. Treat it well. Work on it. Make it grow bigger. Take action.

'So, hope can grow into the reality you want. Not the reality that's imposed on you by the outside.

'With this virus, people have the chance to change the way they think. To realise what is more important: that fancy car out there? That you can't go anywhere in, because you're supposed to stay at home?

'Or is it the people around you? That you have to learn again—because of your 'prosperous' life—to get on with. Striving to nourish your children, that you put in this world out of love?

'Or are they a hindrance, just: "How can I get rid of them?" And it's not like that thought comes into your head for a split second when that little one did something incomprehensible—like destroying some of your property, you know?

'We're talking about the continuous thought, "I wish I would not have them. I wish someone else would take care of it. I wish they would just go away." They won't. You created them. And you say they are the fruit of love. So, treat them that way. Your fruit of love.

'Be sure to show them the ropes for this life. If children damage their property, parents think "I could kill that one," for a split second. It is necessary to teach the child how far they can go.

'There are boundaries in living together. You need to learn how to get along with people. And how to treat things that someone has put hours (or weeks) of their lives into creating.'

'Or years,' she said. Mari had taught her a lot about respecting the labour in property. She understood the concept as a child. But had somehow lost her respect for things as an adult in the throw-away society. It was spiritual to be anti-materialist.

'Or years of work,' he agreed. 'It's about respect. Teach them respect. Treat your surroundings well. Whether humans or even things. You will be rewarded.

'Do you understand?'

'I do.' Esteem of the work people put into her surroundings. When did that change? When cheap, pretty items were mass-produced in China, that working people could afford? *What about respect for the Chinese workers? Living in dormitories, far from home, with their children and old people left in the countryside. Things are not working well there. Nor in Bangladesh, where most of our clothes are made.*

Years ago, she asked Monica about the idea that everything is conscious. Aedgar talked to Nerida about it in 2016. She asked Monica because she wanted her opinion, but also because she wanted to talk to Mari about it. *Maybe our lives could be better if we changed the way we think.* Mari would listen if the idea came from Monica.

'Aedgar says that, for example, this table has consciousness,' Nerida said then. She tapped the wooden table.

'Well, of course.' Monica waited a beat. 'How would it keep being a table, if it doesn't know it's one? It needs consciousness to hold the atoms together.'

'If you have a dog you treat badly, one day it's gonna bite you,' Aedgar said. 'Or someone else if you're lucky. Treat them well. They will stay with you. They will be a delight.

'A society needs some rules, so humans can live, all of them, as a society. To take part in things; each person provided with their share of participation.

'If you have someone on top who uses everybody else to take more out of the society, whether it be power or paper with numbers on it, you destroy that society. Because you will have others in that society who say: "I wanna be like him." Or like her. And "I will do exactly the same thing." You have an awful lot of those around. They try to out-do the ones up there by being nastier. We could say dumber.

'They don't do their part. All they do is try to please that one up there. So it says, "Aw, come on. I lift you up to be on my level." Until that one then pushes their mentor out.

'We see it as a big kindergarten where no one has rules or responsibilities. Where no one feels "I have to bring in my part." People feel, "Why should I? If those up there don't?" There's that envy. Envy and greed are the worst. Envy makes people greedy when they haven't been before.

'Are there any other questions? We think we went a bit far.'

'I liked it.' She did. They took her beyond the limits of ordinary thinking. She felt invigorated by the energy they brought.

'Good,' the spirit said. 'We hope you're not the only one.'

'Me too.'

'Can be a bit controversial.'

'Yes.' Nerida couldn't process the possibility of decades of race wars. *I will try to figure that out later*, she thought.

'Now,' she said, 'I'm sorry to ask about these vaccines again. But the ones that are made to use messenger RNA? Are they the ones that could harm people in the longer term?'

Even if she doesn't do it as a full-time job, Dr Nerida will still have to give people the anti-COVID vaccinations. Perhaps she will be made to take one herself, to be allowed to work. *How to reconcile that with what Aedgar says?*

'You are fighting an enemy. Let's call it that,' he explained. 'You take some parts in your body. You change something in your body, within you, to fight that enemy.'

'Yes.'

'What's that good for? It means you fight the enemy at the enemy's level. You don't want to fight it within your own body.'

Of course, you fight a disease within your own body, that's what the immune system is for, she thought.

But then, there's strength in keeping an enemy outside of yourself. M'Hoq Toq taught her once to put a psychic shell around herself to be able to work in a hostile place. *Maybe this is a bit like that. Stop the baddies getting in.*

'Those things mutate, as you know. They can evolve in the wrong direction. And once it's in the body there is not much you can do about that.'

Is he talking about the virus mutating once it's in your body? Or contracting a mutated form of the virus?

'So, they say, "We're only changing those cells. We're only fighting there, at that special spot, where it attaches."

Okay, she understood that. They called it the spike protein. Those vaccines cause the body to create SARS-CoV-2 spike proteins, so that the immune system learns to fight it.

'It's a wrong way to think. Further down the road when the struggle with that virus is finished, that creation will look for other things that are within your body. Because you put it in your body.'

Nerida thought, *Does he mean that some aspect of the vaccine would look for something else to attach itself to? Something else to fight?*

'Previous vaccines used this enemy to train the body, so to speak, to do it itself.'

Okay. I get that. Vaccines provoke antibody production against the disease.

'And get rid of it and fight it.'

'That's right.' She was with him now. She remembered something she read on Wikipedia, 'The vaccine transfects molecules of synthetic RNA into immunity cells.' It stuck in her head because 'transfect' was a new word. The image she had in her head was like microplastics getting into the immune system. *But now you're just making shit up. Focus.*

In an ordinary vaccine, Aedgar was saying, 'You have cells that fight that body, but they are still your body's cells. Once that enemy's gone, they'll be done with their work. You know?

'But these other things change something significantly within the body. You have changed something.

'And the makers of these injections have literally no idea what this is gonna do in two years from now or even one year from now.

'So, the virus goes off. It happily mutates and changes to a different host.'

Maybe SARS-CoV-2 will fall in love with mosquitoes, she thought.

'The virus is gone. But you are stuck with those other changes in your body. Do you understand?'

Nerida tilted her head. 'I think so. Are you talking about the mRNA vaccines in particular? Or does that apply to all of the anti-COVID vaccines that are being used?' She seemed to recall that some were using an adenovirus coat, the shell of the virus, to deliver the material. The kind of technology that killed Andy.

'Most of them,' he said cryptically. 'There are quite a few.

'One, single one, could—we don't say it is—it could be promising if they did a lot more work on it. We repeat, a lot more work. Not something you could do within days or weeks. It would probably take another year. Or two.'

Nerida understood that he had objections. She couldn't get her mind around what his objections were, except that having a vaccine made a permanent, unpredictable change in the body with, according to Aedgar, no benefit beyond the placebo effect.

'It's awkward,' she said, 'for a doctor to be opposed to the use of these vaccines. I've spoken to colleagues and told people who've asked me my opinion. I've said that these vaccines are not adequately tested, and we don't know if they're helpful at all, or harmful. I am apprehensive.'

'Well, all we say is that you asked. We gave you an answer. It is up to you, my dear.

'You could package your response as some scientists do.' Aedgar made his pompous authority voice. '"Oh, in general, yes, yes, yes. But there might be something that's a no, no. But in general, yes, yes, yes!"'

He made her smile now. *That's exactly what they do. Clever observation, Aedgar.*

'"But at the end, maybe no."

'We hope that some humans can read between the lines, if you tweak it that way, to find out what we actually said.

'You don't change important things within your body to fight something that's outside. Because the body will be changed—and not just temporarily.

'That external enemy moves on happily.

'You will have another one come. And then they change their so-called vaccine again. You will end up with a whole battery of changes to your DNA. And all these viruses or other pathogens walk off, happily, each with a new partner, so they can replicate somewhere else.

'They are conscious. You've heard it before. "I would like to have as many children as possible. Human beings will allow me to do that. This is what I go for."

Nerida saw a small cockroach heading to the kitchen compost bin.

Aedgar went on. 'It is not like, "Oh, there is Grandpa Joe. And Aunty Paula. Oh, we'll take them because they're useless anyway." This is not how it is.

'It's like, "Oh, how lovely. They will provide us with a whole new generation. We love you."

'Until death. That's how it is. This is the form of consciousness, "We love you because you give us all these opportunities."'

Nerida recalled flies in the desert. *They try to get into your eyes. They want a drink.* And *to deposit maggots there.*

'It's not like you're being punished. "You've been a very bad person all your life. We go for you. Oh, you've got a different colour, we go for you. You've got different eyes. We go for you." No, that's not how it is.

'It's like, "We love you for all the opportunity you give us. We are eternally grateful for your offer." They don't see that it was never offered, you know?

'It's like, "Oh, that's wonderful! Let's go there!"

'So why would you change anything in a body, so that then you have it, this thing with its overwhelming love for human beings? And then have to carry it around in your body? This is not the way to go.'

Does he say that the virus itself stays in the body when the vaccine is injected? I'm not sure about that.

Aedgar was on a different tack. 'They should look for things in nature that are useful to fight that thing. In plants, for example. We've had this discussion before. Go with it.'

It's true that researchers would be better off working on a treatment for the sickness. Why have they given up on that? Doctors are still trying everything we can think of.

'Don't go using things you haven't even started to understand,' Aedgar asserted. 'You don't have the technology or, sorry to say, the brains to do this. Our friend would say it's like the Sorcerer's Apprentice.'

'Yes.' Nerida thought of the Disney cartoon with the lazy apprentice Mickey Mouse. His magically animated brooms and mops became monsters, turning his life into a nightmare. *Mari loves that story. Maybe Aedgar can see it in her brain.*

'It's always there, that Sorcerer's Apprentice dynamic.'

What does he mean by that? Using technology without enough knowledge spirals into disaster?

'It's quite obvious to us. Probably to some others of your race, the humans, as well. Cause if you change something within your body to fight it, those little things, they love you so much—they will adapt to your body much quicker than you can respond.'

Finally, she asked, 'So the vaccine will actually make people more vulnerable to the illness?'

'It could be a consequence. We're not saying it. We will need you, you know?'

Maybe he is okay with me not quite understanding. Perhaps it was their intention, she realised finally, to leave her with limited understanding.

'Stay out of trouble,' he said. 'But don't tweak what we say. Just put it into conversation.'

Breezily he mimicked, 'And then someone came along, someone I usually don't know. They told me that story and I thought, "It could be interesting."

'Or,' in his satirical, autocratic voice: "There is in general, yes, yes, yes." Raised a pointed finger. "But this one thing, no, no, no. But in general, of course, yes."

'Down the road they will say, "No. We should have never done that."'

Nerida thanked him. She felt well cared for. And she enjoyed the spirit's perspective on her colleagues and science. She had a sense, too, that Aedgar was protecting her. *Maybe if I knew the full story, I would go mad. Maybe I would be like Skete Parlour, vilified and terrified. A full-on anti-vaxxer compelled to tell my terrible, unscientific truth.*

'You are welcome, my dear.'

'When we lived in a mining town to work in 2015—'

'Yes.'

'M'Hoq Toq said, I think, that there was a conscious virus, dug up out of the ground—'

'Yes.'

'Which could cause something beyond a plague, a pestilence.'

'Yeah. There are quite a few of them,' Aedgar said coolly.

'So, it's not just this one that's been created? That was just a taste?' She had a metallic taste in her mouth as she said it.

'Yeah, that's just a tiny, tiny hint.'

Nerida sighed.

'You understand that there's a lot out there on the planet you live on. A lot of pathogens that were never touched before. Or they were frozen over, heated up, frozen over, heated up, dried out, to stop them. It was in places you would call 'safe' because no one ever went there.'

Nerida nodded.

'Then someone discovers something,' Aedgar continued. 'Testing for whatever that was. "Oh, something magnetic out there."' He imitated an oafish voice.

'They go for it. They dig stuff up. In areas where no one ever lived. And they ship it all over the world. Because it's all about the quantity. Paper with numbers on it. Prestige or power.

'They dig up other things with it.' He arched a brow.

'There are—used to be—dense forests on this planet that had their purpose. Maintain climate, keep things fertile, all of these things. No one ever went there.

'Some people lived there that were very well adapted.

'But then others came. Started cutting it down. Quantity. Paper with numbers on it. Prestige. Power. Of course, as they move further and further in to the forest, they take things out that they can't see.

'Once they realise what they've done, "We dug something up. It's quite bad," it will be too late.

'When they finally have something that makes it possible for them to see or to measure it, it will be too late.

'Plenty of people have already died. "One of the trees fell on its head." That human, you know?

'Not entirely true. Maybe that person was too weak in the first place. Was not adapted to the climate. Should not have gone to this area, ever. Ended up there. Stunned by something.

'Everybody says, "Yeah, he got hit by a tree."

'We're sure that happens now and then.

'(We are not talking about you, my dear).

'Mostly, though, they died from something else. Will the ones of low intelligence tell the world? They're going for power and prestige and all of that. They're not going to publicise it. "Some people in there died of a disease that we can't name. We don't know how it works. We don't know how to deal with it."

'Will they ever tell the rest of the world? Probably not.

'People will find out, though. Sooner or later. In this case, maybe not so much later.

'These things that make people sick have consciousness. "We found the perfect host." "Go for it." Consciousness can mean communication. Trees communicate. So why does anyone think viruses can't? Or bacteria for that matter?

'There's a whole load of bacteria out there on your planet. You get in touch with that? Game over. We can tell you that.'

'Do humans have to go to the end of the world for greed, prestige, power? We don't think so.

'Do you have to go back to living in caves? Why would you?

'But going to interfere with the moon because you've destroyed the planet you live on? And then you're looking for other planets? Don't. Don't.

'You will interfere with much more than your little brains can even think of.

'There will be things you can't measure. You don't know how. It's going to hit back at you. You have no idea. You think there's no harm there. Because you, at the current moment in time, can't see it or you can't measure it. Doesn't mean harm is not there. We can promise you it is.

'As we've said before, we will always make sure there's that tiny bit missing that you would need to conquer, as you say, other planets.

'You can't mess up this planet and think, "That one's done. I can't get more prestige, paper with numbers or power out of it. I just go somewhere else."

'You are not alone in this universe.'

Nerida was consoled. That there were guides helping to keep the worst aspects of humanity in check.

'Your first mistake is that you talk about it as a Universe. It's not. Even "multiverse" can't describe it. You understand?'

'If I can't understand it, I can accept what you say. I trust you. I appreciate the good work you do,' she said.

'There will be a lot of humans out there who read or listen to our words, who will say, "That was a waste of time." All of them should be very glad that for us it's not considered a waste of time, trying to give you little hints, information to enable you to survive. Nourish that hope. It's out there.'

'I understand.' She spoke slowly, 'To nourish that hope, given that the present trajectory is so frightening, and dismal, can we talk about ways to cultivate our own minds?'

Aedgar said with a half-smile, 'Are you trying to get us to say all these nice things?'

'Yes.'

'So we can make you feel better. Even though you just look out the window and you can see it's not?'

'Yes.' She laughed with a cry in her voice.

His voice was warm. 'See, there are a lot of young ones out there. We appreciate them. Some adults belittle them. "These are only children. They don't even know what they're talking about."

'To the children, I can say, you startle them, you make them think, then they feel like they have to belittle you.

'A lot of you young ones act out of fear of the future. Don't act out of fear. Because you are right.

'Don't fear those old men and women that tell you, "you are just children."

'Think about different solutions.

'Because one day you will be old enough to take over.

'And you might go and stuff them into "nursing homes." Then they can experience firsthand what they created for the older people that did not have enough power, status, or paper with numbers on it.

'You're on the right track. Keep working on it. You don't need to create mass demonstrations, putting yourself and others at risk. But keep your networking up. Listen to ideas. Try to study all these things that you need to know.

'You're on the right track. You are right. Those are wrong.

'Was that enough my dear?'

'That was beautiful. Thank you.'

'Keep going, young ones,' he said. 'Keep networking. But try to get some holidays off your devices. This is not the whole solution. Stay in touch with the person right next to you.'

He was quiet. Nerida was feeling emotional.

'Is there anything else, my dear?'

'I would like to call you wise,' she said.

Aedgar sighed. 'It's a bit much. I mean, you are a human being and you're calling us wise? Thank you, anyway.'

She laughed. 'Thank you for your wisdom. And thank you for coming and sharing it with us.'

'You're welcome.'

'And thank you for looking after the love of my life.'

The room was quiet. Mari returned slowly and sleepily.

'Hey, darling.'

'Hey.'

'It's dark.'

Mari blinked. Looked out the window into the night. 'Yeah, I just realised.'

CHAPTER 59

Lennox Head, Bundjalung Country

Sunday March 14, 2021

Across the ocean in America, people marched to
commemorate the death of Breonna Taylor, the young medical

emergency technician shot dead by plainclothes police who forced entry into her apartment.

The wrong apartment. In Louisville, Kentucky.

'It reminds me of David Gundy's death,' Nerida told Mari as she sliced a tomato at lunch. 'A young Aboriginal man shot in his bed at Marrickville, when I lived there in inner-city Sydney. The Special Weapons and Operations Squad,' she saw the question on Mari's face, 'like a SWAT team. Smashed his door down, just before dawn. They had no reason to be there.'

'When was that?'

'1989. Ruby was four years old. Jim was two. I was a single mum with a head full of dreadlocks. Living in Public Housing. I was scared walking them to childcare.'

'I loved your dreadlocks. What do you mean, though?'

'The police hunted for an Aboriginal man with dreads all day one Wednesday. He was accused of shooting a cop, so you knew he wasn't going to survive.

'It was on the radio all day, how they were hunting him. I was glad to be a short, round, fair-skinned woman. But I was anxious about being on the buses to Uni, walking around in the city. I kept my hair wrapped.'

'So did David Gundy have dreadlocks?'

'No. He wasn't the one they were looking for. He didn't look like the guy, but they shot him dead anyway. In the early hours of the Thursday morning.

'It was all so bloody predictable, the way they were revved up. The cop said it was an accident. That the loaded gun pointed at David accidentally misfired. No consolation to the people that loved him. He was a dad, you know?'

She got up to get the salt. 'They changed the name of the SWOS a couple of years later. After they got busted for playing Russian Roulette with Aboriginal kids in the park near Redfern.

'Breonna's murder reminds me of Fred Hampton's death, too. One of the Black Panthers. 1967.'

'Why? You weren't even born till the year after that.'

'They shot him in his bed. Said he was armed. But he was in bed with a book. That's all. Another pre-dawn raid. They came in a gas company truck.'

'Why do you carry this history? I don't understand.'

'It's what I was born into.'

Mari reflected, chewing on a toasted bread roll. She buttered the last piece. 'It's not a competition. You always say that.' She paused, collecting the crumbs from her plate.

'I know which concentration camp my mother's father was in. We know that from his tattoo. I don't know much more. I wonder if I suffer less because I don't know.'

'No. I think you suffer more because you've got patterns in your body that respond to trauma you don't know about, can't talk about. We know that your mum nearly died herself as a baby, of deprivation and starvation.

'That influences you through epigenetics.'

'But how much trauma can a person take?' Mari raised her voice. 'I've had enough in one lifetime, just my lifetime, for anyone.

'Locked in the cupboard by nuns, beaten by a priest. Left in horrible pain from unnecessary operations by your colleagues.'

Nerida flinched, feeling echoes of Mari's pain in her own body.

'And I can't help feeling that re-hashing the stories of suffering and victimisation over and over makes it all more likely to happen again, not less,' Mari concluded.

Her vision was still spotted, as if through greasy glass, even if she saw very well between the spots. She'd been able to spot a whale's blow from the balcony of the orange house when they went to Narooma, Nerida noticed.

Mari went back to the eye specialist who found she'd had a small retinal detachment. Her vision gradually returned, and the pain lessened in frequency and intensity. She questioned the metaphorical meaning of the vision loss. 'What did I lose sight of, that my body has to tell me?' she asked Nerida. 'How do I grow my vision back?'

The MRI images of her head fascinated Mari when Nerida showed her the images on her computer. Examining the septum of her nose, they saw serpentine curves where it should have been straight.

'I got hit in the nose playing handball.'

'What, when you were a kid?'

'Maybe fourteen? The doctor straightened it while I was awake. You know, clunk, clunk.' She mimed it, pushing her nose from side to side. 'Looks like it wasn't a great job.'

'Yeah. It's no wonder you snore. But your eyes look normal. And your brain is perfectly beautiful.' Nerida leaned past Mari to use the track pad. Detailed patterns of her favourite shell came into focus on the big screen.

'Your neck shows years of hauling tanks and dragging people around. Look. Signs of the surgeons who've been there too, tying up your bones with wires, trying to fix you after all the years walking tilted on one foot.' She examined the spinal cord at the base of the brain, the perfect flower of the white matter. 'No emergencies there.' She rubbed Mari's shoulders.

The neurosurgeon on the Gold Coast agreed. Mari had an appointment to see her at the end of June.

'If they're waiting more than three months to see you, that's a good sign,' she told Mari.

In Lennox, Nerida saw online that the land they wanted at Greenough had been sold to someone else, even though they made an offer on it. They had hours of umbrage.

The next day, though, the News announced with fanfare that a chemical treatment plant was to be built near Greenough. It was a processing plant to produce ammonia and urea from natural gas, the reporter said. Construction has started on the gas pipeline from the south, past, or through, Green Head and Greenough.

'Perhaps it was for the best that we didn't get that land,' Nerida said, stretching.

Green Head had a fight against fracking on its hands they found out, too. 'Just as well we didn't buy there,' Mari said.

Nerida agreed. 'I know we'll be engaged with whichever environment we live in. I would like to avoid buying into a fight that will consume us, if we can. We have other important things to do.'

Nerida's son Jim sent a text, 'Great news Mum. We're coming home!!! Need to get away from COVID. I love the USA but Oz safer now. Haha glad we can get away. Phone date on Tuesday??'

His voice was excited but edgy over the phone. 'We've gotta get out of here. I love you, Mum. LA's insane, Mum. Tens of thousands of people homeless on the streets. Drug addicts and filthy people coming to Church expecting us to feed them, sleeping on the pews. They could do more to help themselves. Honestly, they're disgusting.'

Nerida remembered her son, then, camped on her lounge for more than a year when he was twenty-two. When no one else could tolerate his broken, addicted, abusive personality. The way he used people.

He stole anything she had that would sell for drugs. He was injecting ice at the time. He'd disappear for days, then come back to sleep in the living room for days, coming down, begging her marijuana, diazepam, anything chemical.

She never had anything. She was political then. And she was in her last year of medical school. She couldn't have drugs in the house.

Didn't need that television, anyway.

But even she reported him to the police so that he left after he sold their washing machine. And she came home to find him on the doorstep of her apartment with traces of ice and a syringe. It was the beginning of making firm boundaries with her son.

'Cindy wants to come to Australia. It's a big country. Not much COVID, eh? We have friends there already, through church. We might have to stay with you awhile. Seems like there's a housing shortage there. The houses are expensive!

I know you wouldn't want us on the streets, would you, Mum? You're such a compassionate person.

'The thing is, Australian immigration need a guarantor for Cindy. To pay her medical insurance and so on.'

'Well, that would be you. You're her husband.'

'That's the problem, see. Because I've been declared bankrupt twice now. I wasn't really bankrupt, you know, it's just what the accountants tell you to do to get out of tax. But because of that, and because I don't have any savings, they won't accept me as a guarantor. It needs to be a relative. They need three hundred thousand deposit.'

'Three hundred thousand? I don't have that kind of money, love. No one I know does.'

'But you're a doctor. You could earn it if you tried. If you took some kind of decent job with better people. Worked a bit harder. Or you could get a mortgage on your house.'

He knew how to play her.

Nerida was called lazy as a child when she had a slow and thoughtful approach to things. She worked twice as hard as anyone the rest of her life, to prove that untrue.

'Well, we were thinking of getting a mortgage to repair the orange house. It needs a new roof, the weight-bearing beams need replacing. Needs new windows and doors. I was going to ask for a mortgage for three hundred thousand to do that. But we really need those repairs done. And we need a place to live, Jim.

'I want you to be safe.

'But I can't mortgage our house for you and Cindy. Mari wouldn't agree to it. I'm not sure I would, either. You already lost the house you had before you met Cindy because of your gambling.'

Jim snorted. 'How did I know you would bring that up? You know that the bank treated me unfairly then. They wouldn't give me a break when I was at my lowest point.

'You're my mother. I was always the one who missed out. Now you're the only one who can help.'

Nerida said nothing.

Then, 'You have money coming in with your work. How much do you have saved from the condos you sold in Bell Gardens?'

'Oh, that fell through. Honestly, we have the worst building inspectors here. The bureaucracy is unbelievable.'

'What about the subdivision in Nevada?'

He took a moment to remember. 'I was gazumped on that. It was all snapped up by an off-shore company. One of my former colleagues sold the whole division for, like, five times its value.'

'Money laundering, I guess,' she said.

Nerida looked down the hallway where her wife was painting, serene, totally absorbed in her work. 'Look, Jimmy, I'm not sure we can help you. I'll talk to Mari about it. You might have to move out of LA to somewhere quieter, where the rent's cheaper. You can commute to work.'

'I'm out of work, Mum. I'd need you to pay our airfares, too.'

'Why would you?' Mari asked the whole kitchen, later. 'So he can use you up again? And his bigoted homophobic wife can have you fund her shopping addiction? He does nothing but hurt you, Nerida, over and over again.'

'I wonder what he's here to teach me, then,' Nerida said sadly. 'What am I to learn out of this?'

The magnolia flowers unfolded in the rain, their perfume washed away, but their thick cream petals were resilient. The rain and wind came and stayed every day for weeks and weeks. Broken leaves and fallen palm fronds fell into the pool but the flowers held on, bouncing under the drops, bruised to gold.

The peewee visited every day. Sometimes a pair of them came, their feathers fluffed up for protection from the rain.

Nerida felt connected to her totem black and white birds. The magpies and currawongs sang in the mornings, lifting her mood.

The peewee challenged his reflection in the silver base of the pool fence. He came to battle himself over and over. Every day. 'Stupid bird,' said Mari. 'He's going to hurt himself.'

'Is there an acupuncture point to bring down blood pressure?' Mari's brows knitted. Her jaw clenched.

'Sure. Why?' They sat on the lounge together watching television. Nerida looked at her wife closely. Touched her cheek and forehead with the back of her hand. 'You're hot.'

'I can feel my pulse in my eyes. Pounding.' Mari touched her temple.

'*He Gu* will bring the heat down out of your head. You know, Colon 4.'

'This one on my hand?'

'Yes. Let's do it.' Nerida went to get needles.

Mari's pulse settled after the needle was in. 'It's not thumping and racing anymore,' Nerida said.

'My eyes are better,' Mari said. She fell asleep on the lounge with the fine needle in her hand.

As Nerida undressed to shower, she watched her wife on the bed. 'You're still unwell?'

'I feel like shit.' Mari looked pale.

If she has chest pain or fever when I get out of the shower, I'll have to take her to the hospital, Nerida thought. *I hope it's not COVID.* They still had no way of knowing whether they had COVID-19 back in Fitzroy last year. If it was, Mari might be suffering long-term effects. Or she could be reinfected.

They kept an eye out for Coronavirus cases or clusters in the district, but that thing could be anywhere. Nerida stepped under the warm water, tried to wash worry away.

CHAPTER 60

Bundjalung Country, Lennox Head NSW

Monday, March 15, 2021

Nerida woke to see the giant full moon setting through the window, so white it seemed translucent. After yoga and meditation, she opened her eyes to early sunlight cutting across the pool water, each ripple in the net of light coloured gold and orange. Magpies warbled. The rain had cleared. Her tomatoes, some split by the storm and flood, ripened. The lime tree was covered in tiny fruit.

There were no toads in the pool, not even dead ones.

Mari had been drawing these past days, sketches and colour plans to finish her triptych. If she wasn't yet ready to get out her paints again, at least she was drawing. She sketched boxes and cubes, as well, designing a house should they need to rebuild the orange house or sell it and build elsewhere.

Cooler nights might spell the end of the toad season.

Nerida went inside the house. 'I need that plastic bag we used for the washing,' she said to Mari, who was rubbing spices into a piece of beef for roasting.

Mari still had shadows around her eyes. She was not feverish, though. Her skin was its usual tan, her cheeks and lips rosy. Sleep and the acupuncture had chased away whatever made her sick the night before.

Rubbing herself with a repellant, slipping on her leather shoes, Nerida opened the glass doors into the small yard, screwing up the courage to open the pool skimmer box.

There were three large toads in there. One looked up at her with dark slits in its golden eyes. Another hung bloated, caught on the flap of the skimmer. A third was also probably dead, sitting under the water on the pile of leaves in the basket.

She used the golf club to lift the living toad out. It leapt into the pool and swam. She cursed it. Then said, 'I see. You're making it easier for me.' *Scooping a big toad out with the net is easier than trying to lift it out of the skimmer box.* It was large, probably five or six years old and a female. *I can tell you enjoy your swim, but this life is over now.*

The toad wriggled in the blue plastic net but stilled when she put it on the ground. Nerida killed it, targeting the neck and head, in two blows. She buried it and the other toads in mulch and soil. Smells were buried, too.

Once the big ones were out, the filter box was full of leaves and the macerated bodies of smaller toads.

She put her hand in the bag and reached into the turbid water to pull the basket out. She didn't have gloves long enough to reach the basket without wetting her skin. *You'd need veterinary gloves,* she thought.

She pulled a handful of the decomposing mess out before realising her arm was wet. There was a hole in the bag.

Am I imagining that stinging burn on my arm?

The toad poison, if that was what it was, came off with soap and water.

Later that day, Mari suggested a channelling session.

Aedgar greeted Nerida with his usual charm.

'What can we do for you?'

Nerida took a deep breath. 'Well, you might be able to sense that it's very wet here.'

'It's not like steam or vapour in the air. It is more like real rain coming down.'

Nerida agreed. 'Some of the houses might wash away.'

'That would be a bit too drastic. We think the soil under them might get washed away. In the long-term, cracks will appear. Buildings too close to waterways might get, as you said, washed away. The water removes the ground from under them.'

'We have another house we call the orange house,' Nerida reminded him.

'We might have heard about it.'

'Yes. We have a man coming to see if it's going to fall down the hill. Or whether it might remain secure enough. You know, remember that it's a house.'

'It might not have been reminded of that enough,' he mused. 'It might not happen immediately, falling down, we mean. But it needs some urgent maintenance of an invasive kind. This is not like just putting different, new wood around the outside.

'You see obvious cracks, but that's not the main problem. They are more likely to be superficial. It's the less obvious problems that will turn out not so well.

'There are problems inside some of the material. We have not seen anything like that material. It has a bonding problem. Something's got in there that's not supposed to be there.

'We think it started out with air bubbles. Air bubbles around some of the material. And then other things from the environment got into it, leading to rotten material inside. It's not obvious, not at the moment. It's not in the areas where you think it might be.'

The orange house is rotten in places we haven't yet thought of? This is so sad. And frustrating. 'I guess the house might need to be knocked down.'

'We would not think the whole thing. Some parts of it. Mind you, we're not talking about small parts of it.'

Rain hammered on the paving outside. The pool was a blur of blue.

'We think we discussed this issue with you before as a metaphor of some sort.'

'Oh, yes.' The conversation was in early 2013 at Mutitjulu, the Aboriginal community at Uluru. They lived there then.

Talking about his own work with Nerida, Aedgar had emphasised the importance of attention to detail.

'They use this mix they call—concrete,' he said. 'If you have even a bubble in it, it will impact the material's strength. If you put the weight of a high-rise building on it, a small bubble can cause the failure of the whole project in the end.

'It might not happen immediately. It might take a long time to appear as a problem, but if it does, it can be devastating.

'So it was a tiny thing someone didn't pay enough attention to, because they thought it's not important, in a big project.

'But the bigger the task, the more attention you have to pay to the details. In the execution and in the planning. If people don't take small or tiny things seriously enough, that can cause failure.'

Talking about their orange house now, eight years later, he said, 'You have a base. You pour a base. You got air in it. You will create weak spots.'

'That's right.' Back in 2013, Nerida was impressed with Aedgar's study. From England in the 1500's to learning what concrete and skyscrapers were, was quite a leap.

He continued to survey the house. 'We would not say that bad vibes work on the house. It's more like Nature chiselling away on mistakes that have been made.

'The place itself we would call fortunate.'

'The piece of land there? Yes. It's a nice spot. As long as you don't fall down the hill,' she said.

'It doesn't feel like it all would slide down the hill. It has issues, which, if all was done well in the beginning, should not have become issues.

'Humans have always built on mountains. You could see the weather coming. You could see enemies approaching. Or you could see your friends arriving to visit. So, it was always fortunate to have a place up on a hill.

'There were just not the right skills involved in the building.

'It can be fixed but be aware that the problem is not in the areas where you think it would be. You should keep that in mind.'

The susurrant murmurs of the palms blended with the sound of softer drops on the roof and in the pool. Calm acceptance washed over Nerida.

'Is there anything else we could help you with?'

'You may be able to sense that next to us here is a swimming pool for recreation.'

He moved the head towards it. 'Why would anyone do this? There is a natural pond below where you're living.'

'That's right.' *But no one can swim in the wetlands down the street. Even if it smells fresh, the water is labelled unsafe. As the surrounding land is built on, with project homes, a new supermarket, new carparks.*

'That pond attracts some creatures you would not like, already,' he said. 'So, you magnified the problem by putting (what did you call it?) a 'recreational' pond in here. A mistake. Should not be there.'

Nerida inclined her head. 'I've been killing toads that come to the pool. Killing is an unusual thing for me to do.'

'They're poisonous toads that were brought from another country to eat beetles. There were too many beetles because there was too much sugar cane. They didn't eat the beetles. But now there are too many toads.'

Aedgar exhaled sharply. 'Humankind interfering with nature—'

'That's right.'

'Always a bad idea. They call it "science."'

'A lot of it is trial and error. Mostly error. Because the trials don't go all the way. If they went all the way with their trials, they would not have brought these animals here.

'You have a few examples of that on this island. Very unfortunate.'

True, that. She thought of prickly pear, eroding rabbits, ferocious feral cats.

The million camels.

She saw a farmer on an agricultural program who got up to shoot camels every day. Because there was no abattoir to butcher the camels, their bodies rotted in the dirt, breeding flies.

They were a pest because they drank all the water he wanted for his cattle. One of the camels killed a cow and drank its blood for moisture during the drought. That hideous image made her feel better about only having to deal with toads. *At least you don't need a gun to kill a toad.*

'We don't like the word 'humankind,' because humans are mostly unkind,' Aedgar said, dryly. 'With their surroundings. Even amongst each other. They've always interfered, or tried to interfere, with poor results.

'There have been a few examples where they continued their trials until they got a better result than error, after error, after error. They started to rethink the whole question from the beginning,' he conceded.

'In the case of these reptiles, the trial was erroneous. They built on that. Instead of going all the way back to fundamentals.

The creation of troubling issues often starts right in the beginning. The further the project advances, the bigger the error gets.'

Nerida agreed. 'Yes. Growing nothing but sugar cane, for miles and miles and miles, is a mistake.'

'You need to change what you plant,' he said. 'Work with nature, not against it. Be guided by nature.'

Myna birds squawked outside, attacking wrens to chase them from their nest in the bushes.

Nature can be horrible.

'What about the toads? Should we just swim with them in the pool? Forget about them? Leave them be? They kill the other frogs. They kill everything. That's why I'm killing them.'

Aedgar considered. 'Well, it's a good thing to kill them. They should not be here in the first place. But it would take a lot more to reverse that error. We would not normally advise killing other species. But this one came out of an error that was called science. It needs action and intervention to reverse that error. Letting it be won't help.

'We feel a bit sorry. They introduce new species, the sugar, then they've brought in yet another species, the toad, supposedly to take care of this. They have still not learned that you can't interfere that way.'

Nerida prompted, 'Can we make medicines out of them?'

'Poisons can make potent medicines. But it would need a lot of work. The toxin is too…faceted. You would need to single out some parts, discarding the rest.

'We can think of three parts,' he raised three fingers 'that could be very potent medicine. But if there are ten parts, and three are usable, it would be a lot of work to separate the medicine out.'

The mynas were splashing in the pool, dive bombing insects. *It's a pity they don't eat cane toads,* she thought. Mynas were an aggressive pest too. Throwing native birds out of their nests. *Maybe humans don't like them because they're too much like us.*

'They don't have many enemies here, those creatures,' Aedgar said. 'So, you'd need to find a way to stop them reproducing. This would be the only way. And even then, it would take a long time to get rid of them.'

So many of them. Toad nests were all over the grass lawns along her street. She stepped on tiny toads every time she went into the front yard to get mail or take the bins out. Walking by the wetlands to the shop was unpleasant. The path was littered with toad bodies. The smell of their decay came in sudden bursts wherever she walked out of the house. Sometimes the drain in the shower smelled like them.

'You can't call it 'castration' because there's nothing there to be cut out,' Aedgar mused. 'You need some kind of chemical.'

'An acid,' he decided. 'The effective degree of acidity would depend on the area: temperature and the moisture in the environment would dictate the necessary acidity. It's a fine line. You'd need to spray or douse big areas where they breed. Or where they move through.'

Nerida suppressed a mental image of hundreds of toads on the march in the long grass down the road.

'There's a lot of toad poison in the ground. You should not have agriculture in an intense breeding ground. It would take decades, in some areas centuries, to grow it out of the ground.'

That's a new idea, and an unpleasant one. I love sucking on sugar canes. Do toads taint them?

'But that's something that will be discovered a long way down that road,' he said. 'You could grow other things. Trees. But you should not grow vegetables or fruit.'

'We might have to reforest those parts where the toads have been,' Nerida suggested. 'That's not a bad thing for the planet. We need more forests.'

'Yes, it would help with your CO2 problem, as well. Acid. Acid will be the key to it. It will not harm humankind, or animals. It's the poison that they've produced that's a danger.'

He spoke as if he could see it. 'It's as if the poison is activated already when they come out to the surface. They don't need to reach a stage of growth or development to have that poison. It's integrated already when they are produced.'

Nerida knew that. The toxic tadpoles were produced in 20-metre strings of tens of thousands of eggs. Both killed almost all animals that usually eat frogs and frog eggs. Even crocodiles.

Aedgar was thinking it through. 'They'd have to spray huge areas all at the same time. Three times in (what you call) a year. And then, two times a year for the following year and then once more in the third year. But in all areas, huge areas at the same time. This will be a challenge.'

'We're not up to organising things like that, yet.' Nerida said. 'But we'd better be.' It was grim to reflect on more agricultural land being damaged. *We have little enough.*

Aedgar concurred. 'You don't seem to be up for a challenge requiring you all to do one thing at the same time, in large numbers. It's not on your agenda.'

'Unless it's kicking a ball or hitting one with a bat. Large numbers of people can come together for that,' Nerida observed.

Sports people kept travelling throughout the pandemic, within Australia and internationally.

A gay couple whose surrogate child was born were not allowed to go to her. A son could not be united with his dying mother across a state border. But a dirt-bike rider went from Queensland to compete in Spain.

Surfers came from Brazil, hugging their fans in a dangerous delusion that the pandemic did not exist. And couldn't hurt young people, anyway.

Aedgar nodded. 'Yes. But that's not productive. It's more destructive. Even centuries back they've done things like this to entertain and keep small minds happy and content.'

Jousting tournaments. Bear-baiting. A monkey strapped to a horse, both to be savaged by bulldogs. Tudor England was barbaric.

'They got entertained so they would forget that they've got nothing to eat. Or because there was no hope of going to fight in a war. So, there was entertainment. It was about creating common enemies within their groups. You understand?'

'Absolutely. Still the same.'

'Yeah. Nothing has changed.

'Don't let your fellow humans describe themselves as progressive. They love that word. We don't think they understand the meaning.'

Nerida said, 'There's a lot of excitement around the vaccines against COVID. It's like a horse race, the way people talk about the different types,' she said. Even as a doctor, she found it hard to find material about the different vaccines. The only studies about them were funded by the drug companies themselves.

He said, 'It serves as distraction and entertainment. Still. We think one has bits of promise. The rest are useless.

'But how would your (how shall we describe them?) creatures of no intelligence explain, to huge groups of humans, that they can't provide a solution, prevention or treatment, against this disease?

'So, they've made something else that has shortfalls and can be dangerous.

'They tell people about these mixtures, "It's all the same. It has a different name. It was created in a different place on that planet. But the result will be the same." It won't.

'Many years from now they'll say, "What were these people thinking? Did they think at all? Who put so much pressure on them to produce in a short time? Something useless?"

'There is time pressure.

'People could use help in staying away from each other. That would help a lot. More than their so-called medicine.

'Because it's not medicine. It's a distraction. "We have to keep all of them down. We have to give them hope. We have to give them the idea that we are the greatest creators on this planet. And everything will be fine."

'We don't think it will be.

'They will have ongoing fallout from what they get into people at the moment. It's the tiny air bubbles in a foundation. Once you build on it, it's gonna crack.'

Nerida understood but felt uneasy. It was scary to think that the vaccines could cause harm. *But having COVID is worse.* She understood why people, including her colleagues, were willing to trust and try the shots. Would she vaccinate them? Or refuse? Nerida didn't know if her world had gotten vaster or been reduced to a pin.

Aedgar persisted. 'It's that trial and error. You have a trial. It ends in error. You don't start back at the beginning because you are pressured for time.

'So, you try to build on the error. The whole thing turns out to be an error, so what are you gonna do, if there was nothing good in your work to begin with?

'You need to change your foundation.

'Are they doing this? No. They won't.

'There are some bright minds out there. They are silenced at present.

'Others say, "We can do it. In whatever timeframe works for you."' He mocked servility.

'This is not how Nature works. This is how they end up with a trial, then an error, another trial with another big error.

'They have one that's promising. A bit. But it needs a lot more work for this promise to come to fruition. Using it before then turns the promising thing into an error, as well.

'You need to wait. Figure out which part works. And which part we can do without. Concentrate on this.

'We know time is everything you think about here. It's the most important thing, the most precious, the most expensive stuff you can have.

'But it's not stuff. It's not even existing in a way you think it exists.

'So, they save on something that does not exist, to please others with invidious motives.

'It's very hard for us to look at.'

Clouds outside were breaking up, letting low beams of sunlight through. A flock of white cockatoos flew across the sky, going to their tree.

'Sometimes, it's fascinating. Yeah, about a thousand years (as you would call it), they've used the same methods. Did it ever work? No.

'Five hundred years ago (as you call it), they had a similar issue. They acted the same way as they do now. It did not work then. It does not work now.'

Is he comparing the anti-COVID vaccines to the nosegays, miasmal smokes and beaked masks doctors used during the plague in 16th century

Europe? He must have been alive during the 2nd wave of the plague in Europe, she realised.

'It's fascinating,' Aedgar observed. 'In all those centuries—what have they learned? Sadly, not much.

'Always trying to please someone, rather than to help. To help fix a problem, get rid of a real threat—it's not on their agenda.'

Did he just learn that word, 'agenda' the way he learned about concrete in 2013?

'You don't mess with Nature for the sake of something that does not exist. Or to please the ones on top. The ones without intelligence.'

'Hmm. Or for lots of money,' she commented. She knew how desperate laboratory researchers could be for funding. The search for a vaccine against SARS-CoV-2 was something governments and companies were prepared to generously fund.

'We don't think that's an important thing, either. We can see some of your areas don't seem to function without it.

'But now they're using more paper, more ink. They print more numbers on the paper. But there is nothing behind it. So, it's worthless.'

'It will be,' she agreed.

'Yes.'

'Quite soon.'

'Yes.'

'We've seen that before, as well,' Nerida said. Mari told her when she was a child in Germany, she found a paper with faded printing and asked her father what it was.

She had told Nerida, 'Dad was reading the newspaper and looked up. "A million Marks," he said.

'That was exciting. "We're rich then!" I said. I might have been eight years old.

'Dad said that it bought a loaf of bread for a while. Other times you needed more. He said people would take a bag packed with cash and come back with something little, a piece of sausage maybe, in the bag. It didn't affect the village so much because people traded things.'

Aedgar brought her back to the present. 'Yeah,' he said. 'It repeats itself. Every generation thinks, "We are so progressive. We are so much more intelligent than the last generations." Yet they make the same mistakes.

'For us, it's challenging to watch, in some areas. In other ways it can be amusing.

'You watch a child going up a step. Trying to jump. Falling down. It looks funny. And then they get up and do it again. You can count how many times it takes them to do something different. To try in a different way.

'Some of these incidents you can watch endlessly. It's funny. And then it gets really sad.'

'You can see what they've done with the creatures here. They've got no enemies. That creates an even bigger imbalance in everything else. You have all these stinging insects in huge amounts. It's an imbalance. It should not be like that.'

Nerida scratched. The cane toads killed the goannas that ate them. Less of the giant lizards meant more rats. More rats in the district meant more fleas. They'd seen fleas in their bed. They usually bit Mari. But Nerida had mosquito bites like welts that lasted a week. 'It makes it almost unbearable to go outside,' she said.

'Yes. You have a dense forest, high mountains. All these things live there. Leave them alone. They have their habitat. They leave you alone. Encroach into the habitat and they have to go somewhere. We don't think they want to harm you in the first place. But they've got nowhere else to go.'

'How does the virus fit in to that scheme of things?' she asked.

'It's trying to reproduce. It found the humans a fertile ground to reproduce. That's all this virus is interested in. That's the consciousness it's got. "How can I make more of myself?" Having consciousness is not like being intelligent.

'You can have a thought: "All I wanna do is reproduce."

'That consciousness exists in your fellow humans. Or, "All I wanna do is eat." Or smoke. Or drink. So, you're all a bit like viruses in some ways.'

Nerida chuckled. She didn't eat bread. Otherwise, she'd smell it and look up half an hour later, having consumed a loaf or more. She remembered, too, the drive to get laid. It was a major influence

on her life, for better and worse, in the years when she was subject
to stronger doses of hormones. It drove her to shop for a new dress
for a single occasion, pull razor blades over her legs or rip her
eyebrow hair out with wax. Suddenly she understood what he
meant by the consciousness of a virus. *It's conscious the way a rabbit is.
Or a dragonfly.*

'Some people think, "It's going to go out there and kill all
those sinners." It doesn't have that understanding,' Aedgar said. 'A
person is something that moves and is alive and is a promising
breeding ground. The virus doesn't know where that breeding
ground is, where it came from, what it is going to do. Where does it
live? Does it have a lot of paper with numbers on it? Does it live in
a castle? Does it wear a crown?

'No, they don't. They can't think like that. They have a
consciousness. It's not the same as yours. All it tries to do is
reproduce.'

Nerida doodled stars on her notepad. Realised they looked like
Coronaviruses.

Aedgar's voice deepened. 'And it was created to do so. There
are dark minds behind it. It was created by human beings.

'And it was created,' he sighed deeply, 'for a purpose. The
creators knew it would kill. What they did not know was that it has
consciousness. Because you can't create consciousness. You have
no control over that.

'It was 'seeded' in different areas on the planet. People say it
got out of a laboratory somewhere. But it was put out there, seeded,
before that. This, and the way humans move around, helped it.

'You understand?'

Nerida tried. 'So, when they say that it came out of a lab in
Wuhan, it was already seeded on five different continents? Was it
seeded in Wuhan?'

'Getting out there was an accident,' he replied. 'It's manmade.
It was produced there. The thing escaping where it was created—
we would see that as an accident. It was not meant to go out in
their own area. Why would anyone do this?

'But someone had access to it before then. And it's been
seeded, we think, yes, in at least five different places. If you look
where you have huge outbreaks, you can see if it's a rich country.

Not talking about paper with numbers. Or that people own, or live in, castles.

'Value, those people thought, is hidden in the ground. Or even in the surrounding oceans. "We can have this if we eradicate the humans in the area. We can go in and have it all. No one is going to fight us."'

'That was the motivation of the people who made it in the first place?' Like the neutron bomb. Kill all the people. Take the stuff you value.

'Correct. You have everything provided there, except living beings. And then, you come in and take it over. You understand?'

'Yes.' *So, it was made as a weapon of war. But someone else, someone other than the evil scientists*—as she thought of them—*used it as a weapon.*

'And preferably without doing damage to your own part of the world. It's a small part of the world. And people would say, "Oh no. They are not intelligent enough to do this." As we told you before.'

Nerida took in a sharp, hard breath.

CHAPTER 61

Home at Lennox

Same Day

He explained, 'If you have information, wherever that comes from, that someone else has created that weapon, you just go and get the item, one way or another. It does not mean you produced it. You have the information.'

Nerida was disorientated. *So, is he talking from the point of view of those who acquired the virus as a weapon now? How can a great-hearted spirit like Aedgar....?*

Okay, I know he would say they have no physical body. But is his perspective so broad, so distant that a loving, compassionate spirit like Aedgar, can slip into the perspective of a terrorist organization? And expect me to follow?

Perhaps he sensed her resistance. 'You know, we've heard sentences from your field of expertise. Like, "Medicine is not about knowledge. Medicine is about knowing where it is written."'

'Mhm.' She'd heard that before.

'The solution to your problem—you need to find that. You need someone or something to give you the hint to find out what you need to know. You understand?'

She sighed. 'Maybe.' *Not really.*

'You don't need the facilities to produce things if you have knowledge of where it is produced and then the knowledge to get it. "How do I get it from there to here, and from A to B? And what or who do I use?" You don't have to do it yourself. You get others to do it. That works in your favour.'

'Okay.' *I'm in a Dan Brown novel now.*

'Now, you're told "We are all one. We're all in this together." All of that. It's not quite like that. They blame someone for it. That's how it works. You create a common enemy.

'While the one who's done it is sitting in a corner giggling. At how everybody else is ripping each other apart.'

It's a noxious image, she thought, *a titillated, mass-murdering dictator.*

Aedgar continued. 'Everybody is distracted. Those of no intelligence all say, "We've got other problems now." While in the backroom they make decisions that are not popular. Even damaging. Or dangerous. This happens all over the world.'

'Right.' *He's reminding me about the sonic exploration and the coal-powered stations. But this might be my last chance to ask about Sars-CoV-2 before writing the book.* 'Let me ask about the way the virus appeared in the world. It came out of Wuhan as an accident. It had already been seeded in other places because other people planned to use this as a weapon.'

'Yes.'

'And—'

'It's manmade.'

'It's manmade. Yes.' *He keeps saying that.*

Perhaps he senses that I can't accept it. The ramifications of this idea—of me being given this information—are too much for me to process. There would need to be a criminal investigation. There could be a war.

She took a deep breath, placed her feet flat on the floor.

I don't know why I should be shocked. Biological warfare was used against the Kooris when the British arrived, intentionally and not— the First Fleet gave people smallpox. Last century, Stalin used it. Roosevelt started the production of ricin to be delivered in artillery shells. Saddam Hussein used germ warfare in the 80s. *It's still going on.*

'But you say it has consciousness,' she continued. 'So, did the virus wake itself up where it was seeded already? After it came out of Wuhan?'

'It evolves,' he said. 'You can't see it as a lonely little virus sitting somewhere. Viruses are tiny. You should know that.'

'Yes.' *What? Viruses were talking to each other?*

'You can have a huge number of them in a drop of water.'

'Yes.'

'And when they reproduce, they evolve. You might say it mutates.'

'Yes.'

'It does that. See it as evolution. It gained those extras and went out of control.

'It was made in what they call "a controlled environment". What they don't have control over is the mutations, that thing evolving. And it got consciousness. It's conscious.

'Not like, "I know your name. I'm going to get you." It's like, "Oh, I can feel vibes. I can—" And it's reproducing. That's all it's about: reproduction. And it got out of control.'

Nerida took a step back.

'Years ago, we were at the island where Mari got sick from the birds. She had bird 'flu. M'Hoq Toq was talking to me then about new kinds of viruses evolving.

'He said a conscious virus could evolve that did not have greed as an aspect. Its consciousness, responding to the thoughts of those who created it, contained an element of revenge. Or the possibility of it.' She was scared to ask about this but felt compelled. *Was there something like a mamu following Mari around? Her mind whirled.*

Aedgar spoke more gently. 'For now, there is consciousness. We would not call it revenge. It might look like it. But it's not. It's all about the fastest, easiest or most convenient way to reproduce.

'It loves water. It loves the heat. It loves the cold. Not too cold. Not too hot,' he summarised. 'Boiling temperatures, extreme cold, can kill it.

'But it can survive for a very long time in water. In ice too— because that's only a degree or two below freezing.

'Or on a surface someone touched. You put it in a fridge. It stays there for ages on a surface. Until you get it out and it's like, "Oh, something warm touched me. That's a good one."'

That's creepy. Maybe Mari's right, washing everything that comes into the house. Damn. I thought I was the scientific one.

'It goes to the pores of your skin,' he continued. 'It goes into your eyes if you wipe your face.'

I'm starting to feel a bit paranoid myself. How does a person live with this thing?

'It's there if someone coughs on you. But that's not the only way. As soon as you get too close, it just gets you. You need distance from someone else to keep it away.

'I'm not touching your hand. But I'm getting very close to you now—'

'To touch my elbow,' she said. He made an elbow bump, then extended Mari's arm.

'Two stretched arms shaking hands—'

'That's safer,' she said.

'It's a bigger distance,' he confirmed. 'If you then sanitise or disinfect your hands, it's all right.'

So, Dr Khumalo back at Fitzroy Crossing was right. She'd offered her elbow. He declined it. 'I shake hands or nothing at all,' he said, when he returned from South Africa. People said he was attending funerals there.

Aedgar continued. 'That thing can live for a long time in other materials. What if two hours later, you touch your elbow? Then you touch your eye? There you go. That's how easy it can be.

'You go and eat a salad that's out in the open all day. You pick something from here, something from there. Or someone else does that for you. That's not safe. If it's around, it will get you.'

Nerida felt grateful for their rented accommodation, cane toads, damp rot and all.

CHAPTER 62

TIME SLIP 6: Past

Sydney, Eora Country

October 19, 2000

Nerida was meeting Keira for coffee in Newtown.

Coming off the crowded bus, she wove her way past the harried people on their tight lunch breaks, noticed the homeless, claiming their spaces on the narrow footpath.

She gave an orange twenty-dollar bill to a young man sitting with his head on his knees. She sensed his empty stomach the way a dolphin could with their sonar. Nerida had just got paid. She gave generously, then, to one needy person, then told others for the rest of the fortnight that her coal-biting budget was done.

Summer warmth reached down, even into Newtown's narrow streets. It was easier to navigate the city since the Sydney Olympics finished a few weeks earlier. In the lead-up to the Olympics, cameras were put up at every intersection she crossed through the city. The government put them up for security and traffic-control. *I feel under surveillance everywhere I go now. What times we live in!*

Her long walks through parks, blocks and districts, one of the great pleasures of her life in the inner city, no longer felt like her own. She felt observed when she went into a political meeting, or to a workshop to paint banners and placards. She probably was.

Keira had claimed a tiny, wood veneer table outside a cafe. She looked well.

Nerida kissed her soft cheek and gazed fondly into her little black eyes.

Her straight black hair shone in an angular cut. She had pictures of kittens on her jacket.

'I couldn't last in medicine. Did you hear?'

'What happened?'

'They would make no allowance at all for my illness. When I had to go to hospital, they wouldn't allow a re-sit of exams I missed.

Somebody in the faculty, at least, didn't want an HIV-positive doctor.'

'I'm so sorry. That must have been awful.' Nerida understood what it was like to be unwelcome and unwanted at University. She had that experience once or twice.

'I've landed on my feet.' Keira stirred sugar into her coffee. 'I've got good work and a lovely man. We're sharing a terrace house in Erskineville. I couldn't be happier, really.'

She's only twenty-two, Nerida thought. *Only five years older than Ruby.* 'Look how resilient you've become,' she said. Nerida was drinking roasted dandelion root with soy, considering her liver after last night's pay-day feast with the kids of fried chicken and chips.

'I wanted to see you to tell you. I've done a fair bit of research. I think I know what happened to Andy.'

Nerida leaned forward. The noise of the street fell away.

'First, some background,' Keira said. 'KLH is Keyhole Limpet Haemocyanin, a protein produced by a mollusc.

'It has five parts and contains copper. It is slightly larger than bovine albumin and is a great antigen.

'Essentially, this protein is readily recognised as foreign by the host immune system by its size and shape. And is actively removed once detected by the immune system.'

Nerida nodded. This must be the crustacean protein Andy was injected with in the experiment he was paid to join at Uni. *When he joked about growing a prawn head.*

Keira spooned cocoa-coloured froth from her coffee. 'KLH is used to help develop vaccines and cures.

'It can be bonded relatively easily to other molecules. And the introduction of the hybrid—KLH with that other molecule—can generate an immune response. That is, you could tie a viral capsid to it and use it as a viral vaccine and possibly an anti-viral treatment. Are you with me?'

'Yes.' She remembered reading about this technology, even talking to Andy about it. 'The capsid is the shell of the virus, with the viral DNA taken out. The body recognises the virus without being harmed by it. So, the KLH triggers an immune response by the body?'

Keira nodded. 'It's possible that some of the KLH that was injected into Andy bonded to a neural peptide and created a form of neural antigenicity where his immune system attacked his nervous system. This is consistent with what we know of Andy's condition.'

You would have been a brilliant doctor, Keira. Damn that University faculty for not supporting you.

Keira put down her cup and used her hands as if balancing her arguments. 'Things that work with this theory? It's how KLH works as an anti-cancer drug: local exposure leads to a targeted immune response. And, KLH has been implicated in other forms of dendritic and neural apoptosis.'

'So, this stuff has been shown to kill nerves?'

She was reaching back to her science training, for words crowded out by the medical terminology she'd learned since. 'Apoptosis is programmed cell death where the cell plays a role in its own demise. And dendritic cells are part of the body's immune response. Am I remembering that right?'

'Yes. That's right. 'Keira rubbed her mouth, as if shy about what she'd said. 'In humans, Andy would be the only known case—at least as far as I can tell. That's what's against us.'

Nerida looked up as a waiter presented her with a plate of tomato on toast. For once, she wasn't hungry.

'This could be the simplest solution,' Keira pressed, 'hence most likely.'

'Can we sue the bastards?' Nerida thought of Andy's mum, Carleen, whose life was almost destroyed by his suspicious death.

Keira cocked her head. 'I've been thinking about it. If there are no previous cases arguing negligence on the part of a research team, it would be difficult.'

'But not impossible?' Nerida asked.

'Well, subsequent acts of parties involved indicate a fair measure of guilt,' Keira said.

Andy's files, stolen before his family went to collect his things. The key gone from the chain around his neck.

'What do you think? If only I had a few letters after my name, this would stand up in court and we'd celebrate bringing them down,' Keira said.

Nerida had a few letters after her name. She already had her science degree by then. But didn't know how she could speak up for Andy. The cover-up seemed so complete.

'That opportunity will unfold. It might take time. We'll see.' She squeezed Keira's arm, trusting her words could make it so.

Lennox Head, NSW. Bundjalung Country

Sunday March 15, 2020

The afternoon light made orange borders around ripples in the pool outside. 'Mari has an idea of waves of the virus spreading, getting bigger and closer together. But everybody's hoping now that it's gone to sleep. Or it could be completely gone.' *Including me,* she thought.

At breakfast that morning, Mari had made a looping wave with her hand as she spooned coconut sugar into her coffee, explaining the concept of bigger and bigger waves of the virus.

Nerida, inhaling the steam of her tea, barely suppressed her annoyance. 'You say these things. It's all bad news. Don't you ever think things could get better?' she had said. *It's not always easy living with a Cassandra. Or Eeyore.*

The back of her neck prickled. She focused now on Aedgar.

'It's not going away,' he said. He contemplated. 'We would describe it as a *ripple* effect, going in the opposite way. You throw a stone in the water and get ripples running out,' he demonstrated waves flowing from a centre. 'This one came from the outside and its waves are coming closer together.' The fingers rippled into a crescendo in the middle of the imagined pond.

'We haven't seen the worst of it yet, then?' She leaned her elbows on the table, tapped her forehead with her fingers.

Aedgar's tone was patient. 'In some areas they have seen bad things. You live in a fortunate place because it's far away from everywhere else. If you keep it that way. You have a lot less people on this island than in other places.

'It's not about being an island, though. English people live on an island too, but the population is much bigger and it's a lot closer to other countries.'

The geography is significant. Here, and in your neighbouring country with the cloud, it was imported. It is imported by travelling inside people. It can travel on surfaces that you might not even think about. And it can travel in cooled things.'

'Food and water?' Nerida asked. *As if I'm not anxious enough already.*

'Yes. You take it out of that environment. Put it in a shop. People take it home. This is what's happened when sick people say, "But I haven't been anywhere."'

'There are scientists out there that know about this. We are sure.'

'Uhuh.' She thought about Mari then, who insisted on washing everything they brought into the house. All the groceries were washed with soap and water. Then showers and fresh clothes for themselves. Shop clothes and masks were washed in hot water. Grocery shopping had become a substantial fortnightly commitment.

Aedgar said, 'Keeping the scientists quiet is about preventing a panic.

'Do all these decision-makers have an idea what happens if the rest find out about it? "We inject something into you." The trial-and-error approach. An error built on the first ones because of time pressure. You know?

'You know you're distracted. You might be feeling safe.

'The only thing that keeps numbers down now is people keeping distance. Then they think, "I'm tired of this." Or, "It doesn't help, anyway." Well, it doesn't help from one day to the next.

'But you don't mess with Nature. And you can't predict what's gonna happen in Nature. Especially not if you have interfered with it.'

Nerida rested her chin in her hands.

'A lot is out of balance. You would not have to handle locust swarms and all of that if you'd worked alongside Nature. Nature will give you the information of what to do, what to plant, when. If you need wood to build a hut, you take some wood. Not all of it.

'Not the whole forest.' He gestured as if he was planting seedlings. 'And every time you take things out, you plant new ones.'

'Yes.' Dark red and green leaves rustled in the wind outside around the pool.

'You rotate through these areas too. You take what you need in the area where you live.'

'Mhm.' *You told me this already, Aedgar.*

'If you start thinking in paper with numbers, you take out more than you need. To sell to other places. This is not how it works.'

He paused.

'You might call it "Knee jerking Nature."'

Her eyebrows slid up. 'Knee jerking Nature?'

'Yes.' For once, he sounded unsure.

She smiled. *His study of colloquial English has let him down.* She responded to the image in her head. 'Like kicking Nature in the balls, is that what you mean?'

He nodded. 'If you do it, it will be painful. You get results that you did not ask for. If you kick it too hard, it will never come up again. In many areas you are at that point.'

'Yes.'

'Needs to be understood.'

She lifted her chin. The smell of roasting meat filled the kitchen. 'Thinking about meat…'

'Meat?'

'Yes,' she said. 'Would you say that a household can have one or two animals, if that's the kind of diet you need? We don't have to have thousands of animals denuding the earth. Do we?'

'No. It's all about numbers and money. They say, "We just produce what people need." But people don't need to eat meat, for example, three times a day. Or every day. That's not necessary. It's all about the amount and the balance.

'And then you produce mountains of soybeans. Send them to a factory to produce something that looks like meat and, in a distant way, might taste like it. What good is that for Nature? It means you don't rotate your crops, either. You are focused on a specific market. Same crop.'

'Monoculture.' She'd seen that. Hundreds of kilometres of canola in the south and west of Australia. Hundreds of miles of soybeans when she visited Illinois. Now she was surrounded by river flats thick with toady sugar cane, on every piece of arable land.

'Same problem,' he said. 'There are a few people feeling sad for animals. Many don't understand that the ways you grow and consume all the vegetables, seeds and grains, deprive the animals, too.

'Think about doing things *in measure*.

'Keep the balance. You can eat a small piece of meat, for example, two or three times a week. You don't need huge amounts. You will grow out of your shape, your form.'

He spoke softly.

He can tell that I'm sensitive about 'growing out of my form.' She had been in and out of her best shape many times. *That's a non-judgmental way to put it. Bless him.*

'It's not healthy. Everything you get too much from is not good for you,' he said.

'People running and running and running and running like crazy doesn't make them healthy in the end,' Aedgar added.

'You can't lay on your bed all day doing nothing. This is out of balance, as well. But running around like someone's chasing you for hours every day, that's not a solution. It's another problem.

She smothered a laugh. 'Mhm.'

'People playing with weights and heavy ropes and machinery—that's not healthy.

'Just do what you're supposed to do. Do your work around where you live. Don't sit in your car and drive everywhere. Walk. And you'll have exercise. You don't even have to pay for it. That's a new concept. But no one would ever advertise that. There's no money made from it.

'They make small enterprises where they do, and concentrate on, only one minor thing. Sometimes it's good to concentrate on one little thing and you get really good at it.

'Yeah.' Like her brother's home brewery. Or Mari with her cakes.

'But they make people lift that weight. And charge them money for it. And then they make it look good and interesting and fun. "You should do it because your life will be so much better."'

'Yes,' said, Nerida, giggling.

'We don't think so.

'And this is how people create jobs out of things that should not be jobs in the first place.'

Why not? People find a way to make a living however they can.

'And then, there's this virus going round. All these little shops closed.'

'Yes.'

'It was never supposed to be a business. And then they're out of their business. They're all moaning. "I've lost it all. I put everything into it."

'Well, for a long time, you might have got an awful lot out of it. Selling something to people that they could do everywhere else for free.

'It hit back at them.'

This is the way I thought when I was twenty, she thought. *Before people made a religion of 'entrepreneurship.' Before I was supposed to build a platform. My younger self had some good instincts.*

'Now they could think, "I should do something different." Because others might think, "I can make my own coffee." And "I go somewhere and eat something that someone else has cooked. As a treat."

'Some of you need to keep working, working, working so you can pay for someone else cooking for you every day; someone else taking care of your offspring every day. Someone else to drive your offspring to places that they need to be, (in your own opinion). What kind of job do you need to pay for all this?

'And then it comes down to, "I've got no time." Yeah, you've got nothing of something that doesn't exist.

'Rearrange the way you think.

'Have some exercise. Plant some things, even in small pots, that you can eat. Or plants that grow to look beautiful and smell good. They make you happy. That's as important as eating.

'But going to a shop that does nothing but cut off the heads of those colourful things, grown to make you happy, what's the point of that?'

I feel a bit sorry for the florists, now, she thought.

He kept going, 'When no one spends the paper with the numbers for those beautiful cut-off heads, they throw them out.

And then they complain, they haven't got enough business. Shouldn't have been a business in the first place.

'People look for ideas. "How can I make money out of my neighbour?" They go for it. They say, "I'm self-employed. I'm running my own business." This is not true. This is like *piracy*.

'You buy, cheaply, things that are heavy. You make people work with those things. You might have the premises so they can be out of the rain,' he conceded. 'Or people go out to the park. So they don't have to pay for the venue. They might have to transport all these ugly weights to that venue. But then they watch other people work with them. And charge them for it. "I'm a self-employed businesswoman." Or businessman. That's not how it's supposed to be.

'Because people are not working together. They don't help each other. They pretend that they help you to be healthy.

'There is probably, amongst some scientists, some idea of how many bad things happen in bodies of those people that lift the heavy things and pay for it. They get injured by doing so.

'If people do their work at home, they get exercise.

'But when they go out in the park, paying money with others, they are pressured by other people. "That one lifted it ten times more than I did! It hurts like hell already. But I have to try to get five more times." And then they get injured. While the other one still goes another ten times. What's the point?

'People yell at others, pretending to be in warfare. "I am gonna kick you up to the moon and into space if you don't do it ten times more." And they get paid for it.

'Yes.' Nerida could see his point, even if she still thought he was unfair to florists. Maybe even to personal trainers. *Medicine is a business, too. Should we all be working for each other without money like Bartgrinn and M'Hoq Toq did as travelling healers? I don't know how that would work.*

'We would think there is something deeply wrong with a society like that.

'But people think it's normal. And they think they do a good thing: shaming others for being different.

'Should not happen.'

'Humanity is drifting further and further away from each other.

'So much so-called work is not about helping people.

'There is always that thought in the back of your head that, "One day you're gonna repay me. Because I helped you." Or, at least, a long time from then, "Well, you can't kill me because I helped you all back in those times."'

'Hmm. Is there something wrong with that? It's part of my motivation in my work sometimes, as a doctor.'

'That they won't come to kill you?'

'That they won't hurt me. They'll keep me.'

'Some people,' he said kindly, 'do their work for the love of humans.'

Nerida felt an upwelling of love in her chest.

'They have empathy. They can't see other humans being in pain, suffering. They feel that urge to help.

'Empathy makes for a good profession. You find more empaths in health, in professions like yours.'

'Yes.' *I never expected to meet so many compassionate people in medicine.*

'But there are always those that do it for other reasons. You find very bad people in your profession, too.'

'Yes.'

'The ones that think they stand above others. They don't have any idea what kind of work other people do. They have the same mindset as the ones that make other people lift heavy things and charge them money for it.

'You'll find them everywhere. They call themselves CEOs, managers. All they can think is getting more paper with numbers on for themselves or getting it for their company.

'So others can say, "Look at how successful that person is." They don't really care about who's working there. Or what kind of work they do.

'Yes.' She'd experienced that.

Managers who had no conception of the importance of the healing, often lifesaving, work that she and the others at the clinic or hospital did.

It was happening to the prisoner support team, Pick Up, whose book she was writing.

The Pick Up workers had their office taken away and were denied access to their vehicle, without consultation, when they came back to work after holidays in January.

The CEO of the service worked exclusively with a new doctor who promised to make a lot of money.

'We might get our book finished just in time for the project to cease existence,' one of the staff told Nerida.

Her friend, who had worked as a community doctor for over twenty years, was moved out of his long-term clinic room without notice or consultation, too. And sent abusive emails. 'I get at least one horrible email a week,' he told Nerida.

She could see the health of the team members declining, even at online meetings. They were twitchy, haunted. The kindest, most tolerant people in the world, being undermined, mentally tortured by mismanagement.

'They are in all sorts of professional groups. You find them everywhere,' Aedgar said. 'They go for paper with numbers on it. They push to maximise what they get out. Taking out whatever wealth they can, without any of that paper with numbers reaching those people that do the work, where it belongs.

'So, you have the narcissists. They always go with the empaths.'

'Right.' *This is a new concept.*

'They work with them to make themselves look better. No one can tell at first sight, then, "That's a horrible person." They want others to think, "They work in health. Must be a good person."'

'They're a kind of a parasite on the empaths?' she asked.

'Yes.'

'I've come across that.' She had sour experiences with venal, corrupt management. In one of the remote communities she'd worked in, the manager was a barely functional alcoholic. He did a lot of damage. *Definitely a narcissist,* she thought.

'Everyone in your profession, who's an empath, will come across that.'

'They use us,' she murmured.

'If you delve a little deeper into where they came from, they all have skeletons in the basement. All of them.'

'Indeed. They've all done terrible things.' Another of her managers had driven away, by bullying and bureaucratic insanity, a dozen dedicated doctors and nurses. The manager formed a belief that clinical workers were not needed.

Nerida found out later that she was relentlessly pressured by her own boss, a director. The director had embezzled millions of dollars and wanted long-term staff, especially the intelligent, ethical ones, sacked. To try to hide her crimes.

'There is a surge in those people now,' Aedgar said. 'It wasn't like this before. You had people to help those who worked directly with sick people. Supporting them. Taking the work off them to ensure that they could concentrate on a sick person.

'But then came all these people who saw this as a business opportunity. "Why hasn't anyone seen how much paper with the numbers on it can be made here?" And, "We can have huge, shiny buildings everywhere so people can see we are really good. We are really successful."

'But they take it out of the ones that do the work.'

Nerida could relate. 'And there's great opportunities for the virus in those huge, shiny buildings,' she said.

Aedgar disagreed. 'You take that virus idea too far. It has consciousness. It's not like, "I'm going to get those ones in the shiny buildings." But after a pause he said, 'It is very likely to be there because there are more people in a small space.'

'That's what I mean,' she said. 'And they go up and down in elevators and they're breathing from the same air source'.

'Yes. It jumps on the jacket.' As he touched Mari's elbow, she imagined him in tweed. 'They touch the other people's sleeves. Then it can go to every level in the shiny building.

'It sits there waiting for someone and says, "Wow. That looks like a great place to have babies."

She noticed that the last light was gone from the day.

'It's been an enriching conversation,' she said.

'Likewise.'

'Our first book will be out soon.' She grinned.

'Soon? We have heard that before—'

'Might even happen this time,' she said.

'It might have been quite some time ago.'

He's right. I've been promising to get a book out since, I dunno, 2015? I wasn't ready. I'm ready now. She ducked her head. 'Indeed. Purple and gold, for the cover.'

'Oh, we like it. Peacock and gold could be good, too.'

'Maybe peacock for the next one.'

'Yes, indeed. You can go with green, with orange. Even black. Gold goes well with everything. If you have a lot of dark chapters, you could use black.'

'Well, this book could almost use the black,' she added.

Aedgar said, 'Yeah, people might mistake it for the Bible.'

She laughed. 'That'd be bad.'

'It's just another collection of mind-bending stories,' he mused. 'To influence people.'

'That's the idea. Finally, we might see some fruit from the trees we planted all those years ago.'

'You should not be scared if you see too much of it,' Aedgar said quietly.

'Okay.'

The night was black outside the windows. *Dark inside, too,* she noticed. The kitchen was lit by the green lights of the microwave and wall oven.

'Don't interact with those that have wrong ideas about it,' he said.

'Okay.'

'Is there anything else, my dear?'

'I'm afraid I have to let you go.'

'We will always come back.'

'Thank you. Please do.'

Aedgar whispered, 'So, until another time, then.'

In the quiet darkness, Mari shook her head, took a breath as if coming up from deep water.

'Where is my love, my Mari?'

She roused. 'Hmm?'

'Good session.' Nerida smoothed her hair, palmed her cheek.

'Good.' Mari closed her eyes. Opened them wide. Smiled.

CHAPTER 64

Lennox Head, home

Friday March 19, 2021

Nerida woke content. Her body was well, and her head was quiet.

I won't do yoga. I want to get on with writing the book. Hungry, though.

She cut up banana with blueberries, scooped on yoghurt. Scooped fragrant coffee into the pot to brew. Pulling the chia jar from the pantry, it fell from between her hands with a crash. Shards of glass and a half kilo of tiny, black seeds exploded across the kitchen floor.

Looks like I get to do my yoga after all, she thought, bending to pick up the glass splinters. *What's with all the breaking?*

Last night, preparing dinner, Nerida put a bowl of cold potatoes into the microwave. A loud crack came from the humming oven.

'Oh no,' said Mari. The bowl had silver crack through one side of it.

After dinner, Mari knocked a bamboo breadboard onto the floor. It broke with a loud smack, too. '*Duppl*,' she called herself.

'Damn,' Nerida said, contemplating the pile of scattered seeds mixed with swords of slivered glass. 'We lived here a year and a half without breaking anything.' She noticed then that her feet and shins were stinging. They were spotted with blood where bits of glass had hit her.

It's time to leave. I guess we're in danger of cracking up. She wrapped the broken glass carefully in newspaper and put the chia seeds on the garden. *They might grow here next spring.*

The last of the tomatoes were ripening, the vines withered. She washed the blood off her legs carefully. The little cuts knit fast.

When Mari rose, she made them coffee. They watched the German News together. Mari explained the stories to Nerida, who could read some of the headlines.

A Native woman in Greenland explained that she would be exposed to radioactive fallout if rare earths were mined by an Australian-Chinese company in the land behind her place.

The Indigenous people need the mining because there are less fish now, so they need a new industry, the mining company CEO explained.

A young Greenlander fisherman said that he loved his work and wanted it to continue. The government raised the fishing quota so that people could haul more fish out before the mining started.

'And poisons the fish. Right.' Nerida said. She went back to her desk.

At least the writing went well. She had started work on putting together transcripts of her conversations with M'Hoq Toq and Bartgrinn. She updated the website with extracts of what the spirits said about the pandemic.

A few people sent notes of encouragement. She worried that she would lose her editing job if the website became popular. *What if these messages will always be for a select group of people? That could be all right.*

Perhaps she should offer the writings to just a few open-minded friends. Sometimes she wanted the spirits voices to stay underground. *Maybe they can grow and communicate between minds like mycelium connecting tree roots.*

She felt guilty for feeling that way. But she'd experienced prejudice, and not just for her culture or sexuality.

Nerida was brilliant enough to be offered a role as a University Professor in 2018.

She and Mari thought about settling down. But the university found her reviews of spiritual books and the aedgar website. 'You keep some quirky company,' the Dean said. 'We would love to have you on board… as a senior lecturer.'

'So, you'll offer me a job that has me working just as hard for about a third of the money, and much less status,' Nerida replied.

'My spiritual beliefs don't affect my ability to work.' As she said it, she realised it was true. 'All sorts of people, with all sorts of spiritual or religious beliefs, work in academia. Will you have the same problem if I eat Jesus' body in a cracker and drink his blood in wine every Sunday? How is that less magical?'

'They were all insane workaholics trying to prove their value, somehow,' Mari commented when Nerida came from the Uni. Nerida looked at her. 'What do you mean?'

Mari chatted to Med School academics as she waited outside for Nerida, sitting on a bench like a Romany fortune teller.

'Several of them stopped for a chat. Very insecure, unhappy workplace. One told me how he uses his train commute for work.

'Another, how her car is turned into an office, so she can record lectures while she's driving. Do they have to prove that being a teacher is as valid as working in a clinic? Something wrong there.'

'It would have taken over my life. I can see that. We'll just keep doing what we do.'

Driving from the University that day, ravens followed the car. Nerida was taught by her father that ravens accompany travellers to keep them safe and offer reassurance. *Perhaps I did the right thing. Maybe my connection with the spirits helps keep me on my path.*

Two years later when the Coronavirus hit, hundreds of academics were fired when the gargantuan market in overseas students, overwhelmingly from Asia, shut down overnight. Nerida was glad then to be working on her modest projects.

And thrilled to continue to publish channelled material. Despite her fears, transcribing and putting the conversations with spirits together energised her. She liked being in her small office, with her carved boab nuts and the black and white pearls she bought in Tonga on her bookshelves. She'd never had a home office before.

She could be disrupted, though. 'There's a new enquiry into the blood clots caused by that vaccine,' Mari called from the lounge.

'Yeah, all right.' Nerida was typing out one of her conversations with Aedgar about the vaccines. Reading it, she felt right in the middle of what her colleagues were calling 'vaccine hesitancy.'

I know myself as a scientist. Why is this happening to me?

Would I decline the vaccine if I didn't have those conversations with Aedgar?

No. I'd want to demonstrate my trust in science. I'd be like my medical mates, posting my jabs on social media.

But she talked to educated people who also had reservations about the vaccines, even without the input of non-physical beings.

'I like to use medicines that have been shown to be safe for thirty years,' one of her doctor friends said.

On the phone, she asked her parents to wait six months, 'Until we know more about them. Australia still has low rates of community transmission. It could be a different story in places where the infection was rampant,' she acknowledged. 'Wear your masks. Keep your distance from people,' she told them.

Later that afternoon, Mari came to Nerida's desk to report, 'A man died today in a Brisbane hospital from COVID. They've got fifty people hospitalised with it in Queensland. Like, just overnight.

'And then they say they've got no cases, because they're not transmitted through this community,' she said. 'They don't count people who are in the quarantine hotels or nursing homes.'

So, Aedgar was right when he said you won't hear about the numbers... This is one of the ways they do it.

'They all got off a plane, then. They'll be from Papua New Guinea,' Nerida said.

The enormous state funeral of PNG's first Prime Minister in mid-March was probably a super spreader event. Mari predicted it when they saw it on the news then.

By the end of March, PNG's cases doubled every week. Health workers there didn't have the capacity to test many people, so that was a massive underestimate. Most sickened and many died in remote villages.

Papua New Guinea was Australia's best mate when it came to mining. But a huge Australian company wreaked environmental disaster when their tailings dam failed early in the century.

Before that, through the 90s, a war was fought with Australian mercenaries to impose an Australian-owned mine on Bougainville Island.

Nerida and her comrades used to demonstrate against it. A nurse she knew was fired on by Australian mercenaries taking medicines to Bougainville in a small boat. She'd been pulled over by police in Canberra and charged with drug offences for having boxes of antibiotics, blood pressure and diabetes meds in her hatchback. They confiscated her phone, harassed her contacts.

'Now they send three health workers with boxes of vaccines. For, what, about ten million of the world's poorest people? Who are really sick now? They send the vaccines they've stockpiled. The ones they're not sure whether they're safe anymore.' Mari was angry. Again. *Still.*

Nerida murmured agreement. Outside the window a kookaburra laughed. *The rain will be back this afternoon.*

The news confirmed that time Mari devoted to channelling was worthwhile. They were hours from her life she would never get back, after all.

And she was determined not to be told directly what she had channelled. She never read the transcripts of the conversations that Nerida spent hours typing and editing to put on the website. She would never read the book.

Mari didn't want to compromise the integrity of the channelled messages with her own opinions and personality. It took years for Nerida to respect that. It meant there was a built-in separation, a loneliness in their marriage, despite the power of their love, and despite having a crowd of highly intelligent beings as regular company.

But Nerida was better rested and had a broader perspective since working from home fulltime. She and Mari laughed more.

Gradually the shadows under her eyes resolved. Nerida became more tolerant of watching or hearing about the news. They watched the news from America over lunch a few times a week.

They created a routine of coffee together in the mornings. Nerida looked forward to Mari getting up. She interrupted her work then, rose to greet her with an embrace.

Mari's eyes were better since she started washing them with the eyebright tea Nerida made.

They made progress on the orange house, asking an engineer to arrange repair the corroded beams supporting the house. But still considered whether they should sell it, find a more accessible place.

They talked about finding land with decent soil, away from fires and fracking.

'I can still grow food on the balcony at the orange house,'
Nerida said. 'A few metres of raised garden beds will be enough if I
manage them well.'

Mari knew about growing food. She topped up her coffee from
the pot. 'Dad's parents, Hans and Rosa always had food growing.
They had two pigs and a cow. They had a horse until it kicked
Rosa. Then they got another cow to pull the cart.

'Any extra milk or food went to the pigs. The animals made
compost. Hans knew how to slaughter and butcher them. Sausages
and salted meats always hanged in the cellar. The wood in the
house downstairs smelled like ham.'

'Like your parent's place, that seemed to have ham fat in the
wooden beams?'

'That's right. Hans and Rosa had fields, too. As kids we used
to go and help dig the potatoes. One of the village men plowed the
field with his horse and others helped plant the potatoes. They got
paid in potatoes.'

Nerida saw a light in Mari's eyes. 'There were plenty, then?'

'Yeah. The soil was good. There was wheat. Rye too. There
were always bags of flour around. They took it to the local mill,
downtown, you know?'

Nerida enjoyed visiting the village mill when they lived in
Germany. The place had an industrious air and was fragrant from
the wood, stone and grains.

A fine mist of flour covered everything. Sacks of spelt and rye
were stacked against the shop walls.

Going there was a break from the tough job of being carers for
Mari's parents: suddenly so ill, suddenly dying, both shockingly
disabled. Needing more than they could give. Mari lived beyond
human capability in those days.

Nerida looked out the window. The lettuces needed picking
before they bolted. Passed over her grief. As Mari passed over,
around and through the many wounds of her grief, fifty times a
day.

'They made their own cakes and bread,' she reminisced.
'When I was a child, there was a communal baking oven
downtown. A big one, glowing red in the back, made of brick and
clay. It was a place to be in the winter. Women took their dough.

Sometimes they had time for a chat. The whole village smelled of the bread, or apple cakes, on Fridays and Saturdays. Or onion tart if there was a feast coming, like celebrating the harvest.

'We kids had to go and fetch the milk. It made us strong.'

Even you, little Mari, with your congenital problem with your legs. You walked up that hill with the milk jug, got to feel strong and useful sometimes between all the surgeries, after all those times learning to walk, again and again.

'There were fruit trees. Cherries and apples and pears and prunes.'

You broke your arm falling out of the apple tree once, trying to prove yourself to the boys. Prunes?

'You mean plums?'

'No, there were plums and then the little yellow ones. Plums and prunes were different.

'Dad planted a tree ten years ago. He was always looking for that bumper crop of the little yellow ones.

'They always had a garden. Mum loved flowers, so they grew those, too. The cherry tree out the front of the house blossomed every spring. The fruits made us happy.

'There were berries up on the meadow. Too many kinds to name. I don't know all their names in English.'

In the afternoon Nerida looked at upcoming jobs in the Bush. She declined offers of well-paid jobs doing nothing but injecting people with the anti-COVID vaccine all day.

But she wondered about her clients in the remote places. Would she vaccinate them? They lived a long way from the cities, with plenty of space around.

But they were at high risk if the virus got into the communities, with their overcrowded housing and widespread chronic diseases.

She decided that, as she did with medicines she wouldn't use herself, she could facilitate people making their own, informed choices. If people wanted and believed in the vaccines, she would give them.

She resolved to become an expert in the evidence. She couldn't help a bias against giving the injections, though. Or waiting longer, at least before taking it. It was a dangerous way to think for a doctor.

Sometimes she couldn't decide if her spiritual conversations expanded her consciousness or reduced her world to a narrow, blind box.

Her parents had the vaccine. And her mother was sick in bed for days, had to go back to the doctor for an injection to stop her vomiting. Her Dad was fine. Both felt safer.

Meanwhile, the news bulletins emphasised all day, every day, that the vaccines were the way out of the crisis. Nerida remained conflicted.

CHAPTER 65

Walking on the beach early in the evening, Mari relished the pink light reflecting on the wet sand. Nerida played in the frothy ocean, the water still warm on her feet.

A little mound rose in the wet sand as a wave retreated. 'There's a pippi in there,' Nerida dug her toe in to scoop out the mauve and white shell of a tasty mollusc. She tossed it back in the waves. *Plenty to eat at home.*

Mari walked confidently on the wet, packed sand, taking photos of the waves. She was working on a painting that was all about light on waves. She took Nerida's hand to help her balance in softer sand. They stayed until the last reflected purple was gone from the clouds. The constant roar of the grey-green waves cleared their heads.

There was shocking news when they came home. An Asian-American woman was beaten in a random racist attack on the street in New York. On television.

That's a huge Black man trying to beat the life out of her! Oh my god, look at him. He's out of his fucking mind! And there's the Black security guard, closing the door on her.

'It's a hint of the nightmare Aedgar said would unfold, if the course is not changed in America,' she said to Mari. 'Marginalised people hating each other, killing each other in spiralling racist terror. I can hardly bear it.'

'You'd better get that book out, honey, if you think it could change things,' Mari said sternly. And squeezed her hand.

CHAPTER 66

Lennox Head, home

Friday March 30, 2021

Next morning, Mari put her head in the door. 'Take a break. Come and see.'

On the deck outside sat a green tree frog, a wise-eyed native. 'He's a beauty!' Nerida said.

Mari took photos. 'Maybe I'll sketch him to paint a portrait.'

Back in the kitchen, Nerida sliced an apple and poured herself tea. 'Did you drink that equisitum tea I made? It's good for your eyes and your lungs.'

'It tastes disgusting.'

Nerida was exasperated.

Mari refused herbs, refused even plain water. *How many foul-tasting things were forced in her as a child?*

'The puffers don't work,' she explained. 'None of the medicines I've tried with you for years did any good. You've been gasping and wheezing every night.

'This works, doesn't it? I've put a bit of honey in the pot for you. Just half a cup of tea, morning and night. It's your medicine. Maybe an extra dose when your cough's bad. Okay?'

'Okay.' She poured herself a shot. Grimaced as she swallowed it.

'I don't know what we'll do with the orange house at Narooma. I still don't know whether we should try to fix it or rebuild it or sell it,' Nerida said.

'It seems to me that we really don't want to sell it,' Mari reflected, drinking cordial to recover from the herbs.

Outside, the peewee battled his reflection. 'Maybe he does that to remind us how useless it is to fight ourselves,' Nerida said. As they watched, he stopped pounding the ephemeral enemy and trotted around the paving stones, looking for bugs, tilting his head to look up at them sometimes, like a child wanting to be sure their carer was watching.

Nerida sipped tea. 'I got an email this morning. I've been asked to go and work for two years as the doctor at the Cocos-Keeling Islands.'

Mari's face was open.

Encouraged, Nerida said, 'I couldn't help thinking about it. Maybe we should think about it. It's a special place.' *We'll go diving and snorkelling. Maybe get a tinny, go boating around the atoll after work.*

'I'd be working fulltime again. I'm not sure how much that would delay the books. I'm better at writing now. I've got more discipline, more of a routine. Maybe I'd be able to do an hour or two a day. We wouldn't really know if it would work until we get there.'

She thought of what M'Hoq Toq said, that if a place is right for you, you can work all day and night and still feel good. But if it's not for you, it can look like paradise and feel like shit. *Mari seems to have that response to the place they chose in Lennox Head.*

'It's always hot there,' Mari said. 'We said we wouldn't go to a place where it's always hot to live again.'

'Yep. And there are geckos and mosquitoes and sandflies. You got very sick last time we were there.' Nerida looked into her wife's eyes. 'That bird flu nearly killed you.'

'I would stay away from the birds if we went there again.'

Nerida warmed her hands around her teacup. 'My main reservation is that we would be away from my parents. And Ruby and Seb.'

'They'll come to visit. We saw more of them when we lived in the remote desert than we have living in the same state. Because it's like they feel that they could drive up and visit us anytime. And it's not such an adventure, when we live here, I guess.

'We might not be there when the baby is born.' There was a place inside Nerida, a bud of blossoming wonder, since Ruby was pregnant again. She didn't talk much about it, afraid of jinxing the pregnancy by wanting the child too much. It made her happy to dream of the little one, though.

'I'm not touching that one. Only you can decide on that,' said Mari.

Nerida nodded. 'Maybe we can start at the islands after the baby is born. We'd have a regular wage. We could buy Mum and Dad business class airfares to Perth.'

'Maybe we can find someone we like to rent the orange house,' Mari suggested. 'Someone who'd enjoy it and look after it a bit.'

'Mum would help us find someone decent. We'd have to fix the corroded steel beams.'

'And the windows,' Mari said. 'But we won't save a lot of money you know. Island life is expensive. We'd have to get our own ATV or golfcart. Last time you took the one they gave us to work. I got stuck.'

Even if she talked of difficulties, Mari looked pleased. 'We couldn't take anything that would be damaged by mould. It's so damp.'

'And I don't think the pay is so great anyway,' Nerida said.

They sat still a moment. The peewee had met his mate and they were dancing and singing on the pool fence.

'But I love the people. Their cultures.'

'They were kind to us last time, including us in things. Like inviting us to a wedding,' Mari added.

'I'd catch fish,' Nerida said.

Mari reached out, rubbed Nerida's earlobe, and smiled. 'It is a place of gorgeous colours. You know how I love the Indian Ocean. And I can take my medicinal cannabis there because there are no cars on the island. No police either.'

'Could you safely drive a golfcart or a tinny?' Nerida teased. 'I'll send them my CV and then we'll decide, when we know if I've got the job or not.'

CHAPTER 67
TIME SLIP 7: Into the Future

Gunditjmara Land. Formerly southwest 'Victoria.'

Friday March 28, 2036

Unpacking the tiny house behind the car is easy. Nerida does the heavy lifting. And tasks close to the ground. Mari does jobs needing powerful hands, attention to detail and finesse.

'Lovely spot, eh?' Nerida unpacks the table. 'See the cherry tree's full of fruit? The apple tree there?'

'That looks like sweet potatoes on the vine,' Mari points.

'We can roast a couple. Sprinkle them with truffle powder we got in Gundagai. I'd like to eat some of the smoked eel we brought from Tae Rak, as well.'

'Truffles and smoked eel together? Really?' Mari frowns.

'Okay. I'm just thinking about the choices we have.' Nerida kisses her on the cheek, slips her arm around her waist. 'I'll get drinking water.' She pulls two jerry cans off the tiny house trailer, fits a fresh filter of charcoal and moringa husks into the mouth of each. Carries them to the rainwater tanks.

Mari picks up the narrow hose where they parked. Turns a spigot to clean dust and mud off the car.

'Don't get that splashed on you. That groundwater's full of poison,' Nerida cautions, hauling one of the jerry cans back.

'It's good enough to fuel the car,' Mari says. 'I'll get the electroliser out to fill the hydrogen tanks after I finish here.'

'Don't use it on the fine spray. It's got gas in it.'

Mari gives her a look that says, *Do you think I've never done this?* 'Yeah, go away. There's uranium and methane and other shit in that water.'

'I wish they knew more, back then. And not just pretended that they did,' Nerida says as she walks off.

Later, Mari pulls out sourdough bread made with a culture she first grew at Uluru twenty-five years ago. Nerida has sweet potatoes baking in the ashes of their fire.

'Can you do my dressing before we eat? Then we can wash our hands and forget about.'

'We should go back and see the dolphins in Kalbarri this winter.' Mari washes the wound on Nerida's breast with goldenseal tincture in clean water. 'It never was the same after the cyclone. But the dolphins are there.'

Nerida shakes her head. 'We missed the deadline to be allowed to travel over there. They only let about three hundred people go. We can go next year. Ouch, that hurts.'

'Sorry. I can't believe that idiot burned you with the laser. He could have killed you.'

'But he didn't. It was an accident.'

Nerida flinches as Mari, using self-sterilising scissors, snips burned skin from the edges of the hole. With her chin on her chest, she sees a pink hole where her colleague burned through her shirt and bra. It happened in less than three seconds. 'It looks nasty, but it's clean. It'll heal from the bottom up.'

'There are no accidents,' Mari growls. 'I know you like surgery. But just stop it. No more, okay? You'll be seventy soon. Leave it to the young ones. Let this be a lesson.'

Nerida enjoys the quick resolution and healing her laser work offers patients. 'It's not major surgery.'

'It's major enough when an *Arschloch* hits you with a laser that was turned up way too high. Were you operating on a cow, or what?'

The setting sun lights up the tops of the mountains. Nerida changes the subject as her wound is dressed with special seaweed. 'The Dreaming stories here tell of earthquakes, even a tsunami.

'A massive volcanic eruption changed everything around here five thousand years ago. Gunditjmara people understand how the planet changes, how to adapt.

'After the lava cooled, all those thousands of years ago, they engineered fish and eel traps and holding ponds in the lakes and channels. There was plenty! So much food they built houses and stayed. You see why I've been wanting to try this eel?'

She opens the bundle of leaves, smells the smoked meat inside.

'Gunditjmara people won the rights to their lands back in the 1980s,' Nerida goes on. Smacks her lips. 'Massive legal battle

against a mining company. Nobody talked about it. The gougers
didn't want urban Aboriginal people to know they won a Land
Rights case in a coastal area.'

Mari says, 'Didn't work. You know about it.' She raises a glass
of merlot. 'Well done to the Gundipmara.'

'Gun*ditj*mara. Keep practising. It's a big island.' She stirs the
coals with a stick.

'Bit of a difference between the five-thousand-year-old stone
houses around here and the ruined apartment blocks we saw in
Naarm, blowing away in the wind.' Nerida unwraps a sweet potato,
easing it onto a bamboo plate with the eel.

Mari eats her bread hungrily. 'What are you gonna do?
Apartment buildings with their disease-prone elevators and central
air conditioning. Landlords saying they couldn't afford to make the
buildings safe.

'Some of those apartments had no windows that opened.
Don't you think that was a bad time?' Mari says.

'People lived in those boxes. I remember a public health guy
saying apartment blocks were like vertical cruise ships. Early in the
pandemic, after the cruise ship disasters. Everybody thought that
was such a radical, extreme image. He was on the right track,
though.

'It was the economy that forced them to keep opening
everything up. Still believing everything could be as it had been. No
thought that the economy should change.'

Nerida's brows knit. 'Did you see those kids at the market
yesterday in their hoodies?'

'You look after a lot like that, don't you? They're good, those
fancy hoodies with the built-in oxygen delivery system,' Mari says.

'So fuckin' sad. It's a hard life for them.' Nerida sighs. 'Do you
want a potato? Very sweet.'

'Thanks. I'll have a taste.' Mari opens a jar of pesto, made
with basil and toasted mealy worms. They trade it sometimes on
their travels. It's a simpler exchange than medical care or the
channelling they do when needed.

The coast is abandoned. The women travel and stop in places
like this. As long as the sweet potatoes and apples grow. Settled

people live further inland, away from the rising water and destructive storms.

The gougers, the mining companies, had to pack up and leave. Humans need the land to live.

'Shall we go to those mountains tomorrow? People say there's good swimming inland, just west of Gariwerd.' Nerida looks for stars as the night closes in. Snuggles into her scarf. *We'll climb into our cosy bed soon.*

Shaking her head, Mari's face is lit by the fire. 'We should go to Gariwerd itself. They're fake, those hills. They're made of mine tailings. The lake was a pit. A *Drecksloch*.'

'People say it has a kind of beauty. But it'll be centuries before its energy's restored.' Nerida agrees, holding her knees. 'Just because they put trees on it doesn't mean it's healed. Might take a hundred years.'

'You know they put some kind of soap in that lake to make the particles sink to the bottom. Now the water tension's gone. You can't swim. You'd sink like a rock.' Mari puts a small log on the fire. It flares up, entrancing.

'But we should head to the lake even if its soapy. Remember that young woman trading the smoked eel?'

'What about her?'

'She gave me a message from Greg! He's staying in shack in a valley up behind that artificial lake. He wants us to visit him.'

'Aah, Greg! Why didn't he send the message psychically?'

'I guess it was more fun to track us down through the eel people. He likes to create a bit of serendipity.'

Stars come out as the white embers turn orange and red.

'It could all be so different if we'd listened to the actual scientists. Not the minions of the mining industry. Or people paid by gas and coal,' Mari muses.

Nerida agrees. 'If only people listened to Aedgar and M'Hoq Toq, back then. Or even, as you say, independent scientists. They didn't have to believe in spirits and channelling.'

'What do you mean by independent scientists?'

'Well, the ones that didn't lie for a living.'

Mari tosses her head, points her finger over the fire for emphasis. 'Scientists in those times weren't paid to lie.

'They were paid to not give one hundred percent of the information. You have that tiny field of expertise. You don't know what your neighbour's tiny field is.

'So you can't cope with answering questions that might be easy for someone who never attended high school. You know? That narrowness. That's what passed for science.'

She sounds like she's channelling Aedgar now, Nerida thinks, but doesn't say anything. *As Mari gets older it seems like they blend their energy with hers sometimes. I hope that doesn't get us into more trouble.*

'It took years for me to accept other ways of receiving information and learning than science,' Nerida said. 'And I had you, my most important person. Massive shake-up, your channelling!

'Science was precious to me. Still is. Clean water and hygiene, electronic communications, freedom from religion, bridges and airplanes: all of these began with science.'

'Science gave us dirty air and water, too. Corrupted by greedy monsters,' Mari says.

'Anything's warped by thinking of nothing but money,' Nerida counters. 'I had to expand my consciousness. So did other scientists. Look, science isn't bad or good. It's a tool.

'Like, money's not good or bad. Needing it made us go to interesting places, do things we wouldn't have done.

'When money was low, I was pushed to look after people. I learned. Did healing I might not have done, otherwise. Needing money made you finish your paintings and sell some. We made money from our books. Eventually. Enough to keep writing, even when things got, hmm, difficult.'

'Fucking thought police,' Mari says. 'I'll never forgive them for the way they treated you. And it was a supposed friend, that *daube Henne*, who called me brain damaged. She gave them enough to lock us up.'

'Yeah. My terrible son played his part, too. One day we'll write about it in another book. Telling our stories is our best opportunity.'

The orange sky is becoming mauve.

Mari relaxes. Cogitates. 'An opportunity to expand their mental horizon. I like that Hermann Hesse quote. Do you remember? "People with courage and character always seem sinister to the rest."'

Nerida is soothed to see her wife philosophical about the attacks, the damage done to her. To them. 'Let's be sinister together, then, my lovely witch.'

She sucks the fat from her meal off her fingers. 'Hesse also said that only the ideas we actually live have any value.

'Like the healers and Elders, or the wise young ones we meet. Remember the artist outside the art gallery, warning people about the cannibal beings under the salt lake? Making his paintings, telling everyone. How right was he about that?

'We're living our ideas. Humans are the brink of developing our superpowers. People like you and Greg show them more clearly than most...'

Wiping pesto onto the last bite of bread, Mari smiles. 'Want some wine? Look at you, all inspired! What brings that on?'

'You know, scientific revolutions have happened before. We're living through one. There's gonna be upheaval in a time of revolution.

'We met brilliant people at the summit last week...' She takes a glass of red. Raises the glass. 'Let's enjoy the power of being embodied. We're still around for a reason. Healing times ahead, my love.'

'Maybe there's a way to regrow my foot,' Mari acknowledges. Science will help her grow one like a starfish.

'I like that they play music to my cells. And talk to them all day. They have that recording of my voice encouraging them. They're good in their blue ceramic dish. No plastic. It's all about the vibes, isn't it?'

'It's all about what works,' Nerida replies. She shifts from her side of the fire to sit beside Mari.

Mari's team has begun growing new body parts, a new foot and ankle, using her specially nurtured stem cells and five-dimensional printing. The ankle, then a new foot, will be grafted onto her leg in five stages over about eight months.

'It's worth a year's work,' the scientist had said, his thick, black brows sliding up his forehead. 'We analysed your cells. Your life expectancy is another thirty or forty years if you don't succumb to an accident.'

Mari lifts her leg, massaging the stump above her prosthesis. 'Who would think that could heal?'

Nerida feels cautious hope for a body with less pain for her wife.

'You make me happy, Mari. Even when I'm not, you make me grow. You subject me to alchemy. Love and change are the only constants.

'You're my companion in all of it.'

Mari rolls her eyes. Smiling, they put their faces close. Shutting their eyes, touching foreheads, noses. Laughing lips.

'I love you,' says Mari. Pulls her wife close. Kisses her hair and forehead.

'*Gitayn yurrung-ga gati-nun,*' Nerida murmurs in her ancestor's, now her own, language. She points with her chin. 'The moon's coming up over that hill.'

The stars dim as the nightmarish baroque-pearl moon, broken and scarred, rises on its crooked path.

APPENDIX

Glossary of less-usual words

Adenovirus: A group of common viruses that infect the lining of
        your eyes, airways and lungs, intestines, urinary tract,
        and nervous system. They're common causes of fever,
        coughs, sore throats, diarrhea, and pink eye

ambos: (Aust. slang) Ambulance officers (often paramedics)

Anangu: (pronounced arn-ung-oo) The name used by members
        of several Aboriginal Australian groups, roughly
        approximate to the Western Desert cultural bloc, to
        describe themselves. The original meaning of the word
        is 'human being, person,' 'human body' in eastern
        varieties of the Western Desert Languages

APY Lands: Anangu Pitjantjara Yankunytjatjara Lands. A cross-
        border region in the southwest of the Northern
        Territory, the northwest of South Australia and into
        Western Australia. See also NPY Lands.

Aussie Rules: An Australian football code. Elements of it come
        from 'marngrook,' a Gunditjmara game using an egg-
        shaped, leather ball.

Arschloch: (German language) 'arsehole'

ashwagandha: Commonly known as Indian Ginseng or Winter
        Cherry, used to treat stress

ATV: All Terrain Vehicle

Bettflucht: (German language) 'escape from bed'

Biripi: (also spelt Birpai) The language/culture group whose
        land lies on the Mid North Coast of New South Wales,
        including the current-day city of Taree on the
        Manning River.

boab: A bottle-shaped tree related to the baobab of southern
        Africa, including Madagascar

brolga: A common, gregarious wetland bird species of tropical
        and south-eastern Australia and New Guinea.

brutha: (Aboriginal English) 'brother'

Bundjalung: The language/culture group occupying the north coastal area of New South Wales

bush: (Aust. slang) Any sparsely inhabited region in Australia

canna: A flowering plant, with large foliage

canthus: Either corner of the eye where the upper and lower eyelids meet

cenote: A natural pit, or sinkhole, resulting from the collapse of limestone bedrock that exposes groundwater

CEO: Chief Executive Officer. Acronym adopted in the '80s meaning 'boss.'.

Chauvin, Derek: (see Floyd, George)

CKI: Cocos-Keeling Islands

coal-biting: (Koori English) Begging for sustenance, usually asking for money

cockies Cockatoos (Australian native birds)

Colchicaceae: A family of flowering plants

cousin-sister: (Aboriginal English) A cousin or more distant relative in a sisterly relationship. Can be a more formally defined relationship in some strict Aboriginal kinship systems.

cow cocky: (Aust. Slang) dairy farmer

CPR: Cardio-Pulmonary Resuscitation

croc: (Aust. slang) 'crocodile'

CV: Curriculum Vitae. Work summary to apply for a job.

D-Dimer: A protein fragment (small piece) that's made when a blood clot dissolves in the body.

Danggu Gorge: A gorge on the Fitzroy River in the Kimberley region of Western Australia, in the traditional lands of the Bunuba.

Daube Henne: (Swabian) lit. deaf chick. Roughly equivalent to 'bitch'.

daughtergirl: (Aboriginal English) A young woman or girl in a 'daughter' relationship. May be a niece, daughter-in-law or adopted daughter.

Den knüpf i an de Eier nuff: (Swabian language): 'I'm going to hang him by his balls.'

Des kotzd mi à: (Swabian language) 'That pisses me off!'

Dhanggati: The language/culture group occupying the area
            around what is known as the Macleay Valley on the
            Mid North coast of New South Wales
Dharug: The language/culture group occupying the area from
            the west of current-day Sydney, north to the
            Hawkesbury River, and west to Mount Victoria.
Dhitiyn bayiratikal marrung: (Dhanggati language) 'He's a good
            singer'
Dhunuwi yalaan: (Dhanggati language) 'sunset'
didgeridoo: A wind instrument made from hollow wood,
            developed in northern Australia
Diné: (Diné language) 'The people.' Members of a native
            American language/culture group. Known in English
            as 'Navajo'
donga: Minimalist, portable accommodation hut, commonly
            used at mine sites
Dreamtime: A term devised by early anthropologists to refer to a
            religio-cultural worldview attributed to Australian
            Aboriginal beliefs.
Drecksloch: (Swabian language) 'shithole'
Duppl: (Swabian language) 'silly'
echidna: A native egg-laying mammal with a spiked, dome-
            shaped body. Sometimes called a porcupine
écru: (French language) The colour of unbleached linen
ED: Emergency Department
Eora: The language/culture group occupying the area of
            current-day Sydney
Epigenetics: The study of how behaviour and environment
            change how genes work
EPIRB: Emergency Position Indicating Radio Beacon. Used to
            help search and rescue authorities pinpoint a person's
            position in an emergency.
equisitum: Horsetail plant
fella: (Aust. slang) 'fellow'
fibro: Cheap building material containing asbestos
FIFO: 'Fly in, fly out' describing working arrangements for
            miners.

Floyd, George: A 46-year-old black man murdered in
Minneapolis, United States, while being arrested on
suspicion of using a counterfeit $20 bill. Derek
Chauvin, a white police officer, knelt on Floyd's neck
for nine minutes and 29 seconds after he was
handcuffed and lying face down.

folie à deux: (French language) 'madness [shared] by two,' also
known as shared psychosis or shared delusional
disorder (SDD)

frack: Hydraulic fracturing. Considered a less invasive
method of extraction of natural gas for fuel

Fukushima: (Japan) Site of a nuclear reactor disaster in March
2011

Gariwerd: (Jardwadjali language) A mountainous area in
southwestern Victoria, also known as the Grampians.

Gitayn yurrung-ga gati-nun: (Dhanggati language) 'The moon's
rising over the hill.'

Goldman, Emma: (1869–1940) An anarchist political activist and
writer.

Goori: Demonym for Aboriginal people of the NSW far north
coastal region. See Koori

GP: General Practitioner, Family Physician

grasdackel: (German language) 'moron'

Gunditjmara: The language/culture group occupying an area on
the southwestern coast Victoria, including the current-
day city of Warrnambool.

Gundungurra: (also Gandangara) A language/culture group of
south-eastern New South Wales, occupying the area
from the southern Blue Mountains to the Southern
Highlands.

Gundy, David: A young Aboriginal father accidentally shot dead
by police in his bed in Sydney in 1989. A judicial
enquiry concluded that 'Police had no right to be in his
home at all, much less to point a loaded and cocked
shotgun at him.'

ICU: Intensive Care Unit

IV: Intravenous (through the vein)

Ivermectin: Inexpensive anti-parasitic drug, originally used for
livestock.
jeez: (Exclamation) 'Jesus!'
Jigalong: A community in the Pilbara region of Western
Australia, around 1250 kilometres northeast of Perth
and 520 kilometres southeast of Port Hedland on the
western edge of the Little Sandy Desert. Traditional
Owners:Martu
Jimblebar mine: An iron ore mine located in the Pilbara region of
Western Australia.
Kalbarri: A resort town at the mouth of the Murchison River, on
Western Australia's central 'Coral' coast.
Kata Tjuta: (Pitjantjatjara language) 'many heads.' Also known as
The Olgas. A group of large, domed rock formations
or bornhardts located about 360 km southwest of Alice
Springs, in the southern part of the Northern
Territory, central Australia.
Kim Jong-un: Leader of North Korea (DPRK) since 2011
kookaburra: Native bird with a characteristic laughing call
Koori: A shared name for Aboriginal Australians from the
approximate region now known as southern New
South Wales and Victoria.
Kriol: Shared Creole language of Aboriginal people across
different parts of Australia. The 2011 census for Kriol
speakers is 4,000, but linguists estimate the real
number is closer to 20,000. Kriol is used in churches,
education and the Kriol edition of the Radio News.
Kimberley Kriol is a distinct dialect.
Kumpupirntily: About 320 kilometres east of Newman
(Parnpajinya), it is the site of a proposed mine for
Potash, granted approval in 2020. Named Lake
Disappointment in English in 1897. Kumpupirntily is
where cannibal beings live under the surface of the
saltlake, as described in Chapter 18.
Kununurra: A town in far northern Western Australia located at
the eastern extremity of the Kimberley
lillipilli: Native tree or shrub. It bears abundant, brightly
coloured fruits.

loo: (Aust. slang) 'toilet'

Mabo decision: The June 1992 ruling in by the High Court of Australia recognised that a group of Torres Strait Islanders, led by Eddie Mabo, held ownership of Mer (Murray Island). The decision overturned the fiction of 'terra nullius' and led to a framework for all Australian Indigenous people to make claims of native title.

malachite: An opaque, green-banded mineral which forms crystals

mamu: (Pitjantjatjara language) evil spirit or pathogen

Martu: Aboriginal people of a big country west of Newman. Their territory includes Kumpupirntily, see above.

Meanjin: Derived from the Turrbal word for the river peninsula where the city Brisbane is located

mob: (Aboriginal English) people. Sometimes used in 'that mob' or 'those' mob, when talking about a specific group. Or 'my mob' as in my clan or tribe.

moringa   Also known as the drumstick tree (for its seed pods) or horseradish tree (for the roots). Tropical, drought resistant. Cultivated for medicinal and other traditional uses.

mozzies: (Aust. slang) 'mosquitos'

MRI: Magnetic Resonance Imaging

Munsee Lenape: A subtribe of the Lenape, originally constituting one of the three great divisions of that nation and dwelling along the upper portion of the Delaware River, the Minisink, and the adjacent country in New York, New Jersey, and Pennsylvania.

murrungbu: (Dhanggati language) 'Thank you'

Muru-ora-dial: Aboriginal clan occupying the area of Gooriwal (current-day La Perouse in Sydney), around the north head of Botany Bay

Mutitjulu: An Aboriginal Australian community in the Northern Territory located at the eastern end of Uluru. People living there are mostly Pitjantjatjara but there are also Yankunytjatjara, Luritja and Ngaanyatjarra.

myna: A common bird, introduced from southeast Asia. It is a
            pest, which aggressively pushes native birds from their
            nests.
Naarm: The Wurundjeri name for the area now occupied by
            the city of Melbourne.
Navajo: (see Diné)
Ngaanyatjarra: a language/culture group of Western Australia.
            They are in the Goldfields-Esperance region, as well as
            the Northern Territory. They are closely related to the
            Yankunytjatjara and Pitjantjatjara.
NGO: Non-Government Organisation
Noongar: A grouping of several Australian language/culture
            groups in the south-west corner of Western Australia,
            from Geraldton on the west coast to Esperance on the
            south coast.
NPY: Ngaanyatjarra, Pitjantjatjara and Yankunytjatjara
            lands. The NPY Lands span the central desert region
            of South Australia, Western Australia and the
            Northern Territory, covering 350,000 square
            kilometres and encompassing 26 remote communities
            and homelands. Comparable to the APY Lands.
obs: Routine medical observations, e.g. blood pressure,
            heart rate, temperature.
Palyku: Aboriginal Traditional owners (TOs) in or near
            Newman in the Pilbara. Newman is near the boundary
            with Banjima and Wawula countries, as well.
PCR: Polymerase Chain Reaction. A method widely used to
            rapidly make millions to billions of copies of a DNA
            sample.
peewee: A small, inquisitive, black and white bird. Also called
            the peewit, magpie lark and mudlark
Pertussis: Commonly called whooping cough. A bacterial
            infection which can be fatal in babies. Immunisation
            confers protection.
phosphorylation: In chemistry, the attachment of a phosphoryl
            group to a molecule. Critical for many cellular
            processes in biology.

Pilbara: Region of the mid-north of Western Australia covering
             over half a million square kilometres. Contains some of
             the oldest rock formations on Earth, including world-
             heritage listed petroglyphs (rock etchings). It is an area
             of extensive mining, pivotal in the Australian economy.
             There are more than thirty one Aboriginal cultural
             groups in the Pilbara.
pippi: (Also 'pipi') A shellfish commonly used for bait or food
Pitjantjatjara: (pronounced pigeon-jarrah) A language/culture
             group of the Central Australian desert near Uluru.
             They are closely related to the Yankunytjatjara and
             Ngaanyatjarra.
PPE: Personal Protective Equipment (eg face mask, sterile
             gown)
Promethazine: An antihistamine drug which makes people sleepy
resus: 'resuscitation'
Ricin: A poison that can be made from the waste left over
             from processing castor beans. Has been used as a
             biological weapon.
RNA: Ribonucleic Acid.
roo: (Aust. slang) 'kangaroo'
sats: 'saturations,' referring to oxygen saturations, a
             measure of oxygen in person's blood
schee: (German language) pretty or beautiful
scheisse: (German language) shit
schlürfen: (Swabian language) shuffling
sheoak: Native trees with dense, hanging needles
songlines: A journey across country described by song as people
             travel
tachy: 'tachycardic'
Tae Rak: Gunditjmara name for Lake Condah in present-day
             southwestern Victoria
Taylor, Breonna: A 26-year-old African American medical
             worker shot dead when white plainclothes policemen
             broke into her apartment in a misguided drug raid on
             March 13, 2020.
TB: Tuberculosis
telly: (Aust. slang) 'television'

temp: 'temperature'

Tet-Tox: Anti-tetanus immunisation

Tetanus: Infection by a soil-borne bacteria with a high rate of mortality

tinny: (Aust. slang) A small open aluminium boat.

tip shop: (Aust. slang) a shop selling materials recovered from landfill to reduce waste.

tjanpi: (Pitjantjatjara language) A type of spinifex grass, used to weave baskets, fibre sculpture and other objects.

Tramadol: Analgesic medication

Uluru: A sandstone monolith in central Australia, sacred to the Pitjantjatjara. (Also known as Ayers Rock.)

Valproate: Anticonvulsant drug, usually taken to avoid fits or seizures in epilepsy. The level of valproate requires monitoring by regular blood tests

vino: (Aust. slang) 'wine'

Whadjuk: The language/culture group in the south-west of Australia, including the site of the city of Perth.

whitefellas: Non-Aboriginal people, usually of European descent. Can be mildly derogatory (but not always).

Wiradjuri: A language/culture group of central New South Wales, occupying a large area west of the Great Dividing Range, from the Murray River to around Mudgee.

Xi (Jinping): President of the People's Republic of China (PRC) since 2013.

Yankunytjatjara: A language/culture group of the Central Australian desert near Uluru. They are closely related to the Pitjantjatjara and Ngaanyatjarra.

yarndi: Marijuana. From Wiradjuri 'nyaandi' ('thingamajig,' 'what's-its-name').

Yuin: A grouping of several Australian language/culture groups in the South Coast of New South Wales, from Botany Bay in Sydney, to Eden.

yuwa: (Western Desert languages) 'Yes.' Also 'Uwa'

yuwayi: (Dhanggati language) 'Hello'

Zoster: Herpes zoster, commonly known as shingles

About the Author

Miki Mitayn is a writer of Goori, English and Irish ancestry. She works as a scientific and medical writer, as well as a clinical health worker, to support her family and her love of storytelling.

Born in Sydney's western suburbs, Miki has lived in the USA, the Black Forest in Europe, in Australia and the Pacific.

She began writing fiction in 2015. *The Conscious Virus* is her first novel.

Follow Miki on her Facebook page
https://www.facebook.com/aedgarbooks
And on Goodreads:
www.goodreads.com/author/show/21646577.Miki_Mitayn

The Aedgar Wisdom Series

The Conscious Virus is the first novel published in the Aedgar Wisdom series.

Chronologically, it will eventually be the fifth book in the series of ten. The contemporary nature of TCV made it push itself to the front, demanding to be out in the world in 2021.

The first novel in the series, *Aedgar Arises* tells the story of how Mari and Nerida met, how they went to live in the desert. How and why Mari learned to channel. What was Aedgar like when Nerida first met him? Did they like each other? It will be published in 2022.

To read extracts from the spirit conversations featured in the first five books of the series, visit www.aedgar.com

Keep up to date on the publication of new books, extracts and special offers. Join our mailing list at www.aedgar.com/contact